Antonio's Life

By José F. Garcia

PublishAmerica
Baltimore

ISBN: 1-60703-290-2
PUBLISHED BY PUBLISHAMERICA, LLLP
www.publishamerica.com
Baltimore

Printed in the United States of America

Acknowledgments

I wish to thank those members of my family no longer living, whose very rich lives served as the basis of this book. More than my words, these are their words. I only hope that I have done them justice in my representation of whom and what they were. As a young man, I was impacted first by their strength and then by their kindness. That seemed to have been the common thread that bound them all and gave them their identity.

Next I wish to thank the living members of my family whose unwavering love and support I have enjoyed and appreciated. Their love causes me to feel sad for all of those whose families are not equal to mine.

Most especially, I wish to thank my wife Janice Garcia for her patience and support as I wrote this book. Her help in guiding me and suggesting changes to the scenes I wanted to project, I believe added great quality and honesty, and made the emotions all the more real. She also had to bear the presence of the many voices speaking to me while she was trying to sleep, and would not relent until their words were on paper, regardless of the time of day or night.

Lastly, I wish to express my gratitude to my mother now deceased, who in this book is represented by Lola. By the way she lived her life, by the way she raised her children and by the way she loved her family, made us all the better people. Having been raised and guided by Leandra Bermudez de Garcia has been for me the greatest honor and privilege that anyone could hope to experience.

CHAPTER 1

"How could they have surrendered? Did they even put up a fight? We knew the Americans would win, but hell, they must have surrendered before firing even one shot. Dam the Americans. The reason why I came to Puerto Rico was to get away from people like them. I guess I did not travel far enough. I should have gone with Xavier to Argentina."

"A big difference between my brother Xavier and me is that he hated people like the Americans for no specific reason. He hated them out of general principle. Most of the things that he thought he knew about them that made them worthy of his hatred came to him through rumors, jokes and many hours in conversation with people that shared his contempt and hatred for them. What is the value of knowing how to read, if you are going to rely on rumors and believe all the nonsense you hear. Why bother learning to read at all," Antonio Barradaz said to his friends. He was not having a good day. Today of all days to have this news was beyond awful. Today he had planned to celebrate his twenty first birthday. The celebration would be much like all other birthday celebrations for him and his friends. They always drank more and faster than they should have, and ate far less than required to equalize the alcohol in their blood stream. But that could not be helped because when they pooled the few coins they had to buy food and drink for the party; drink always won the contest. Antonio who was in a position to contribute more than a few coins didn't, lest he be misunderstood by his friends. The party was of no great consequence. Usually five to seven of his friends would squat around a fire and just drink pure Rum. Since it was home made there was never any consistency in the volume of alcohol content from one bottle to the next. As a consequence it was anyone's guess how long it would take them to get drunk. Since there were no glasses they would either pass the bottle around or use coconut shells from which to drink. The only Problem was that the shells could not be put down since they would tip. Something they never forgot no matter how much they drank. They were more likely to spill blood than rum.

There were never any women invited. Mainly because there were only a few who would accept, and the ones who would were not really welcomed company. Besides, their presence almost always lead to a fight. As luck would have it, the girls got prettier as the night progressed and by the time they reached beautiful; the boys were too drunk to hurt each other in a fight. So instead of trading punches they traded insults and since no one remembered anything the next day, no harm was done to body or to pride. Although not literally, Antonio was for all intents and purposes; and orphan. But that fact was not going to keep him from doing what he had been doing on his birthday since he was fourteen years old. He had great plans for a small celebration. With a little luck one of his friends would show up with a small pig to roast. But his enthusiasm for the celebration died when he learned that General Toral and Admiral Cervera, the Spanish commanders of army and naval forces in Cuba, had signed an unconditional surrender ending the Spanish-American war.

The way Antonio figured it this may have been the first time these self aggrandizing warriors had to fight opponents other than peasant children and women. A real fight. Not like the fights their soldiers were known to have had in the whorehouses when they refused to pay the women because the ladies had failed to deliver a satisfying encounter. Even those fights they lost. Maybe the ladies should have tried to collect from the officer's wives for the service provided in wearing out their husbands. "I wonder what stories they will tell back in Spain about how bravely they fought. I can just imagine the orders to the troops. It must have been something like if we see many we run, if we see a few we hide and if we don't see any, attack at will." Antonio told his friends as they all laughed in agreement. Antonio, who had never been to a circus, knew that it could not have been any funnier than Spanish troops on maneuvers. The Spanish army he thought had spent so much time in abusing defenseless peasants and natives that whatever fighting skills they may have had were lost, assuming they had any at all to begin with.

As he stood at near the shack which was made of palm tree branches layered over split palm trees that were dug three feet into the ground. It had

6

no walls, only a thatched roof, which suited the occupant just fine. The whole structure gave the appearance that it was about to fall over which in fact it had more than once. Not because of poor construction or weak materials but because in the Caribbean Sea region when the hurricane winds came no matter the quality of construction, structures fell. It was either up to the wind, the rain or both. It did not matter, but you could expect it to fall at least once during hurricane season. The good news was that it did not take a lot of time or materials to rebuild. The only real piece of engineering that had gone into building the hut was the digging of a drainage ditch that would cause the water to flow away from the posts. However, no ditch digging was going to suffice when challenged by the torrential rains that you could count on in the Caribbean. This was not the best shelter, but it was just as the owner wanted it. Once, Antonio tried to talk him into building a more permanent structure, one with walls. But Orovis, the owner refused by saying that the one thing he knew was that everything was temporary so why search for permanence, and walls were not needed because he had nothing to conceal.

Relieving himself from all the liquor he had drunk the night before, Antonio was trying to figure out what the time was. In fact they had just quit playing dominoes at five that morning. Someone had brought a small table and four chairs and they had played all through the night. For most people, including them, the rooster signaled time to rise. On this morning it signaled why bother.

It was around one in the morning when Raul had come up the road with the news. He had been working with a crew that was unloading a merchant schooner at the port of Mayagüez, when one of the hands told him he had seen the Spanish flag taken down at the Morro fort in Havana, followed by the American flag going up the pole to replace it.

"Dam it all," he thought, "I did not come all the way from Bilbao with our great Basque traditions only to live like a slave to people who do not speak my language, and I swear by the old mighty I am never going to speak American." Barradaz had been a Basque name for as long as the Pyrenees have been mountains. If it had not been because his father had taken a younger woman for his wife, a Spaniard at that, and from Madrid to make it worse, with their better than thou airs, he may have still been in Basque country. But as she established her domain over her household she gave Don Gregorio the ultimatum. "If ever you wish to be inside of me so that I may give you sons; the ones from your last woman must go. I just don't feel like loving when they are but four feet away from us when we do it. It was bad enough that they sat outside our window our first night. I just can't and I won't. You decide."

This was nothing new. Ever since time has been recorded, stepmothers have been scheming to discard their step children. Except that in the case of Martina, Don Gregorio's new wife, she did not even pretend that she had any motherly instincts towards his children. In fact everybody knew where they stood the first time she set foot in the house. "This place is just too small for all of us; some of you will have to go." Her warm personality was filled with so much of the milk of human kindness that it just exploded out of her.

Don Gregorio decided that Martina, the new wife, would give him many more sons and besides it did feel good between her legs. His own father, Antonio's and Xavier's grandfather had done the same to him. Except that Don Felix had used up five women before he could no longer perform his manly duties. But not before he had fathered twenty five children. Possibly more, but he only claimed twenty five. What could you expect of a seventy year old man who marries a fourteen year old girl? His death had been sweet and sudden.

Don Gregorio's third wife who was Antonio and Xavier's mother had been used up long before her time. She reached old without going through middle age. It was not clear if she had ever married Don Gregorio. It seemed that her life had been about abuses all along the way. First her brothers had abused her in ways that brothers should not abuse their sisters. Then she was beaten by her Father frequently. It was her Father's way to vent his rage against life. He never vented against her brothers because they fought back. By the time Don Gregorio came around promising a better life to Iluminada, Mina, as she was called by everyone, did not have to consider the proposition for very long. She was seventeen years old and had agreed to everything that Don Gregorio required, including calling him Don Gregorio, so long as he promised never to beat her. She could take abuse, but it was the beatings that she would not stand for. He never beat her but did abuse her in ways that would have made beatings more acceptable. Either by accident or deliberately Don Gregorio could be and was extremely cruel. Never a term of endearment, even while making love when men will say anything to women to get their cooperation if not their enthusiastic participation in the act. Mina never felt loved by him or by anyone else and as a consequence was incapable of giving love to anyone even her children.

When she went to live with Don Gregorio, neither her father nor her brothers came looking for her. Don Gregorio never asked for a dowry as it was the custom because he knew that one would not be obtained. And rather than create a pretend confrontation with her relatives he thought he would get the dowry out of her in other ways.

First came Xavier followed within a year by Antonio, whom she nicknamed Anton. Xavier, whom she did not love as much as Antonio, was just Xavier. For some reason she never bothered to give him a nickname. Maybe he was guilty of having too close a physical resemblance to his father. Her favoring of one more so than the other had no effect on the bond between the two brothers. They were always together and if ever one was threatened the threat would be met by the two of them. No matter who or what. You took one on you got the other. And the village knew it. They drew close out of necessity more so than out of brotherly love.

After Mina gave birth to the boys, one after the other, she just dried up. Don Gregorio gave it all he had as often as he could but to no avail. Just like That, she dried up. His reaction was that of resentment because it brought his masculinity into question. After all, Basque men were supposed to be the strongest in every way. That is why they were superior to the Spaniards, with their effeminate ways.

So here she was, undesired by her husband and unwanted by her family whom she had not seen in the nine years since she had gone to live with Don Gregorio. Mina was filled with her own demons that kept her from being close to her boys or to anyone else. She had no religion to fall back on, no faith to sustain her and no confidence on her own strength because she did not have any.

The only thing that she had been good at was making babies and that did not last very long. She never did enjoy the act of making them but she so much loved the idea of the result, that the vision of babies in her mind replaced whatever pleasure she should have received from copulating with Don Gregorio. But even when the babies were born her attachment to them was neither long nor strong. There was a void in her soul that could not be filled by anyone or anything. The one characteristic that was peculiar in Mina was that no one ever saw her smile.

Her death was the one thing that made sense about her life. That was the reason why no one wept when they went down the ravine to retrieve her body. There seemed to be no sadness about her death, only acceptance, as if suicide was the only sensible and natural course of action for her.

Antonio and Xavier never did understand their mother. They had spent very little time with her and never felt the attachment that sons are supposed to feel towards their mothers. Her death was of no great consequence to them. And not knowing how to act during the burial, they relied on others to show them. And since no one acted mournfully neither did they. It was not as if they were going to miss her warmth and kindness because they never felt any from her. She had been so consumed by the caring of Don Gregorio's eight children from his previous women that she had little time for her own sons. It may have been different if she had demanded that Don Gregorio dispose of the children from his wives, but she never realized that she could have demanded such a thing because she was Basque and not a Spaniard. That was not the attitude of Martina, who followed her into Don Gregorio's house and who wasted no time in reducing the size of the family.

It seemed to Antonio that for all of his twenty-one years confusion had been the overwhelming dynamic. He was born in Spain but was not a Spaniard, he finally learned Spanish and was sent to Barcelona to work for his uncle, but there they spoke Catalan. And he never did find his uncle because he had moved on to parts unknown.

He would often walk by the port of Barcelona from which Columbus had departed for the new world, and wondered what it would be like to leave Spain. Antonio was thirteen when he and Xavier were sent to Barcelona. To no specific address and with no specific assignment. The instructions they received from their father were along the line of "Why don't you boys head on out east towards the Spanish coast. Just follow the sun and you will run into Barcelona. Once you get there, ask for Barradaz."

Although he was only thirteen, or because he was already thirteen he knew what was being told to him. Only the week before his father had poured him and Xavier a cup of wine and told them in as clear as language can be, "You boys are old enough to understand that this house will only have one master, and he is speaking to you." With that they understood that ready or not, masters of their destiny they would be.

He and Xavier remembered their father's parting words. He did not say go with God, and he did not say good luck. He said, "Don't shame me." They guessed he thought his name had some value or that theirs was an honorable family. Don Gregorio had always believed that people should share. That is why he did not mind helping himself to his neighbors' goats. Never close neighbors. Never for the purpose of raising a flock. Always to feast. And to ensure protection, he would invite some of the neighbors to participate. That way everyone could partake of the goat and share in the crime. Honor was to him but a concept. One that came and went based on the day's needs.

There had been that one time when one of the guests, a man who had been visiting a neighbor turned up at one of Don Gregorio's feasts and recognized the goat he was eating as one of his own. This particular goat had only three legs and one and a half ears. Those pieces of the goat's anatomy had been taken by a wolf that for some reason had no been able to complete the kill. When the rightful owner had eaten his share of goat, he recognized it as his own, and called Don Gregorio a thief.

True though the charge was, Don Gregorio tried to deflect it and defuse the situation by asking the owner if he had enjoyed his meat. When the owner said yes but asked what the hell that had to do with anything, Don Gregorio said that he should be grateful that he was not being charged for the labor and preparation of the feast. Everyone laughed at the same time, recognizing that Don Gregorio was trying to avoid a conflict. The owner of the goat, not knowing when to quit, called Don Gregorio a thief but insinuated him to be a stupid thief. Otherwise why would he have stolen the least appealing from the herd of goats.

Now this was more that Don Gregorio could tolerate. No, not being called a thief, but a stupid one. That was unforgivable. And so out came the knives. Don Gregorio being 20 years younger, and not as drunk as his accuser, made short work of the killing. He got away with it because defending his honor was more important than the man defending his property. Also, because the Spanish authorities generally did not consider a Basque killing another Basque, a crime. And this was the Basque name their father asked Antonio and Xavier to honor.

The Basque people had the misfortune of being born between France and Spain, and were not really wanted by either country. The Spaniards, not knowing what to do with them did nothing for them. It was and always will be in the nature of the Basque people to be different, to be independent and to do things their way. The Spaniards realized that the way to keep them under the crown's control was to keep them poor and ignorant. Something the Spaniards were good at. They proved this with the Aztecs, the Mayas, the Incas and the Taino Indians. Keep them Ignorant but religious, was the policy.

It all seemed so confusing to Antonio. Although he knew that sooner or later he would have to find his own way in the world because he had seen everyone else in the village do the same. He knew nothing of the life that he was about to enter but knew that it had to be better than the one he was leaving.

Soon after he arrived in Barcelona, Antonio realized two things. First, he could not read and second, he needed to learn. Back in the village he had left, reading was of no consequence since there was nothing to read. All business transactions were made based on barter and trade. Human interactions did not require reading skills. Whenever there was to be an announcement of consequence usually along the line about how the Spaniards were going to help the Basque people. These were made by the town crier. He would stand on a bench at the village plaza and read an announcement usually from the mayor or the council. It did not matter from whom the announcement came, Antonio was always certain that somebody, if not everybody was getting hurt. The hurting came in the form of a tax for the queen, or for the church or for the sheriff. It did not matter since everyone felt royally injured.

In most of Spain one could count on the goodness of the Catholic Church to bring some form of education to the poor people. But you had to be considered people to start with. And that excluded you if your name was Barradaz and you were Basque. For some reason, the priests and the nuns had no interest in teaching the Basque children to read or write. They seemed content to round up the children into the church every Saturday morning, feed them breakfast and read them the catechism. The same prayers, the same stories the same explanations would all come from the little book they held as they read it to the Basque children.

They were expected, and required to repeat and memorize but never to read. They probably thought that if the children could read the book, they would figure out by themselves that unless you were filled with faith, it would make no sense to them at all. Moreover, the children could start asking questions that the Spaniards did not want to answer. The Spaniards had seen in their colonization of the Americas what happens when people have knowledge. There is a big difference between ignorant and uninformed. It did not take too long for both conditions to change once people were exposed to information and began to question authority. There the missionaries went too far in imparting knowledge to the natives. Too far to the point that they natives started asking questions about why if we are all the same in the eyes of God, why are we made to feel the lesser. Or, when it comes to humility why is it always the Indian and not the Spaniard being humbled.

The lessons at the church were held in a form of segregation. The Spanish children, usually the sons and daughters of the Spanish dignitaries and functionaries who ruled the region, were taken to a different room for their instruction. Antonio's curiosity drove him to sneak a peak into the room and there he noticed that every one of them had a book in their hands and were moving their lips in unison, repeating just as Antonio had but freezing their eyes on their books rather than looking at the nuns. At this point Antonio had not realized they were reading since he did not know what reading was, but he did know that they were not the same.

It also struck Antonio how the Priests and the Nuns always looked down at the children as they taught the Saturday lessons. If there were no seats, the children would sit on the floor and the teacher stood and looked down at them. If they were seats, the teacher would stand on a stage or on a ladder, anything but equal to the students. Antonio thought that there must have been a reason why they were always looking down at them. In fact there were several. One reason was so they could make the children feel smaller and inferior. The other was so that they could see all infractions and deal with them in their own ways. Most nuns carried sticks. Large and sharp ones to whack and to jab, often at the same time. With the stick you at least knew what to expect.

Not the same with the small wooden blocks. One of the priests must have been a Jai Alai player because he could reach for a wooden block throw it at the head of a child and before they knew that they were even doing wrong they had been hit. On the rare occasion that he missed and hit the wrong child the priest would say that it served him right because if he had been paying attention, he could have ducked.

Somehow it did not make sense to Antonio. Especially when they read things that made reference to Jesus calling for the children to come to him because theirs was the kingdom of heaven. "I guess the kingdom of heaven must not be for Basque children otherwise why I am always getting beaten up by these people. I think that when they say turn the other cheek, it is mine and not theirs because whatever cheek I turn is the one they hit, and all of this for the love of God."

Antonio was nothing if not curious. He realized that he was as smart as any of the children of the Spaniards. He also knew that he did not know as much as they did about as many things as they did. Marisol the niece of Don Ismael Machado liked to remind him how ignorant he was but he did not mind because he knew the dumber she thought he was the more liberties she allowed herself with him. She would find the opportunity to be alone with him, and played with him every chance she had. In fact she once laughed all the time she stimulated and serviced him as he pretended not knowing what was happening to him or what she was doing. She sure felt superior over him. In fact Marisol was absolutely convinced she was using this stupid Basque boy for her pleasure as he was pleasured by her over and over again. She did teach him a great lesson; you do not have to know how to read to be pleasured by a girl so long as you let her go on believing that she was smarter that you. The strange thing was that she seemed to draw no enjoyment from what she was doing to him or he was doing to her.

By the time he and his brother arrived in Barcelona, Antonio was thirteen and full grown. He had been in serious fights, he had been on his own for a while now, he had been tested and felt he was a man. Still, he knew there was much to learn and had much growing up to do and he needed to read in order to achieve both.

It seemed that everyone in Barcelona could read. He had never seen so many printed papers everywhere all the time. Journals, periodicals, announcements. They even had places where they sold books. It amazed him that people actually paid money for these books and did not seem to get enough of them. Unlike his village where people spoke of nothing else but animals, crops and deaths, in Barcelona everyone spoke about everything but animals, crops and deaths. It was something to feel the excitement of people arriving at the ports with new books and journals and giving them to one another as gifts. And seeing people respond to books with greater joy than if they had received money.

While scrounging around the docks for whatever work they could find, Xavier suggested they split up because that way they would cover twice as many ships, and hopefully one of them would connect with someone or something. "Look Anton, I think it is better than watching each other find nothing," Xavier said. The older brother was right. It was Xavier who first saw the Argentinean freighter, although he had no idea that it was Argentinean since he could not recognize the flag nor read the name of the ship; Las Pampas. She was a combination freighter and passenger ship. Most ships were one or the other. This one however was not much of either. Too small to be called a cargo ship and too filthy to be a passenger liner.

Xavier did not know nor did he care. He just grabbed one of the tie lines that was thrown for tying to the stanchion at the edge of the pier. The amazing thing is that he caught the heavy rope in midair. An experienced hand would have let it hit the ground, picked it up and secure it to the stanchion before the winch picked up the slack. Not Xavier. He grabbed it in midair and dropped it on the steel post as if he was throwing wheels at a round peg. He had no idea what he had done, or what he had done was about to do for him.

The Las Pampas crew boss was watching and first smiled at the stupid kid who would not allow the heavy rope to hit the ground before picking it up. But then he realized that the kid was stronger than most everyone in his crew. Possibly stronger than himself. He continued to watch Xavier and soon realized that the boy was trying very hard to make a good impression because he never stopped moving, he just found something else to do. Helping stewards, handling trash and connecting pumps. It was obvious that this boy had no idea what he was doing but whatever he did he did it well, and with a purpose. The boy reminded him of himself when he first went to sea.

He had been on his own since he was twelve and now at fifty he had been the crew boss of the Las Pampas going on twenty two years. His real name was Roger, after the man who had fathered him. Not his father, who raised him but the one whose seed was planted in his mother. She was a 'mestiza'; a half breed, and he an army officer. The British army took a dim view of their officers fraternizing with the Argentinean peasantry even if just for sexual gratification. And so the time honored tradition was followed and about ten pounds were paid to Patricia for her troubles and that was that. She somehow was proud of having been bedded by the English soldier. Her son hated the thought of it. As soon as he could, he left his mother, went to sea and changed his name to Rogelio, because while he could do nothing about his English blood he was not about to go by an English name. He just hated the idea of having English blood in him as if having a Spanish name was to change anything, or having Spanish blood was any better or make things different.

Rogelio blew his whistle to get Xavier's attention who at first thought he was in trouble followed by a sense of dread when Rogelio signaled for him to go to the upper deck. With Xavier in front of him, Rogelio realized that the boy was bigger in bulk and taller than him. Rogelio, through life's experiences had learned to judge people at first glance. With him it was a simple equation he either liked or disliked the person. There was no in between, no ambivalence. Everything to him, including people, was black and white.

In Xavier he saw right away the defiance of a Basque and the aggressiveness of a boy hungry for anything and not just food. He liked the boy. He asked Xavier, "When was the last time you ate?" Xavier thought for a few seconds and said, "Not counting my nails, it has been a while."

"Go below; tell Pedro the cook that I said to feed you and to keep you there until I come for you." instructed the crew boss. "And who are you?" asked Xavier. "My name is Rogelio, El Jefe" (the boss), said Rogelio as he turned to yell at the boon operator about the pulleys being too tight for the turn that he was trying to make and the weight straining the net. Xavier looked at him for a few minutes, watching Rogelio yelling orders at various crews doing different things. He had never seen anyone so engaged in so many things at the same time, nor had he ever seen so many people respond with so much precision to orders that were so scarce in detail but great with purpose. He just knew that he liked the action.

When he got to the mess hall the crew was already working, cleaning up and preparing the galleys for the return trip and no one paid attention to him.

As he stood there listening, he first realized that there were many languages spoken by these people. It all sounded like Spanish but not exactly. When he first heard Rogelio speak he had to adjust to the rhythm of his speech. He had never heard an Argentinean speak, or a Chilean, Brazilian or Paraguayan. There were two Paraguayans in the crew, he later learned and they were not speaking anything approximating Spanish. Whatever it was they spoke only they understood it. Eventually he did learn they spoke Guarani, an Inca dialect. All these dialects were being spoken in front of him and he tried to understand them above the noise of the mess room. At best he could only pick up every third word but he did understand when the cook said, "Who are you, what the hell do you want, and why don't you answer me?"

"I am Xavier, and Don Rogelio sent me to ask you to feed me. He will come down later to get me. In the meantime he said that you would feed me." Scowling, the cook replied, "The only ones who eat in my mess room are men who work and have earned their food. What are you prepared to do to earn your food?"

"Give me the hardest job that you need done," said Xavier as he did all he could to remain in the Mess room. He knew that so long as he was there he was near food. Once they threw him out he was out. And this is the closest he had been to food in a long time.

By the time Rogelio came down to the mess hall to see Xavier, two hours of steady work had passed and he had still not eaten. Rogelio said, "Come with me," but Xavier did not respond. "Follow me," Rogelio spoke again. And again Xavier did not respond except to say, "I am not going anywhere with you or anyone else until I get fed or paid. One or both of those things needs to happen. I have been working like an African except that I know they get fed if not paid, and I have not had either. So there you have it." Xavier sat down.

Overwhelmed by hunger and rage he had that look that said I don't care. Too tired, too hungry and too angry to care. He had a look that screamed dam it, all I want is some respect from you people. Having been around men in all conditions, Rogelio knew desperation in another man when he saw it, and he saw it in Xavier.

That is when he said, "What do you mean you have not eaten?" He walked to the store room and returned with Pedro the cook's ear squeezed between his index finger and thumb, and with Pedro's toes barely touching the ground as he followed. In the deepest voice that Xavier had ever heard from any man, Rogelio said to Pedro, "Did this man not tell you that I wanted you to feed him? Answer me and the answer better make sense, because if not, you may never see your ear again." Pedro the cook, weasel and coward that he was, knew about Rogelio's voice when he used the specific guttural sound. It was profound without being profane. Worst of all he knew that there would be consequences.

"I did not understand what the hell he was saying. Hell, I have never heard that accent before." Best he could think in the spur of the moment. One thing Pedro knew about lying, something for which he had a gift, was to keep it simple and say as little as possible. So he said no more and looked with pleading eyes at Rogelio and Xavier. And then his eyes stopped moving and locked on to Rogelio's eyes. Expert that he was, he knew that wandering eyes were another dead certain give away for a liar, so he kept his still.

The next two words settled the issue, "Feed the boy, and feed him well. In fact feed us both. Bring the Jug of Rioja wine and serve us." At this point Pedro the cook understood that ordering someone to serve them would not do. He needed to make things right with Rogelio and so at once he was maitre'd, sommelier, chef and waiter. None of this was lost on Xavier. He may not have realized it at the time but he was receiving lessons on the effective use of power. More implied that explicit. Strength he learned is not exercised or demonstrated trough violence. Not always anyway. Sometimes character is stronger than force. Brute force is fleeting, it lacks in intelligence. A beast can have force but a man has character. Supported by the fact that he had the best meal of his life, he decided that strength through character would be his way from then on. And with this lesson began his new life.

Meanwhile Antonio had hired out to a baggage handling unit at the Port. The job required the pick up and delivery of luggage from ship to shore and shore to ship. He had no problem with the heavy work it was the light work that killed it for him. He needed to read names and numbers on the tags and could not read either. Because he was smart enough to know that he did not know, he worked with another carrier who would lead and Antonio would follow. The carrier was Miguel, who was Catalan. He liked Antonio so well that he actually spoke Spanish to him. At first Antonio did not know what to make of Miguel. They had met while Antonio was hanging out and about the docks trying to figure out how to get in and look for work. As luck would have it, Miguel saw him as he was taking a break from his twelve hour shift. Shifts were a misnomer because at the docks you worked until you were done. The concept of ten hours work for ten hours pay had not yet arrived in Barcelona.

Upon first laying eyes on Antonio, Miguel knew exactly what and who Antonio was. One more Basque boy lost in the big city. Nowhere to go, nowhere to be and important to no one. "Mi hijo what are you looking for?" Miguel called him my son although he was only two years older than Antonio. "Work of course," he answered. "What else is everyone looking for."

"A place to sleep is what you need because there is no more work tonight my crew unloaded the last of the bags, tomorrow is another day but tonight you have to eat and sleep" Miguel was living at the house of the sisters of the Sacred Heart where in exchange for room and board he did all that needed doing. Miguel said, "Do you believe in Christ? do you believe in God? Do you believe in the Virgin Mary and the holy trinity?" Antonio stood there not knowing what to say and so Miguel answered for him. "Repeat after me, with all my heart and all my soul" Antonio repeated as told. "You will be asked that where we are going and no other answer is acceptable, so please say it again." And Antonio did, over and over. Little did Antonio know that he had met the smartest person he would ever meet for the rest of his life. And he would remember it. He remembered it so well that every son he fathered was given Miguel as the first or middle name.

Before leaving with Miguel, Antonio said, "My brother Xavier went on that ship over there and has not come out. I have to wait for him. Miguel grabbed him by the arm and said, "You are likely to be standing here all night. That is the Las Pampas, and she is sailing in the morning. Believe me if he is working on board he is not coming out until morning. Come with me, I know one of the hands, we'll ask around." Having said that Miguel approached the ramp and yelled, "Permission to come aboard," the cargo master looked at Miguel, recognized him and signaled him aboard. When hearing Miguel's request he sent him to the crew boss and there he found Xavier.

Miguel also knew Rogelio and explained that Xavier's brother was in the pier looking for him. "Oh hell, I forgot all about him. I need to see him. Don

Rogelio, I just need five minutes to say goodbye. I don't know that I'll ever see him again." Rogelio said, "If you may never see him again, you better take more than five minutes. Come back in one hour. Be sure to tell the watch that you are coming back, otherwise he may not let you board."

"I am going to Argentina. Can you believe it? I am going to cross that ocean and get to Argentina. Don Rogelio has offered me a job in his father's ranch. He is an old man who needs help." Xavier explained to his brother. Rogelio knew right away that Xavier was not, nor would he ever be a sailor. But he saw the potential for a strong ranch hand for his father who because of Rogelio's preference for the sea had no one to help him run the ranch. Their ranch was roughly twelve hundred acres. Small by Argentinean standards but large for a small family to run. During dinner with Xavier, Rogelio learned that Xavier knew nothing about ships, but the same was not true about animals. He had been around them all his life and actually liked being around cattle and horses. At the end of the dinner, Rogelio offered to take him to Puerto Plata and there put him on a train for Mendoza. He would send a telegram to his father and would give a letter of introduction to Xavier.

All of this was bewildering, exciting, challenging, everything but frightening. He figured that the way he had lived in Spain so far, his worst day in a foreign country could only be better than his best day in his own. One thing he had always known either because he felt it, or because others always reminded him; Basque are not Spaniards and are not wanted. "I can not take you with me and I don't know if I am ever coming back. But if you want to Maybe we can communicate that way." Both knew that this was their final goodbye. Xavier could not read or write and neither could Antonio. Writing was not an option. They knew that the probability of ever seeing one another again was the same as that of ever seeing their father. And they knew that would never happen. They shook hands kissed each other's cheeks twice. Locked eyes one final time and moved on with their lives.

CHAPTER 2

Everything all around them was opened everywhere. This being Saturday evening and near midnight, Barcelona was just awakening. People gathered around the Tapas bars consuming all of the specialties. These were small dishes prepared as a pre dinner snack. The Serrano Hams hanging from the rafters, the pungent sardines, the shrimp covered in garlic, the olives drenched in spiced olive oil and the anchovies rolled and pinched with toothpicks all were stacked along the counters. The patrons would simply help themselves to as many of the dishes as they wanted and ordered the wine and the beer from the waiters. Somehow the waiters kept track of who had taken what and how much of it, and when it came time to settle the bill, it always worked out. Unless a patron disagreed in which case he would pay what he felt was owed and he would be invited to frequent another plaza because that one was now off limits.

Within the waiters up and down and around the plaza where all the restaurants were, one next to the other, there was a network that shared information about patrons. If ever a patron mistreated a waiter by being rude, not paying for food consumed or failing to tip adequately, the word went out. From there on and until the misbehaving patron improved in manners, service would be awful. The way the tables were laid out all waiters could see all customers in the plaza shared by all the restaurants so there was no way that anyone in disgrace could escape the treatment. There was no set rule covering how long the patrons would suffer the consequences of their actions. It was as long as it was. Miguel stood next to Antonio watching him watch the action, realizing that this was all new for Antonio. The scene did not remind Antonio that he had not eaten in a long time. Instead it caused him to think about how people should live as opposed to how he was living.

There was joy in these people's life. He did not necessarily think them to be rich; they just had lives richer than his. In particular he was struck by one special girl. She was very pretty and he could not guess her age since he had no frame of reference about young and attractive girls. She may have been in her late adolescence. Her demeanor was that of a person older than her years. With her were two gentlemen who were clearly friendly and familiar, one more obsequious towards her than the other. He wandered where the chaperon would be, because there was no way that a young lady would be out that late in the evening accompanied by two men without one. Unless one of them was her brother and so he filled the role of her protector.

She wore a beautiful chiffon dress and a shawl around her shoulders both ivory white. Her striking black hair contrasted dramatically as it fell on her shoulders covered by the white shawl. The dress fit her figure in a way that indicated a young and firm body without revealing much. Everything about her was fluid, her features, her motions and her demeanor all spoke of class and wealth. It also spoke of loveliness. Antonio never one for dreaming, at that moment began to form the dream that would drive him in everything he did. His dream was not about the Catalan girl as he thought of her, it was about the lifestyle that would allow him to be noticed by others as she was noticed by him. To be so comfortable in that world, so as to indicate that he belonged and anyone who looked at him could tell. This whole experience lasted but a moment, but Antonio could have stood watching her until he could turn to stone.

Miguel nudged him and they moved on. Everything was opened except at the convent. It was locked tight and the only way to enter was by jumping the fence. This was difficult to accomplish but for the experienced, and Miguel was very experienced. The reason experience was needed was because the top of the cement wall was filled with glass from broken bottles from one end of the wall to the other. The nuns had brought in a mason to place the broken glass all along the perimeter. The locals would make jokes about the security along the lines of would the broken glass serve to keep intruders out or the novices at the convent in. Many of the novices in the convent were sent there because of their religious calling but others were sent because their families could not afford to feed them, or because they were incorrigible and their families hoped that by making a contribution to the church, the nuns would turn the misguided ones onto the right path. Some of the girls who arrived at the convent did not stay for very long. Soon after they realized that the way of the habit was not for them, they would start plotting their escape. Once in a while when a girl realized that the convent was not for her, the nuns would place her in service with one of the families that attended the church. For many that was more preferable than returning home or walking the streets, which for some was the only option. The only opportunity for outside contacts came during the Sunday masses when the church courtyard would be filled with worshippers and many young men whose sole purpose for visiting on Sundays was to inspect the girls. The nuns fully aware of their intentions and the temptations at play during the service would be exceedingly vigilant, but there were too many boys and girls to watch and one way or another temptation would prevail upon discretion and another novice would be lost to the ways of the world.

"Do what I do and grab where I grab, I mean put your hands exactly where I place mine." Antonio did exactly as he was told and after grabbing hold of the wall at the precise spot where the spacing between the glass allowed for a hand to be placed, he leapt to the courtyard. From there they walked to Miguel's cell. The room was called a cell because it was where visiting monks would stay. Often when waiting for their ships to depart for Africa or the Americas, the monks would lodge with the sisters and since they had taken a vow of poverty, the cell was a fair reminder. In truth, a cell was something that hole in the wall aspired to be. It had no window and no ventilation and it reeked of the odor of every human being or animal that had ever passed through it. Miguel slept in more of a cot than a bed. Beds usually have mattresses. The cover that rested over the boards that replaced the leather straps that at one time must have been part of it, or something but not a bed, was so thin as to be almost translucent. In a corner there was a candle that at full light would not be sufficient to do anything but keep him from bumping into the wall. In the corner there was a hammock made out of burlap sacks that were tied at either end by ropes. Miguel picked it up and took it outside where he gave one end to Antonio and grabbed the other. "We have to shake the bugs and God knows what else out of this hammock. Shake it hard otherwise they will cling to the burlap and express their displeasure at being evicted in the middle of the night by biting you." Once he was satisfied that the hammock was cleared of bugs Miguel took it inside and hung it from two hooks protruding from the main beam in the cell. Recognizing that Antonio was too large for the hammock he told him, "You take the bed. In that hammock your arms and legs will take turns hanging over either side and if they hang from the same side at the same time you will surely crash to the ground. Now don't argue and take the bed." Antonio said, "I am too tired to argue, so I will not, but I am taking the hammock and that is that." With that he jumped into the hammock and was asleep before Miguel could say another word.

For Antonio this was an improvement over the park benches he had been sleeping in or the crates he slept on at the pier after the police ran him off the park. Although Miguel had offered to share the cot, Antonio preferred the hammock. He after all was familiar with hammocks because he had been sleeping in them all his life. The hammock did offer one problem for which there was no solution, Antonio was big in everyway.

He was full grown. At thirteen, he was already six feet one inches tall and weight over two hundred pounds. The only way you knew he was still a boy was because he did not yet shave. Otherwise he was a fully developed man. This also included his very large feet. They were larger than a foot measure and no hammock was going to cover them. This would prove to be a problem his whole life. Finding the right fitting shoes or boots would be an expensive proposition and since he refused to spend any more money than he absolutely had to, for all of his life he wore only boots. And for a time he thought there was no need ever to own more than one pair at a time. Although he did not realize it at the time he was learning the lessons that would ultimately define him as a conservative man. He understood that to be a conservative one needed to have something to conserve.

By the time of the first bells, Miguel was already up and dressed. Since Antonio had little to change into in his traveling sack, Miguel took him to the room where the garments that had been donated by the wealthy Catholics were stored. These were of course the garments that had been rejected by their servants and their servant's relatives. Style was not a concern, but size was. There were very few items that fit him, in fact none that he could find. As a happy coincidence Antonio had not yet developed the young man's vanity usually associated with people his age and so he did not care what he looked like. That was until he noticed the smile in Miguel's face when he saw the clothes Antonio was wearing. No matter, it was what it was. After washing up by the fountain outside the entrance to the church they started their chores for the day. The first order of business was to get the sacristy ready for the altar boys. The first mass would be at six followed by one every hour until the Noon mass. By the time they arrived at the kitchen the breads for the six masses and communions were already baked by the Nuns. Fortunately one of the loaves was not shaped well and could not be used in the mass so that it became their breakfast. When they sat down, the sister at the oven brought them sausages to go with their bread and coffee. The first nun looked at Antonio with a welcoming smile and another one said, "Don't feel that you have to eat all of it at once. Chew the bread slowly. Don't you realize that this is our daily bread for which we always say thanks? It is a gift from God. He gave it to us and the least we can do is to enjoy it in his holy name." Antonio did not know what to expect but this certainly was not it. "What is your name my son," the nun asked. "I am called Antonio" he replied. She said, "Yes, Antonio is your name, but here you will be called Anton." Antonio said, "Only my mother has ever called me by that name, how did you know?"

"I am Sister Maria de la Dolorosa, and I am your mother now. That is how I know. I know more than you think I know and will know more than you think I should. It is what I do. I have been directly by the Holy Virgin Mary to be your mother and since I have pledged my life to her, your mother I am." At this point Miguel spoke and introduced Antonio to all of the Nuns explaining how they came to meet and how they had shared the cell. Not disclosing that they had jumped the wall since they had arrived after midnight. Sister Maria said to no one in particular, "This is a day for celebration. Miguel has brought us a new son. Full grown and obviously strong. Anton," she said, "Will you lead us in the morning prayer," and with that she handed Antonio her prayer book. Antonio had felt lacking for not being able to read, but never embarrassed. Never until now. Recognizing at once what was going on and mortified that she had caused Antonio's discomfort she said "Forgive me I realize that you do not read Catalan. I can tell by your accent that you are Basque. Never you mind. I'll pray for all of us."

Miguel looked at Sister Maria and back to Antonio and knew that there would be no need to ask for anyone to teach Antonio to read. He remembered how he had become the sisters' project when he first arrived and they found out he could not read. He became their enthusiastic project. It was almost as if there was a competition about who could teach him best. Nuns were either trained in nursing or as teachers. And Miguel had needed both health care and reading lessons when he arrived four years before. After breakfast they walked to the sacristy where they delivered the jug of wine they had picked up from the storage room adjacent to the kitchen. Antonio carried the loaves of bread in a basket he picked up next to the table in the kitchen. He covered the bread with a cloth given him to him by a novice who looked no older than twelve. She smiled shyly at him when she handed him the cloth and said, "I am Renatta. I am your sister and God's child." This she said in such a natural way that it moved Antonio to look at her and say, "I too want to be a child of God just so that I can be your brother."

When they arrived at the sacristy the six altar boys who would be attending at the first two masses were already changing into their vestments. Close in age and demeanor, these were the sons of mothers who hoped that their boys would go into the priesthood because that way they were assured paradise. Some of the boys were answering the call of God, others were there for the free wine they could get. Others were there because sometimes in a hot summer day they could get a peak at women's breast when they held the communion plate as the priest blessed the recipients. Altar boys sneaking a peek needed to lean back away from the priest because if he noticed them peeking, an elbow to the kidneys would remind the sinner just how mortal sin could be. Unlike the church he had attended in Bilbao, the church in Barcelona allowed him to sit with the Spaniards. In fact, he sat up front behind the nuns.

By the time they processioned into the church the word had spread about the new boy helping Miguel, and everyone of the nuns and novices smiled at him. Everyone of them saw in him a project for salvation and education. The mass was in Latin and although Antonio did not understand a word of it, he did enjoy the pomp and circumstance and all of the rituals associated with the service of the Eucharist. When communion came, Miguel held Antonio and told him, "Stay with me, I'll explain later." Since they had returned to the convent so late Miguel had missed confession and was not eligible for communion. Antonio on the other hand had been baptized but that was the extent of the sacraments that he had completed and could not receive communion.

The mother superior, Sister Graciela de la Cruz looked like someone who had not missed many meals. Although large and imposing and stern in appearance, she frightened only the priests who may have attempted to boss her around or to demand some service from one of the nuns without going through her. From time to time a young and ignorant priest would arrive at the convent with the misguided notion that priest ruled and nuns served. For the most part the Monsignors or the senior priests would brief the young ones on protocol. The few who would not listen would find themselves wishing for service in the jungles of Guatemala instead of the convent in Barcelona. After the mass had ended she asked for Antonio to be brought to her for a conversation. She mainly wanted to assess his needs and how best to help him. By his demeanor she could tell that although he was not afraid he was apprehensive, tentative about looking at her or speaking to her.

They sat on a bench and she began by asking Antonio to account for all thirteen years of his life. There was not much to recollect and most of what he did remember was not pleasant. Like most people, the pleasant memories replace the unpleasantness of life, and so Antonio could cover his whole existence in less than ten minutes. Among other things Sister Graciela was an expert in human beings and she could read Antonio like an open book with only a few pages. He was so prepared for harshness and difficulty and so expecting of it that anything other than what he expected threw him off balance and made him defensive. At once the sister sensed Antonio's demeanor towards authority and religion, but especially towards her as a nun. It was nothing personal, after all they had only just met. But she knew that unless she could break through the barrier built in the past, there would be no future for her with him. "Anton, tell me about your religious upbringing," she said and met his stare. "Were you raised in the faith, were you baptized, have you ever confessed, have you had your first communion, have you been confirmed?" More of his blank stare gave her the answers to all the questions. "With respect sister, the nuns that I have known were nothing like the sisters here. I have been here one whole day and no one has hit me yet. I walk around ready for the first blow. This God of love that you and the others speak of all the time has never loved me. This Holy Mary mother God that you all serve has never been my mother. So with respect, please sister don't be angry with me because I do not trust any of you." She said, "Yet."

"Anton, can you tell me what you want. What you want right now. Not tomorrow but right now," she asked. He paused and thought for all of five seconds before telling her that more than anything he wanted to be able to read. To read books, to read newspapers, to read announcements. He actually thought that different reading skills may have been required based on what one needed to read. "What else do you want?" she asked. Not having thought beyond the first question and his greatest need, he had no answer. She said, "Anton, we will teach you to read, we will teach you numbers, we will feed you and clothe you, but you must do something for me." She paused to look at him and saw the look in his eyes that said here it comes, the price to pay. "What I want you to do for me is to forgive all of those who hurt you especially those in the church who hurt you. I will not ask you to forget them but I do ask you to forgive them. You are not responsible for their behavior but you are responsible for your conduct. Do you understand that if you allow them to influence your thoughts by continuing to live in anger you have allowed them to defeat you."

"Anton you are and must be bigger than they are. Please know this, you are plenty big but height only makes you tall. God wants you to be big and that speaks of your character. We will reach your mind to teach you the things that you must learn but you must let God enter your heart so that he can help you be who you want to be and stop being who you have been."

CHAPTER 3

Almost two and a half years had passed and Antonio could read and write with ease. He could also add, subtract, multiply and divide. His discipline and desire to learn everything that was being taught to him were qualities that even he did not know he had. But once he started to learn he got hungrier and thirstier for knowledge. And he could teach others. He was very good with children, especially the ones from the poor families who would line up outside the kitchen waiting for their breakfast. For many of them this would be their only meal for the day. Sister Graciela seeing how long the children would stand in line waiting for their food came up with idea to put their time to good use by holding morning catechism classes. They way it worked, a group of no more than ten would be taken to a small chapel just to the side of the entrance and there they would be taught while their breakfast was being prepared. When they moved on to breakfast another group would take their place and this would be repeated throughout the morning every day.

One morning, Antonio curious as ever stepped into the chapel and saw that the nun teaching the class sat at eye level with the children. He remembered what it was like when he sat for the same lesson in Bilbao. He thought about his catechism classes and smiled because he had moved beyond the bitter memories of his childhood. He was learning to be the man Sister Graciela wanted him to be. Bitterness will make you the lesser for the experience she had taught him. And so he had moved on, feeling sorry for those so insecure that they felt the need to look down at others. On this particular morning the nun scheduled to teach became ill and Antonio was drafted into service. From the moment he sat with the children he felt the rewards of doing good for no better reason than it was needed. Beyond that day, he would look for every opportunity to be around the children sometimes at the cost of skipping his own breakfast before going to work at the docks. He could scarcely recognize himself. No doubt neither could anyone else who had known him prior to his arrival at the convent. Miguel would marvel and take pride in the change that he was witnessing in Antonio. He felt proud because after all it was he who delivered Antonio to the sisters. When Antonio found out some of the children could not yet read he added reading to catechism classes and soon everyone was reading.

On a Sunday afternoon with all their chores completed Anton and Miguel went for a walk to the plaza. As in every Sunday, unless it was raining, the plaza was jammed full of people. All the shops all the restaurants, all the bars and all the bookstores were opened. And that is where Antonio dragged Miguel, to the first book store he ever entered. It was not too long ago that he had seen people buying books and could not figure why they would spend money on such a thing. Now he wished he could buy every book on the shelves. He picked up a copy of Don Quixote De la Mancha by Miguel Cervantes Saavedra. As he looked at the authors name it struck him that he had two last names, in fact most gentlemen he had met at the docks or at the convent all had two or three last names. Why did he only have one he wondered. Some day he would look into that. As he held the book and walked out of the store with it he made sure that everyone would see the book in his hands. It said to the world, 'I can read.'

The changes in Antonio had not escaped Sister Graciela either. He had not changed much physically. There was no way that he was going to get much bigger or taller, or stronger. The changes she had noticed were that he started to shave and his voice that had been husky when they first met was now deep and deliberate. He also started to pay attention to his appearance. He took care of his good clothes and looked striking when he wore them. He felt different and it showed. He would look at people in their eyes when he spoke or was spoken to. She realized that he was coming into his own. Comfortable and confident. She also noticed that others were noticing him.

The church held a Saturday fair for all of the parishioners and their guests. This event which was held annually commemorated their patron, Saint Jacinto. On that particular evening Antonio and Miguel manned the rings in the bottles stand. To play the game a player was required to buy three wooden rings that were to be tossed a distance of six feet at a box full of equally sized bottles that were tightly aligned in a square shape. Every ring in a bottle would win a price. At any one time during that afternoon their stand was packed full of girls waiting to play and would only hand their money to Antonio. He however, was either oblivious or was pretending to be, and ignored all of the flirtatious energies being spent on his behalf. It may have escaped him but not Mother Superior.

The next day for Sunday mass Miguel and Antonio changed into their Sunday clothes after preparing the sacristy for all the masses. At ten minutes until ten, the nuns entered in procession as customary, Antonio and Miguel followed and sat behind the sisters. As he looked around waiting for the priests, the deacons and the altar boys to enter, Antonio was looking to his left and froze his stare upon the girl that he had seen at the Tapas bar before arriving at the convent that first night. She looked exactly the same maybe prettier if such a thing were possible. She noticed his stare and smiled as she stood for the entrance of the priest which signaled the beginning of the mass. He had not seen her since that evening at the plaza because she had been away at boarding school, but had thought about her often. She was accompanied by a man who was not with her the evening he first saw her. Sister Graciela who could see everything around her all the time looked at Antonio who immediately directed his eyes to the prayer book and started with his responsorial chants. The sister looked at the girl upon whom Antonio was fixated and had to admit he had great taste. She seemed not to have any connection to Antonio since she did not look at him again. She was however lovely and the sister understood about the emotions of an almost sixteen year old boy, especially one as well developed as Antonio. Her own son had been but fifteen when he died.

After the mass Sister Graciela made it a point to find the girl and the man with her who was her father. After exchanging the morning greetings she called on Antonio to join them. To her own surprise he was as affable and warm as he could possibly have been. Where did his shyness disappear to she wondered. Sister Graciela said, "Anton, I want you to meet Don Genaro Gabriel and his daughter Mercedes. Don Genaro, this is the young man who has been teaching reading and writing to the children who come to breakfast every morning. We are very proud of him. This is Antonio Barradaz, a born scholar. Not yet educated but a scholar nonetheless. We are very proud of our Anton," she added, "Don Genaro is the senior member of our district

Council and a very good friend of Saint Jacinto's. Mercedes was baptized and confirmed here, had her first communion with us, and God willing will be married here as well." Mercedes was the first one to speak and in the most unpretentious voice said, "Anton I am very pleased to meet you because if Sister Graciela speaks well of you it is because you are worthy of praise. The reason I know this is true is because she never spoke so glowingly of me." At this moment she released his hand and hugged the Mother Superior with the warmth that indicated there was much history between them. "Young man," said Don Genaro, "will you be going into the seminary?"

"Will you study for the priesthood?" Not knowing what to say Antonio said nothing. Instead it was Sister Graciela who spoke and said, "No Don Genaro, if we continue to take the best of our boys into the priesthood where will the likes of Mercedes find great husbands. No sir. This one is destined for the world and when we turn him loose upon it, the world will be the better for it." With that the conversation ended and they moved on to visit with friends. Sister Graciela said, "Anton will you have lunch with me today? Don't worry I'll ask the priests to clean after themselves. We don't want them to get too spoiled. I have heard from our sisters in Mexico that the priests we are sending to them are spoiled rotten. Come to my suite at one thirty."

According to her rank the mother superior enjoyed a suite of rooms that included her sleeping quarters, her office, a combination sitting and dining area and a small balcony overlooking the garden from which most of their vegetables came. Lunch was served in the balcony and was waiting when Antonio knocked on her door. As soon as he entered she asked him to sit down across from her. The lunch consisted of two kinds of bread, several pieces of sausage, one of them being blood sausage, a regional favorite, cheeses and a basket of peaches. She surprised him by serving him a glass of wine saying, "This wine should taste better than the wine served with communion and besides you do not have to hurry and sneak a drink, we have all afternoon." He smiled at her and they both knew that it would be foolish to pretend that Mother Superiors did not know everything about everything all the time.

"Anton, tell me, what did you think of Mercedes," she asked. Caught off guard he had to think of the answer. Not an answer, but the answer. For he knew that anything less than the truth would not do.

"I was struck by her kindness and her openness; she is nothing like I had imagined she would be. Today was not the first time I saw her. I saw her at the plaza about two years ago, she really made an impression on me then and a bigger and better impression today."

"Were you surprised that she is not much different from the rest of us? Were you surprised by her kindness? Were you?" she asked. "Yes and no," he answered. "Please explain," the sister asked. "Well, Sister Graciela since I do not know her; I can not form a judgment either way. I choose to think that as pretty as she is she must be kind, what reason would she have to be otherwise. On the other hand, were I expecting her to be unkind I would not have been as disappointed as I was pleasantly surprised she was kind. Sister Graciela, I have come to know that there are the kinds of people that enjoy being kind to other people and then there are the other kind of people."

The sister stared at him taking his answer in and reflecting on it. "Anton you are as our merciful lord told me you would be. Filled with a great heart and an even bigger mind and if we can get you to continue to develop both the world around you and those with whom you share your life, your friendship and your love will be the more fortunate. Anton it is not by accident that we are in each other's lives and luck had nothing to do with it. We come to be together by the grace of God. When a nun takes her vows she is required to have no life other than the one she has pledged to God. Even your previous life ceases to exist. In my case it was easy. I was not always a nun. At one time I was a wife and a mother, and fully committed to my family.

My son was fifteen when our barn caught fire and my husband who went in to rescue him perished along with my boy. Anton, please do not speak. I must tell you these things so that you know that I have known love, satisfaction, physical gratification, I have known them all and I have also known despair. It is only because my neighbors held me back that I did not burn with my husband and my son as I had wanted. But if I had burned with them I would never have known the pleasures of serving our lord Jesus Christ and his Father our God. Anton, I was placed in this earth at this moment in this place to be here for you. And Anton, I do not believe that a greater purpose would have pleased me more."

"I have seen the way the girls look at you with a hunger in their eyes that either you do not yet see or choose to ignore. But the time is coming when the forces of the flesh will do battle against the forces of the spirit and the winner will take your soul. As a nun I have taken an oath of celibacy, but Anton I have had my experiences after all my son was not born through Immaculate Conception, it was through copulation with my husband whom I loved and respected. And as a married couple we exchange our humanity to create another human being, a child of god, our son. Anton, think about this, of all the species of the earth only humans mate face to face. Why do you think that is? Animals can do the same. There is no physical reason why they can't. But they don't. Why is that Anton?"

He was absolutely consumed by emotion and could not speak. The sister continued, "Anton, the reason only men and women mate face to face is because God gave us the gift of reason so that we can make a choice and having made that choice we look at one another as we exchange pleasures, and through that process on those occasions we glorify our humanity and glorify our God, and because of that he rewards us with a new life in his image. You see Anton your humanity is a gift from God and you must never let anyone make it less than that for you, nor should you ever make it the less for a woman. Do you understand what I am saying to you?"

It had been a long time since Anton had last cried and in that moment he could not contain the tears that filled his eyes. His heart, his soul and his spirit at that moment were transformed and the love he felt for this good woman was more than he could understand himself. He felt like running for shame because he felt unworthy of her. His eyes were so swelled up with tears that he could barely see. At that moment Sister Graciela touched his hand and said, "I asked you here to feed your body, but first I felt the need in you for your soul to be nourished. Let us say grace and share this beautiful afternoon."

CHAPTER 4

Antonio and Miguel had built quite a reputation at the docks for honesty and consistent reliability. Whatever they promise they would deliver and the bosses at the docks who represented the various shipping lines knew that from the two of them they always got more than required and better than expected. There was a maturity in Antonio and Miguel that was far greater than their years. No one really knew their ages or much about them. They knew that they were not particularly religious although they lived at the convent with the nuns.

They had leadership skills that could not be taught. Theirs were strictly natural. It was evident when at the start of the day the crews were assigned to the day's in-bound and out-bound ships. Early in the morning the various shipping lines would line up the crew bosses for the day's assignments. They always gave the first choice to Miguel and Antonio because they knew that the best hands wanted to work for them. And as the assignments were given and the crews were selected, Antonio and Miguel had the very best of the hands available. It was interesting to anyone watching the selection process unfold that most of the hands were older than Antonio and Miguel. More interesting was to notice that they called them Don Antonio and Don Miguel. This was not demanded or required. All other crew bosses were called by their first names or some corresponding nickname. If ever there was a place where time was money, the docks in Barcelona were it. The available hands had figured out that the best organized bosses would eliminate wasted time and effort and that translated into more money for them since they were paid based on the numbers of pieces of luggage they handled. They also knew that with these two bosses there were no second chances. If ever a piece of luggage went missing they would track at what time it went missing, figured whose hands were near the missing piece when it went unaccounted for, and that man would not return to the docks.

Their management and operational styles were almost identical in that they built reciprocal trust with their laborers. Antonio, larger in size and bulk and with a commanding voice never felt the need to raise his voice to anyone. Either in praise, correction or criticism he had the same somber tone of voice. He was always in control and had such a commanding presence that when he spoke the crews responded in whatever form it was expected. They had come to appreciate that the respect they afforded him was earned. Miguel on the other hand was not small but was not as big as Antonio. In his own way his command of people was effective. He never felt the need to insult a man in the process of correcting him. If a man had made a mistake, Miguel would not use the word stupid, instead he would say something along the lines of "What you did lacked in diligence and in the future I expect better from you. Do I make myself clear?" and through those comments he would address his concerns and preserve the man's dignity.

By the time Antonio had reached seventeen and Miguel was nineteen they felt themselves masters of the universe. They earned what for them was plenty of money. Voluntarily they were paying a small rent at the convent and Antonio had moved to his own cell. The sisters would chastise him because when he was given his own cell he took the hammock with him. Never knowing when the bed could have been taken from him, he said, "The hammock will always be with me. I can not hang a bed between trees but I can always find where to hang my hammock." The nuns relented on their insistence but demanded that he should have more than one hammock, so that on occasion they may clean it for him. They were also concerned about the effect that the curved sleeping position could have on his back. It never concerned him.

On the Saturdays that they got off work early they would venture out to the plaza after washing up and putting on their best clothes. This consisted of a plain shirt, cotton slacks and a jacket. Sister Graciela had prevailed upon Antonio that he needed more than one pair of boots. Leather needs to breathe or it will rot she told him. This he knew to be true because his own boots were rotted. The sister asked a parishioner who was a boot maker to make him a pair of boots. Since she knew that he would not go for a fitting, she got him to stand barefoot on a piece of paper and traced his feet. This she gave to the boot maker and from that outline he produced Antonio's first pair of Valencian leather boots.

On this Saturday evening around eleven they sat at a Tapas bar that looked over the plaza where the tables were set. This was so natural for them that it was hard to believe that only four years before they had stood outside looking in. Now they sat inside looking out. They looked and felt like everyone else because they were. Mercedes saw them before they saw her.

Since there was better lighting in the bar than at the tables it was easier for her to see them. She approached them and said to Antonio, "Are you still Sister Graciela's favorite, have we lost you to the seminary? Is there still hope for the girls?" Both Antonio and Miguel jumped to their feet to acknowledge her presence and before either one could respond, she grabbed both their arms and walked them to her table. Making the introductions she said "This is Martin my brother and his fiancée Irene. They are to be married soon. I am their chaperon this evening. And if you would be so kind to sit with us, they will go walk around the plaza alone because I will have you to protect me." Martin and Irene did not have to be given the offer for privacy twice. They leapt at the chance and left for their walk but not before saying, "Please keep our tab open and help yourselves to whatever you wish, although we are leaving you, you will be our guests."

Mercedes said, "Antonio are you not going to introduce me to your friend? Or are you so ashamed of me?" Quickly he regained his confidence, smiled at her and said, "It is my honor to introduce my brother Miguel to you. You should like him he is Catalan like you." Miguel tried to stand to bow to Mercedes and before he could she offered her hand, shook his and asked him to please sit. "I did not know you had a brother here in Barcelona." Antonio said, "Miguel is my special brother. The one God gave me did not work out so I decided to pick my own and he is my brother by choice, what do you think?" She looked at Miguel and back at Antonio and said "You are fortunate to have a choice, and you have chosen well. Miguel, I am honored to meet you." Miguel held the same smile he had been holding since she first approached them at the bar. He was troubled by the absolute certainty that if he said anything she would think less of him. He did not know what she thought of him, but it mattered a great deal. Finally he mustered the courage to say, "Please excuse my silence, I am presently relishing in the pleasure of your company." With that he sat down and looked at Antonio whose eyes were wide filled with an expression that said, "Where did that come from?"

As they ordered Tapas and a carafe of wine, the conversation loosened and they began to feel the comfort that one feels being around people one has known for a long time. "We just came back from the theatre. Have you ever been? If you haven't you must see this play before it closes. It is Don Quixote. A real masterpiece, maybe you have heard of it?" Antonio said, "I have read the book several times, and found it extremely satirical," Mercedes said, "There may never be better satire than the one Cervantes inflicts upon our nobility. Of course we are not supposed to say this so I am saying it between friends. Have you read it too Miguel?"

"No, but I will, starting tomorrow, if the sisters give me the time." Mercedes looked surprised as she said, "You mean to say that you are still living at the convent."

"Of course," said Antonio, "But why does that surprise you? Oh I understand. Men our age are living at home with their families or are out to find their fortune in the world. It turns out that Miguel and I are each other's family, and as far as the finding our fortune, all things in due course."

"How about you? How is your father? Are you still living at home or can we expect you at the convent to take your vows?" With that Mercedes broke out into a grin followed by uncontrolled contagious laughter. The kind that caused the adjacent tables to wish they were in on the story. "No my friends, I did give it some thought for about ten seconds when I was seven years old and kissed my cousin." She continued, "I am trying to convince my father to let me go to Cuba. My uncle has a large sugar cane plantation there. I do not know how far it is from Havana but I think I would like it. I just don't want to take a husband before I have had the time to see that part of the world. I have seen Europe and Africa and I now I want to see the Caribbean. Maybe even get to North America. I would like to see what the Americans are like. I did learn English when I was in England at boarding school." Antonio asked her, "What is it that attracts you about Cuba?"

"Mostly that I do not know it," Turning to Miguel, she said, "And how about you, are you going to let me carry on about myself and not tell me who you are?"

"I am Miguel de la Madrid and I want to be very honest with you, this is the first time that I have had a conversation with anyone of your class where

I was not being told to do something or to stop doing what I was doing. I have not been around people like you, ever, and certainly not eating and drinking with them." Leaning forward and with all earnest she said, "And please tell me Don Miguel de la Madrid just what kind of people is it that I am?"

"Better than me, " he answered. "Not enough of an answer. Unacceptable if you are to say that I am better than you, that by definition makes me special. So please tell me how is it that I am special." This time Miguel paused looked at Antonio and back to Mercedes and said. "Miss Mercedes what makes you so special is that you do not realize how special a person you are. One has to have met many unkind people to recognize how special your kindness is. I have had the misfortune to have been around many unkind people most of my life, except for the sisters at the Convent. But they do not count because they are not regular people they after all are sisters. But I am grateful for all of the negative experiences that I have had with people because it makes this one all the more memorable for me."

Mercedes did not know what to expect but she certainly was not expecting this outpouring of admiration from the least expected source. So surprised was she that no reply, no comment or movement came from her. In all of her life she had not heard words expressed in such a way with such sincerity that at that moment something stirred in her. Something that she had never felt before. Whatever it was that this man had made her to feel she did not know what it was, but she did know that she wanted more of it.

At this point Martin and Irene returned with a look about them that confirmed the enjoyment they had from being by themselves. Although surrounded by a multitude, alone nevertheless. Antonio and Miguel stood up and Irene said, "I am honored but please remain seated." Miguel responded for the two of them and asked they be excused because of their Sunday morning duties at the church. Mercedes looking directly at Miguel said, "Well then, we will see you at the ten o'clock mass" As they walked away Antonio said to Miguel, "How long have I known you my brother?"

"Almost four years now, why? said Miguel. "Because I have never been prouder of you than I am this evening," remarked Antonio. "Well Anton, when you introduced me as your brother I figured that we stood for something more than two crew bosses out for a beer. We stand for one another. We stand as brothers. And as brothers we must bring honor upon one another. All brothers may do the same, but they are not brothers like us. They are brothers by accident. They had nothing to do with whose brothers they are. But Anton you and I chose one another, and that my brother is what makes our bonds special." With that, Antonio threw his arm over Miguel's shoulder and there it stayed until it came time to jump the glass encrusted wall.

Next morning Antonio finally figured out what it was that was so unusual. It was so obvious that he had to laugh at himself with the same kind of laugh that he had seen in Miguel's face that first Sunday morning when Antonio wore the ill fitting clothes he had collected from the poor people's locker and Miguel had attempted but failed to contain a smile. These however were not ill fitting clothes that Miguel was wearing. These were the very best clothes he had ever worn. Antonio looked at the boots his adopted brother wore and now he understood why Miguel had taken a small cup of olive oil to his cell.

The boots looked like a great amount of effort had been invested in bringing the luster out of them and with great success. It was clear to everyone at the kitchen that for Miguel this was a special day. They just did not know what made it so special. They wondered if the Bishop was visiting and they had missed the announcement. The shirt worn by Miguel was no doubt new and it surely did not come from the poor people's supply. The same was true of the rest of the ensemble. The black tie, the blue jacket and the black pants were all put together with one purpose and one purpose only and that was to impress. But who did he want to impress was the question.

When Miguel entered the kitchen everyone and everything came to a sudden awkward stop followed by exclamations from everyone at the same time. All offering very complimentary comments but none more earnest than Sister Maria who said, "For the first time in my life I am questioning my vows to the lord. My son I do not know for whom you are making this effort that has made you so handsome and so special, I only hope that she is worthy of you. May I have a kiss from you before we lose you forever?" With that she walked the few steps towards him, held his face and kissed both his cheeks. The kitchen erupted with multiple degrees of bravo exclamations followed by requests from several other nuns saying "I am next, no I am next" and so on. Miguel grinned from ear to ear relishing the attention and the love he was feeling from every one of them. When finally everyone calmed down and one of the sisters handed Miguel and Antonio each a cup of coffee, Antonio asked what the occasion was. Miguel replied by saying, "Tell me Antonio, if the queen of Spain were to invite you to her castle would you not wear your very best?"

Well she has not invited me to her castle, but today God expects me at his house, and can I dress less to be in the presence of God than I would to go before the Queen?" He looked at Antonio with a smile that said, and that is that. Antonio reminded him that on the day of their first communion two years earlier they hadn't dressed as well. Miguel paused for a few seconds and answered Antonio by reminding him that then they were children and now they were men. Moreover, they did not own any good clothes then. Antonio could not refute this undeniable truth, but did say, "But will the lord not think less of me when he sees me next to you."

"No," said Miguel, "Because in the eyes of the lord we are not the same. Since he knows that my misdeeds are more and than yours I have to try harder." Antonio remembered what it had been like for him to take his first communion. Because of his age the preparation had been conducted in private classes by the nuns. Others preparing for their first communion were trained in larger groups of younger people. However on the Saturday evening before his first communion they all went to confession together. They had been told by the sisters what to say, how to say it and what to expect. As they got closer to the confessionary Antonio was ahead of Miguel, and ahead of them was a young girl that they judged to be around fourteen years old. She approached the box, knelt and began her confession. Neither they nor anyone else could hear what she had said, and were in shock when the priest, a man in his late seventies if not older stepped out of the box and started yelling at the girl who rose from her kneeling position and ran towards the nearest exit followed by the priest who continued to scream, "How dare you, how dare you?" at the poor girl who ran out of the church never to return.

The priest returned to his station, looked at Antonio and calmly said, "Let us continue." Antonio looked at Miguel with a petrified look that implored to his friend to go next. Miguel closed his eyes in fervent prayer clearly indicating that he was willing to wait until the end of the world or until Antonio moved to confession whichever came first. Antonio, who up to this moment had never experienced fear from man, nature or God, at this moment felt it in every form from every source. He remembered that during first communion classes the sisters had continually reinforced the message that redemption would only come through the forgiveness of sins and they could only be forgiven if they were confessed. There it was, and there was no way out of this but to confess. Sister Graciela sensing his trepidation gave him a reassuring smile with a slight nod in the direction of the priest, who waited inside the black box, He stood and shuffled more than walked towards his inevitable fate and knelt. Not hearing anything from the other side he had hoped that maybe the priest had fallen asleep after waiting so long, even better he may have died in there. He waited and no sound or movement was perceived so he was about to stand and walk away when the black curtain opened and he saw the shape of a head that seemed to nod in encouragement. A voice said, "Do you wish to confess my son?" Remembering his training he responded with, "Forgive me Father for I have sinned this is my first confession before you and God." Then he paused thinking about where to start, what to say and in what order. As he labored to organize his thoughts and prioritize his sins he was trying to decide if he should start with minor and then move to mortal sins or should he reverse the order. While the priest seemed to appreciate the apprehension of a first time confession he was not willing to wait all evening.

"Yes my son" he repeated. None of the thoughts in Antonio's head could overwhelm the image of the young girl being chased out of the church by the same priest who now wanted to hear his sins. Finally, drawing from the depth of his spirit and bringing forth all the courage that he could muster he spoke.

"Father, I have had bad thoughts and have said bad words." There, he said it. He had done it. He had confessed, in one clean sentence he had met his obligation and was now ready for his first communion. A stunning silence settled in. It was caused by the priest waiting to hear more and by Antonio waiting for his absolution. They would have waited an eternity if the priest had not spoken first saying, "How old are you my son?" This Antonio could answer truthfully and forthrightly, the question was why was he asking the question. What does age have to do with anything? He wondered if the same question was asked of the fugitive girl. Maybe, he thought that was the answer that caused her to fail. "Father, I am sixteen years old," he almost whispered. The priest reasoned that a boy of Antonio's age would easily move up the sinners scale beyond bad thoughts and words. But sensing the hesitation in coming forth with greater details the priest set out to extricate a confession and so he asked, "Tell me about your bad thoughts." Truth was that Antonio had always been so comfortable in his own skin and with his actions that he genuinely did not know what bad thoughts the priest was after.

So with as much sincerity as he could project, he asked, "What kind of bad thoughts interest you Father? Do you consider thoughts about girls to be bad, or about older women, or maybe it is violent thoughts that are bad, which of those do you prefer father? I have not had many of any of those but if you could help me by sharing yours, maybe I can do better in discussing mine. Finally the priest had heard enough and closed by saying, "For your absolution my son you must say fifty Hail Mary, recite the Lord's Prayer fifty times and say ten acts of contrition."

"Over what period of time father?" Antonio asked. The priest understood that he was dealing with one smart Catholic boy and smiling to himself said, "Before this night is over. Now go and sin no more."

In the procession to enter the church, Antonio always went ahead of Miguel but on this Sunday the order was reversed. This change in the processional sequence meant nothing to Antonio until they arrived at their pew and Miguel sat on the aisle side directly across from Mercedes and her family. Mercedes, her brother and Irene, his fiancée all acknowledged Antonio and Miguel. The Parents, Don Genaro and his wife did not. At the end of the mass as the parishioners mingled outside in the courtyard. Martin called to Antonio and Miguel who walked towards where the family stood.

Antonio spoke first and introduced Miguel to Don Genaro who responded by introducing his wife Doña Carmen who smiled at both but did not extend her hand to greet them. Instead she just smiled and said nothing. The boys on the other hand spoke expressing their pleasure and honor in meeting such a distinguished lady, and slightly bowed their heads as they looked at her eyes. Carmen Alicia Gabriel was not accustomed to being looked at directly by those she considered of lesser class or position. In fact she had dismissed servants for having the audacity to look her in the eyes as she spoke to them.

It simply was not acceptable and she believed it to be an act of insolence. Her discomfort made everyone uncomfortable and so it was Mercedes who first spoke. "Are you going to see Don Quixote as you said you would? You absolutely must, if you think you liked the book you will surely like the play. And do take Miguel with you it will do him good to laugh. Maybe it will take some of the seriousness from him." Martin explained, "These two gentlemen joined us for Tapas last evening when Mercedes, Irene and I went out. He went on to describe his understanding of Antonio's and Miguel's situation at the convent. To which Mercedes offered, "Mamá, this one is Sister Graciela's favorite and she said so." At this point Martin spoke and said it was time to leave since they had reservations at El Meson De la Rambla. This was the meeting point where the important families of Barcelona congregated on Sunday afternoons and where they enjoyed four hour dinners. "Would you consider joining us as our guest?" said Mercedes. Since no one spoke to support the invitation, it was clear that only she wanted their company.

Sensing their discomfort Miguel responded with the excuse that they had promised the sisters to help them move some tables in a classroom that was to be painted the next day. "Maybe some other time then," said Martin. "Nonsense," said Mercedes "This is the Lord's Day and your day of rest. Please do not offend me by rejecting our invitation, I insist." It was clear that only Mercedes was insisting, and to limit the family's anxiety caused by her impetuous invitation Antonio said, "It is not possible for us come this minute we do have some commitments to the sisters, perhaps another time." As if a game was being played where the ball is passed from one side to the other, Mercedes hit it back when she said, "Then you can join us for dessert, please know that I will not accept any more rejections from the two of you. What have I done to deserve this treatment? I thought we were friends." Since it was hopeless to continue to argue they agreed to meet for dessert around three at El Meson.

Walking back to the kitchen where lunch awaited them Antonio asked Miguel if he planned to wear tails and a plumed hat for dessert and coffee with Mercedes. "Perhaps one of the members of the queen's court will lend you his coat and hat, maybe even a sword. Lets go find one." Miguel had to smile but also recognized that Antonio knew how important it was for him to impress Mercedes.

At three in the afternoon they joined the Gabriel family who ordered a nuts and berries tart covered with an orange glaze. Two chairs had to be added to the table since the parents had hoped more chairs would not be needed.

Carlos Primero was the cognac of choice for the gentlemen and anisette for the ladies. As the conversation unfolded among the family Antonio and Miguel could not help feeling excluded because the topics discussed were foreign to them. Mercedes sensing her parents' efforts to make her guests feel unwelcome, engaged them in conversation by saying, "Tell me what a day in the life of Miguel de la Madrid is like." Miguel jumping at the occasion to respond said, "My life is the result of a great mistake. You see before my father passed away he promised that I would be remembered in his last will and testament. One day as expected I was called to the reading of his will. There the executor of my father's estate read the part of the will that stated that I, being his favorite son was to receive fifty million best wishes. And so I left there to search and I must admit that I am still searching."

"Searching for what," asked Irene. Miguel replied "I am searching for the bank that will change my fifty million best wishes into fifty million pesetas." At that moment everyone including Don Genaro burst out laughing. Antonio said, "You see, Miguel has no need to see Don Quixote, he is living his life." By telling the story Miguel succeeded in gaining the center of attention of the gathering. It may have escaped him, and almost everyone there, the way Mercedes looked at him. However, it did not escape Doña Carmen who at the end of the evening as she prepared for bed said to Don Genaro, "I will write to my brother in Cuba to tell him that Mercedes will be going for an extended visit."

CHAPTER 5

By the time Antonio and Miguel arrived at the docks and reported to the office to receive the day's assignments things were already backed up and productivity was degrading by the minute. The port superintendent was dealing with the problem the way he dealt with all problems, by yelling at the section bosses, threatening them and cursing at them with every profanity that his vocabulary held, and there were many. As always, nobody paid attention, choosing instead to focus on the logistics of dealing with too many ships, not enough berths and the demands of too short a turn around. What made these problems more difficult than usual, was that usually they threw more bodies at the schedules and that would suffice. However, more bodies would have made no impact on the backlog. If anything more bodies would have only added to the confusion, diminish productivity and possibly cause the accidents that occur when too many people move too fast in a very small space. Like marbles in a glass, that will inevitably crash.

One solution would have been to expand the port which would have entailed dredging and building new piers, which everybody knew should have been done but as always as with all government decisions, the changes required were slow in coming, took too long to implement and were obsolete upon delivery. In the meantime the number and size of passenger ships that were coming to the pier continued to rise and now they were stretched to their limit. Backlogs cost ship owners a great deal of money. In instances where operators had leased ships from owners, they were forced to pay by the day.

It did not matter whether the ship was at sea loaded full of passengers or waiting to dock or depart. The owners did not care because they collected their fees regardless. The operators on the other hand cared a great deal since it was possible to incur losses through dock delays equal to or greater than the income from cruising.

This could spell disaster for the operators and they did what everyone did which was to hire agents whose job was to bribe, threaten and offer what ever it took to the dock masters to get their ships serviced. This had always worked but not this time. There simply was no space and no time to add berths to the port. Antonio and Miguel approached Don Mauricio, the chief superintendent for dock operations, who was in what could be called, a state, and asked him for a little time off to see if they could help. From his body language Miguel knew to expect a reaction of shock and disbelief. The superintendent did not disappoint. He was incredulous to hear such a thing and in a very loud voice said, "How dare you on the worst day in the history of the port of Barcelona to walk in here and say this to me. You, the crew bosses on whom I rely the most and now you tell me you are deserting me." The anger reflected in his eyes was a combination of fear and rage. He was deathly afraid of the consequences of his failure to service the ships. He knew that many if not most of the passengers were people of great influence and his failures would be known to people who could and would make his life more difficult that it needed to be. His rage was the only management tool at his disposal. The only thing he knew was to scream at people hoping that the decibel count in his voice could somehow make the situation better. Instead it had the opposite effect.

Seeing what he believed to be a great opportunity to offer an idea that he had been contemplating for a long time, Miguel decided there would be no better time than the present to offer it. He also sensed that Antonio was about to apologize for the interruption, but he gave him a look that said, "Let me talk to him, trust me I know what I am doing." The one thing that their brotherhood had foster was absolute trust and confidence in one another. Antonio responded to Miguel with a slight nod and stepped back a half a step so that Miguel could have control over the moment. One of the most important observations that he had made in the convent was that only the priests raised their voices never the nuns, but the nuns were always in control and won every argument. Because of that experience Miguel knew that he needed to gain control before he could be heard, and so he spoke softly and deliberately. And getting closer he said, "Don Mauricio, Antonio and I will come up with a plan that will improve the crews' productivity at less cost. We may have a way to reduce the time to load and unload with the same number of hands, possibly fewer." At this moment, almost whispering those words, he gained control and had the superintendent's attention. It is now seven o'clock, will you please give us until two this afternoon to hear our plan. If we can do what we think we can you can turn over the baggage handling to us and you can concentrate on the traffic problems."

"Get back by two and your plan better be workable in every way," said Don Mauricio as he turned to yell at someone else for no better reason that he knew not what else to do.

About a quarter of a mile west of the piers there was a small beach and that is where Antonio and Miguel retreated to work on their plan. While walking to the beach Miguel said, "Thanks for the trust, for not questioning what I was saying to Don Mauricio, had you done so we would not have the opportunity that has been handed to us." Antonio did not respond but knew that while Miguel may have been grateful there was no way that he could be surprised because they had backed each other since the day they met. This he knew for certain. He also knew that he had no idea what would come out of Miguel's lips next.

They sat on the sand across from one another and using a stick Miguel began to draw a schematic of the port and the lanes the ships used to enter and exit, and the corresponding berths. When he was satisfied that his sand drawing was accurate he said, "I have been looking at this for a while. The basic problem is that there is no organization, no rhythm to the flow of work and a lot of wasted time and motion. The handlers grab the bags they can carry onto the deck turn them over to the ship's stewards, then walk back empty handed. Since they are paid by the bags they collect a chit from the steward for every bag they have carried. The more bags they carry the more they earn. The waste comes in the time returning to the line empty handed and the time they stand until the next bags are handed to them. Our plan will be to use push carts that we will use to load the luggage off the passengers carriages as they arrive, push them to the loading ramp and instead of carrying them up the ramp to the steward's station, we are going to form two lines from the push carts to the decks and hand bags from handler to handler in a continuous motion." Antonio looked at his brother amazed by the clarity of the plan and wondering why he had not suggested it before. Miguel smiled at him and said, "Was it not you who once told me all things in due course?"

"This is the right time." Antonio said, "Your plan covers the efficiency part but what about the cost?" Miguel had also thought about the cost issues and reasoned that the port would be more than happy to pay twice as much as they currently spent in exchange for cutting the loading and unloading time because it would increase berth space which in turn would allow more ships in and out and more than double the fees collected by the port. After explaining this business model to Antonio, he continued, "I have explained how the port saves and makes money with our ideas the question is how are we going to make our money." Antonio suggested that they should collect a fee of five percent of all daily payments to the crews for organizing and managing the whole process, plus training the crew bosses on the new system. His plan was to collect a fixed fee from the port based on the number of bags handled, but instead of paying the men for each piece they would be paid an hourly wage that could be more than they were making through the chit system. In effect collect a daily fee based on volume and since the volume was bound to increase everyone could earn more. This eliminated the collecting and returning of chits and had a smoothing effect over daily income and expenses. Miguel also thought as Antonio did but wanted Antonio to offer his idea so that it could be their plan not just his. The only remaining concern was in getting the crews to go along with it, and Miguel thought that through as well.

Realizing the gravity of what they were about to do they paused to offer a prayer and asked God for his presence at the meeting with Don Mauricio. They remembered Sister Graciela's admonition the time she said, "If you remember to take God with you into whatever the conflict is, it will never be a fair fight. No Matter the odds, no matter the opposition the fight is never fair if God is with you." This is why they decided to invite God to the meeting.

The superintendent stood by the window looking out to sea in frustration as he saw the number of ships anchored waiting to be serviced. Some had already unloaded passengers through shore boats but the passengers were still waiting for their luggage. Don Mauricio was at his wit's end by the time Antonio and Miguel returned at two o' clock as promised. Miguel said, "Don Mauricio, we are ready to speak with you if only we could have some privacy, some of the items we will discuss are only meant for executive's ears, your ears only sir. Based on what you see and hear you can determine who else should see this plan, but for now this is only for your eyes and ears."

With his ego sufficiently stroked he was ready to listen in private. Asking permission to use the scheduling chalk board, Miguel drew the plan he had drawn in the sand. Taking greater care to explain the time and motion concerns. He knew that greater detail was required in the explanation because Don Mauricio was not as smart as Antonio and because it was his head in the noose should the scheme not work. Following the discussion on logistics they presented the payment plan. The plan was for the port authority to pay directly to them an amount equal to one and half time as much as they had been paying all handlers at peak capacity. They would then assume responsibility for paying all crews. Effectively replacing the port authority as the employer. This they presented in tandem and while one spoke the other one thought of supporting arguments. It all seemed thorough and completely well thought out. The superintendent paused and thought that at the end of the day things were so bad that there was no way the plan would make them worse.

"How do you plan to put this in motion?" he asked, indicating that he had accepted it. "Before we address that question, Don Mauricio it is of great importance that you lend your name and the importance of the office you hold to the plan. Your name associated with the plan will carry great weight and the crew bosses will listen, after all who does not listen to you." At this point they were making it up as they went along and suggested that they intended to invite all crew bosses to a meeting at the small chapel in the Convent at Saint Jacinto's on Sunday afternoon. Getting permission from Sister Graciela would be Antonio's responsibility. After all, what was the use of being the favorite if you were not taking advantage of what the status offered. By Don Mauricio's authority all crew bosses were required to attend the meeting the following Sunday at three in the afternoon. The sisters looked upon the meeting as an opportunity to meet people who may not have visited a church since baptism or first communion. The reason they selected the chapel as the meeting place instead of the courtyard or another place was because they knew that people tend to behave with civility and decorum while they are in church. So they hoped.

As scheduled and as expected because of the importance of the issue at hand everyone who needed to be there, was. Better than Antonio, Miguel understood the cultural and emotional forces that could derail the decisions that needed to be made. He understood that this was a group of mostly

Catalans who would out of hand reject a Basque suggesting how they would work, especially a change so dramatic with such great impact on their future and their livelihood. For most of them working at the docks was a family tradition. It is what had been handed down from generation to generation and while it was not much to outsiders, for those at the docks it was their tradition. "Antonio you must let me do all of the talking even when it concerns you, even if it offends you. If ever there was a time for you to trust me this, more than any other is that time." If brotherhood ever meant anything to Antonio this was about absolute trust between brothers. While Antonio may not have understood everything about everything he did understand what his brother meant. Antonio left through the side door and reentered the chapel and stood at the very back of the crowd. There was barely enough room for everyone to sit comfortably.

The chapel was quiet and somber, this was a church after all and while many of them did not attend with any regularity they never forgot what was the conduct expected in the house of the lord. Miguel began by saying, "In this place at this time the only one who lords over us is the lord himself and he expects nothing but honesty and good will from all of us. This is not about me versus you this is about what our lives are going to be as a result of our decisions today. Most of you have known me since I was a child running water buckets so that you could drink during breaks. There is not one single job or task that you do that I have not done myself. I tell you this because I believe that if not your trust I believe that by my conduct I may have earned your respect." He had to make this point clear to the men and so he paused to let them reflect on his credibility. "Don Mauricio wants all of us to help him solve the problems of delays while waiting to load and unload ships. He has devised a work plan that changes the ways we have done things for these many years. The concern is over the number and size of ships coming to Barcelona and our inability to service them. He is not interested in adding more crews because that is not the problem. What he wants is better productivity and results from the crews he has, even if the authority has to pay more." He paused to gage his audience's demeanor. Their response was neither positive nor negative, they responded with silence and attention. As he spoke he looked at everyone straight in their eyes trying to figure out what was behind them. He walked them through their recent history at the docks.

Reviewing the pattern of increased time at work, faster motion required with no appreciable difference in their earnings. As he explained this was as a result of the continued practice of adding more hands to the tasks because the authority knew not what else to do. Eventually as he pointed out they would spend more and more time waiting to grab luggage resulting in fewer chits from the stewards. More of this is what is going to happen unless we join together in a bold plan. I will present this plan to you and I have but one request and that is that you let me finish before you throw anything at me." Some smiled in response others nodded in a tacit agreement to listen.

Miguel explained the use of the push carts and the new loading and unloading process. "Many of you will ask why is this a good idea, or you may ask why should we try this now. Well the answer is simple, an opportunity has been handed to us and this is the time for us to gain control over our lives by demonstrating that we can take it upon ourselves to deliver the service that is needed as we always have. The principal difference is that we are stepping up instead of letting it be just somebody else's idea we can make it our idea by doing better than expected. We can deliver more than has ever been expected of us because of us not much has ever been expected. This is our time."

At this point he could sense in his audience the most human of concerns, the one that leads to the question about, "What is in it for me?" He continued, "We think there is a way for us to work together and benefit ourselves and the authority. Usually whatever helps one hurts the other. Our plan is to make a list of all the luggage when it is taken from the passengers and the wagons that deliver them to the docks. We will then load them on the carts. It will take four men per cart to deliver them to the loading ramp where the crew will form two lines and pass the luggage from one handler to another. When the bags are on board the ship's steward signs the list that was made when the luggage was placed on the deck. Instead of waiting for the chits from the steward, we turn the lists in at the end of the day. By the way, it is harder for luggage to go unaccounted for when it gets counted twice. Right now we are paid by the piece based on the number of chits we have collected. The problem is that we spend as much time waiting to grab bags as we do carrying them.

Sometimes we make more other times we make less. Our idea is to pay everyone equally based on the day's work. If you push the carts today, tomorrow you load luggage at the ramp, or you may be maintaining and fixing the carts. Wheels and crates will need fixing from time to time, but if we keep them well maintained we can reduce the down time that would affect what we earn. We will assign an hourly wage to every man that will correspond to a greater amount that we now collect on a good day. At the end of the day wages will be distributed. Crew bosses will be paid on a different scale than the handlers, but that amount will be determined by how much more we collect at the end of the day. His audience sat in absolute silence not knowing whether to approve or reject the plan. More or less they were waiting for someone to speak. Arturo, who was originally from the region of Galicia, had been working at the docks for over ten years, so it was to be expected that he was not about to relinquish seniority without a fight.

Since he had been told that this meeting was at the direction of the superintendent, he needed to proceed with caution. He stood up to be recognized and spoke to the audience instead of Miguel. "Will this not reduce the size of the crews? Some of us will lose our work, what about that?" He was asking what he knew everyone wanted to know. After waiting for the murmurs and the noise to subside Miguel said, "On the contrary. This will keep the authority from hiring more handlers which will increase our wait time and reduce our pay." Arturo pressed on by saying, "What about those who are waiting to come to work at the docks. What will happen to their jobs?"

"If you are so concerned for them you can give them yours," someone yelled and everyone laughed heartily. Everyone except Arturo whose demeanor and stance told Miguel that he could and probably would cause great trouble if allowed. He knew that Arturo needed to be reckoned with because although he acted like, and was a bully, he always stood up for his people and had their loyalty.

"Look men," said Miguel, "This plan will not be perfect on the first day but if you support it for two weeks, the authority will evaluate the results and decide on the future. Unless we do this, Don Mauricio will do as he always does, which is to bring more bodies to our already crowded docks and then we all lose." He closed the meeting by asking them to suspend their disbelief and to meet at the dock one hour earlier than usual on Monday morning. He did not ask for a show of hands since he figured that those who agreed would be there and those who did not would not. He did know that a majority supporting the plan, would convince the superintendent to go forward with the experiment. Either way it did not matter since he had done all he could. Antonio tried to speak to some of the men in the courtyard but thought better of it. Miguel had explained the changes as best as the changes could have been explained and there was nothing that he could add that would change the men's minds either way. As Arturo left with his crew he looked at Antonio in a way that said that he was not going to give up his position easily and that Miguel could expect trouble, possibly in the form of violence.

CHAPTER 6

Early that evening they went to the plaza just to be around people and to try to relieve their minds of the impending events the following morning. Not knowing what to expect at the docks, they knew they needed to be ready for anything, since anything could happen. It had been Miguel's idea to go to the plaza, although clearing his mind was not his only interest. They had not been at the service attended by Mercedes family and he missed seeing her.

There was a heavy cloud cover that spelled rain, and as result the plaza was not as crowded as usual. This being Sunday and the day before returning to work, many people retired for the evening after their Sunday dinners at the plaza. "No matter," he thought if he saw her he saw her. If he didn't, then he would not be laying in his cot wondering if she had been at the plaza that evening. For the last five minutes she had been studying him well aware that she was the only reason he was there. His searching eyes and his walk clearly showed his one and only purpose for being there. She too had looked for him in church and experienced a disappointment similar to his when she did not see him across the aisle. By nature Mercedes was an introspective and thoughtful person, although her beauty and playfulness said differently. She enjoyed having people seeing her the way they wanted to see her except for those people who really mattered to her. She knew intuitively that Miguel knew who and what she was. A very serious person when it came to her heart. Lost in thought as she was, she saw him walking towards her in a most deliberate way. His walk had purpose and determination. His stride spoke of a sense of urgency to be near her. Antonio, whose legs were longer than Miguel's was keeping up but not without effort.

"Miguel and Antonio allow me the pleasure of introducing you to my cousins Cecilia and Catalina. When you get to know them better, they may let you call them Ceci and Talina. They are visiting us from Malaga and will stay until the end of next week. My dear cousins I have the extreme pleasure and distinct honor of introducing to you two of the most important men in this plaza. And why are they so important you ask. Well I will tell you why. They are important because now that they are here we can be certain that we can have a carafe of wine in safety and security in the knowledge that no one will dare disturb us. The other reason for their importance is because unlike most other men who love to hear about themselves these two will want to know about you." No one could have guessed that the three girls were related, even remotely. They were short in stature and plumb if not stout and they did not have any of the style that made Mercedes so special.

Miguel grinned with a look of embarrassment and pride at the same time, spoke first. "Ladies will you consent to allow us the honor of being seen in your company if we promise to guard your well being and ensure your comfort with our lives if necessary." Mercedes laughed and said, "I can tell that you finally read Don Quixote. That is what one could expect him to say were he here at this time." Still looking at Miguel she said, "Antonio, since you are not the Sancho Panza type, we will name you Don Rodrigo, El Cid, the great defender of the faith."

Soon after they sat and before they consumed their cups of wine, Mercedes said, "Miguel will you walk with me to the linens shop I am thinking of changing the covers in my bed and want to look at some material. Antonio, you would not mind protecting, and possibly entertaining my cousins for a short while, would you?" Unaccustomed as everyone was to that side of Mercedes no one responded. She continued, "Miguel, you have nothing to worry about, a walk with me will not constitute an engagement to marry. It is just a walk." It may have been just a walk to Mercedes but it was far more than that to Miguel. As for the marrying, Miguel thought, "Don't be too certain."

Much to their surprise most of the crew bosses were already at the docks when Antonio and Miguel arrived one hour ahead of schedule. There seemed to be an atmosphere of positive if not curious energy among the men as they milled around waiting to be told what to do. Miguel had drawn schematics of what he called work stations. These were strategic points of control from where the flow of work could best be managed. Since most of the men there could barely read and write, the work needed to be described through diagrams that indicated directions and flow of traffic. The diagrams were rich in symbols and every crew boss had a symbol that corresponded to his work station.

Miguel did not have to look to see who it was that was approaching him because he knew it, and he also knew what was about to happen. Without turning to look at him, he said, "Arturo let me show you the work stations concept." He could feel the eyes, the attention of the crews drifting from him and towards his back. "Let me show you today's assignment for you and your crew. The reason I say for today is because we need to meet right here at the end of the day so that we can decide how we can improve the work flow for tomorrow." As soon as he finished speaking Miguel realized that he had been speaking to himself because everyone was waiting for Arturo's next move. They were not kept waiting long. Arturo was not inclined to be told what to do, and that was not the reason he was there. "And who the hell gave you the authority to lord over us as if you were the queen herself? Whatever the superintendent wants done we can do it without you and your Basque bastard friend assuming control over our lives. Do you actually think that we are so weak and so stupid that we would go along with your scheme. The way I see it, you are trying to take over the docks and I am going to stop you, even if I have to gut you like a hog." By this time Arturo had removed his jacket and a knife was in plain site. A wide circle began to form with expectation that a violent and bloody contest was about to start, one that could explode and involve everyone there with potentially grave consequences.

Antonio realizing the spot Miguel was in, decided that it had gone far enough. He stood next to Miguel and said, "I have done what you asked of me. I now ask you to do what I ask of you. Stand aside. He is nothing but a bully and a coward. I see it all over him. He had to wait until there was a crowd because he does not have the courage to confront us alone and he hopes that if things get out of hand they will intervene and stop the fight he plans to start. He just doesn't know that there will be no fight to start or to finish. Trust me my brother, and leave this to me." Antonio approached Arturo getting so close until they were within a foot of one another, since he was not armed, Arturo's knife remained in his belt. Antonio saw the rage in Arturo's eyes and knew that it was there for the sole purpose of hiding his fear. They locked eyes and neither one spoke, neither did anyone else. They seemed suspended in time. Finally Arturo spoke and said, "Well are we going to fight or are we going to dance?"

In a deep and deliberate voice Antonio said, "Arturo, when these men left their families and kissed their wives and children this morning, they walked out of their homes with the expectation of returning this evening. We have it in our hands whether they do or not. When these men left for work this morning, possibly they were kissed by their wives who had no idea that it may have been their last kiss. It is up to us whether it was or it was not. It is not the same for me. I am an orphan. No one needs me and no one will miss me." Antonio sensed a change in Arturo's stance. Less threatening, less challenging but still guarded. With his hands remaining on both sides of his waist he continued. "These men have an opportunity to better themselves as a consequence of what happens or does not happen between us here and now. Arturo, I too can get a knife and you and I can walk into that empty warehouse where no one can intervene, no one can stop one of us from killing the other. Because I can assure you that only one of us will walk out there alive. My preference is to live and so I have no choice but to kill you. My preference is also to not kill anyone since there will be consequences. But trust me Arturo, I am willing to kill you. Because of my love for Miguel, I will kill you. The question for you to ask of yourself is this. Do you love these men enough to kill or be killed for them? It is all up to you."

Antonio knew that he had reached Arturo and that the question of blood and violence was no longer there. The question now was how to save face and how to make the next move in a way that would make a friend out of an enemy. "Lets give this plan a chance to work. Whatever it lacks, you can help us make it better. Many of these men look up to you, they trust you and they need you to lead them. We can not let them down. Arturo, I want you to do something for me. I want you to hit me and knock me down. I will not strike back you have my word on that, but when I am down I want you to kneel next to me as if saying something to me, then help me up and shake my hand. No one needs to know what was said between us. I offer my oath to the almighty that this conversation I will take to my grave." By now, Arturo not realizing it, was absolutely under Antonio's control. The transference of power had been so subtle that he actually felt comfortable with the outcome.

He hit Antonio on the top of his head causing him to fall more from losing his balance than from the force of the blow. As soon as Antonio hit the ground Arturo's hand was on him picking him up. The crowd remained motionless waiting for Arturo to reach for his knife, and for that reason were confused when Arturo turned and yelled, "What the hell are you looking at, lets get to work."

The rest of the day was not without its problems. It was only natural when people have done things one way all their lives and suddenly they are asked to stop working individually and start working as part of a system. In spite of the start up problems, everyone could see how things would work for the better. It only remained to see what they could earn under the new system.

Miguel and Antonio worried about the same. They knew that if the superintendent did not follow through with his commitment to pay as agreed, they would not live to see another day at the dock or anywhere. Don Mauricio did not disappoint them. At the end of the day every handler and crew boss walked away with more money than they had ever received for their labor and were not as tired. The review meeting was held as planned and Miguel and Antonio could sense the excitement that follows people who enjoy doing a good job and seeing things work better for everyone. The only recommendation, and it was a good one, was to set up a color code that would align colors with work stations so that workers would know where they belonged on any given day. They would approach Don Mauricio to buy them a number of handkerchiefs of various colors, to be worn around the neck. These were to be distributed every Monday as the crews reported for work, and returned on Saturdays as they collected their pay for the day. One of the hands offered that he would take them home to be washed for a small fee, and return them on Mondays sorted by color, ready for distribution.

Miguel would take responsibility for buying the handkerchiefs so the new process could start the next Monday. Having accepted the recommendation and reviewed the implementation of the color scheme there was nothing else to discuss. "Where do you want us tomorrow?" Arturo asked with genuine enthusiasm in his voice, looking at Miguel. He responded by saying, "Tomorrow will bring what it will, but tonight we should worry about how soon can we get a glass of wine to celebrate this day." The remaining of the week continued with great success and more improvement could be observed as everyone became more familiar with the workflow. All things considered, Miguel and Antonio had much to be proud about. Their system had worked, no one had been injured and everyone made more money during that week than at any other time working in the docks. Life could not be better.

No one could remember a Sunday when Sister Graciela had missed the early morning service. This Sunday they were to attend two masses. She had reserved to herself the honor of leading the convent to mass and communion. It was her practice to designate who would sit next to her during the mass.

This was her way of singling out the sister whose conduct was worthy of recognition and as they prepared to enter the chapel that nun would be asked to stand behind the mother superior. Everyone at the convent was anxious about her absence this morning. It was usually she who waited on all others to arrive for the procession. In fact, the nuns used to play a game to see who could beat Sister Graciela to the procession line. It was six o'clock and everyone began to wonder about Sister Graciela's absence. It was not like her to be late. Sensing that things were not right, Sister Maria thought of sending one of the novices to see about Sister Graciela but decided to go herself to the apartment, thinking that Sister Graciela would not want anyone else to see her if she was indisposed. After knocking at the door and not hearing a response, she crossed herself and entered the room. As she entered there was not much light in the room since the windows were closed. She moved in the direction of Sister Graciela's bedroom where she found her lying on the floor between the bedroom and the sitting room, her gown stuck to her body, covered in sweat. Sister Maria rushed to the balcony that looked over the courtyard and shouted for the nuns to get Father Luis who was a doctor. Father Luis had been a doctor for many years before joining the priesthood and now served at the clinic managed by the Little Sisters of Charity. It took the doctor no more than two minutes to arrive at her side since he was already inside the church where he was to officiate in the morning mass. One of the novices trailed him with his medicine bag in her hand. By the time he entered the room, the sisters had lifted Sister Graciela onto the bed and had removed her night gown which was soaking wet from the fever.

When he entered the apartment, Father Luis found her already awake, alert, and wondering why all the fuss and why were they late to mass. The clock on her wall showed that it was five minutes past the six o'clock hour. After they cleared the room, they stood outside in the courtyard to wait for the priest to finish his medical work. The doctor examined her as best he could and could not find anything evidently wrong with her. For the time being he attributed her condition to a fainting spell pending a more thorough examination. This was not inconsistent with women her age. Although no one knew her true age since she never disclosed it. "Sister, I know that you do not take orders from priests that are below the rank of bishops, but it is as your doctor that I order you to rest all day," he said with a smile in his face that made it more a request than an order. "I will return to serve you communion, but now please do as I say and rest." As he left, Sister Graciela spoke to him with a request to ask Sister Maria to return to her bedside after mass for a review of the planned activities for the day.

That afternoon, Antonio and Miguel requested permission to visit Sister Graciela. The doctor had left strict orders that she was to have absolute rest because he knew that it was what she needed most at that time. Only he could authorize visitors in her chambers. But he was more a priest than a doctor and the priest in him knew how much the Mother Superior loved the boys and thought that a short visit would pleased her greatly. She always had smiles for them and at this time smiling would serve her well. "Yes it will do her good to see you but please show no alarm in your faces, else she will herself be alarmed. Remember she is very tired and your visit must be brief. If she allows you, do all the talking so she should only listen. More than anything she will benefit from your love and affection and from your prayers."

Antonio entered first and stood next to Renatta, the novice who was attending to her along with Sister Maria who had gone to prepare a light lunch for Sister Graciela. Her color seemed almost normal and she wore the exhaustion of an old woman who had an episode. They both stood next to her bed and Antonio spoke. "Sister Graciela we came here with the intention of dropping on our knees and say prayers for you but it is evident that it is us who need prayers from you. If you feel half as good as you look we have greater cause for celebration than for grief."

"I am glad you have not forgotten the lesson that I taught you about celebration and grief. It is through those choices that our lord relies on us to show faith in our judgment. Receive my blessing; May God bless you and keep you my sons because I do not want to keep you from your afternoon at the Plaza." Miguel looked and Antonio with a look of surprise that she would know about their Sundays at the plaza with Mercedes and her friends. Sister Graciela said, "It surprises me that you are surprised that I know these things. Don't you know by now that I speak to the angels that guard over you. For that I am truly surprised. Go, be on your way, my lunch is here and I am starving." Smiling they both looked at her with eyes that reciprocated the love they were receiving, proving the doctor right, she needed smiles.

The following Sunday found Sister Graciela fully recovered and directing everything as usual. As the procession was getting organized to enter the church, Antonio and Miguel noticed the presence of new novices waiting to take their places in the line. The group seemed larger than usual since there were four new members in the procession. At once Antonio recognized Marisol, the girl he had known in Bilbao. Not once since he had left home had he ever thought of her in any way. In the context of who he now was compared to who he was then, there was not much to think about. He had succeeded in leaving his past behind in every way, even in memories. Over five years had passed since he had seen her last and not much had changed in her. She was still well shaped and pretty to look at and although she was only a few years older that him, she did not look youthful. He did notice that she seemed uncomfortable as she stood with the nuns and novices, and more so when she looked around and saw him. She did not seemed all that surprised to find him there, in fact she appeared more pleased than startled to see him. Although there was no way for him to know this, she was pleased to see him. Antonio had not been full grown the last time they had been together but had not changed much if at all since she had last seen him. He looked away from her as the bell tolled calling all to mass and signaling the start of the procession. As they started to walk, she looked behind her trying to establish eye contact, but he was in conversation with a nun.

As always when they entered the Church, Miguel searched the pews trying to find Mercedes. Since the family always sat in the same pew they were not hard to find. Much to his disappointment she was not there. Some of the family members were there, but not Mercedes. Antonio could see the disappointment in Miguel. It was all over him. His shoulders drooped and his eyes that had projected great excitement and expectation were now only showing sadness and concern. As he looked to the pews Mercedes' brother and Irene his fiancée acknowledged him with a faint smile, but no one else even looked at him.

The sermon on that Sunday was based on the adventures of being a Christian. The priest offering the message was speaking about the pleasures and privileges afforded to those who accept Jesus Christ in their lives, and live accordingly. He spoke of the parable in the bible that spoke of the difficulty of a rich man getting into heaven. He also spoke of the difference between being wealthy and being rich. He said those who did not know the difference could never be both at the same time. As these words were spoken, Miguel looked at Mercedes family and he could tell they thought those words were for everyone else but them. He smiled inside and felt sadness for them and for Mercedes.

At the end of the service Antonio and Miguel approached Don Genaro to offer the morning greetings and to make a discreet effort to find out why Mercedes was not there. "Indisposed," was the answer and as if to change the subject he added, "I have been hearing of some interesting changes and marked improvements in the operations of the docks. It seems that more ships are being serviced faster. I also heard from the Superintendent of the port authority, who is a friend, that he has turned over the entire baggage handling service to the two of you." Antonio replied, "To me and Miguel who devised the entire plan and succeeded in getting everyone to trust him in implementing the new system. It was all Miguel's doing. I am almost embarrassed to be given any credit because none was earned by me." Don Genaro seemed to have lost whatever interest he had on the topic. He wished them both a good day and walked away. Both Antonio and Miguel were not surprised that they were not invited join them at El Meson for dinner that afternoon. They would have been shocked if they had been asked. No matter, they thought, "We can go anywhere we want."

Miguel was called away by one of the nuns who asked for his help. And as he walked away, Sister Graciela approached Antonio whose face showed a combination of concern and confusion. "Don Genaro seems to have left rather quickly. Is everything all right? If I did not know better I would think he had been offended by you and Miguel. But that is probably my imagination because I know how well mannered the two of you are. After all I should know. I am your teacher."

He placed her arm inside his elbow and asked, "Anton, could you please join me for lunch this afternoon, say at half past two. Would that be too much of an inconvenience? I hope not. It has been much too long since we have spoken at length and I miss our conversations." Ever since their first lunch Antonio had grown to treasure their Sunday afternoons at the Mother Superior's apartment. There had been several lunches but all at irregular intervals. He never knew when he would be asked to join her. The invitation always surfaced after church on Sundays and Sister Graciela always had a purpose for the lunch. He went to find Miguel to tell him that he would be with the sister, but could not find him. "No matter," he thought "We will meet for our walk to the plaza later."

Not once had he been late or early to her apartment. He made it a point to arrive precisely at the expected time. It was exactly two thirty when she said, "Come in Anton, the door is opened." This was a beautiful late spring afternoon. The kind that even an atheist would have to agree that only God could create such a day. He entered and saw that she was seated at her favorite place overlooking the garden. She was serving the wine as he took his seat. She said, "This wine has waited a long time to be appreciated, let us not keep it waiting a minute longer."

As they began to enjoy the wine that unlike the sacristy wine that came in a jug, this was a fine bottle of French wine that a parishioner had given to Sister Graciela, who had saved it for a special occasion. For the sister her afternoons with Antonio were always special. From the beginning he had owned the mother's heart laying dormant within her. She had learned that her maternal feelings and emotions had not dissipated with her son's death. If anything the death of her son had increased her longing for him. All of those feelings that were awaken in her the first morning she realized she was pregnant. All were now back and belonged to her Anton. She had a certain reverence about wine because as she explained, wine meant a lot to Jesus. She asked, "Why do you think they ran out of wine at the wedding in Canaan? Because Jesus and the apostles were there," she answered her own question with a grin.

The first hour was spent eating their lunch which consisted of various kinds of cheeses and sausages and a basket of fresh bread. His serving had the more spicy sausages and hams. Her doctor had ordered her to observe a bland diet for a while. In a separate dish she served him anchovies in seasoned oil, one of the region's specialties. "I think the doctor wanted to restrict my consumption of wine so he limited me to one glass. And since he did not specify what size glass, you will note my glass is twice the size of yours."

They first talked about the docks and the developments there. She knew it must not have been easy to do what they had done. She understood all about jealousy, envy, malice and mistrust. She had made it her life's mission to fight them all. "How did you and Miguel managed to accomplish what you did without bloodshed. Without a fight or fights, or were there some and the angels did not tell me." He thought about her perceptions and her insights into people in general and men specifically. "It came close to getting out of hand sister, and believe me I had no idea how it was going to turn out, but at the moment where it could have gone bad I remembered that you had told Miguel and me about trouble, conflicts or fights. Remember that you told us that if we were to take God with us to a fight, the fight would not be fair? So that is what we did, we had God with us and the other fellow did not stand a chance. I never even threw a punch. I did not have to. It was over before it started. He never knew what hit him." He was interrupted by her laughter that more than expressing her enjoying the story, it indicated her pleasure with the story teller.

This was not in her agenda, but she had to recognize that Antonio was full grown and that since he had much to learn about life, it would be best to learn by living it. She brought up the point about how the time for them to leave the convent was approaching. He knew that she was not suggesting he had to leave, but that it was time for him to join the rest of the world outside the walls of the convent. Besides, it was time for another to take his place so he could learn the lessons taught to Antonio. This was not remotely the same as when his father had told him to leave his home. That was a cowardly and selfish act. This was all about love. "You and Miguel are more than ready to find your way. I could suggest you consider the priesthood but that would not be fair to some special women whom you will one day honor with your names."

She took a deep breath and a sip of wine and leaning forward so as to enhance the intimacy and the importance of the moment she said, "Anton it is inevitable that you will have experiences as you seek to find the special woman that God wants for you. He does not always places her in front of you with the sign that reads I am the one. Would it that it be that easy. It is so important that in the process of finding her, you do not lose yourself." At this moment choosing to forget the doctor's order she paused and held up her cup so that he should serve her more wine, never taking her eyes from him.

Not wanting to lose the intimacy of the moment between a mother and her son. "Remember that even without intent or malice those that are hurt by us are hurt just the same. A way to tell you are an adult is that your I'm sorry will be less frequent and far more costly. Children have the luxury of acknowledging their mistakes by a simple I'm sorry. The same is not true for adults. As you go through life Anton, it will be in your hands to make memories or regrets. Both will be with you all of your days. Many pretend to have lived a life with no regrets, but they know it is not true. They know it and God knows it. Some go trough their lives making amends righting their wrongs so that they may sleep in peace. But Anton, better it is to take responsibility for your actions by always being in control so that when the time comes you can walk away from the opportunity to hurt someone." Not surprisingly, Antonio did not speak, did not drink and did not move. He simply leaned back on his chair and waited for more.

"Anton, for a woman, few are the hurts more painful than losing her self respect as a result of having been used by a man. The sad truth is that when a man uses a woman her participation in the act or event that causes the pain is equal to his or greater. Many are the girls who think that it is a game and so they are flirtatious and coquettish and that no harm will come of it. Some even surrender to the pleasures of the flesh not realizing that love is a gift to be shared with the special one God has for them. Not realizing that when they give of themselves what they have given may not be retrieved and then they have less to give to the next and to the next until the day they are empty with nothing left to give. They are the ones who inspire sadness and are in need of mercy because their lives will be full of regrets, when they could have been full of great memories." She paused to look at his reaction trying to measure how much of what she had said was understood by him. After all he was only eighteen years old. True though it was, that he had been at the convent for five years and that he had grown before their very eyes he had much to learn still. She and the rest of the nuns had taken care of nurturing Antonio's development because he needed it the most and had the greatest promise of going forward into the world as an instrument of God, practicing what he had learned through them.

Sister Graciela continued. "Anton, of all of God's gifts to us which one do you think is the most important. Never mind, don't answer that. It is an unfair question and there isn't one correct answer. For me it is Kindness. Kindness, to me is his greatest gift. His to us and us to others. Kindness Anton is how God expects us to express love. Kindness is wanting better for a loved one than we want for ourselves. Kindness is finding the positive way in which to express a negative thought. His last deed before he died at the cross was an act of kindness. Remember in the New Testament lesson when Jesus looked to the heavens and spoke to his father saying forgive them father for they know not what they do. And through those words expressing kindness towards those who were inflicting so much pain on him. Anton, the reason I tell you this is because you have a kind heart. I have seen it when you help the children with their reading and writing. I have seen it when you go out of your way to help others. You have a great and kind heart and that is a gift from God. Why he chose to give that to you is for him to know and for us to celebrate. My duty as I see it is to do all that I can so that others may benefit from it by helping you understand who and what you are. You are the recipient of God's gift and it is your duty to let others see it by letting God's love be seen by others through your good works." He reached for his wine and drank from the glass. His look revealed and understanding of what was being said to him confirming his maturity, emotional and spiritual. His capacity to absorb completely the full meaning of the lesson. "Poor Anton, who thought he would only have to endure one sermon today." She looked at the bread basket and remarked that it would be a sin to not eat it all so she asked him to butter her bread.

Sensing that the day's lesson was over, he said, "I have listened to you, to everything that you have said without interrupting. I have to confess that I may not yet appreciate the full meaning of this lesson, but in time I will, I always do. But now I want you to tell me about you. Tell me about your condition. That was a great scare you gave us last week. No one here is saying anything about what caused your fainting or how you are to be treated to prevent another one. Miguel and I even stopped at the book store to find a book on fainting but there was none to be found. The clerk suggested we ask at the university where the medical school would surely have such a book, so we went but they were close since it was late."

"Anton, rest assured that no one takes better care of me than I do for myself. And no one but the Lord knows me better than I know me. The simple truth is that I am an old woman near the end of this life and ready and willing to go to the next one. How old do you think I am?" He had never stopped to consider her age. He looked at her pondering the question. Her face was that of an old woman but her energy, her agility and her ability belonged to a younger person. "Fifty eight years old I guess is how old you are," he said. "I am surprised at you, lying on a Sunday and within a stone's throw from the house of God. Anton, fifty eight is the age of some of my garments. I may have rosaries that old. No my son, I am seventy eight and my time is near. I have accepted that and expect you to do the same. Upon my passing, I need to know that you will celebrate my life. Please, please promise me that you will see to it that there will be no tears when I am buried. Remember what I told you, always choose celebration over grief."

She went on to ask him about his plans beyond the docks and moving out of the convent. More than anything she was curious because she had not known many who had left the convent and remained near. Most novices who took the habit were sent away to other orders or dioceses, or to missions. The ones who left the convent for other reasons moved far away. At this point she was being more the mother than the Mother Superior. He and Miguel had talked about the need to move, the advantages versus the disadvantages. There was nothing they did or would do that would change as a result of where they lived. They decided to stay away from renting a room to share which was the custom for those bachelors who had no home. Instead they would search for a small apartment situated between the docks and the convent, since they were planning to continue to attend the mass at Saint Jacinto's.

Antonio would continue as an active member of the church because he felt duty bound and because he was a believer. To him it was inconceivable to not attend mass on Sundays. He had not missed one since coming to the convent. Miguel also felt duty bound and that would have been enough of a reason for him to attend but they both knew his main reason for going to church was to see her. To see Mercedes Gabriel.

Antonio discussed their plans to move, but also made it clear that neither he nor Miguel had any sense of urgency about this decision. Not surprisingly they both had enough money to allow them some comfort and so they could be selective about where to live. Although after sleeping in the Monk's cells for five years anything would have seemed like an extravagant luxury by comparison. He added that if there was a need for them to vacate their rooms all the sister had to do was ask. "No. No hurry on our part. At least the two of you are very good about keeping everything neat and orderly in your rooms, unlike the priests who may move in there when you leave, and who expect my nuns to act as their maids. That will never happen so long as I draw breath. Maybe I should post a curse, a warning to the new tenants about what to expect unless they clean after themselves." She started to laugh as if she could visualize a priest reading the warning and maybe sleeping with one eye opened.

That evening just after six, Antonio and Miguel met up in the courtyard and went for their Sunday walk to the plaza. Miguel asked how was his lunch with the sister and added that he had eaten in the kitchen. So much he ate he said that he had to take a nap. Miguel who was as calm and collected a person as anyone who ever walked on the earth, was not himself this evening. He seemed agitated and anxious, even to the point of asking Antonio if they could walk faster. Owing to the wonderful spring weather and the soft Mediterranean breezes the plaza was packed with families of all size and ages promenading around the square enjoying the weather. Summer, they knew was around the bend and with it all the humidity that Africa can send to Spain.

Every table was taken and every bar was packed. They first stopped at El Meson, thinking and hoping that by chance they may have still been there. Not seeing them they continued to walk around for what seemed to be at least an hour and not seeing Mercedes or any one from her family, they decided to eat at their regular Tapas bar. As luck would have it there were stools available at the counter. After greeting the acquaintances they had made as a result of their frequent visits, they settled on a carafe of Rioja wine. A sweet wine that would serve to offset the saltiness and spiciness of the various dishes they would consume. Opting to make the best of a disappointing evening they settled to enjoy their food and drink. "There she is," said Antonio, without the need to use her name since there was only one person they wanted to see. Antonio discretely pointed at a table thirty yards away, to their front and slightly to the left. There were five people at the table; three women and two men. One of them was Martin, her brother, the other man they did not know, and three girls, two who were unfamiliar to Antonio and Miguel. After waiting for the opportunity of casual eye contact to open the door to conversation they decided to just approach the table. Antonio thought he had a better idea and ordered a carafe of wine and asked the waiter to deliver it to Mercedes' table. As a matter of courtesy they would be acknowledged and be asked to join them.

When the wine was delivered, the table turned to see who had sent it and upon recognizing them, Martin arose and instead of waiving them over he walked to greet them. He seemed less cordial than on past occasions and while polite, his demeanor lacked in warmth. "Thank you for your very kind gesture gentlemen, but we are just leaving. We are pressed for time because we have to visit some friends who wish to say good bye to Mercedes. She is leaving for a long stay in Cuba where our uncle has a sugar cane plantation. She has been begging for permission to visit for a long time and finally our mother relented." Under these circumstances, protocol dictated that an invitation was needed before they could approach the table. But protocol meant nothing to Miguel who started to walk in the direction of the table before the two other men had realized he was no longer next to them.

Standing before their table, and after an awkward pause he said, "I have come to apologize for our unfortunate timing. We had no idea that you could have been pressed for time when we ordered the wine to be served to you. Please pardon the interruption if I seem ill mannered, I am Miguel De la Madrid, a good friend of Mercedes." His voice seemed different to her. Uncomfortable, not sure of himself. And one thing she knew about Miguel is that he never lacked for confidence. Before she could speak he continued, "Mercedes I could not wait any longer to congratulate you. I just heard that you are traveling to Cuba. How many times have I heard you talk about your desire to visit Cuba and to know that part of the world. Cuba's gain is Barcelona's loss. This will be a sadder less colorful place because of your absence." By this time Antonio and Martin had caught up to him. "Nothing gives me greater pleasure than to see my friends realize their dreams, and for that reason I, no, we must insist that you share a parting cup of wine with us. Please, we insist. This may well be the last time we get to enjoy the pleasure of your company."

Mercedes was by now overwhelmed by her sentiments. She understood the change in his voice. It was filled with pain and anguish. And it cried out from his breaking heart. She now fully realized why her mother had suddenly changed her mind about letting her go to Cuba. The urgency with which the arrangements were made revealed her mother's motive. Her mother, who hated to sail even volunteered to escort her and to return to Spain once Mercedes was settled in Cuba. For a while she had been ambivalent about her feelings for Miguel. First, because she had never been in love, and second she did not know his feelings for her. In the sparse hours they had shared together she had grown to appreciate his intellect and his sense of humor. She could tell a lot about people by the way they spoke, they way they organized their thoughts before expressing them and by the questions they asked. But this evening as Miguel spoke, she could feel his anguish as her own and shared in his dismay as he pretended to celebrate her good fortune. She could see his heart was breaking and had to do all she could to fight the urge to embrace him. It was in the tone of his voice. It was in the language of his body. It did not reflect the joy his words were saying. As of this moment she knew exactly how Miguel felt about her, and for the first time she understood her love for him. When he paused, Antonio looked at him and saw that Miguel was spent. Then looked at her seeking a signal that would reveal if she understood what had been said to her. Mercedes understood very well. She offered her hand to Miguel and said, "Surely we can spare some time for such good friends. God knows when we will see each other again." She filled everyone's cup. Raised hers, paused to measure her words. They needed to be precise without revealing her emotions to the others. She looked directly at Miguel in a way that said that she was speaking only to him, "To sooner rather than later," she said. With those words Miguel received his answer. He knew all he needed to know about her feelings for him. Her words meant nothing to anyone else there but they meant everything to him. He asked for permission to write to her and when she acceded he asked if there was an address that he could have. Her brother intervened at this point and said one would be delivered to the church. With that they stood and parted company. Walking back towards the convent Miguel was not as anxious as when he walked towards the plaza a few hours earlier.

CHAPTER 7

That evening they sat in the courtyard discussing their options with regards to the move. When to do it, how to do it? What furniture to buy? Not much was needed since Antonio would be taking his hammock with him. How would they stay connected to the convent and the church. After all, in many ways the nuns had raised them. The sisters were their mothers and fathers. Settling nothing but an agreement to visit apartments the next day, they turned in.

Antonio entered his cell and without lighting the candle on the corner table, he started to undress removing his shirt. He felt, more than heard her presence in the room. Although dark he could see her shape and hair. She had not changed much in the years since he last seen her. Her hair was long and shiny and fell over her breasts. He stared at the hammock and at the figure laying on it and said, "Marisol please get off my hammock." He did not have to say why are you here or what do you want. They both knew. He felt angry and anxious and at the same time he felt in control. There was nothing to fear from this girl, he thought. "You are not going to pretend that we do not know one another are you? There is no need to pretend, it would be dishonest." With a touch of anger in his voice, he said, "Five years ago you and I were acquainted and shared some intimacies, but believe me when I tell you that you do not know me or know anything about me. The boy you knew in Bilbao is nothing but a memory for you and for me. The little that I remember of him is not very pleasant and easy to forget." As his eyes adjusted to the darkness he could see that she was not undressed but it would not have taken long for her to be that way. She remained in the hammock as she said, "Antonio we can now do it the regular way. Before when I was a virgin that was not possible but now it does not matter. You see it is as a result of my losing my virginity that I am here. That is why I am here I tell you, to be punished."

"No," he said. "That may be why you have been sent here but that is not what you are here for." Her voice rising she said, "You are wrong, what I am here for is to be punished for my transgression. It was not my fault he deceived me, he was supposed to marry me, he had promised. That is why I let him take my virginity. Antonio, the way I see it I am going to have some fun while I am here and deny them the punishment they wish to inflict on me. And as luck would have it, here you are. My old lover." He looked at her more clearly now. He could see a hint of sadness in her face as she demeaned herself through her words and at this moment his feelings towards her turned to pity. "You and I were never lovers. Because we did not know what love was. There was never any love between us. There was never any respect one for the other. We were no better than beasts following our basic instincts. But Marisol you and I are not animals, we are human beings with the potential for great things, if not in the eyes of others, then in the eyes of God." She sat up to look at him as he put his shirt back on. Trying to mock him she said, "So this place has gotten to you, and now you are one of them. Is that it, you hypocrite, are you forgetting what we have done? Are you planning to erase it, to ignore it as if it never happened. I know you enjoyed yourself. I felt you."

"Marisol listen to me, it is not that I am one of them, what is important is that you become one of us. You are a human being. If you let it, this place will transform you, this place will restore you." To this she laughed and said, "So this place will restore my virginity. Is that what you are saying? How can you be so ignorant?" He knelt before her and said, "Marisol this place will restore your honor. Men and women are bound to lose their virginity at one time or another and that can not be reversed, but honor can be preserved forever, and no one can take it from you. Don't you understand that unless you can regain your self respect no one will respect you." Through the moonlight that was now filling the room they could look into each other's eyes. He reached for her shoulders and said "please stand up," as she did he turned to reach for his blanket that rested at one end of the hammock, placed it around her shoulders and said, "Come, come with me."

Holding her hand they walked to the Chapel and entered. Adjusting his eyes to the darkness after walking in from the moonlit courtyard, he guided her to the pew closest to the entrance door. After she sat, he walked to the pew in front so that he could sit across from her instead of next to her.

He could sense the hostility and anger, but also the curiosity in her, wondering what was going to happen between them. He guessed that she was angry at everything and everyone, but mostly she was angry at especially herself. And that she would continue this cycle of blame for the things that had happened and were happening to her.

"Marisol, you are absolutely right when you say that this place got to me, and if you give yourself a chance it will get to you too. When the nuns took me in I was as lost as any man can be, except that I was just a boy. The first thing they did that really confused me was to treat me with kindness and feed me. That, I was not expecting especially coming from where I had come." She once again felt the need to attack him and rail at what the chapel represented.

"How can you believe all of this nonsense? I remember what it was like for you in catechism class. Were you not there just for the breakfast they served, like the rest of the Basque boys? I don't remember you being so religious when you were doing things with me. And although you were only a child or so you thought, you were closer to a man in every way but in years. How long ago was it, five or six years? It may be that I do know you, and certainly better than anyone here. You and I are exactly alike. The only difference is that I stopped pretending that I cared and you haven't. But you will. Let's go back to your hammock and make each other feel good. Or we can do it right here. Would that no be something?"

"What we did was what all children do as part of the process of trying to figure out who they are. It is part of the process through which we are given the opportunity to learn right from wrong among other things. There is no denying that I had pleasure with you and that I behaved as a boy of thirteen is expected to behave. That may explain my conduct but it does not make it right. Your being here is my opportunity to make it up to you for having used you. Marisol it is in your hands, it is all up to you. What happens with you and to you for the rest of your life is in your hands and God's." Her sarcasm bordered on hostility as she said, "Please you are not going to preach to me now are you, no thank you, once a Sunday is more than enough." Her words were biting and painful and he knew she wanted him to give up on her.

Antonio talked her through the process of redemption. He spent some time talking about how hard it had been for him to accept that he could be loved because no one had loved him before. He told her how before one can be forgiven, one must forgive oneself. This he explained, was unavoidable and would require her to examine her conduct. "Why would I want to do that? I have had nothing but misery all of my life. Hell, unhappy is something that I aspire to be. Miserable is my usual state. And for this you want me to be grateful to God." Antonio continued as if he had not heard a word she said.

"Marisol, you say you were sent here to be punished. And maybe those who sent you did wish for you to suffer, but little did they realize that no punishment could be greater than the one you are imposing on yourself. I can't tell whether your anguish is greater than your anger. Either way they are too much to bear by one girl all by herself." Antonio thought that by expressing care and concern she would accept the refuge that was offered to her by the Sisters and the church. And he said, "Imagine the disappointment of those who want you punished. Those who sent you away with the expectation that you would suffer. Can you imagine their frustration when they learn about how much you have enjoyed the experience how much you will have grown. Those who have given up on you, those who have written you off, and those who have discarded you like an old shoe should not rejoice in your punishment. Think about what they will think when they see you return in triumph, with your honor restored, with your dignity intact. They will see that a new person was born. And that the old one no longer exists. There are mighty dreams still in you and great triumphs to be accomplished. All of those are in your power. They are within your reach. Marisol, claim your victory by reclaiming your humanity. Please open your heart so that the love of God and all of us here can reach you. You can be a person that can make others feel the better for having met you. You have it in you to offer hope to those poor girls who despair as you despair. You can be God's gift to the world and all you have to do is to want it. To want to be that person. Please Marisol, let me help you, let the sisters help you, let God save you."

Marisol felt exhausted and spent. She was out of arguments. She did not move and did not speak except to say, "Please leave me alone. Get away from me. Leave me here. I need to be alone, to see if I can speak with God.

I feel some powerful tears coming from my broken heart, and I want only God to see them. Antonio, you have done enough for me, more than I thought

76

anyone could, but you are right when you say that the rest is up to me. I do not know what the morning will bring, or all the mornings remaining in my life, but this I know, they will be my mornings. Antonio, never in my life have I loved or felt loved until now. You say that I can be God's gift to the world, but in truth, it is you who are God's gift to me. I will see you in the morning." Antonio walked around to her side without releasing the hand she was holding, hugged her and kissed her forehead and said, "God be with you." The following morning she was found asleep in the pew.

She had spent the night reconstructing her life beginning with her family. Felipe and Penelope Machado, her father and mother had been well established socially and financially along the Basque Coast for many years. Their prominence was recognized by all and especially the church. Her Uncle on her father's side, Rodrigo Machado had been the bishop of Valencia and it was believed that his church connections reached all the way to the Vatican in Rome. There were four in her family. Her three younger brothers and herself. Although she was the only female, all the favors and attentions fell to her brothers. The times where she had been made to feel special were rare if ever. Her first communion had been just one more Sunday. Her brothers' first communions had been great events worthy of celebrations. Her mother mainly turned her care over to a maid because she was too busy doting on her sons. By the time Marisol was ten years old she felt unwanted and unloved and would do anything to gain attention. The more attention she craved the more severe her punishments. If not in physical cruelty, her mother was an expert in other forms of punishments. She was good at making Marisol feel ignored and worthless.

By the time she was an adolescent she had no self esteem and even less sense of self worth. Next to a girl's wedding day, few days were more important than her fifteenth birthday. It would have been her coming out party. Marisol had been to many of these events where families spent fortunes in presenting their daughters to society. On the day she had reached her fifteenth birthday she was living with her aunt and uncle in the Bilbao region and her big day came and went without any form of celebration. Since she had been sent away, because she was as her mother had said, "Incorrigible," her relatives saw no need to reward her with a celebration of any kind. Soon after that she became the Marisol that now sat deep in thought at the chapel in Saint Jacinto's church. She was exhausted by all the self examination and crying she had done all night and into the early morning hours. She had fought a battle against all the demons that had been with her for longer than she could remember. While she did not know the exact moment they had taken control of her life, she did know when and where she would reclaim her soul from them. This was the place and now was the moment. She rose from the pew and joined the sisters as they were entering the church to hear the mass.

CHAPTER 8

All week Miguel could think of nothing else but Mercedes' departure for Cuba and how to get her address there. He knew that her brother had no intention of bringing it to the church as he had said. No doubt he was following his parents' wishes in doing all that could be done to separate her sister from this unworthy suitor. In fact he wasn't a suitor yet, but why take the chance, end it before it begins, he thought was their view. Their vision for a husband for Mercedes had to do more with wealth and social aspirations than it did with her happiness. They had made a sizeable investment in her education and upbringing and were not willing to stand by and watch her waste it all on a dock worker.

They had had no communication of any kind since the last time at the plaza when she had offered her sooner rather than later toast. How interesting he thought, that so few words could reveal so much. It told him all he needed to know and allowed her to say all she needed to say. While she continued to attend church with her family, they no longer lingered in the courtyard.

Their rush to leave was so urgent, that instead of returning to their pew after communion they simply filed out the door and into their carriage that awaited them, ready to leave as soon as they sat. Canvassing the plaza for sight of her had proven futile since she no longer visited there. No doubt her brother had reported on their encounter and her family decided that no such event would occur again. Mercedes, knowing her mother's penchant for absolute control over her family knew better than to openly resist. After all it was not too long ago that her brother had been forced to break his engagement to Irene. All that it took for it to end was a report that Irene's father's business had suffered major set backs placing the financial viability of their family in jeopardy. There had even been rumors of a potential bankruptcy. This, Martin's family could not abide and so on one day Irene was their future daughter in law and on the next she ceased to exist for them.

Mercedes understood why her parents behaved as they did. It was consistent with who they were. If anything, she would been surprised if they had behaved otherwise. It was Martin's behavior that she found contemptible. He never protested or asserted his feelings for his fiancée. Instead he simply said, "As you wish," and retired to write a letter to Irene. The coward did not even have the decency; the courage to look at her as he gave her the news. What made it even sadder is that Mercedes had grown fond of Irene and resented her brother's reprehensible conduct. These events made her the more certain that Miguel was a better man than any of those in her family. Miguel was enterprising, self made, confident of who he could be and certainly no coward. He had proven this to her and to others by his quiet confidence. Miguel did not have to shout to be heard, nor threaten people to be respected. The respect afforded to him was earned as was her love for him. Mercedes better than anyone understood the dynamics of her family and knew with certainty that any overt expression of interest in anything or anyone, other than the mass would make any effort to communicate with Miguel all the more difficult. The Sunday before her departure for Cuba the entire Gabriel family was in attendance at San Jacinto's Catholic Church. As usual, they occupied their family's pew and heard the mass as if they were the only people there and it was said only for their benefit. Mercedes wondered is she would ever return to this church that had meant so much to her. God only knew how long she would remain in Cuba. After the mass they spent time in the courtyard saying goodbye to friends and well wishers.

Mercedes spoke to everyone she could, delaying her departure until she could find the right person that would help her accomplish the real mission behind being at the church. She hugged and kissed every one of the sisters and every one of them said a short prayer over her as was the custom for a traveler. She had hoped that as all the goodbyes were being said, her mother would become distracted and less vigilant. When she was approached by Renatta who had not yet made her vows, Mercedes looked into her eyes and as they hugged, she slipped a small note in the waistband that was worn by all novices. "For Miguel, for the grace of God make certain he receives this. God blesses the kind, will you do this kindness for me?" Renatta looked at Mercedes and with a smile said, "I have eyes and ears and I also have a heart.

"Mine has been given to God, but that does not keep me from understanding love. Leave it to me." Renatta made the sign of the cross over Mercedes' forehead. Doña Carmen, who at this time was approaching them, stopped not wanting to interrupt what she thought was a devout prayer being said for Mercedes.

The note said, "Confessionary, Thursday, eight in the morning." Miguel read it and began to worry about what could go wrong. What if she could not make it as she planned? Time was running out on them. Failure to meet would cause him to explore the whole island of Cuba in search of her, all one thousand miles of it, which he was willing to do but would have preferred not to. His other concern was over the fact that there were no confessions heard on Thursdays. That was the priests' day for services to the parishioners away from the church. They would visit those who had been unable to attend mass, or those who had stopped attending. Some were infirmed others had just moved away without notifying the church, still others had given up on the church altogether. Thursday was their day to minister outside the walls of Saint Jacinto's.

Miguel appreciated that there was nothing he could do to get Mercedes there as planned. That was entirely up to her. It was for her to worry about how to keep their meeting. Instead he focused on what he could do from his end to make certain that they could use what he knew would be their short time together. Realizing this would be their first real time together since they had never been alone, and this would also be their last time together for a long time to come. What to say, what not to say, what to do or not to do. All these thoughts consumed him and kept him from sleeping the night before. As usual, Miguel spoke when he had something to say and on Wednesday morning, the day before his meeting Mercedes he discussed his plan with Antonio, who was not surprised because he had noticed a change in his brother. But he believed in all things in due course, and that meant that he would have to wait for Miguel to speak when he was ready. Miguel told him he planned to be late to work on Thursday and asked Antonio to find his replacement at the operations control station from where they managed the dock's activities. The main problem and one over which he had no control was that he and Mercedes knew there were no confessions on Thursdays, the question was who else knew.

Thursday morning Mercedes arrived in the company of her maid and the driver. The maid accompanied her to the chapel and sat to the side as Mercedes knelt to pray. She had thought it best to keep her maid in the chapel instead of allowing her to wonder around and possibly speak to one of the sisters who could reveal the fact that there was no confession on that day. What if the maid wants to confess, she thought. "Well then, Miguel will just have to hear her confession." Some of the sisters had seen her approaching the chapel but thought nothing of it since that was the reason it was kept open at all times, so that people in need of prayer could do so at the chapel.

Except for the intercessions candles that were lit near the altar, it was dark. Mercedes approached the confessionary and knelt not certain of whom if anyone was there. The one thing she had was faith and her belief that God expected her to be where she was at this moment in this place and at this time. He opened the curtain and whispered "Mercedes you honor me with your faith and trust in me. Trust me when I tell you that I am more certain about this than I have ever been of anything in my life. Mercedes, please believe me when I tell you that my life has been meaningless, aimless and lacking in joy until I met you. You bring the best out of me. Because of you I want to be the best man, the best friend, and the best husband a woman could ever have. I know the risk you take to be here and I treasure that you would allow me to offer you my heart. Much more than that I do not yet have. But whatever else I do with my life it will be to honor you. Mercedes there is not much time for a courtship between us, but know this, I plan to come after you. I will find you, Cuba or China it does not matter. I will come for you and I will find you. "Miguel," she began. "I have come for no less than your heart, and I leave in the knowledge that yours is mine as mine is yours. Miguel, from this moment forward think of me as your wife before God if not yet before man. I know that you will come for me, and when you do you will find me more in love with you than I am now, if such a thing were possible. I too pledge to you whatever gifts are in me to give. I pledge to you my life. I go from here celebrating our future, confident in the knowledge that God blesses us."

Because of the little time they had she quickly explained that while her uncle's farm was away from Havana, they had a residence there near a place called the Malecon. "It is a great walkway that follows along the bay. Writing to one another will be extremely difficult and ensuring that we will receive our letters will be impossible. Instead, I will walk by the Malecon every day between five and seven in the evening. I will do this until we see one another. The rest of our future I leave in your hands to plan. The thought that you are coming for me makes my departure more bearable. I know that you will come for me I just want it to be sooner rather than later." With this she crossed herself walked to the altar to pretend to do her penance and a short while later left the church for the last time. Her maid remarked about the length of time the confession had taken to which Mercedes replied "Only God knows our sins." As she left the church she thought it was fitting that they had used a confessionary to confess their love.

On the following Saturday both he and Antonio watched her as she boarded the ship to Cuba. Antonio who was expecting a sad countenance in Miguel looked at him and was surprised by his smile. Everything that needed to be said between them had been said all that remain was for the execution of their plan. Miguel thought it would be ironic if he was to sail on that very same ship when he himself would sail for Cuba. He could see the moment when he would meet her in the Malecon. His plan did not extend beyond that at this point. Three things he thought about. One, they would not return to Spain, two, they would not remain in Cuba and three, they would go to a Spanish speaking country, perhaps another Island. "Well," he thought, "All things in due course."

The little apartment they rented was comfortable enough. In fact it was more than they had hoped for. The one bedroom to be shared by both was bigger than the cells they occupied at the convent, and they had been comfortable there. Besides there was no need for more space in the bedroom than required for one bed. Since Antonio had hung his hammock as usual. This room also had a chest with four drawers. Which was just fine because as their income grew they had started accumulating clothes. For the first time in their lives they had more than one pair of socks. They had enough underwear so they could change more than once a week which used to be only on Sundays before church. Their landlady would wash their clothes for a few coins which they could well afford. Because of the size difference between them it was not possible for them to share clothes or shoes. There was a second room that served as the dining room and kitchen. The apartment also had a table, two chairs and a coal stove. The stove was used to cook and to heat the apartment in the winter. The coal was sold to them by the landlord who would fill a small bin once a week. There was a well with a pump in the back yard from where they drew water for their cooking, cleaning and bathing needs. For other sanitary purposes there was a communal outhouse with an external pump that pushed water from a tank that was to be filled with a bucket by the last person to have used it. Sometimes the tank was filled with water, other times it wasn't.

Leaving the convent had been easier than they had expected since all the sisters offered their blessings. In all their time at the convent they had had very little contact with the priests who gave all of their attentions to candidates for the priesthood or the altar boys whom they would have liked to have recruited. Antonio and Miguel did not fall under either of these categories. The physical move was simple since all they had taken to their new apartment was their clothes and a hammock.

Sister Graciela had been approached by Marisol about three weeks after her talk with Antonio in the chapel. She had kept her distance and avoided eye, or any form of contact with him. He understood by her demeanor that her distance was owed more to her embarrassment than to any resentment. She later on while smiling, explained to him the state of bewilderment which thanks to him she found herself in. When she said thanks to him she meant it in the most profound way. He was the only man upon whom she had thrown herself who not only did not take advantage of her but made her an offer for her to be better woman. By his conduct he had demonstrated his sincerity and she had responded with scorn. She had accepted his counsel with regards to regaining her honor but felt uncomfortable being near him, because after all he knew all about her. "Marisol," he said, "I will tell you what was said to me, no one here cares who you were, we just want you to stop being that person and become the honorable woman that is in you." She expressed her gratitude but also spoke of her concern because she did not want to remain there under false pretenses . He explained that it made no sense for her to continue to be troubled by her past. Her confession had taken care of all of that. He said "God has forgiven and absolved you of your sins, it is up to you to leave them in the past and move on to a better life. Marisol it is not possible to move forward so long as you continue to look back. The lord has placed his trust in you, now it is up to you to trust in him."

Because she was concerned about remaining in the convent under false pretenses Marisol felt compelled to speak to the mother superior. She asked and received an audience with Sister Graciela. One of her grave concerns was that since she did not feel the call to serve God as a nun, she could not remain at the convent. The problem was grave because since her family had sent her away in disgrace, she had no place to go. Her meeting with Sister Graciela was in a way another confession. While not revealing the details of her past conduct, the sister was able to grasp who Marisol had been and who she longed to be. Wanting to be a better person was all new to Marisol who could not be expected to simply fall in line and get on with her new life. There was no magic wand that could be waved to make her the person she wanted to be overnight. "Providence" Sister Graciela said, "Is what brings you here at this moment in time. I appreciate the problem that you can not be a novice since that is not your calling, and this after all is a teaching convent. But since you are not called to be a nun, you are going to be a teacher. We will work all of that out. You will share in the duties with the novices and the sisters but will not attend the same classes. Please move your things into the room vacated by Miguel. It has a bed and a chest of drawers. Whatever comforts you need beyond that, you can earn. Sunday afternoon at half passed two I want you to join me for lunch. Please be on time. It distresses me to be kept waiting when I am hungry." Marisol thanked the sister and as she walked away sister Graciela thought, "It is providence all right, that brings me a daughter as I am losing my son."

CHAPTER 9

Spring had passed and summer was upon them with the stifling heat and humidity and the sand which blended with the wind that occasionally blew in from the deserts. It had been three months since Mercedes had left for Cuba and as agreed there was no communications between them. Her family had moved to their mountain home to escape the summer heat and the crowds that gathered at the beaches during the season had filled the city to its limits.

Miguel had thought through the plan to meet Mercedes in Cuba. What he had not yet resolved was the question of where to go after Cuba. The island was too small for them to hide forever. Besides living in hiding is not what he wanted for them. He would make it a point when time allowed, to speak to sailors who were aboard ships returning from South and Central America and the Caribbean Islands. He also worried about how to sustain themselves until they could get settled somewhere. He appreciated that Mercedes was willing to make sacrifices for their sakes, but he wanted to minimize her discomforts. After all she had been raised in comforts. Somehow he would have to accumulate the funds before he went after her.

On one Monday morning they were loading a ship under the Argentinean flag. This one was named The Belgrano and was brand spanking new, in fact she was making her maiden voyage. This ship had more advanced equipment than other ships not as new. One of the advancements was a system of hand operated pulleys that rolled on boards that were extended from the ship to the pier. The system allowed handlers to place the luggage on the belts while two men moved the cranks that caused the conveyor belts to roll. The luggage was delivered right to the push carts and rolled away to be returned to the owners who waited at the terminal. Antonio and Miguel looked at this new system and knew that the days of baggage handlers were threatened, if not numbered. They deferred any discussion on the matter until they could be alone and have time to evaluate the impact that change and progress could have on them and the crews. It would have been clear to a blind man that the ship's conveyor belt would reduce the time and the number of people required to load and unload. Possibly, the ships would handle the process with their own crews and not have to pay the port authority for a service they did not need. In that case the superintendent whose responsibility was to produce revenues from the ships would have some concerns. No doubt the superintendent would figure out how to continue to collect revenues one way or the other. But that would not necessarily include them or the crews. They both looked around in different directions trying to see if anyone else was noticing what was so evident to them. Seeing that no one was paying any particular attention, they went on with their work knowing they had much to think about.

At this time one of the hands that had been working on the Argentinean liner approached them and said, "With respect Don Antonio, the chief steward of the Belgrano, the Argentinean ship docked at the third berth asked me if I knew you. When I responded that I did, he asked me to deliver this note to you." He handed Antonio a note written in the Belgrano's' letterhead . The messenger stood by saying, "Should I wait for you to read it and reply. I will be happy to wait. The Steward already paid me." Looking towards the ship Antonio told the man to go about his business. He had an idea who may have sent the note, after all he only knew one Argentinean.

Miguel also knew who the note could be from. It had to be from the chief steward who had taken Antonio's brother to Argentina some five years before. It was at this time that he realized that not once had he heard his adopted brother speak of his blood brother, ever. Holding the unopened envelope in his right hand, Antonio continued to look in the direction of the ship. "Go. Find a place and read the note. Standing here worried about the best or the worst that it can say will not answer any questions about what you are about to learn. Sooner or later you have to read it, better maker it sooner." Antonio nodded in consent and walked away to find private space to receive whatever news had found him. "Come aboard the Belgrano at four o'clock this afternoon. The deck boss on duty has instruction to bring you to my quarters. It was signed Rogelio, Chief Steward, El Belgrano, The Pride of Argentina. Antonio looked at the ship again. This time he was closer but still could not see Rogelio on the deck. There were many men working at all sorts of tasks that take place on board a ship. They were all uniformed in different styles clothes but in consistently black and white colors. Some gave orders others followed them. By concentrating on those who seemed in command he figured he could spot Rogelio, and he did. Not much had changed in the man, he was as fit as the last time he saw him. The only difference was that unlike the last time Rogelio was not shouting orders.

Instead he spoke to men who yelled orders at others. This told Antonio that Rogelio's position on this ship was of greater importance than on board the Las Pampas, when he sailed taking Xavier Barradaz with him.

Rare were the occasions if any, when Antonio had the opportunity to see the dock operations from a ship's deck. He had never been all that curios about it. Up to now he had not had any need to gain perspective on the way his crews interacted with the ships' crews, manually or mechanically. Until now he had never felt threatened, and he knew well that before assessing a threat one needed to understand it. For that reason he boarded the ship twenty minutes before four o'clock. He stood on the deck a good while observing how the pulleys worked and how the conveyor belts rotated on the rollers. He noticed that the balance was tentative at best. It shifted based on the weight that the belt was carrying. It also appeared that the belts would torque left and right and as the pieces were transferred from ship to shore there was a risk that the luggage could fall to the side, crashing to the pier or falling in the water, with potentially disastrous results for the luggage and their owners. Right at that moment, it occurred to him that Miguel could design and construct a better system, sturdier, more secure and less prone to accidents. The idea was that if they could construct a better system than the ship's, the port authority could retain control over the luggage operations and relieve the ships of any liabilities and consequences of sunk luggage. He made some mental notes which he would later share with Miguel. At precisely four o'clock he set out to find the deck boss who was in charge of the Belgrano's deck that afternoon.

He did not know what to expect when he spoke to the deck boss but it certainly was not the treatment he received. Deck bosses were out of necessity crude and rough men not known to observe any courtesies for anyone except passengers and superiors. "Great to welcome you aboard, sir. I am Francisco San Martin, Deck Boss on duty. Don Rogelio has asked me to take personal care that you are brought to his quarters. Sir, if you would be so kind as to permit me three minutes and I will take you to him directly."

With that Francisco turned around, yelled a number of instructions without using names. Yet the ones for whom the orders were meant all responded as if they had been spoken to by name. Clearly this was Francisco's crew and no one else's. After issuing all the orders to his people, the deck boss turned to Antonio saying, "If you will please follow me sir, I'll take you to Don Rogelio."

The Chief Steward's quarters were situated one deck below, aft of the ship and fairly close to the officers' quarters. After knocking and without receiving an instruction, Francisco opened the door and stepped into a comfortable but sparsely furnished office. It had a desk which was bolted to the floor and two chairs in front. To the right was a combination state and bedroom. There was a medium size cabinet that served as a file and storage closet at the same time. He could tell these were the quarters of someone who wasted neither time nor space. "Please sit if you like. Don Rogelio will be here shortly, he is probably detained by a meeting with the first officer. May I offer you anything while you wait?" Before Antonio had the time to reply, Rogelio entered the room. They looked at one another in silence not so much sizing one another but trying to remember how they looked the last time they had seen each other. This ship was a vast improvement over the one in which Xavier had sailed to Argentina.

Rogelio entered the room, thanked Antonio for coming and invited him to sit down, as he did the same. "This is some ship. It must be four times the size of the Las Pampas, and certainly on a much different class. It seems that your fortune has improved." Rogelio explained that the previous employer had sold his business to the current owners who owned a fleet of cargo and passenger vessels. And did not mix both. The routes they served were literally all over the eastern hemisphere. This covered the North and South American continents, the Caribbean Sea and Europe all the way to Antwerp. What made his situation special was that because of his seniority, he could pick and choose his ships and cruises. At his age he explained it was important to find warm waters every chance he could and he did. "But work is still work regardless of how nice the ship," he added, followed by, "Thank you for coming." Without asking Antonio he turned and filled two glasses with wine, and offered the first the one to him. As he held his own glass he said, "Your brother has asked me to share this wine with you. It is a gift from him. He has sent you a case which I will give to you before you leave. It is from Mendoza, our soon to be famous wine region. The French have a surprised coming to them from Argentinean wines. Just wait and see."

"Your brother has been a blessing to my father and the ranch. If I did not know better, I would swear that he was more Gaucho than Basque. It turns out the Basque and the Gaucho have much in common. Rebellious by nature, largely ignored and abused by the authorities and have a strong desire to be left alone. He has found his calling working the cattle and learning about the grain and the vineyards." Rogelio paused to allow Antonio to absorb what was being said to him. Antonio tasted the wine and said, "This wine makes me realize that I have been drinking terrible wine all of my life except for once when I was served a French wine. I usually drink communion wine, and as you may not know the Catholic Church does not spend a lot of money on fine wines for communion. It basically needs to be red and wet. And that's it."

"I do know of what you speak. When I was a boy and the priest would come out to the ranch to hold mass for the hands. I served as his altar boy, and my step father never allowed the priest to use his good wines for communion."

Reaching into the top drawer of his desk, Rogelio produced an envelope with a letter in it. The only way he knew this was from his brother was because it was Rogelio who was delivering it. Not having ever seen anything written by his brother he was not able to recognize the handwriting. He was surprised to receive a letter from Xavier, because the last time he saw him neither one of them could read or write. Rogelio stood and told him that Xavier had asked him to answer whatever questions Antonio would have after reading it. Xavier thought that it would not be possible to tell all in one letter, and so he relied on Rogelio to fill in the blanks. Rogelio left the office so that Antonio could read the letter in private, but promised to return shortly.

Antonio held the sealed envelope in between his fingers for a while, and thought about the fact that this was the first time he had ever received a letter from anyone let alone from a member of his family. It pleased him that his brother like him, could read and write.

July 1895
Mendoza Argentina
Dear Anton:

The last time we saw one another I thought that we would never be together again. Now I know for certain because the only way that I will return to Spain is if I can walk on water, because after crossing the Atlantic Ocean I swore that not even dead would I do it again. From the moment that we left the port of Barcelona to the moment we reached Puerto Plata few were the moments that I was not asking God to take my life. I actually became a convert thinking that a merciful God would respond to my supplications. He did not and so I am back to being an unbeliever. There is one other way for us to see one another and that is for you to join me here. I know that my description of the journey could serve to discourage you but I know that if I made it so can you. Rogelio is willing and able to bring you on the Belgrano at no cost to you. He and I will pay for your trip. But I am ahead of myself. First allow me to tell you what my adventure has been like.

I do not know very much about Argentina other than what Don José Luis, Rogelio's step father has given me to read. He taught me to read and write but as a condition I had to agree to read one book a month. One of his choosing. It was a struggle at first but now I enjoy it a great deal. After I learned to read, during the week I lived out on the range with Gauchos, but if time allowed I could return to the house Saturday evenings and stay through Sunday. His wife, Rogelio's mother likes to retire early since she seems to not be well. Don José Luis likes to discuss the books that I read long into the night. Frequently we play chess, a game that he has taught me. I have yet to defeat him. Even when he has drunk three times more than I have, he still wins.

When I first arrived I was awed by the beauty of the range. Unlike our country, when I look in any direction all I see is open fields. Just before the time to harvest the grain when it is at its peak golden color it responds to the wind much like a wave does in the ocean. At first I was troubled by how would the Gauchos receive me. Not having been around anyone but Basques all my life I did not know what to expect. The first full day at the ranch Don José Luis rode me out to the camp where the Gauchos were. As I sat on the buggy, he spoke a few words to the foreman, returned and told me to get off and that was the last time I saw him for three months. The foreman took me to a bunk house assigned a bed to me, pointed me to a room full of old clothes and said, Take what you need and meet me outside.

I found everything I needed except for boots. Those I had to buy after a while. The foreman approached me with a horse and told me to remove the saddle. When I did, he told me to saddle the horse. Finally after saddling and unsaddling the horse countless times, he told me to mount the horse. And there was the surprise. Anton, I was born to ride a horse. Next to walking is the most natural thing that I have ever done. I told the foreman my name and asked him for his. He told me that his name was Foreman, and still is.

I had some fights with a few Gauchos who meant to test me more than to hurt me. And after that I was one of the hands. I remember that Rogelio had told me that more than anything Don José Luis, his father respected a man for his sense of honor, his work ethic and his disposition to learn. Honorable conduct is a way of life among Gauchos. Is their code of conduct and it is inviolate. No one makes the mistake of breaking it. No one who wants to live, that is. Gauchos are very skilled with their knives and are never found without one. I mainly decided that I would out work and out perform everyone at whatever task I was given and see what would happen as a result.

I had little contact with anyone outside the Gauchos the first year. Not even women. Especially women. For a Gaucho there is no more serious offense than to have a man speak to his woman without his permission. Foreman had forewarned me about this. So I went one whole year without speaking to a woman, and only then because she spoke to me first.

Towards the end of the first year, Don José Luis spoke to the foreman for a while, about what I did not know, but at the end of the talk he came to me and told me to grab my things and throw them on the buggy. We rode back to the main house where he pointed me to a smaller bunkhouse than when I first arrived. Then he told me to meet him at the house at first light. That is how I started to learn to read and write. Every day for the first three hours I sat in a room. Sometimes with a priest from the local mission other times with Don José Luis. Once I was able to read better than I could write, I was given a horse to return to the range with books to read and paper to write.

For the next six months I worked the range and read the books and developed my writing. I had to be discreet about this since I found out that the Gauchos could neither read nor write. They did not seem to care one way or the other, but only foreman knew about my assignment from Don José Luis.

One day Foreman told me that as ordered by Don José Luis I was to pack my bags and ride to the ranch. It was early in the evening when I returned to the ranch house, but unlike the last time, Don José Luis told me to clean up and join him in the main house for dinner. Cleaning up for me meant to put on the least dirty clothes, which I did. Once at the house Don José Luis began to talk to me about the books I had been given to read, not to test my memory but my knowledge. That evening we spoke until very late and drank a good amount of wine and brandy.

The next morning I was awoken by the cook who told me that Don José Luis was waiting for me outside. When I dressed and joined him he simply told me to mount up and follow him, No breakfast, no food and no drink. He took me out to a small group of young gauchos who were tending a small herd of cattle. Everyone of the gauchos were younger than me. Don José Luis told them that I was in charge of moving the herd to a range fifty kilometers away.

And that began my training in leading and ordering men. As time went on Don José Luis gave me more and more responsibility to the point that today I am his right hand man. I enjoy full privileges and when at the ranch, I sleep at the main house.

I hope to tell you more about my life here when I see you as I hope that you will agree to return with Rogelio. Anton, I have never been happier and can not conceive that I could ever live anywhere but here. There is a place for you here if you want it. We can be better brothers than our circumstances allowed us in the past.

Please come.

Xavier

When he was almost finished reading the letter Rogelio returned to the office and served him another glass of wine. "Your brother confirms that I am a good judge of character. On the first day I met him, I knew that there was a good man inside that boy and I was right. My step father tested my judgment in Xavier by letting him fail or succeed on his own, and Xavier stood the test well. By the way he is now Javier instead of Xavier. My step father gave the name to him because he wanted him to stop being Basque and start his new life with a new name." Rogelio did not ask about the content of the letter. But he knew that Xavier wanted Antonio to return with him.

"My mother and I were abandoned by my real father," Rogelio said. "She went to work at the ranch caring for Don José Luis's first wife who had been ill for a long time. When she died, Don José Luis asked her to remain at the ranch. Eventually he married my mother since they were living as husband and wife, and he took me in. He had never had any children with his wife and so he adopted me as his own. I was everyone's disappointment since the cattle and the grain were not for me. It has troubled me that I was not repaying his kindness to my mother and me. I could tell he hoped that one day I would tire of the sea and return to Mendoza, but as time has passed that has been an increasingly unlikely probability."

"I can assure you that in our house your brother is the heir apparent, and I could not be happier. Both my parents have come to appreciate him and in the case of my step father, to love him. Javier needs help that he can trust. My father wants him to have a family so that he can enjoy a good life at the ranch. However he is concerned that unless Javier can get some help with his responsibilities, because he now runs the entire ranch and all related operations, he will never be able to have a family. My step father does not want to see Javier have a woman and not be a husband to her. That is what happened to him."

Antonio did not speak a word nor did he make a sound. Not wanting Rogelio to stop talking about his brother. He understood that in a way Rogelio had become a brother to Xavier in the same way that Miguel was his. To Xavier's good fortune, it seemed that he may have also acquired a father and a mother in Mendoza, Argentina. Providence, as Sister Graciela liked to say was a strange and wonderful power. It worked for good and worked for ill, it all depended on the recipient. He reflected on the notion that since Xavier's departure he had not given much thought to him. Then again Xavier had not given much thought to Antonio when he left him alone on the pier the day he boarded the Las Pampas and sailed for Argentina.

"What do you think of the offer? Will you consider it? We sail tomorrow. Please give it serious thought. This decision is about your life." Antonio thought that this was indeed a life changing decision, but one that he had already made. "I will give my answer tomorrow. Will you carry it back for me?" Rogelio smiled at that comment recognizing that Antonio was not going to travel to Argentina. He said, "Have it here before we sail. I'll get your case of wine."

CHAPTER 10

Miguel was at his work station when Antonio joined him with his case of wine. Instead of a square box, the case of wine was packed in two rows of six bottles each and secured with twine from which a handle was formed. Antonio carried it the way a managing director carries a briefcase, causing Miguel to say, "Lets get you a jacket and tie and call you a government minister." Antonio returned the smile, placed the wine on the ground and returned to his work.

On the way to their apartment Antonio offered to let Miguel read the letter from Xavier, but he refused saying, "I much prefer hearing about it from you. That way more than knowing what the letter says, I'll know what it means to you. Lets find us a place to have a beer and you can tell me." Being a Friday night, the early crowds were beginning to form in the cafes and restaurants. These were people attending the theater or flamenco shows. Their custom was to have a light snack before the show and a full dinner after. Since they were dressed in other than their Sunday best they had to settle for one of the lesser establishments.

While they drank their beers and ate Serrano Ham and Blood Sausages with bread soaked in spiced olive oil, Antonio related not just the content of the letter but also what he saw in the ship's conveyor belt system. Miguel could visualize it as quickly as Antonio described it and right away began to form ideas on how to improve it. As the conversation continued it took the form of questions and answers, and as Miguel collected the information he needed, he made several drawings of the belts and the pulleys from different perspectives. He had a natural ability to transfer to paper the parts and mechanisms of different equipments. Some people spoke with their hands, Miguel was eloquent with his drawings. When he had it all well understood he said to Antonio, "What will you do? About the letter that is, what will you do?" Antonio told him that he had decided even before he disembarked the Belgrano. "I am staying with my brother," he said extending his hand before walking out of the office.

That evening when they arrived at their apartment at half past ten there was a party in full force in the center courtyard of the apartment building. There was a man playing a forceful Flamenco melody accompanied by a chorus of two girls and a boy. The girls appeared to be in their late teens or early twenties. In the dim light of the courtyard torches it was difficult to tell their ages with any certainty. But while the light may have concealed their ages, it failed at concealing their beauty. They were strikingly elegant and clearly showed their moor ancestry. It was all over them. It was in their figures, in their motions and their voices. The boy who was about twelve, had a beautiful voice and sang as his sisters danced in the energetic and seductive Flamenco tradition.

Their landlady called them to join the celebration but they declined because they were returning from work and were not presentable. She insisted, saying, "If you were presentable this would be the wrong place for you. This is for working people only. Come, join us and bring your wine. Miguel inquired about the cause for the celebration since he was not aware that anything had been planned. "Who wants to be in a warm apartment while we can be outside enjoying the breeze, the evening, the company and besides we can wear ourselves out. This will help us sleep better tonight," the landlady said, "Come let me introduce you to my guests. These are Dolores and Pilar, my husband's nieces, they will be with us for three weeks. Will you share your wine with us?" Antonio agreed and offered to return after he had at least washed. Miguel followed him to the apartment where Antonio opened the case of wine, set two bottles aside to take to Sister Graciela, removed two bottles to take to the party and stored the rest. As they washed Miguel told Antonio to go without him because he wanted to work on his design for the conveyor system he would build, and because he had no desire for female company other than Mercedes.

A few more of the residents had joined the party and were in conversation with the visitors when Antonio returned. After handing the bottles to his hostess he turned and spoke to the boy. "I am Antonio, what is your name?"

The boy, accustomed to being ignored whenever he was the youngest person among adults, stammered, "Manuelito, Manuelito is my name." From his experience with children at the convent, Antonio knew about making children comfortable around him. The first thing he did was to go down on one knee so that he could be eye level with the boy. He asked, "Have you been to the beach yet? Do you like it? Are you a good swimmer?" Without pause, Manuelito said "No. Yes. Maybe." He replied with a smile and explained that he had been at the beach the previous year but not yet since they had just arrived. He had liked it quite well but was uncertain about his swimming skills since he had only been swimming in the pond in his father's farm, but never in the ocean. "I'll give you a better answer tomorrow, if I do not drown" he said, pleased with his answer.

The older of the two sisters, Dolores, broke away from the conversation, leaving her sister to fend for herself with two young men who were contending for her attention. She brought a cup of wine for Antonio saying, "Better drink your wine before it is all gone. At the rate it is being consumed it won't last long." She hugged her brother to her side with a warmth and sincerity that said she was comfortable doing it because she did it often. Manuelito hugged her back and held her until somebody brought a tray of chicken gizzards, baked and covered in rosemary and basil. As he ran to get to the food he offered to bring some back for Antonio and Dolores. They both declined and asked him to eat their share. "You are Basque are you not?" He answered her by saying that he had left his home so long ago that he forgot what it was like to be Basque. She asked, "Why did you not go to the Basque coast instead of coming all the way to Barcelona? It would have been closer. Am I asking too many questions?"

"Your questions are fine. It's my answers that are lacking"

"Your brother has a fine and promising voice. Hopefully someone in your family will see to it that it gets developed," he said. Dolores looked at him with an expression that showed surprise and curiosity. Usually when around men her age she heard comments about how big, brave and strong they were. Or instead of talking about themselves, they would find even less interesting topics for conversation. Never once did anyone express an interest in her little brother. "In my family we too think he has a promising voice, but we have to wait until his voice changes and then we will listen to see if the promise remains. So many children lose the innocence in their voices which makes them so charming when they go through puberty and the charm is lost. Interesting that you would make that observation about his voice, why is that?" Antonio responded by saying that those without any talent should take care to protect those who have it because so often that talent goes to waste unless nourished and cared for. He said that he did not recall ever having a child's voice and the charm associated with it, but he did recall that no one ever asked him to join in song and on the few occasions when he did sing, no one ever asked him to sing again. That, he said, served as the confirmation that he had no talent for singing. At this time he sat on a chair and Dolores sat next to him. "Everyone has talent in some form, it just takes longer for it to be revealed in some than it does for others. Yours will be revealed in due course no doubt" she said. He looked at her with a smile when he heard one of his favorite expressions. "Why do you smile?" Dolores asked. "You are right. All things in due course."

He stood to thank her for her company, explaining that he had a very early day ahead and had something to write that evening. As he extended his hand she held his shoulders stood on the tips of her toes, kissed him in both cheeks and said, "It has been my pleasure to meet you."

Antonio arrived at the dock ahead of Miguel and walked directly to the Argentinean ship. He had thought about what to write to Xavier in the note that Rogelio would take back to Argentina. The offer from Xavier was genuine and certainly kind. It was an opportunity for an entirely new and different life in a new country. One in which he would have no past, only a future. In pondering the offer he tried to think of all the pluses and minuses. There were more of the former than of the latter. None of these could cause him to forget that his brother had left him behind when he left for Argentina.

He simply said, "I am going," without thought to leaving Antonio behind. Since going with him then was not an option neither would it be going to him now. "My brother," he thought, "What is my brother to me? I am with my brother and his name is Miguel de la Madrid." The note he wrote did not take him much time since much time was not needed to reply. When he entered the chief steward's quarters, Rogelio was already at his desk and offered a seat to Antonio. "I have a note for Xavier and I thank you if you will deliver it to him." He continued by saying, "Argentina is not for me and he already has a great family." With this he handed the note to Rogelio who noticed it was not sealed. He asked if he could read it and Antonio responded by saying, "Since you knew the content of Xavier's letter to me, you should see my response to him." Rogelio opened the envelope and read the one line in the note. It read "One Barradaz is enough for Argentina." Signed, "Anton." Without comment Rogelio extended his hand and wished Antonio well.

They had been at the dock a good two hours before the superintendent arrived. This being Saturday he mainly stopped in to check on the day's traffic and the following week's schedules. He had been extremely pleased with the results of the system implemented by Miguel and Antonio and as a consequence was positively disposed to hear their latest idea. Antonio spoke first and reviewed what he had observed on the "Belgrano" and the potential strategic threat that the ship's system represented to the labor force and to the port authority. Don Mauricio had not spent any time seeing the conveyor belts himself but had heard about it from others. He had not given it much thought until Antonio mentioned the possibility of lost fees because of the potential elimination of the need for services provided by the port authority. Don Mauricio appreciated the difficulty of his position if ever he had to explain a decrease in revenues to his superiors who had experienced an increase thanks to the system designed by Miguel. "Go on show me what you have," Don Mauricio ordered. Miguel presented the drawings which he had worked on the night before.

He had a mechanical mind and the ability to articulate processes and systems with great simplicity. Which is always the case when the speaker thoroughly understands the subject matter. And Miguel understood his system better than anyone. It really was a simple idea. The Belgrano's system required two operators running the pulleys, and because of the uneven distribution of force, the motion of the belts was not precise or consistent. Miguel's design required only one operator and as a result the force applied would be even. The brilliance of his system was in building the frame with rollers that were wider on the outside and narrower in the inside. This would have the effect of eliminating the outward shifting bias of the belts. Instead it would cause all bags to drift towards the middle of the belt and reducing if not eliminating the opportunity for them to fall off into the water.

Antonio proposed that by offering the service themselves they could charge the ships for the added efficiency and risk reduction. This offered an opportunity to protect the authority's revenues and possibly increase them. After a few questions were asked only to show that he was engaged, Don Mauricio asked about the building of the system, the time required to build it, and the length of time required to test it. Miguel who well understood the superintendent responded by suggesting that if it was seen to be his idea, his initiative and his leadership that was driving the project, everyone would fall in line and they could have the first one built in no longer than two weeks. The superintendent who never objected to claiming credit for great ideas that were not his, ordered them to report to work on Monday with the completed plan.

Thanks to the day being fairly slow, they were back to their apartment late that afternoon. As they entered the courtyard they were met by Dolores and Pilar who had been waiting for them since earlier. Dolores spoke at both of them saying, "You are being offered a grand opportunity to rescue to damsels from danger. We want to go to the plaza this evening and will be in danger going by ourselves. But we are going regardless. It is up to you to protect us if you wish. However should you not and should anything happen to us it will be on your conscience." Miguel and Antonio both smiled in disbelief. They had never been asked to go out by girls, and these two certainly needed no protection. "Meet us here at ten and we will go to La Rambla. Once we are there we will find a way to keep you out of trouble." Antonio said.

As soon as they entered the apartment they both washed. Antonio laid on his hammock for a nap and Miguel worked on the details of his design. He would have it all documented and ready for Monday before they met the ladies for their evening out. Shy and retiring would not be words one would use to describe Dolores or Pilar. Their demeanor was somewhere between aggressive and confident. Dolores especially was someone who had a natural ability make others comfortable around her. She was flirtatious without being sensual. And she was the first to the door when Antonio knocked. Followed by her sister, she stepped into the courtyard, placed her arm around Antonio's elbow and said, "I feel safer already."

All four engaged in jovial conversation, everyone speaking to everyone at the same time. No one listening, and occasionally stopping to laugh. As they neared the plaza they were approached by a young couple holding an infant. The mother looked weak and had a vacant look in her eyes. She and the man had the features of gypsies although they were not dressed in the usual gypsy way. There was not a great deal of color in their garments. They were ill fitting and were clearly hand me down rags. The man spoke and said, "Ladies and gentlemen please excuse this intrusion, we have not eaten in days, our child is sick and in need of nourishment, so is my wife who is too weak to feed our boy. Could you find it in your hearts to forgive me for begging, and give us any coins that you could spare." All four looked at the family and were touched by the contrast. In front of them was a starving family and a few yards ahead were people enjoying themselves oblivious to the suffering of these gypsies. Antonio and Miguel reached into their billfolds and handed the man not coins but a few bills. Even after helping them they felt uncomfortable in front of the poor family and so they wished them well, and moved on.

After a few steps Antonio stopped and returned to the gypsies to say, "Tomorrow morning come to the church of San Jacinto after five in the morning. I will be there. They will help you." The man looked at Antonio ashamedly and explained that they were not Catholics. "Neither was I. Please come to the church in the morning." As they walked away, Pilar looked back at them and said, "That is really sad. I sure hope that it was not an act and that they do need money to eat." Looking at her Antonio said, "It makes no difference to us if it is or it is not an act. At the end of the day, we are not responsible for their behavior, only for our conduct." They continued to walk in silence. Dolores drew closer to Antonio and said, "You told me that you had no talent, but it is not true. Your talent has been revealed. I have seen it, and it is kindness. This would be a far better world if more people developed talent like yours more than all the other forms."

The plaza was not as full as usual because people had not yet exited from the theaters and shows, and they could choose any table they wanted. They selected a remote table away from the noise that would soon invade the plaza and would cause them to yell rather than to converse. When the waiter arrived and described the specialties of the evening they settled on a tray of assorted Tapas with a combination of salty, extra salty, spicy and extra spicy varieties of foods. The kind that would require more than one carafe of wine for company. After the first glass of wine, Pilar wondered out loud what could possibly be wrong with the women of Barcelona who would allow two handsome men like them to wander around unattached. "Or maybe," she said, "The problem is not with the women, perhaps they are too demanding and as a result their expectations can not be met." She demanded to be told which one was it, the women or the men?

Miguel responded saying, "It is neither. I have a wife. She is in the island of Cuba visiting her family. I am going to join her there soon. So you see, you are both safe with me. However the same is not true of Anton. With him you are not safe. In fact the only reason why I came along was to protect you from him. You said that you wanted us to protect you from danger. You do not know the half of it. You should consider moving away from him and closer to me so that I can protect the two of you should the need arise." Both girls jumped to their feet at the same time and leapt on Miguel's lap pretending to be terrified and begging for Miguel's protection. All four broke into laughter at the same time. Antonio simply looked at Miguel and admired him for his ability to inject fun into any situation.

On the way back they took the long route walking near the ocean before turning back to their street. During the walk, Miguel and Pilar walked ahead while Antonio and Dolores lingered behind. She said, "Anton, do you like to be called Anton instead of Antonio."

"Only by those who matter to me. I want you to call me Anton." She continued and said, "You never did answer the question asked by Pilar. Tell me why is it that there is no woman with you."

"But you are with me," he said. "Would it not be uncomfortable for all if there was another woman holding my other arm. You both would probably tug at my arms until I stretched as if I were on the rack. No. For me one at a time is enough and right now it is you and only you." She looked at him thinking how nice it would be for that to be true. For her to be this man's only woman. After they arrived back at the courtyard, Pilar and Miguel retired quickly sensing that Antonio and Dolores wanted to be alone. She reached up to him and held his face with both hands and kissed him. He had not had much experience in kissing women other than the fraternal kisses he often exchanged with the sisters at the convent, but this was different and he liked it. He felt that she was better at kissing than he was and so he let her lead. She hugged him and asked, "Are you going to mass tomorrow." He explained about their roles on Sundays at the church and that he and Miguel would be at the sacristy very early to prepare for all the masses, but that they would attend the ten o'clock mass with the nuns as they had been doing for years. "Pilar and I will be there at nine thirty. Will the nuns be jealous if we sit with you?" He smiled, kissed her again and said to her "I will see you at San Jacinto's at nine thirty."

When Antonio and Miguel arrived at the church they found the Gypsy family sleeping at the gates. The husband and the wife were huddling the child to provide him the warmth they could not enjoy themselves in the cool morning. They entered without waking them. Miguel quickly returned with blankets so they could be covered when they awoke, while Antonio went to the kitchen to see Sister Maria.

Once they turned over the family in need to the nuns, Antonio and Miguel returned to what for years had been their routine. It started at the kitchen with affectionate bantering and verbal jousting between them and the sisters. As it had been the practice for the passed few years, sister Magdalena served them their bread out of the oven, the sausages and their coffee. This time she offered orange juice since they had received a crate of oranges from one of their missions in Africa. As he ate the bread Miguel commented on the vast difference between freshly baked bread and bread just out of the oven. "We have noticed how partial you are to it. Sometimes we worry that our bread is the one and only reason you come to San Jacinto's."

"Sister Magdalena" he replied, "The lord does not care why we come to church so long as we come." She asked him if he would continue to attend mass at Saint Jacinto's if the bread was not there for him. He paused for a minute searching for an answer. Finally he spoke as he reached for a new roll. "Yes, but I would not enjoy it as much." Satisfied with the answer Sister Magdalena returned to her work.

Sister Magdalena remembered the first time she saw Antonio in the kitchen. She was then almost thirteen years old and remembered how awed she felt by his size. Back then she dealt with the crush she had on him, but now she loved him and Miguel as her sons. It mattered not that she was younger than both. Her name had been Renatta when they first met. Magdalena was the name she had taken at the time she took her vows. Taking a different name reaffirmed the end of the previous person and the birth of a nun. She was a natural and gifted teacher, which was a good thing since the other option was nursing and she would faint at the site of blood. She made her students want to learn because as she frequently explained to them, their failure to learn would reflect badly on her because she was the expert on whatever subject was being taught and was expected to be able to teach. It was not possible for them to fail to learn only for her to fail to teach. Her attitude made all the students work extra hard not for fear of their failure, but her's. As expected of all the members of her order she would soon go on mission. As was their practice her first mission would be outside of Spain.

Having finished their breakfast, Antonio and Miguel went about their chores at the sacristy. Not much had changed since they started their service getting everything for mass. The Catholic Church is all about traditions and repetition and as a result nothing ever changed in the sacristy. Except perhaps the quality of the wine. It was now diluted with water so that the only semblance to wine was the color. The altar boys arrived to prepare to assist the priest and as usual most of them looked as if had not been their idea to be up that early. Left to them, they would have preferred to be somewhere else, namely asleep in their beds.

The procession was almost completed as Dolores and Pilar arrived at the church. Since it would have been disruptive to join the nuns and everyone else processing, they instead sat a few pews behind Antonio and Miguel. Wondering what had happened to them Antonio looked around and behind until he saw the girls, exchanged smiles with them and returned his attention to the priest who was beginning the mass. Sister Graciela, ever vigilant over her flock saw the acknowledgement between Antonio and the girls and she too smiled.

They met at the church courtyard, and Pilar spoke first saying, "It is entirely my fault we were late. I got up early enough but I just could not move. We are not accustomed to rising this early on a Sunday, and if ever we do, it is not to go to church. Please forgive me." At this moment Sister Graciela approached and said, "You are forgiven. Now tell me what you did. My dear children don't you know that by your presence here you are forgiven. However I will not forgive any of you if you do not join me in the dining hall for hot buttered rolls and coffee. Usually we meet in the kitchen before the first mass but since it is closed until the early afternoon, the dining hall it is. Anton please lead them, I will meet you there."

Coffee was already served by the time Sister Graciela entered with a tray of pastries and Marisol alongside her. "Look what I was able to find. One of our parish families stopped at a pastry shop on the way to church and brought us an assortment of pastries. Please, please let us not pretend we are not hungry. Marisol come sit and join us." As she sat Marisol looked directly at Antonio and said, "Anton you look so well, so happy, what is happening that is making you so."

"Hard work and clean living is all," he responded. Sister Graciela was pleased by the absence of tension between Marisol and Antonio. There was genuine warmth and affection between them. This confirmed to her that whatever their issues had been, they were no longer. However the sister did feel a touch of tension on the part of Antonio's friend. "Anton" she said "Now that we are settled will you please make the formal introductions. I do not know what has happened to you since you left us, the two of you. We sent you out gentlemen and you return as mannerless ruffians. We may have to bring you back for more lessons." Dolores and Pilar not knowing Antonio's and Miguel's history with the nun were confused and perplexed by the sister's admonitions and remained silent. "But of course we won't, simply because we can not afford to feed you." Her last remark was accompanied by a smile that set everyone at ease.

Antonio obeyed the command and said, "Sister Graciela, Marisol, I am pleased to present to you the Vincenti sisters, Dolores and Pilar. They are the nieces of our landlady and will visit Barcelona for another two weeks. After that they will return to Valencia. Their little brother is also with them on this visit. Ladies, Sister Graciela is the Mother Superior of the convent and Marisol is training to be a missionary teacher." Sister Graciela inquired as to why their brother was not with them. They explained that their uncle had taken him fishing very early in order to catch the low tide but that they would bring him the following Sunday.

As they enjoyed their pastries, Dolores looked at Marisol wondering if this was her competition. It caught her attention that she called him Anton. Marisol was older than Antonio, but so was she. Antonio did not seem to be especially attentive towards Marisol but still she felt a twinge of jealousy that kept her from being her jovial self. From the other side of the table Marisol was assessing Dolores for different reasons. She wanted nothing but the best for Antonio for whom she had strong fraternal feelings. Deep in her mind she worried that this girl could use Antonio the way she had. That thought she put out of her mind when she remembered her evening at the chapel with him. She thought about how silly it was of her to worry about one so well grounded as he. Miguel inquired if the sister had heard anything from the Gabriel Family. Sister Graciela who prided herself on knowing everything about everything all the time, said, "No Miguel, we have not heard anything about Mercedes. Since her family moves to the mountains during the summer months we will not see them for another few weeks. I will ask then. But it is strange that she has not written to us as she has always done when traveling"

Walking back from the church and with no appetite left after feasting on pastries they walked along the plaza with no other purpose than to feel lighter after a good walk. "Why don't you go ahead and ask me?"

"Ask you what Anton." He was enjoying himself knowing that she had a few questions about Sister Graciela and a few hundred about Marisol.

CHAPTER 11

The building of the frame for the conveyor belts had progressed faster than expected. The lathing of the rollers which required great precision had been the most difficult of the tasks. They were made from oak wood and needed to be identical to the corresponding rollers on the opposite sides of the frame. Miguel saw to this by using a caliper and stopping the lathe every few seconds as it approached the desired size, long enough to measure the rollers at three different points. The results had been so satisfactory that while the first unit required almost a full week to build, the second one only took a day. As a result instead of delivering one, two were delivered for the test. The conveyor belts performed exactly as designed. They were tested with different loads at different speeds and always with the same result. Not a single piece of luggage slipped anywhere but to the center of the belt. Don Mauricio who was extremely pleased with his new system expressed his appreciation by rewarding Antonio and Miguel with a bonus in the equivalent of two week's pay each. "Cuba money is what I call this," Said Miguel as he hid the money in his secret spot in the apartment.

His progress had been slow in building the treasure needed for his journey to Cuba and beyond, once he had Mercedes. So far he had enough to get there and to travel to their next destination. At this stage in his planning he was favoring the island of Puerto Rico. It was known by different names to different people. When Columbus discovered it, he named the island San Juan and the port of entry Puerto Rico. In the years following, Don Juan Ponce de Leon reversed the names.

The sailors who had stopped there spoke of the island's natural beauty and described it as a smaller version of Cuba. From other sources he had heard that the fortunes to be made in Cuba were already in the hands of the rich landowners, but the same was not true of Puerto Rico. Moreover, because the island was one tenth the size of Cuba, the government did not seem to pay a lot of attention or to interfere with the residents. Once he had decided that Puerto Rico would be their destination Miguel took an engineers approach to the planning process. He wrote everything on a note book he had purchased expressly for that purpose. Everything was clearly thought through and re-thought. Everything was clear to him. The only things lacking were the dates.

All through the week, much like a wife waits for her husband, Dolores waited for Antonio to return from work. She was not shy about kissing him in front of others and he was not shy about kissing her back. He enjoyed her playfulness not realizing that she was serious about her intentions for him.

Even if he had not confirmed how he felt about her, she was certain her feelings were reciprocated, even though they had not been articulated by him. On one occasion her aunt allowed her to prepare the evening meal for the family, and to invite Antonio and Miguel for dinner. Everyone understood that this was one of the ways Dolores's was letting Antonio know that she was ready to be a wife. His wife. For all intents and purposes, in her mind they were already engaged. For her the question was not if, it was when they got married. After all other than working on their relationship and caring for her brother, everything they did was done together. Little by little she grew to appreciate Antonio's relationship with the convent and with Marisol.

Although everything indicated that there was no love from him for her in the way that a man loves a woman. She felt that the same was not true from Marisol for Antonio. Neither one of them had given her cause for jealousy in any way. While she did not know their entire history, her woman's intuition told her that there was more between them than what it had been revealed.

Their second visit to the church had been as great as the first. As promised, this time they had brought Manuelito with them and every one of the sisters went out of the way to express their joy at having him worship with them. Both Sister Graciela and Marisol had recognized the intimacy developing between Dolores and Antonio. Both were pleased for him, but concerned for different reasons. Marisol, not being a nun still though of men in the way women naturally do. She believed that Antonio would be a fine husband and father because he was a good man. She did not think of herself for him, but wanted that special someone to be worthy of him. And in her mind, Dolores was not the one. The Sister's concerns were mostly about his youth. Because of his size and bearing most people overlooked the fact that Antonio was still a youngster. Life had denied him his childhood. He had been thrust into the adult world without any preparation. It was by the grace of God that he had come to her and she had been able to give him the bearings needed to follow a course to a good life as a Christian. "Have we done enough?" she wondered.

This girl in his arm was only a few years older, but far more mature in the way that a woman can be because she has to be prepared for a different and harder life than a man's. The need to be a wife, a mother, a friend, a lover and a mind reader are forces that greatly influence the forging of a woman's character, ahead of her years. This, Sister Graciela knew a great deal about. She had been all those things to her husband and son when she had them. As she observed them conversing with others, it appeared to her that Dolores was more in love with Antonio than he was with her. It was in the way she looked at him and was never not touching him. Either holding hands, or by placing her arm around his, she was never out of touch. The sister was troubled by her perception that this could end badly for one or the other, or both. Hearts do not break by themselves and the consequences are serious for those who have a part in the breaking.

Following the mass they all walked in the direction of the plaza with the intention of spending a leisurely afternoon enjoying good food and wine, and the good life they felt they were living. Dolores said, "Would anyone mind if we do not go the plaza, but instead why don't we go to the beach. Let's just buy some cheeses, bread, sausages and wine. There is a basket in the house and we can just loaded it up and take it with us. Let's spend the afternoon at the beach. What do you say?" Regardless of what they thought about the plan, no was not an acceptable answer. Besides no one had a better idea and the plaza would always be there, but summer was passing and the number of beach days would be fewer. Soon the fall and winter winds would arrive and it would be a whole year before they could enjoy the beach again.

In one half hour after returning to the apartments they were standing in the courtyard waiting for Pilar whose habit was to not ever be on time for anything. There was a lot of excitement about this excursion. Especially for Manuelito who was the first one ready and could not contain his sense of urgency fearing the sea would dry up before he had the time to jump in. His swimming ability had improved since he first arrived and he wanted to impress Antonio who had never seen him swim. At the beach, they selected an ideal spot because it was against the concrete wall and about one hundred meters from the water. This gave them the shade needed to keep the food relatively fresh and to avoid being burned by the sun. The girls removed their skirts and blouses to reveal their bathing suits. These were pantaloons that reached just above the knee. This after all was Spain and not France where the rules of modesty were not as demanding. Even before they had folded their clothes, Manuelito was already in the water. "Why are you not changing?" Dolores asked. "Don't tell me you are shy, because you do not have to be in front of us. We live in a farm and in a farm there is no modesty. What we don't see in people we see in animals."

"We can't swim," Antonio and Miguel answered almost at the exact moment. "You go ahead we will watch our food and promise not to drink all the wine." Antonio pointed at Manuelito and said "Your brother will watch over you, we are sure." Both men removed their boots and socks and rolled their pants to their knees. "Go ahead" Miguel urged them, "We have things to talk about."

"Better be about us," Dolores said as she turned to run to the surf.

"What is on your mind Miguel? I know you. Tell me what it is that has consumed your thoughts this week, as if I did not already know." He was absolutely right. Miguel had not been able to break through the problem of accumulating capital for his and Mercedes' escape from Cuba. Comparatively speaking he was earning decent income, sufficient for his personal needs with some left over in savings. The problem was that at the rate he was saving the money required, more than two years would pass before he could leave. "I am just not moving fast enough in getting to Cuba. I know she will wait for me, but I don't want us to be apart one minute longer than necessary. I just don't know that I am doing all that can be done and it troubles me. I can solve any problem. Always have. Yet here I face the most important problem in my life and I can't solve it."

"Why don't we go to Madrid, rob a few banks, return here and send you to Cuba," Antonio said laughing. Miguel took the comment in the spirit in which it was meant and laughed with Antonio. Then he added, "You do not have the same concerns as I have. After all your woman is here and you see her everyday." Antonio sat up realizing that Miguel thought of Dolores and him as a couple. In Miguel's view they were almost married. He was startled by the thought that if this is what Miguel thought, the same must have been what everyone else thought. And while he did not particularly cared about them, he did care about Dolores thinking the same. He realized that he may have gone too far with Dolores and while he never purposely encouraged her emotions, he did not reject her kisses either. As he looked at her playing in the surf with her sister and brother he knew that she was no child, but a woman in love. It troubled him that he let it get this far, after all he had only known her for two and half weeks. And it was not his fault she had fallen in love with him; or was it?

As she walked from the water's edge to the blanket, Dolores' bathing suit clung to her body and revealed her physical attributes that were otherwise concealed by the traditionally modest dresses worn by Spanish women. He knew that she knew he was staring and admiring her because she slowed her pace and walked more slowly as if giving him more time to take her full measure. It was at that moment that he decided not to see her again after that afternoon, if he could avoid her. As they returned to the apartments Dolores felt a change in them. She was just as affectionate but he wasn't. The closer she tried to get the more distant he became. She naturally began to ask herself what had she done. The answer being nothing, she had to think about what had changed in him. She remembered the lustful look in his eyes as she and Pilar came out of the water and walked to the blanket. She had to admit to herself that she had enjoyed the moment at least as much as he had. Then she understood; he was afraid of her. Afraid of what she wanted from him. Maybe of what he thought she expected from him.

The day ended when Antonio and Miguel claimed a very early start the next day and hurried along the steps to their apartment. Pilar and Manuelito walked away leaving Dolores alone and lost in thought. "Tomorrow we will clear the air of whatever it is between us. It can not possibly be another woman because we are together all the time that he is not working. I am convinced that it is not because of Marisol, and it can't possibly have anything to do with Sister Graciela. Maybe I'll speak to Miguel tomorrow. He can help me understand what is the matter with Anton."

The next few days there was little or no contact between Dolores and Antonio. One day he returned from work long after Miguel and she did not see him when he arrived. On another day both of them returned very late and he claimed exhaustion before going to sleep. By the time Saturday came she caught up to him at the courtyard before he left for work and made him give her his word that they would talk that night. That would be their last opportunity since she was returning to Valencia on Sunday.

Saturday after work Miguel did not return with Antonio since he had some design issues with the conveyor system to address. The first two units were already in operation and had proven themselves to be as effective as they had desired them to be. Now the port authority wanted them available in all piers. Both the management and the men wanted them. Since they could handle greater volume faster, the ships' turnaround time had been reduced as had the time in the berths.

Antonio entered the apartment to wash before seeing Dolores. He stripped off his shirt and began to wash his upper body with a coarse cloth. The same one he used every day after work. When he had finished washing he reached for his razor to begin shaving. That was when he noticed her at the door which he had left open so that any breeze coming from the sea could flow through the apartment. This was not a particularly hot evening, but any movement of air was greatly appreciated. As Dolores entered the apartment and moved opposite him, she sensed his nervousness and said, "Please do not make the two us uncomfortable, just relax and finish shaving. This could well be our last time together and I want it to be special." He proceeded with his shave feeling her eyes upon his back. The last few years had been kind to his body. It was that of a man that does physical work every day of his life except Sundays. His muscular definition was well pronounced, and there was great symmetry between his torso, arms and legs. After shaving and drying his face he combed his hair that because of the humidity was unruly. As he finished he thought that maybe he could get Sister Magdalena to cut his hair before mass the next day. He kept it short in the summer and long in the winter. However his hair on this evening was as long as it had ever been, summer or winter. He reached for his shirt to put on but she had already picked it up and held it close to her chest as if she was intending to keep it. He extended his hand to reach for the shirt, she took his hand in hers and kissed it saying, "How did I let this happen to me. I never for one minute thought that one man could mean as much to me as you do. Especially one who is not in love with me." Wrapping her arms around his waist she pressed her lips against his chest as if she could sniff his soul and breathe him inside her. "I do not care that you do not love me Anton. I have enough love in me for the two of us." She took his hand again and led him into Miguel's room. He hesitated in following her but saw the hurt in her eyes and the sadness in her body. Darkness had begun to envelope the room and although the window was opened there was not much moon to light the room.

Dolores began to undress in a way that was more sad than alluring. She was determined to give herself to him for no other reason than her fear that she would never meet a man who would mean as much to her as he did. And the thought that her first lover would be anyone other than him was unacceptable to her. She loosened her long brown hair that now rested on her chest and was barely touching her breasts. She moved it away from her face so that her emotions could not be concealed from him. As she stood naked before him she pulled him towards her as she lowered unto the bed. Not a word was spoken between them as they began to touch and to explore each other's bodies. Her sexuality was being offered to him in a way that was more supplicant than sexual. He was torn at that moment between hurting her by going through with making love to her or destroying her by walking away. She finally spoke and said, "Anton, this is my decision, this is what I want. I know that you do not love me enough to be with me forever but I hope that you love me enough to receive me as I offer myself to you. There will be no recriminations from me because of this moment between us. You are my going away gift to myself. Please do not deny me this memory of you." Gentle as he was when he entered her it did nothing to quench her thirst for him. Her hunger for him was deep and as she reciprocated his thrusts she exclaimed in pain and in pleasure asking him to penetrate her deeper. She wanted to be touched in a place where no man would ever touch her, because she had reserved it only for him.

He fell asleep looking at her and that was the last time he ever saw her. Very quietly she arose from the bed, dressed, and left the apartment carrying her shoes. He did not wake up until the next morning when Miguel shook his shoulders and told him it was time to leave for church. He had seen them in each other's arms and retreated to the hammock where he laid pretending to be asleep as she walked out. He remained and slept in Antonio's hammock thinking it best to let him rest. Not a word was said between them as they walked to Saint Jacinto's. Knowing him as well as he did, Miguel understood that Antonio would say whatever needed saying when he was ready and not before.

They entered the kitchen and sat for breakfast without the usual bantering and joviality with which their Sundays always started. Miguel tried to fill the void and succeeded but not enough to improve Antonio's countenance. Marisol was already at the kitchen when they entered and as always kissed and hugged them both. Immediately she felt the distance in Antonio's demeanor. He did not look at her as if trying to avoid her eyes, so she looked even more intensely at Antonio as she asked if the Vincenti family would be joining them for mass. It was Miguel who answered with the explanation that they were returning to Valencia and would be leaving early that morning. Sister Graciela, who was almost never at the kitchen since she was accustomed to having breakfast brought to her quarters, on this occasion heard the angels telling her to go and be there. She knew they were right and that she was needed as soon as she arrived. She offered her blessings upon all present and as she finished she remarked, "You do not cross yourself anymore when I bless you Anton. Why is that?" Anton excuse himself by saying that he had been lost in thought and had not heard her blessing, but still did not cross himself because he felt unworthy.

Antonio looked at Marisol and felt she was right when she called him a hypocrite that evening when they had spoken in the chapel. He then looked at Sister Graciela who was now standing over him with her hand on his shoulder and a soft and soothing voice said, "Anton, I can tell that you are troubled and there is nothing better for you this moment than confession. Come with me now." He stood and followed her into the chapel where she said, "Wait here." He sat with his hands folded between his knees asking himself what had he done. As he waited for the sister to return, he felt as lonely and as empty as he had ever felt in his life. For most of his life he had endured the consequences of someone else's actions or someone else's mistakes. This time it was all his doing. He remembered that Dolores had told him that she would have no recrimination but that did not exclude his. He tried to justify his conduct by thinking that it had been her choice, her decision. He had acted according to her need and that since he had not forced himself upon her, he had done no wrong. But he knew he had. He had used her by taking from her a piece of her humanity.

Sister Graciela returned and asked him to move to the confessionary where Father Armando would hear his confession. This time it was not about bad thoughts and bad words or other childish failings that he was going to confess. This time there were serious sins and even more serious consequences. He wondered if she was feeling as anguished as he felt. Dolores never went to confession and so no wrong doing was going to be admitted by her. He on the other hand would not have it that easy. He needed his confession to be heard and as he confessed he would have to hear himself describe his actions. No amount of penance would suffice to assuage his anguish. If redemption could ever be found for him he wondered how long would this be on his conscience. The priest heard it all as he had so many times before, but seldom one as painful as the confession that was now being offered. He too felt the anguish and thought than more than acts of contrition and similar prayers, this sinner needed reflection, so he ordered him to kneel through the entire mass that he was attending that morning and to reflect on Jesus' suffering because of his failing.

Antonio did as he had been directed by the priest. He followed the instruction to remain kneeling during the mass but more importantly, he reflected for the whole hour on what had transpired. He was not a coward and was willing to receive God's punishment in whatever form it would come. He needed to focus on the now. He felt he had disappointed all those who trusted him to be a better man but mostly he was disappointed in himself. He had expected better and had failed himself and her. At the moment when values and honor should have dictated the outcome he had allowed the flesh to prevail.

Marisol had been waiting for him outside and approached him as he left the church. "Will you please walk with me to the plaza. I need to buy a book and would appreciate your company. I have asked Miguel not to join us. If ever there was a time when I have felt needed by someone, this is the time and you are that someone." She was speaking as the sister she wanted to be for him. Her intention was not to reprimand but to help him understand the same way that she had understood the power of redemption. She also understood that sometimes more is said by silence than by words. So they walked for one half hour before either of them spoke. She understood that when it came to the impact of sins upon a soul she was the expert and he was the novice. By just being with him she thought Antonio could understand and appreciate that more than anything she wanted to just be there for him. "Anton what is the first commandment" she finally asked. He looked at her with curious eyes thinking, "Where is this going?"

"I am serious, what is the first commandment? Please answer me."

"You shall have no other God before me" he replied. She went on to explain that those who continue to honor God above all else can and will be redeemed. "Anton, no one rises out of bed in the morning with the expressed purpose of disappointing God. It happens most of the time out of ignorance, other times it is just malice but most times it happens because of weakness.

But regardless of why we disappoint God, he gives us another opportunity because he knows that there is better in us than our actions have shown. He showed me that when you were there for me, and now he wants me to be here for you. As well you know, I more than anyone know what it is like to fall. Regrettably we have to fall in order to appreciate the rising. What is important is that once we rise above sin, we need to stay risen. Anton I saw it in her and saw it in you and there was no way to spare you the trial. But I also know the nobility in you. I know there isn't an ounce of malice in your body. It is the essence of who you are. It is your style and it is your substance. Usually we are told to forget experiences such as yours, to put them behind us, but I say the opposite. Hang on firmly to the memory, because that is how we keep from repeating our mistakes." He placed his arm around her shoulder drawing her nearer to him. That simple act of warmth and friendship told her that all that needed to be said, was said.

On Wednesday evening there was a knock on their door. Miguel opened it and was startled to see Sister Magdalena and a novice both looking at their feet not knowing how whoever answered the door would be dressed.

"Please wait just a minute" he said as he closed the door halfway. Antonio was now out of the hammock and in the process of putting on his pants. As he spoke to Antonio, Miguel lit a candle. "I do not know what this is about, but it does not look good." After they were both dressed they asked the women to enter and stood waiting for them to speak." Both women's eyes were swollen from crying, and both Antonio and Miguel knew they were in great distress, and not able to speak. After waiting for them to gain their courage, Antonio spoke to say that it was clear there was something seriously wrong and if was for their help that they had come, they should speak so that help could be provided. "It is because the situation is hopeless that we feel so helpless. There is no other way to tell you, but tell you we must; Sister Graciela has gone to be with our lord." Both men felt their legs fail them as they shook at hearing the news. Neither one of them spoke because they couldn't. And even if they could have spoken they would not have known what to say. They were still in a state of shock when the young nun said, "Come, let us go to the convent."

Sister Graciela's body still dressed in her nun's habit was lying uncovered in her bed. She had retired early saying she was experiencing some indigestion which she could not explain because she had eaten very little during the day. For a few days before her passing she had not felt well and thought that a little abstinence would help her stomach feel better. Sister Maria had been attending to her and watching over her from a distance sort of speak because if there was one thing that sister Graciela did not want or like, was being fussed over by anyone. Around ten that evening Sister Graciela was finishing her work at the desk in her quarters when Sister Maria entered carrying a tray with tea and biscuits, thinking that sister Graciela would benefit from the light snack before turning in. After thanking her for her kindness Sister Graciela had asked her if she would remain and join her in her evening prayers. "I know that the lord frowns on us having favorites, but I can not think of anyone with whom I wish to pray more than you. Besides if he finds fault in my favoring you dear sister why did he not send someone else with my tea. Let us begin, In the name of the Father and the son and the holy spirit." Those were the last words spoken by the Mother Superior because soon after that while still kneeling she crossed herself and collapsed.

Sister Maria reacted calmly and with acceptance because an angel had told her to go and be with Sister Graciela. She was grateful that the angel had spoken to her because it was thanks to the angel that her dear friend did not die alone.

The room was lit by more than the number of lamps and candles that were usually found in the sister's quarters. As the nuns entered the room to pay their respects they brought and left their candles behind. It gave the impression that the room was lit more for a feast than a funeral. Antonio and Miguel thought this as they stood behind the nuns waiting to get closer to view her remains.

Antonio stood over her and closed his eyes to try to recapture from his memory how she had made him feel when in her presence. After looking at her he looked to the right towards the balcony where they had spent so many special hours. He could easily remember the number of times the he had sat with her for lunch and for lessons. On those occasions they would be so involved one with the other that time had no context. It just did not matter.

He reflected on the first conversation he had with her when he arrived at the convent and it made him appreciate what providence had done for him by bringing them together when it did. He also remembered the last conversation they had when she had taken him to confession.

As befitting a person committed to poverty and the service of Christ, her funeral was as simple an affair as it could have possibly been. The funeral mass had to be held in the church instead of the chapel because of the large number of parishioners who attended the service. The mass was offered by a monsignor and the eulogy was delivered by the Bishop of Barcelona who among other things said that he doubted that as many people would attend his funeral because he thought he could never be worthy of as much love as had been earned by Sister Graciela. Believing that those already in glory needed not to be glorified, he commended her spirit to the heavens and commended the living to follow her example of service to God.

On the front pew sat her family who had traveled from Asturia for the funeral. There were two men and a woman. These were two of her five brothers and one of her nieces. More family members would have attended but they were farmers and work on a farm does not stop for the living or the dead especially during harvest time. By their clothing it was evident these were people who only wore jackets and ties on special occasions and those would be weddings and funerals. They had asked Antonio and Miguel to sit with the family since this was how she regarded them, and they would be pall bearers together.

At the end of the service, the monsignor spoke to thank everyone and to inform them that as requested by the family only the members of the convent and the immediate family would attend the burial. He also said that since she was to be buried on the church's ground they could if they wished, pay their respects at her grave on another occasion. Her grave site was selected by Sister Maria. One that she thought would have been selected by Sister Graciela had she had the opportunity to do it.

Following the burial, they all retreated to the courtyard where everyone lingered not knowing what to say or do. The members of the family realizing that this would be the last time they would see these people tried to engage everyone in conversation, sharing memories of the sister and telling stories about what she had been like before becoming a nun. Marcos, the youngest of sister Graciela's brothers approached Antonio and asked if there was a place they could speak in private. Antonio suggested the sister's private quarters.

The two men were comparable in size and appearance. Their bodies were those of men accustomed to hard physical labor. By looking at Marcos anyone could easily tell he was a farmer. He had the skin of a man who spent many hours under the sun and the tough hands that corresponded to his profession. Style wise they were very similar. They were both direct and used to looking at a man in the eyes when speaking or spoken to, and accustomed to getting straight to the point. When they entered the Sister's quarters, Antonio noticed one of the two bottles of Argentinean wine that he had recently given her from the case sent by Xavier. He picked it up and held it in his hands as he explained to Marcos how it came to be there. "You should take it with you for your return trip home," he said as he handed the bottle to Marcos who replied by saying, "No, let us drink it here and now, to honor her name and her memory."

"You may not realize how much she loved you. She wrote to us every week of her life, never missed a week. Regrettably, we were not as consistent in responding. These last few years she mentioned you often in her letters.

That is why we were not surprised when she asked us to sell her farm. She wanted you to have the money instead of the farm because she did not want to tie you with a farm. She planned to leave the money to you in her will. We thought of buying it ourselves but more cattle, pigs and wheat is not what we need. We have more than we can manage. Since we had just sold it, she did not have the time to put this in her will but that will not keep us from fulfilling her wishes. "This is yours" he said as he handed Antonio an envelope. It contained a draft note from the National Bank of Spain made to bearer.

Antonio held the note in his hand and for the very first time in his life cried inconsolably. He cried uncontrollably. He cried because he realized how much she had loved him. He cried with so much force that he felt lacking in oxygen as his chest heaved with pressure. He cried because he remembered how he had disappointed her. His heart raced and jumped as if it wanted to come out of his chest. Marcos moved towards Antonio and embraced him and through that gesture expressed his feelings better than words could ever have. At that moment, they were members of the same family feeling each other's pain.

Antonio stepped away and stretched out his arm, but before he could speak, Marcos said, "If you are about to tell me that you can not accept this gift, I ask you that you honor her memory by doing as she wanted you to do. By putting this money to good use. What form will that good take is unknown to us. Only God knows, but since she trusted you, you can do no less but to try." Antonio nodded, shook hands with Marcos one last time and walked out of the room.

After the funeral they walked back to the apartment without either one saying a word to the other. This was a Saturday and a light day at the docks and so they would not have to return to work until Monday. The systems they had implemented at the docks were so efficient that it could operate without them for a day or longer. After removing their jackets, they sat at the table in the apartment. Miguel served them both the remainder of a bottle of wine that had been opened the last time they had an occasion to celebrate. That seemed so long ago that if they had tried neither could have remembered. "I have something to show you" said Antonio as he handed Miguel the envelope. When he saw the bank draft Miguel did not know what he was seeing since he had never banked but he did read the very large number written on the face of the instrument. He continued to stare at it trying to decipher what it meant. The first thing he did was to close the door because he realized that the note represented a very large amount of money. The second thing he did was to ask what it meant to them. "What is this about, this is a fortune, what will you do with all this money, what will it mean to you?

This changes your life, where will you go, what are you going to do?' He would have continued asking questions if Antonio had not stopped him saying. "This my brother, changes nothing between us. This is Cuba money. Lets go get your wife. Let's go get Mercedes."

CHAPTER 12

The following days on the docks turned into a blur. While they had not yet left, their minds were already in Cuba and beyond. As diligently as they could, they examined their plans, their time tables and how to turn over their responsibilities at the dock to the best man for the job. This was all so sudden and of all the issues to deal with, they had not given much thought to replacing themselves. This would be one more item to be added to their planning list. Most important, they agreed was absolute secrecy for as long as possible.

Since they knew that Don Mauricio was friends with Mercedes' father, they would not have been surprised if he had not been asked to keep his eyes on them. That evening while they ate their dinner at a bar near the apartment, they started what would be one of many reviews of their plan. Since Miguel had projected a longer wait in his time table to travel to Cuba, he was now working at a much faster speed in identifying concerns and action items. He knew that there was a ship departing for the Island of Santo Domingo every other Saturday. This ship's first stop would be the Island of Cuba where it would remain for two days before sailing for Hispaniola or the island of Santo Domingo, which was the new name given to it. There, it would wait for passengers who would travel from Puerto Rico and other islands to board the ship on their return to Spain. Ideally, they though, with any luck they would be able to link with Mercedes and continue on their journey without delay. One of the main concerns was the ship's manifest.

By maritime law all ships were required to file a manifest with the port authority before being cleared to sail. The manifest included everyone and everything that was transported from the port of origin to the port of destination. They had no concerns over having their names listed on the outbound ship. Since most of the crews new them it would have been foolish to travel under any name other than their own. Still they would do all that it was possible to not be seen as they left. They decided to buy passage for

Santo Domingo. That way, their intention to stop in Cuba would not be disclosed and their ultimate destination would not be revealed. And since they planned to sail for Puerto Rico under assumed names, they could disappear, or so they hoped. Securing their identity papers in Barcelona was a fairly simple process but securing false names was entirely a different matter. All things in due course they decided. All of these decisions were made the easier because they had enough funds to sustain them for quite a while. Antonio had made it abundantly clear when he admonished Miguel who was having reservations about how would he ever pay it back. "Listen to me now because I never want to discuss this again. This is our money and we are brothers and partners." He went on to say that if Miguel thought that he was going to stay behind and miss out on the adventure he was wrong. Besides, he added, the money was left to him with the instruction that he put it to good use, and right now he could not think of a better purpose.

Contingencies are those things that we do not think about until the need is upon us, and as a result the outcome is unpredictable. Now they were entering the what if part of the planning process. Starting with what if it was not possible to leave for Cuba as quickly as they hoped. What if Mercedes was sick and could not travel. What if she had changed her mind which was suggested by Antonio with a slight grin as he said it. "Then we will become kidnappers," replied Miguel.

What would they carry with them for their new life? Taking into consideration that Puerto Rico was several degrees south of Barcelona, which offered a strong reason why the region was called tropical, they concluded that most of their clothes were not of much use in the tropics. And since the only other thing that they owned was Antonio's hammock and several books which he was not leaving behind, packing they concluded was not much of an issue. "Other than our suits, there is almost nothings for us to pack."

"We don't own any suits, we only own a jacket each" said Miguel. "But we will." Antonio said that he refused to let himself or Miguel be seen by Mercedes in no better condition than when they last met. Once again they turned to the contacts they had made through the church in finding someone who would make their suits.

They decided to work backwards from the date of departure to the present time. They would leave in two and a half weeks. At the dock they looked at the scheduling board and selected the "Candelaria" for the journey. This was one of the newest vessels in the Spanish commercial fleet. It had the speed of a man of war with the comfort of a cruise ship. Of course none of the planning could address Antonio's concern about actually crossing the ocean. Remembering Xavier's experience, he had some worries about how his stomach would respond to the motion of the ship. He was not a man who would take counsel of his fears, but this was an unknown. Little did he know that Miguel had the same concerns and was relying on him to see him through the potential ordeal. At the end of the day it mattered not since there was no way they were not going.

That afternoon they reported to the port authority's office in response to a request from Don Mauricio. Not knowing what it was about they had no choice but to wait until he was ready for them. He did not keep them waiting long when the secretary showed them to his office. They remained standing until Don Mauricio asked them to sit. He enjoyed the deference shown to him by his underlings and through these little gestures he liked to remind them who was superior and who was inferior. The last time they had been here was when they turned over the final design of Miguel's conveyor belt system. The port authority had filed a patent application which had been granted by the Royal Office of Patents and Inventions and soon became the standard for luggage handling for the authority. This had brought great credit and recognition upon Don Mauricio who had contributed absolutely nothing to the design of the system and even less to the building. "I have great news for you; upon my recommendation the port authority has authorized a special distribution of funds to you and the crews. As I knew it would, the implementation of the new luggage handling system has had a very positive impact on revenues and I thought it only fair that everyone should be rewarded." As he reached into the safe and pulled a very large and bulging envelope they wondered how much had he kept for himself. "Please see that this is distributed to the men in a way that is equitable. I trust your judgment and know that you will follow my wishes as if I was doing it myself." They thought that if they were to follow his example most of the money would remain in their pockets. After expressing their surprise and gratitude for his largesse, they retreated to their work station.

They counted the money and determined that if evenly distributed it would be the equal of two days pay for every man. As they settled on a strategy to distribute the funds, Miguel struck upon an idea for how to select their replacement who needed to be identified, and soon. At the end of the day they called all the crew bosses to their location, handed each an envelope with money and instructed them to split it among the men in a way that was fair and equitable as had been directed by Don Mauricio. They were handed the amount of money corresponding to two day's pay for every member of their crews. Further, they instructed the crew bosses to distribute the funds before the men left the docks. That left them all little time since they were beginning to shut down and assemble to collect their pay for the day's work. Each man assembled their crews and distributed the money as directed by Miguel. He and Antonio stood by as the distribution was taking place watching the men's reactions to the additional pay. Some were pleased while others were extremely pleased. Miguel had seen what he wanted to see.

All bosses gave their crews the equivalent of one day's pay and kept the rest, except for Victor Gutierrez who gave each man in his crew two days pay. That was also the amount he had given to himself. Looking at him, Miguel said to Antonio, "We have found our replacement."

The next day they returned to the superintendent's office and asked for brief audience. As they entered his office and before he could offer, they declined the invitation to sit because they would not be staying long. Knowing how the superintendent enjoyed it when deference was shown to him, they said, in recognition of the importance of his time. Holding his cap in his hands Miguel spoke saying, "We feel duty bound to share a concern with you, and that is the lack of management and operational depth at our level. An operation as important as yours can not and should not rely on just two men. We worry about continuity, about having men who can step in and take over our positions. Men that can serve you well as more responsibility and power is given to you. Don Mauricio there is no doubt that in recognition of your exceptional leadership they will give you greater responsibility and when that happens we must be ready to respond." Hanging on to every word, Don Mauricio could see the day when he would be called before the queen to be knighted. He could see the size of the fortune that he could amass as a result of the increase in bribes that he would collect. This was all good news for him.

"What do you require of me gentlemen?," he asked. At this moment Miguel realized that he had succeeded in his purpose. He asked Don Mauricio to authorize Victor Gutierrez to work as their assistant. This would allow them to prepare him for greater responsibility so that when more responsibility was given to Don Mauricio as it was sure to happen, he could respond in a moment's notice by having a strong management team in place. Their plan was to make certain that everyone would know that Victor's selection was Don Mauricio's choice and not theirs. This would reduce the jealousy factor that would undoubtedly play among the crew bosses. And would raise no immediate concerns when they stopped showing up at the docks. This would give them a long lead time before anyone knew they had left Spain.

For the balance of the week, they included Victor in their processes exposing him to the kinds of things that he would have to master. Victor was a Catalan. Born and raised in Barcelona. He had a self assured quality about him that caused them to trust him with greater responsibility as the week progressed. He was older than Miguel and seemed equally wise. He was very deliberate in all things he did. They had never seen him display any temper nor show any fear of anyone. They were now ready to replace themselves at the docks.

They secured their papers to sail on the Candelaria through an agent in yet another effort to conceal their plans until the very last minute. Instead of seeing Don Mauricio to inform him of their leaving they would simply not show up for work one day. Since Victor was now well trained and prepared to assume their roles, the dock operations would not suffer in any way. Moreover their direct contacts with Don Mauricio were so few and far between that it would be a long time before he realized they were no longer running things.

One evening they invited Victor to join them at their favorite Tapas bar after work. And there, after a few glasses of wine, they explained in great detail the financial arrangements through which pay was distributed to the bosses and their crews. Victor understood that they would not be coming to work every day or at the same time as they had always done. Instead they expected him to take over in their absence whenever they were not at work. This was all well understood by Victor, who also understood and liked the five percent of the total day's pay that would be his and his assistant's, if he wished to have one. He immediately thought of his oldest son whom he had been trying to place at the docks without having to dismiss anyone. He trusted his son and knew that he was smart and would do a good job. More importantly sharing the five percent with his son meant keeping it all in the family without taking money from any one's pockets.

Don Mauricio's announcement of Victor's promotion had the desired effect. Grumbling was kept to a minimum because after all it had been the superintendent's decision and the promotion had fallen to one of their own instead of an outsider. The evening ended with Victor offering his solemn oath that none of this would be discussed with anyone. If and when asked by Don Mauricio he was to say that he did not know when they would return but until then he was in charge.

How to say goodbye to the sisters at the convent was a different matter altogether. There could be a great many questions to which they would have to offer careful answers. The least said the better was their plan, but that only had to do with the answers, the questions would be beyond their control.

They waited until the Friday before their departure to visit Saint Jacinto's church for what they knew would be their last time. Customarily, the Friday evening service was held by all the members of the order. It was their version of a social event. They gathered in the dining room after the service which usually ended around eight o'clock. Sister Maria who had been elected Mother Superior by the sisters, followed by the Bishop's appointment, ran what could have been construed as a lighter ship than her predecessor. Since the service on Friday evenings was strictly for the members of the order, Antonio and Miguel met them as the nuns entered the dining hall. In the early days when they were youngsters and on the few occasions that they were around, the sisters would ask them to wash and dine with them. At any one time there were forty to fifty nuns at the dinner. It was readily evident to them that nuns in the dining room behaved differently from nuns in the church or in public. They behaved like women. They laughed, they gossiped, they told funny stories, they had fun. Sister Maria wisely recognized this as their time to let their hair down figuratively, and to connect with each other as the sisters they were.

When Sister Maria saw them she said, "Sisters if I may have your attention, this is a much too infrequent honor, we have our prodigals with us this evening. Since it is too late for confession we have to assume they are not here for penitence. And if not for penitence, we then have to ask the reason for your presence with us. Anyone care to offer a guess."

"They miss us" one of the sisters said. "They wanted safe female companionship," said another. "No" said Marisol who although not a nun was allowed to dine with the sisters, "They have something to tell us." With that comment everyone turned to them with inquisitive eyes. Some thought there may be a wedding or such similar announcements. It was Sister Maria who said, "You are leaving us are you not?" She had been wondering why they had ordered suits to be made by one of the parishioners.

The room was quiet enough that they could hear each other's breathing. Antonio and Miguel had been there when many of them had been novices. They had in many ways grown up together. This departure was no less painful than losing a member of their family. Whenever one of them left on a mission, there was great celebration because they knew this was the fulfillment of their calling and that they would be together again. Such was not the feeling at this time. Antonio spoke to say that they were there to say goodbye and to ask for their prayers. He added that it had been Sister Graciela's expressed desire that they commit themselves to doing good. And although it was not yet clear what they were going to do and where they would do it, they would notify them in due course. Miguel added that he hoped that all they had learned from them would serve the purpose of demonstrating to all who came in contact with them that they were worthy of being called Christians. As they looked through the room they saw smiling faces, and grim faces and questioning faces. The only truly happy face they saw belonged to Marisol. Sister Graciela insisted that they stay for dinner saying that they would be her honored guests.

"You are going to Cuba are you not? Don't even think about denying it," said Marisol. She had pulled Antonio aside for a bit of privacy. Incapable of lying to her, he simply nodded. "You may think that this is about Mercedes and Miguel and that is partially correct, but it is not the only reason. That is the reason Miguel is going, and I am going with him because he is my brother. And so yes I am going with him, but I am also going for me. Ever since I learned to read, right here, sometimes in this very room, I have focused more on knowledge than on information. And even more than knowledge I have gained understanding. I have read Cicero, two books on Charlemagne. I have read Plato's Republic and Socrates. Reading has opened my eyes to many things but mostly to the unjust society in which we live. I am supposed to honor and serve the queen like everyone else, but I ask what has she done for me. I see people, undeserving people, benefiting from the ideas and hard work of others. I see their lives get better and better all the times, while my life does not change because it has nothing to change to. It is not just Barcelona, it is the country. It creates many barriers to ensure that the powerful remain that way and the weak even weaker so as to reduce any possible threat. You mark my words, this country is headed for a revolution. The French had theirs and ours is not far behind. I do not know what waits for me wherever we end up, but I do know that it has to be better than this.

My one and only regret is that I will not see you or the sisters again and you are my family. I feel that I have already achieved as much as I could have in Barcelona and I have no doubt that I could stay at the docks the rest of my life, but the knowledge that I have acquired has served to widen my horizons and I feel compelled to fulfill my destiny, but not In Spain."

Marisol responded with a smile that not only expressed her agreement with his plans but also celebrated his vision and the purpose for his life. She held his hand and said, "You told me once that in me there were mighty dreams and great triumphs yet to come, but I tell you that mine will pale by comparison to yours. When you feel the time is right, please write to me right here. If I am not here they will know where to find me. And I would not be so sure that this is the last time we are together." She was hugging him one last time when Sister Maria said, "Save some for me." At this time the sister had Miguel with her and asked Antonio to join them. Sitting at her table she spoke to the two of them. She told them that as a result of her calling she had been denied the benefit of motherhood, but on the other hand had allowed her to be the mother to many more than she could have birthed. "And as I look at all my children few have given me greater pride and satisfaction than the two of you. Anton, I remember the morning when Miguel first brought you to our kitchen. I remember how we rejoiced by the thought that God was giving us a gift. And through that gift and opportunity to demonstrate our Christianity. Any one can claim to be a Christian but not everyone can practice it. This is what happened to you in the Basque country. You met people who were bad at it and could have turned you against our faith and our Lord. But we kept that from happening."

It was no accident that Miguel reached out to you on the same day your brother abandoned you, and luck had nothing to do with it. It was through providence that all was arranged. The reason I tell you this at this time is because you need to trust providence and you need to allow it to sustain your faith. When you feel most abandoned, when you feel most alone and desperate turn to the lord and let him lift you. You both represent our best work. Go to where you must and do us proud. Now kneel so that I can bless you." No response was expected and none was needed.

They simply rose from their knees, kissed and embraced the sister and walked out of the convent. On the way out they stopped and looked at the safe spot where they would jump the fence when returning late to the convent. It seemed like a life time ago. Before going to the convent, they had stopped at the bank where Antonio had withdrawn enough cash to see them through the next few months, and asked for another draft note to cover the remainder of his funds. That way he would simply deposit it in a bank in Puerto Rico whenever they got there. Before leaving the convent Antonio reached into his billfold, drew a handful of bills and handed it to Sister Magdalena saying, "For your first mission."

CHAPTER 13

On the Saturday of their departure they arrived at the boarding plank of The Candelaria dressed in their suits and long before anyone of the crew would have been on deck, they simply boarded. They jumped over the low and small chain that laid across the boarding ramp and proceeded to find themselves a spot in which to hide until the boarding process started. All they were carrying with them was a small sailor's locker which was easily carried by Antonio. It contained a few clothing items, their work boots, several books and of course Antonio's Hammock. Since passengers were not expected until seven in the morning, arriving at five ensured that no one would see them board. Although they were fairly certain that no one would recognize them dressed as they were, why take the chance they thought. Their names would be on the ship's manifest but unless someone was specifically looking for them the probability that their names would be spotted was extremely remote.

At precisely seven in the morning the ship's steward took his position and almost as soon as he did, he found himself face to face with the first two passengers. "Where did you two come from," he asked. "From over there" responded Miguel pointing in the general direction of the dock's entrance.

As he looked at their boarding documents and logged their names on the manifest, the steward noted that they must be in a real hurry to get where they were going but on a ship everyone leaves at the same time regardless of who boards first. He said that with a laugh. Antonio responded by saying that since they were traveling steerage class they hoped that being first would give them the best berths. The steward smiled with the recognition that these two had never sailed before, because otherwise they would have known that in steerage there was no difference. One berth was as bad as the other. Antonio had given some thought to the motion of a ship as he had watched so many arrive and depart. Because of his observations he believed that the best location would be as close to the center of the ship as was possible. When he made the request the steward ignored him until he heard the ruffle of a few bills being offered to him. "The center berth is yours gentlemen," he said. They retired to claim their berth, changed out of their suits not wanting to wear them any more than absolutely necessary and waited for the ship to sail before returning to the main deck.

As scheduled, the ship sailed out of Barcelona at noon headed for the strait of Gibraltar. Miguel made the observation that it was interesting that the last piece of Spain they would see; Gibraltar, belonged to the British. Within one hour after passing Gibraltar they could no longer see land. They were both affected by the sea in the same way. It did not make them sick, but it did make them hungry.

One of the stewards told them that the ship carried one hundred and eighty eight passengers. The passengers traveling in what was called Royal class seldom if ever came in contact with those traveling in steerage. Either by design or by choice the two classes of people were isolated by physical barriers and schedules. They did not dine together or at the same time. Royal class passengers had wonderful meals served to them in great splendor.

Steerage passengers bought their food at the lower deck canteen. One would have thought they could have purchased the food left over from the Royal class dining room. But that was not to be the case because that was the food served to the kitchen staff.

Canteen food was the kind that had been prepared long ago and was kept on board ship until it was consumed. Antonio ate a pickled egg that he swore must have had prehistoric origins. There was some variety in the fare offered to the lower deck. One day it was bread and sausage. The next was sausage and bread. Miguel and Antonio soon learned that it paid to make friends with the kitchen staff. Not the chefs, but the staff. The people who made the food to be eaten by people traveling in Royal class. The kitchen staff was quartered at the bow of the ship, which was the tightest and darkest section. To get to their quarters they had to pass by Miguel's and Antonio's berth. After striking the kind of conversation that conveyed some familiarity with hard work and sympathy with the members of the kitchen staff, they were able to secure some desserts one day, pasta the next, and finally a healthy serving of roast pig. They made a very smart move in not only paying the staff to bring the food to them, but to having the hands join them in eating it. This did not reduce the cost of the food but it did increase the volume and quality. By the end of the first week they were eating the same delicacies served to the Royal class passengers and probably enjoyed it more. Not once were they affected by the motion of the ship other than to lose their balance when they had consumed too much wine.

Other than the impatience of one who has dreamed of the journey and the future for what it seemed an interminable period of time, the trip was pleasant enough. They played harmless card games with other passengers and learned to play chess from one of the stewards, which helped to pass the time.

The winds had been consistent and favorable and for the exception of a few rainy nights there had been no inconveniences to note. From one of the crew they learned of their arrival date. It seemed they would be entering the bay of Havana in three days time. Soon the next phase of their plan would begin to unfold. The most important phase; getting Mercedes to Puerto Rico.

The Candelaria entered the port of Havana and they were greeted by the imposing sight of a fort named El Morro. This was the symbol of Spanish power in the Caribbean Sea region. El Morro was built in the sixteenth century as part of Spain's military strategy to secure its possessions. Its guns were positioned in a way that would engage invaders at sea long before they could threaten the city. By the time the enemy's ships could reach a point where they could offer a threat they were for all intents and purposes, not battle worthy and would usually retreat. The alternative was to land at a distant point and attack by land, and sailors were not good infantrymen. The fort had walls that in some places were thirty feet thick. More than once it had withstood many direct hits from cannon fire that only nicked the mortar without inflicting any serious damage to the viability of the fort. Looking at the imposing structure they wondered how English and Dutch pirates had the courage or the foolishness to attack it. Especially considering that if captured the Spaniards would hang them from the tower and their bodies allowed to remain swinging in the wind until the remains fell off the rope. This would serve as a reminder to those considering similar attacks that could see through the telescopes the consequences of attacking a Spanish fort or breaking Spanish law. This had the desired effect on the invader's enthusiasm for an invasion.

The fort served both as an army garrison and as a prison. It was Antonio's and Miguel's fervent desire not to end up in it.

It was on an early Friday afternoon when they finally docked and disembarked. Filled with excitement they proceeded to look for a rooming house where they could store their locker, wash and go to the Malecon to begin the search for Mercedes. As they left the ship anyone looking at them may have thought they were drunk. After spending seventeen days at sea they had acquired 'sea legs.' They were so accustomed to the rocking motion of the ship that when on firm ground they wobbled more than walked until their legs could adjust. Noticing this, they enjoyed a good laugh on themselves. After securing a room near the bay, they changed into their suits to begin their search for Mercedes. Just like in Barcelona, Friday evening in Havana brought the crowds to the walkway where people paraded enjoying the breeze from the sea before sitting for dinner.

Antonio and Miguel sat in a café that was positioned across from the wide walkway and seemed to be placed closed to equal distance from either direction. They sat there until around one in the morning when the crowds began to thin out, and the only people out were the ladies of the night and their patrons. Cuba was a more open society than Barcelona and people seemed less discreet and more uncaring about their conduct in public. Antonio and Miguel smilingly rejected several invitations for company, with a simple shaking of their heads. Would it not have been something for Mercedes to walk up to them while they were engaged in conversation with the working ladies. They decided to retire for the night hoping for better luck the next afternoon.

While walking back to the rooming house they were startled by a very pretty blond woman who ran out of what it appeared to be a private restaurant or club. She was being followed by a man who was chasing after her and yelling in a language neither one of them could understand. While they did not understand the language, they could denote the anger and hostility in his voice. It was clear to them that the man was going to visit violence upon the woman. When he caught up to the blond woman, he grabbed her, turned her around and slapped her across her face. He did this while standing in front of them as if they were not there. As he grabbed her to hit her again, she looked at him defiantly as if to say, "Go ahead and reveal the coward that you

135

are." Her lips were covered with a bright red lipstick and droppings of blood. In contrast to him who was a big and rough looking man, she was a small and gentle looking woman. She wore a dress that was about to come off her shoulders and reveal her breasts but she did not seem to care. Modesty would not be her priority when visited by violence.

When the man raised his hand to strike her again, driven by reflex more than thought, Antonio moved behind him and bear hugged him while moving him away from her. As Antonio was dragging the man away from the woman, Miguel stepped in the middle so she could not be struck again. The man now trapped by Antonio's firm hold yelled at him, "Let go of me, I am American." The man struggled to free himself but the more he fought the tighter the grip. Antonio held him wanted to hold him until he felt the threat to the woman was neutralized. Miguel had a different kind of problem. Since he did not speak her language he could not communicate their intention which was to keep her from being hurt by the man. Miguel did not know if they were husband and wife, brother and sister or complete strangers, and had no way to find out.

She had a similar dilemma, not knowing if she was being assaulted or protected by these men. Miguel, in his futile effort to calm her down, reached for her hand as she withdrew from him, stepping back and to the side to look at her assailant being held by the tall young man. At this moment she decided that these were not rescuers but assailants themselves. She stepped around Miguel and ran to where Antonio was holding the man and proceeded to strike Antonio who could not release the American and defend himself at the same time. Instead he turned the man in the direction of her blows which caused him to yell at her with greater anger than when the episode started.

She meant to help the man because she thought he was being attacked, not realizing, because of the language barrier that she was being helped. She continued to pummel and hit both Antonio and the man until Antonio finally released him at which time, the man gave him a fiercely hateful look before returning to strike the woman again.

At this point Antonio and Miguel shrugged their shoulders in disgust as they walked away, with the understandings that not all problems have solutions and that Americans must be crazy. This was their first hostile encounter with Americans but was not to be their last.

Their rooming house offered breakfast at a reasonable price and a much different fare than what they had eaten before. The bread was just as good as any they ever had and so was the coffee, but fried bananas covered in honey, fried thick slices of bread covered with beaten eggs and coconut shavings dipped in sugar cane syrup, took some getting used to. They were in total agreement that the previous day's experience had been unsatisfactory in every way. And that doing more of the same in the same way would yield no better result. Their strategy of sitting at a café looking at every person walking by needed to be changed. Instead they decided that beginning in the late afternoon they would cover the Malecon walkway by each starting at either end and walking towards each other. That way they would double the odds of making contact.

Dressed in their casual clothes they decided to explore the docks and start working on their exit plans. This remained an important and unanswered question which they had postponed pending their reconnaissance once they arrived in Cuba. Walking on the pier they saw a ship flying what they recognized to be an American flag. Seeing the flag caused them to talk about their experience with the Americans the night before, wondering if the people involved were aboard the ship. Antonio remembered the way the man looked at him just before he struck the woman again. Remembering the man's hateful look he hoped they would never meet again. The next thing they saw confirmed that there was a God, and he liked them. One pier over from the American ship, there was the Belgrano flying the Argentinean flag.

"Your brother smiled when I handed him your note. He was more amused than surprised. Wait until I tell him about this." They were sitting in Rogelio's quarters who was as surprised as them by the act of providence that caused them to be in Cuba at the same time. Getting on board the Belgrano had been difficult because Antonio never knew Rogelio's full name. When asked by the master of the deck on duty what they wanted, they simply blurted out "We are here to see Rogelio."

"Which one," he asked. Evidently there was more than one Rogelio or the deck master was a great keeper of the gate. Since Antonio never learned Rogelio's last name he responded with the next best answer. He said "Rogelio, the Chief Steward. Tell him Antonio Barradaz is here. I am his brother's brother." Looking suspiciously the man asked if he was Rogelio's brother, since he heard the remark about his brother's brother he reasoned that if one is a brother to one then he must be a brother to the other, in which case this man must be the Chief Steward's brother, but that is not what he had said. Antonio and Miguel could see confusion all over the man's face as he was trying to decipher the riddle. In the interest of not spending all day on the deck of the Belgrano, Miguel spoke saying "Please go and tell Rogelio that Antonio Barradaz and a friend are here to see him."

They did not have to wait long for an answer to their request for an audience. Rogelio himself came running down from the main deck because this he had to see with his own eyes. "Antonio, you are a long way from home," he said in greeting them. "Home for us Rogelio is where we happen to be standing. Surely you remember Miguel De la Madrid, my brother and partner in crime." The introduction caused him to smile and to say that if they were partners in crime and crime was the reason for their visit he asked if he could be an accomplice. He then suggested that they discuss their crimes in the privacy of his quarters. "Come," he said, "let us go to my cabin."

They gave Rogelio the condensed version of how they came to be in Cuba and their subsequent plans, they presented him with their dilemma, thinking that if he did not know the way around a manifest, no one would. The dilemma was matching the departing vessel, sailing to Puerto Rico on a schedule corresponding to Mercedes' availability. Better to segment the problem was Miguel's suggestion. "Break it into smaller tasks and review them all." All of this was being discussed under the assumption that Rogelio would agree to be their accomplice in the enterprise. Not only would he cooperate, Rogelio was willing to handle some of the logistics. The Belgrano was not going to Puerto Rico but a sister ship was. It was not an uncommon practice for Chief Stewards and other crew members to temporarily change ship assignments provided the captains were both in agreement. Rogelio's request would be based on the fact that he had never seen Puerto Rico and that was enough of a justification.

The Belgrano was scheduled to sail to Curacao and Venezuela, returning to Santo Domingo before heading to Spain. The Bernardo O'Higgins a ship named for the Chilean national hero was sailing to Puerto Rico in three days time. Rogelio would speak with his counterpart and make the swapping of ships arrangements. As they discussed the plan, the logistics did not worry them because they appeared to be well under control. And they trusted

Rogelio to find the way to bypass the manifest. It was the unknowns that troubled them. They needed destiny on their side. They hoped that providence would be on their side, but if there was one thing that Miguel understood was that hope was not an affective strategy. The meeting closed with the understanding that they would meet at the same time the next day to review and refine the plan if warranted, after further consideration over night.

After changing back to their suits they returned to the Malecon and as had been decided one would walk east and the other one west. They would continue to walk past each other until she was spotted. Whoever spotted Mercedes would follow her, the one not following her would know she had been spotted because he would not see the other as they were supposed to while crossing the Malecon. In that case, the one not following Mercedes would know in what general direction to go. In the event of a total disconnect they agreed to meet at the café where they had sat the day before.

It was during the third turn around that Miguel spotted her staring at him. He stood still and fought the urge to run to her which would have been precisely the wrong thing to do. She was sitting with a young lady who had a strong family resemblance to Mercedes, causing Miguel to think they may be related. All the time that he was standing she was staring directly at him, almost smiling. Miguel turned to walk to find Antonio, when he saw him already walking in his direction. Antonio had been looking at them as they were looking at one another. They both noticed a slight reaction on her part when she saw Antonio standing next to Miguel. There would have been no way for her to guess that Antonio was part of their adventure. And it pleased her as much as it surprised her.

Antonio and Miguel had the feeling that Mercedes may have also had a plan, and that sitting in the crowded pastry shop in the late afternoon was part of it. After all, she was smart and they had to consider that she may have spent as much time in what if thinking as they had. Taking advantage that the shop was packed and not a table was available, they approached her table, and after apologizing for the intrusion asked if they could share their table since there were no other seats. In exchange for their favorable consideration, they would consider it an honor if they could be allowed to treat them. Antonio pouring out the charm and with his biggest smile asked if they could sit down. Proceeding to sit before the ladies responded, he said "I am Jorge Garcia and this is Pedro Alvarez we are returning to Spain and wanted to see Cuba before going home. May we please know your names." Mercedes introduced Gloria her cousin and extended her hand first to Miguel and then to Antonio.

She could tell that her cousin was favorably impressed by Antonio and taking advantage of this dynamic she suggested they go to the counter and order pastries and drinks, while she and Miguel held the table. As they rose to go and make their selections, Miguel called on all his control to keep from embracing her. Her look for him indicated similar emotions and that answered the question about her changing her mind. Not wanting to waste any of their brief private time he spoke saying, "We are going to Puerto Rico in three days. There is an Argentinean ship named the Bernardo O'Higgins. It sails at first light on Tuesday. We will meet you outside your house and escort you to the ship. This may be the best opportunity that we may have for a long time, but if it fails I am willing to wait for as long as necessary. I have lived for you and only for you since the day at the confessionary and will wait for you as long as I have to."

"My love," she said "I too do not care too wait one minute longer to be with you." She suggested that after their pastries they excuse themselves and leave. Her plan was for the men to follow them unseen to her house so that they would know where to meet her on Tuesday. She would enter trough the gate where they would meet when he came for her. It would have to be no later than four in the morning because the maids would begin their day at five o'clock, and would be alerted if she was seen up and about at that hour. That was all the time they had to discuss the plan before Antonio and Gloria returned to the table, which was good because simplicity was the best solution to their complex problem.

Mercedes noticed that Antonio sounded differently, and then realized that he was concealing his Basque accent, trying to sound like a Catalan. They made light conversation about several of the day's topics. Gloria said that they were receiving an increasingly large number of American visitors which was good because they spent money like no one else, but also raised concerns that the Americans may have had additional intentions towards Cuba, beyond entertainment. At that moment Miguel stood and Antonio did the same. Explaining that they had some matters to attend to and regretted abandoning such charming company. Gloria who could not conceal her disappointment offered her card to Antonio and asked that he feel free to call on her later on during the week. Antonio could not resist the temptation, so he received the card without releasing her hand, bowed and kissed her fingers in a way that indicated the promise of more to come. She was flushed with her feeling of a potential relationship with this handsome man. "You are incorrigible," Miguel said, as they walked away from the table to set up their observation point.

Gloria, her voice filled with curiosity said to Mercedes as she looked at them walking away, "Those are two very fine gentlemen. I pray that we may see them again. Do you think we will? What do you think about yours?" Mercedes smiled privately and asked her, "What do you mean mine? He is not mine. We just met." Gloria responded by saying, "True that you just met, its just that I thought you two would make a fine match just as I feel the same about Jorge and me."

"One never knows," said Mercedes to her cousin, "One never knows." Sunday they met with Rogelio and walked towards one of the bars that populated docks all over the Caribbean Sea region. The patrons were a mixture of everything and everyone. This was a melting pot of races. Mulatto women sat with white men, black men sat with white women, and black women sat with white men. Argentineans ate with Cubans, and Venezuelans sat with Spaniards. Rogelio described his plan for their departure, which called for them to be onboard by five in the morning. He would meet them at the loading plank, hide them in his quarters until the ship sailed. He would maintain three sets of manifests. One with their real names to be given to the captain and one without to be given to the port authority. The third which would be identical to the one given to the port authority, would be used to replace the captain's manifest after he married them. Miguel's eyes bulged out of their sockets when hearing of the wedding. Rogelio said that it was a matter of conscience since he had arranged for them to use the suite usually reserved for newlyweds he could not allow them to share a bed if they were not married and since the ship's captain had the authority it would all be proper and correct. After all, he asked, were they not Catholics.

Once satisfied with all the arrangements, and before departing they had decided to avoid seeing Mercedes and Gloria for fear of making a mistake.

The best way to avoid saying the wrong thing was to not be in a position to say anything. "Besides, we have lots to do before we leave."

"I can not think of a thing that we need to do before we leave. We have thought of everything, of that I am certain." Antonio smiled and almost laughed at him and then said, "You are wrong. You have not thought of everything. You have not thought about shopping. We must go shopping." Miguel examined all the details in his mind and finally surrendered and asked, "Shopping for what?"

"For a wedding dress and all that goes with it. We will go to a ladies dress shop, find someone Mercedes' size and get her to help us with the selection." Miguel stood amazed at Antonio. His plan was right, he had not thought about a wedding dress, but Antonio did. "How do you know about these things?" he asked. "I read a lot," Antonio answered.

CHAPTER 14

By Tuesday afternoon they were far away from Cuba and even farther from Spain and Mercedes' family. They had made it to the ship just before five in the morning, and as planned, Rogelio met them and secured them until the ship sailed. Mercedes had reduced the possibility of early discovery by claiming exhaustion the previous evening before retiring and requesting that she not be awakened until she awoke on her own. Accordingly, her aunt gave instructions to the household staff that Mercedes was not to be disturbed. She wrote a note which she left behind. It simply informed them that she was safe but had departed for points unknown. She added that in due course she would contact the family. Lastly, she wrote that she would not ask or forgiveness since none was needed, but that instead she would ask for their understanding. Since stealth was of the essence, she carried only as much as she could pack in a canvass bag.

Mercedes had given some thought about what the sleeping arrangements would be once onboard ship. She was more curious than troubled because although they were married in the eyes of God, they had kissed only once, and that was the morning in which she had made her escape. Not knowing what to expect she suffered a case of mild anxiety and confessed to Miguel that she felt like a nervous bride before her wedding night. "That is because we are to be married this evening. One of the stewards will take you to your suite where you will find your entire wedding trousseau. It is a gift from Antonio. I will dress in Rogelio's quarters and will not see you until we are before the captain who will marry us. After that your suite will be our honeymoon suite and then we will see what we will see."

At seven o'clock that Tuesday evening they stood in a private room, inside the main dining room. This was a room where dignitaries, diplomats, cabinet members and the like dined in private and without disturbing interruptions caused by the general public. The private dining room was built in exquisite elegance. Clearly a room for royalty or for those of comparable wealth and status. The walls were built of mahogany panels that had been polished and waxed to a bright sheen. The luster of the wood panels glimmered when reflecting the candle lights from the sconces on the wall, and the beautiful Italian chandelier in the center added greater resplendence to the atmosphere. As customary, Miguel, and Antonio who was the best man stood by the captain as Mercedes waited to enter. She approached through the room's private entrance so as to not reveal that a wedding was taking place. Since it was not possible for her to be attended to by a maid of honor or a bridesmaid, she turned to Rogelio and asked him to stand in that role. He was at first amused by the request but agreed so long as his name would not be entered in the registry under bridesmaid, because if known he would never live it down. He was already playing the role of the father of the bride and was escorting her to the groom and the captain.

The dress looked splendid on her and it fit to perfection. The shopping plan had worked extremely well and they had found a girl whose size and shape was very close to Mercedes'. There were not that many choices available in either size or color since most dresses were made to order and those that were not would have required some if not a great deal of alteration and they had no time for either. They settled on a beige colored dress with a mid-length train more suitable for a cotillion than for a wedding. Beige was as close to white as they could find, given the time constraints. The dress was cut low but not revealing and at the point her dress met her cleavage sat a single pearl on a necklace that Miguel had bought as her wedding gift. He had purchased the necklace from the same jeweler where he bought the rings. Rogelio surprise them with a gift of his own. He had sent some of the staff to search for fresh flowers anywhere they could find them. He told them not to exclude churches and cemeteries in their search and to not return without flowers. He had them place some in the private dining room where the wedding would take place, and the rest in the suite with a note asking her to fashion her bridal bouquet. The note was signed "Rogelio, Your maid of honor." She had protested to Miguel that it was unfair because she had not been given the opportunity to reciprocate. He assured her that sometime in the next fifty years he would give her the opportunity to make it up.

When the door opened and Miguel first saw Mercedes in her wedding dress he was first stunned by her beauty and by the moment. There was not an orchestra playing a hundred violins, but at that moment he could have sworn he heard them. He was overwhelmed by the realization that this exquisitely beautiful girl had selected him to be her husband. This girl who had been educated in boarding schools, and had attended the finest cotillions in Barcelona, and was raised by one of the wealthiest families was about to become his wife. It was not dreamlike, for him it was a dream come true. One that he had never ever dreamt could be possible.

Mercedes stood at the door remembering that when she had participated in her friends' weddings, the occasions had been filled with doubt and uncertainty. Mostly, the brides had been anxious and filled with fears for their futures. And yet thirty feet in front of her stood a man that she had only known for a short period of time and somehow she felt as certain of her actions and decisions that had led her to this moment as she had about anything in her life. She felt a touch of sadness for all those whom she knew had not married for love. And felt elated that she was marrying the most worthy husband anyone could hope to have. This she knew with absolute certainty.

The captain who had not ever conducted a wedding ceremony was more nervous than either Miguel or Mercedes. And since he was a bachelor he lacked even the experience of his own wedding. They all laughed when she made the short walk to where they stood, and noticing the captain's nervousness she said to him, "Please captain don't worry, you will do just fine, it will be over soon." As they exchanged vows and rings they were both enveloped by a feeling of grace and joy that could not be described only felt. Both Antonio and Rogelio performed their functions with distinction, including holding the rings without dropping them by Antonio and holding the bride's flowers by Rogelio. Not one second after the captain declared them married, and even before he instructed Miguel to kiss his bride, Mercedes had given her flowers over for Rogelio to hold, reached for Miguel's face and kissed him softly, and as her lips lingered on his she whispered "I love you my husband." To which he responded by saying, "I love you my wife."

The captain's gift to them had been the special dinner he had arranged for the wedding party in the same room in which they were married, with his compliments. As they settled to enjoy their first course which was a very creamy pumpkin soup with sprinkled rosemary and small basil leaves on the surface, served with their first bottle of wine, an Argentinean chardonnay, Rogelio momentarily excused himself. Discreetly entering the captain's office he went directly to the cabinet where he had placed the manifest with their real names on it, and replace it with the one where their names were changed. This was crucial for their need for secrecy. Had the captain wanted to see the manifest before the marriage certificate was completed he would had seen their correct names. However, once they were married the likelihood that he would ask to see the manifest again was fairly remote. Nevertheless, the correct manifest was purposely misplaced by Rogelio until their return trip to Cuba.

After the magnificent dinner the captain asked to be excused and after thanking the bride and groom for the privilege of conducting their wedding ceremony, he retired. Rogelio remained at the table and listened as Miguel and Antonio told of their lives starting with their meeting at the dock and Barcelona. Their lives with the nuns and their achievements at the docks. The conversation then turned towards Mercedes and what her life had been like while she waited for Miguel to come for her. It turns out that she had gone to the pastry café starting one month after her arrival, every afternoon, because it offered both the visibility and set the stage for a casual encounter when he came for her. The problem was that they had been approached more than once, and more than once had to tolerate the company of some fairly insufferable men. She spoke of her disappointment in her family and of her confidence in Miguel. When she was done, an uncomfortable silence settled in, which was the signal to retire. Time to start their married life, they thought. They stood to say their good nights, Rogelio decided to retire as well but Antonio wanted to walk on the deck before turning in.

It was between eleven thirty and midnight, when Antonio started his walk. The moon was at its brightest that evening and one could almost read by moonlight, he thought. There were several young couples promenading on the deck trying to find whatever form of privacy was available. He noticed one of the ship's crew members inspecting the ropes on the life boats. He was slightly built but powerful at the same time. He was a bit bowlegged, and walked as if his upper body weight was causing his legs to push out from the knees below. "Let us hope we don't have to find out if the winch will work if we had to lower the boats to the sea," he said to the man. "The emergency drills always call for women and children first, but never say who goes second or third. At any rate, the crew goes last according to status. For that reason I am sure that there will not be any space for me. So I do not spend a lot of time worrying about it. Besides I can probably swim to Boriquen," the man said. Antonio had never heard that word and did not know if it was another island or another boat. "What is that word again, the one you just said." The man smiled and said, "I don't blame you that you do not know that name. Long before the Spanish called it San Juan, and then Puerto Rico, the Island was called Boriquen. It was the home of the Tainos. People who descended from the Arawaks. I am Taino, and I was raised in Boriquen. All my life I have lived near the sea, but not too close on account of Huracan. When he comes in anger you do not want to be anywhere near the sea. He will take you with the wind and the waves never to be seen again."

"Huracan," another word that Antonio had never heard before, and so he asked the man to explain what it was, but not before saying, "My name is Antonio what is yours."

"Orovis. I am named after Morovis and Orocovis two of the most honored chiefs of the Tainos. They were brave warriors who fought the Spanish to their death, taking many with them along the way." He went on to expand on Huracan the god of wind, relating what it was like to catch his fury. There was no escaping Huracan when he was angry, he said.

"What was your life like before the Spanish?" Antonio asked in his attempt to keep the conversation going. Orovis explained that he had been raised by the Spanish priests in a mission. He never knew who his parents were or maybe he just did not remember them, or if they were alive. Since talking about their culture, their history or their past was cause for punishment by the priests. They were forced to forget about their ancestors and about their gods. There had been a sexton named Mariano, whose real name was Aracobo and he was Taino. It was through him that we learned of our real history. Many did choose to forget who they were, but not him. "I formed a group to sustain our culture so whenever we could, we would meet to recount the history of the Taino people, and to worship our Gods. They would punish us for speaking Arawak or behaving in any way that would reinforce who we were. We used to discuss the stories about our chiefs,

Guaynabo, Arecibo, Adjuntas and many others. It was important to remember who we were because the Spanish would not even allow us to keep our Taino names. Instead they gave us Christian names."

"Me they called Andres. Once a week they would take us to a room where a priest would read to us from a book. I could not tell you the name of the book because we never read it since we never learned to read. Finally I rebelled one too many times when I would not allow the priest to hit me. He was about to strike me with a stick because I had painted one of our holy symbols, the snake, on my chest and was doing the same on my friend's chest. As he raised it, I took it away from him and struck him several times. Unlike us Tainos, who took our punishment in silence, as warriors, he screamed and whimpered like a cowardly pig. All the while I was speaking to him in my language. Finally I stopped not because I thought he had enough but because I was spent. It was as if I was avenging my ancestors. What I could not understand was why he was so angry. I was just painting a snake on my friend's chest to honor our God the serpent. The serpent is even mentioned in the Christian book. When they read us the story about Eve being seduced by the serpent, it told me that even the Christian God recognized the importance of the serpent God. Otherwise why did he not use a rabbit. No, he knew the importance of the serpent God.

I never understood the idea of only one God because to whom, would you turn when he is angry to intercede on your behalf. None of it made a lot of sense to me. After that incident I could not stay. I went to what was then called Toa Baja and Vega Alta, the two villages from where my people came, but found no one but Spanish and Africans. I guess when they ran out of Tainos to abuse they brought in the Africans. After that I went to the docks and started working the ships that sail the Caribbean Sea."

"What did happen to your people, did you ever find out?" asked Antonio. "Surely somebody must have survived, after all, you did."

"I thought the same," he replied. "But after searching through many villages I had to accept that there were no Tainos left in Boriquen. It is not hard to understand why they disappeared. Death was welcomed after the treatment of the Spanish. They were obsessed with gold and diamonds and there was little of it in the island. After a while they had to recognize there was no treasure in Boriquen, so they moved on to victimize and erase other races from the face of the earth. Finally, I gave up and went to the docks, where I have been ever since. There my life was better but I have learned that everyone must have someone to look down on. And it does not get lower than me, that is why I never worry about the lifeboats. Because there would not be any room in it for me." Antonio said to the Taino, "Orovis, your story is just like my story. Tomorrow I will tell you about my people the Basque. I need to get some sleep. Can we talk again tomorrow? How about right here tomorrow night? Will you be here?" Orovis nodded his agreement. Antonio walked away after saying "Good night and thank you. Tomorrow I want to learn more about Boriquen"

Morning in the Caribbean does not ease into day from night. Instead it explodes with the brightest sun seen anywhere on earth. One moment it is not there and the next is as bright as the day is going to be. It shines brightly even when it is raining. Rain in most places is usually preceded by clouds that eventually burst. This is not true of the rains in the Caribbean they come when they want to, and with no warning. Instead of rain or shine it is rain and shine. Antonio looked out his cabin's window and saw the brightest rain he had ever seen. Rainbows crisscrossing one another all over the sky. One more vibrant than the other. Antonio felt moved by what he was seeing and felt great about his decision to come.

In their suite Mercedes and Miguel De la Madrid were feeling equally pleased but for different reasons. The fears and uncertainties about their being able to fulfill their love by realizing their marriage were now behind them. She had great confidence in his ability to achieve whatever he set his mind to. Because of that, she had no concerns about their future, and she told him so. She had marveled at the works of providence because how else could it be explained that a girl of her upbringing, so distant from his world could have come to fall in love with a man so different from her. She appreciated why she had fallen in love with him, because he was a man of substance. More of a man than any she had ever met. But by contrast she had been just a shallow wealthy girl. One who had never been challenged by life's difficulties, untested in ways that she would certainly be in the future. She hoped that she would measure up to his standards. At that moment she felt sorry for all the people who having had the opportunity chose to not appreciate her husband, "Their loss is my good fortune," she thought.

They had just gone to sleep before the sun rose on the horizon, but were not tired. Their first night as husband and wife had been one continuous exchange of kindnesses and pleasures. That night had been about laughter and curiosities satisfied. They held nothing back in exchanging pleasures and discovered great comfort in their ability to please one another. This was Mercedes' first sexual experience. She laughed at herself when she thought about her fears and concerns about the first time. Her mother had warned her about the violent nature of men when they consummated the sexual act. "Brace yourself and the pain will pass. Keep your eyes closed. That way you can reduce the fear and anxiety that will overwhelm you. Above all remember that the act is to be endured, ladies do not enjoy it," her mother had admonished her. Mercedes wondered if that had been her mother's own experience. Looking back she realized that her fears could have been well grounded if her first lover had been someone other than the man she chose. And thus far she thought, "I have chosen well."

Miguel had different concerns. Always the planner his mind was filled with the hundred questions to be answered once they arrived in Puerto Rico. They knew very little about the island, almost nothing and certainly no one, and while that was not necessarily a bad thing they could count on no assistance from anyone. They were in effect new borns in a new land. He closed his eyes and drew on the memory of the past six hours. Once in bed dressed in their nightgowns they both acted according to the timidity and modesty they felt. He had snuffed out the candles before they both undressed, put on their night gowns and slipped into bed. Their lovemaking began almost with the fear of not doing the wrong thing as if such a thing were possible between two people who loved as they did. Their passion soon overcame their fears and carnal hunger replaced it. Losing their inhibitions and allowing their lust to equal their love they progressed with their inquiries in the dark. Touching and feeling, sensing each other's souls, they progressed to consummate the act.

The nightgowns, which purpose was to promote modesty served as obstacles for the pleasures they sought. It was Mercedes who pushed away from him, stepped down from the bed, lit a candle and stood in front of him allowing her nightgown to fall to her feet, as she showed her naked body to her husband for the very first time. Miguel was overwhelmed by the site of her and could have lain in bed looking at her the rest of the night until she spoke and said, "I want to see all of you my, husband." He stood across from her with his eyes filled with tears. He felt overwhelmed by her gift. She was giving of herself to him, and he was feeling unworthy of the gift. And in the same way she was honoring him at this moment he swore to honor her all of their lives.

A few minutes after eight in the morning they met for breakfast, where Antonio was already at the table. When they first entered the room. Antonio and Miguel exchanged a look that said one was very happy and the other was happy for him. Miguel remembered the night he had seen Antonio with Dolores and wished that his brother were not alone. His suit had been stored away and he was wearing his usual work clothes. Miguel was more casually dressed than Mercedes, because she did not own any work clothes. She had not needed them since in her family's circle manual work was left to others. "As soon as we get to Puerto Rico I must buy clothes more suitable for my new life. These that I am wearing are no longer appropriate. And once there, where are we going may I ask."

Mercedes' question brought reality into their midst. First they agreed that upon arriving in Puerto Rico they should secure rooms until they could get their bearings and select their ultimate destination. The captain had informed them that they could expect to dock in the port of San Juan in the mid-morning on Friday. That left them with more or less two and a half days to work on their plans. Antonio told them about his conversation with the Taino and his intention to talk to him at length during the rest of the voyage. The Indian had mentioned a region that could be an option, provided that it was away from the port of entry. Should anyone come looking for them, they would concentrate on the populated centers. All the more reason to go inland as soon as possible.

Since leaving her aunt's and uncle's house she had not thought for one moment about the reaction to her disappearance or their response. No doubt they would first go to the authorities and demand and island wide search for her. They would probably demand that the entire military garrison should be assigned the task. Next, she thought, they would question Gloria about any contacts, events or incidents that she could remember could arouse suspicion. Possibly Gloria would mention the men at the pastry shop, but she would remember that her interest was greater than Mercedes' who seemed to not be interested at all. Next, letters would be sent to her parents who would with any luck would have disowned her and not look for her. In due course she decided she would contact them. "All things in due course," she thought.

What had actually happened was that as she had hoped, Mercedes' aunt, Doña Conchita entered her room a few minutes before two in the afternoon. By then, Mercedes had been at sea for six hours and was fully immersed in the preparations for her wedding. Worried that she may have been ill but wanting to grant her request to be allowed to sleep, her aunt waited for as long as she could before knocking on the bedroom door. Concerned by the absence of a reply to her knocking, she opened the door and was startled by what she did not see. The bed was empty and unmade, and there was no Mercedes. At first, she thought that Mercedes must already been up and somewhere in the house, and for that reason she was not alarmed. Instead she sent one of the maids to find Mercedes and ask her to join her in the garden for tea. Both Gloria and her mother were in the garden when the maid informed them that Mercedes was not in the house. Because it was unlike her to go anywhere without her cousin, they were now concerned. Gloria and Doña Conchita returned to Mercedes' room to try to find out where she may have gone. It was Gloria who first saw the note on the night table next to the oil lamp. She read it and handed the note to her mother who upon reading it almost fainted.

Doña Conchita's first concern was about the scandal. How to find her while keeping her disappearance from their friends. "Surely," she thought this would reflect poorly on their good name in the island, not to mention the impact that this incident would have in Spain. Next she sought out her husband, whose concern was first about how to retrieve her. No doubt he thought that she must not have gone too far. After all Cuba was an Island. He called on the commanding officer at the army garrison to request that all other garrisons be notified about the disappearance of his niece, and that road blocks be posted on all roads leading out of Havana. He asked that the situation be dealt with as a kidnapping. Colonel Gallardo, the commanding officer of the Havana military district had greater concerns than to chase after wealthy little tramps, but did not say so. Instead, he offered to send soldiers to effect discreet inquiries of the local rooming houses and hotels. "In the event that the initial search yields no results, we will expand it to adjacent districts. In the mean time, I suggest you visit the port authority. In the event she left by ship, her name will appear in the manifest. If she is not listed, we can rule that out as a possibility and we can presume that she is still in Cuba"

One week later, with all options exhausted, there was no choice but to write a letter to the Gabriels in Barcelona for the purpose of advising them that the niece they had left in their care, had simply disappeared. Beyond that, there was nothing to report. They had examined all ship's manifest for all outbound ships sailing from Cuba to every possible destination. They had done everything but conduct a house to house search in Havana, but she could not be found. Worst of all, the secret had been revealed and they were no longer thought of as a respectable family. This left everyone in great distress, except Gloria, who was envious of Mercedes.

Doña Carmen Gabriel knew at once, "She went with him, she ran away with the dock worker. We will find him and he will tell us where she is. Wait until I get my hands on him. God knows what he has done to her by now. No matter Genaro, we must find him and then we will find her." He was in full agreement with his wife about what to do, the question was how to do it. He first went to the convent where he learned that neither Miguel nor his Basque friend had been seen for several weeks. They informed him that they had stopped coming to the church since Sister Graciela's funeral. Next he went to look for Miguel at the docks. Surely his good friend Don Mauricio had done his duty and as requested had kept his eyes on Miguel.

"Why of course I have done as you asked of me Genaro. I know their every move. Him and Antonio, the Basque, I have kept a watchful eye on them. I even know where they live. They share a small apartment not far from here. But tell me, why do you worry about them? Have they done anything wrong? Nothing has happened to your daughter, has it? Tell me now and I will make them sorry they were ever born?" Feeling relieved and reassured Mercedes' father answered none of the questions, but instead asked some of his own. Mainly he wanted to know if anything had changed about their behavior. He asked if their work schedules had changed in any way that would raise concern. Had anyone seen them in the company of women, he asked. Not receiving any answers he finally said," Bring him to me now. I want to see Miguel de la Madrid. I do not need to see the Basque, just Miguel."

"Victor Gutierrez at your service sir." The man standing before Don Genaro was obviously not Miguel de la Madrid. At this point, Don Mauricio believing there had been a misunderstanding said to him, "No Gutierrez, we do not need you, I asked for Miguel de la Madrid to report to me at once. You go back and tell him to come here right away." Now fully realizing what was happening, in his most innocent form said, "I am terribly sorry Don Mauricio, but neither Miguel nor Antonio have been to work for close to a month now. I thought that you knew since you appointed me the assistant manager, just before they left."

At this moment Don Genaro was absolutely certain that Mercedes and Miguel were together, the question was where had they gone. Also at this moment the only benefit of knowing where they had gone was mostly for curiosity's sake, because he appreciated that he had been bested by a clever opponent. How they had done it intrigued him because there was no way they had communicated since Mercedes had gone to Cuba. Of that he had made certain. Further, he thought that if they had succeeded to this point, they were more than likely not going to make the kind of mistake that would make them easy to trace. He asked for copies of all the ship's manifests in the last thirty days, and there he saw their names. They had sailed for the Island of Santo Domingo and once there they could have sailed in a hundred directions, maybe even returning to Spain. Regardless, he knew they would not be found. After explaining all of this to his wife; Doña Carmen, he said, "We have to accept the fact that our daughter has gone with that man."

"We have no daughter, from this day forward, I never want to hear her name mentioned in this house, is that clear," responded Mercedes' mother.

Rogelio entered the room and asked if he could join them for coffee. Mercedes thanked him for his excellent service as maid of honor, but he corrected her by saying that it had been his honor to have served as the father of the bride. He explained that since he was not married and probably would never be, and he had no children and probably never would, last night was the one and only time he would be so honored. Next he asked about their plans once in Puerto Rico. As they explained their short terms plans he suggested a guest house on Tanca Street that had been recommended by one of the officers. "It is called la casa de Asucena. It is named after the owner and the flower whose name they share," according to my sources. The house is situated on a corner property and has a small garden in the rear. It is a short walk from the docks to the house, unfortunately all of it is uphill. I would not recommend that you stay there any longer that is necessary for you to move inland where it will be easier to disappear. In the event that your family hires private investigators to track you, they will not go beyond San Juan in their search"

The three of them looked at Rogelio recognizing that they were all thinking alike. This raised the question that others may think the same. In which case it would be best to go at once after choosing their destination. "I expect to be in Argentina in two month's time and will spend three weeks at the ranch in Mendoza. My family will enjoy hearing of this adventure, but none more than Xavier." Excusing himself because of the need to meet with the captain and the officers to discuss the disembarkation plan, he stood and left the room.

Miguel knew that it was time to get back to what if thinking. To engage in some serious contingency planning. Everything so far confirmed that they were good at it, but they would not be well served by a false sense of security. The best way to proceed was to identify options and list positives on the left side of the page and negatives on the right. The idea was to select the options that offered the most positive alternatives and then focus on a plan to execute them. When it came to what if thinking, they found that Mercedes was equal to the task. Feeling that all was under control, Antonio left them to go walk on the deck.

That evening they dined by themselves in the main dining room, making certain to avoid contact with anyone who would ask polite but impertinent questions of those who were trying to preserve many secrets. Fresh sea bass was the main course selected by all three that evening. The ship's crew had fished during the day, kept their catch alive in sea water and as a result the fish was absolutely fresh. The sea bass was covered with a batter that contained many herbs and spices. The waiter removed all the bones in the fish with a style and grace that could only be described as art. He served it on a bed of boiled and mashed breadfruit with a dash of ground cilantro, finishing with a light mango and brandy sauce over the fish. After proclaiming their appreciation both for the meal and for the service, they commenced to enjoy it while the thought lingered on the back of their minds wondering when they would eat like this again. "Did I forget to tell you that I have never cooked," said Mercedes. "Just a little detail that I think you should know before we arrive in Puerto Rico in the event that you should like to return me to my family." They all laughed at the same time, while Miguel realized that he had not included cooking as an item on his planning list. When dessert was served the only one with room left to eat it was Mercedes, who among her many surprising qualities could eat more than anyone they had ever known.

After dinner Antonio went in search of Orovis who as promised was around the life boats waiting for him. Antonio had saved his dessert in a napkin and offered it to him. He was surprised that a Spanish could be kind to him, since the number of kind Spanish he had known were few and far between. Orovis thanked him and continued the conversation where it had stopped the night before. "You should see the region between Vega Alta and Toa Baja. It starts after crossing the Plata River, followed by a small mountain that lords over a beautiful valley. I like it particularly well because there are mountains around it that shield you from the winds of Huracan when he is angry." His people had lived in the region all their lives until soon after the arrival of the Spanish. His village, he remembered was a cluster of huts they called Bohios. These were shelters with only a thatched roof and no walls. Tainos never needed privacy for anything because whatever they did was there for all to see. It was only after the Spanish came that they had been forced into modesty and clothes. He said that he realized that the days of the Taino were over but had hoped that he could live as his ancestors had lived until the day he could be with them again.

Antonio was not a total stranger to Orovis' sentiments and aspirations. In many ways they were searching for the same things. Mainly an opportunity to live as they pleased, and with no one pressing them to follow rules that made no sense and in no way made their lives better. He thought about the history that he had read about many cultures. And in everyone of them he learned that whenever a society was enjoying themselves someone would come along to impose rules to control or to outlaw them.

Without consulting the others he decided to offer Orovis the opportunity to join his party by serving as their guide in leading them to the Vega region, which sounded appealing to Antonio. He discussed their interim plans with Orovis and offered him the job of taking them to the region. His idea was to pay him for his services to take them there. And once there he could choose to stay or to return to the docks as he wished. Antonio hoped that Orovis would guide them and stay because he believed he had much to learn from the man. Besides, he knew that history was written by the victors and that anything that he could find to read on the history of Puerto Rico and its people would be biased towards Spain. With Orovis he felt he could learn the true account from one of the survivors of the Spanish largesse. Orovis accepted on the spot, and asked Antonio to wait for him at the end of the pier in San Juan.

CHAPTER 15

When they entered the bay of San Juan the very first structure they saw was the Morro Fort, the very same one they had seen when they had arrived in Cuba. "Are we back to Havana?," Antonio asked. "I certainly hope not," said Miguel. "No my dears" said Mercedes, "Spain built the same forts in different places in the Caribbean for the same purpose everywhere; to defend against pirates and other invaders. Let's just hope they don't confuse us with Dutch pirates and fire at us." The Morro fort connected with another fort named St. Cristobal, in a way that their guns could deliver interlocking fire across several miles of the waterfront. It had the effect of raining hell upon their enemies over a very long span of sea. This offered and undaunting challenge for those foolish enough to attempt a run at invading Puerto Rico through the port of San Juan. At this point the captain took personal control of the helm and demonstrated his skill in bringing the ship to its berth with the ease of someone who had docked many times.

After saying their goodbyes to the captain and Rogelio, they went ashore where Orovis waited for them. After the introductions they left in search of the Asucena guest house on Tanca Street. Orovis offered to take everyone's luggage but they declined and asked him where was his. "I am wearing everything that I own, except for my walking stick." Upon his insistence, Mercedes allowed him to carry her canvas bag. She already liked the dark skinned little man with the bowed legs and the chest of a much larger man. He already liked the sweet woman whose kindness showed in her eyes.

As they walked off the ship Antonio and Miguel stopped to look at the baggage handling system operating at the dock. It was as far from a system as any process could be. There was more wasted motion than anything else, and confusion seemed to reign. Antonio suggested that maybe they should stick around and help them with what they knew from the port of Barcelona.

"Difficult to move forward when we are looking back," answered Miguel. "You are right. Lets go," replied Antonio.

At the Asucena they had no problems in securing rooms, except one for Orovis. They simply would not allow Tainos or Africans in their establishment, which everybody knew, the owner explained. "No one allows them on their properties, it is simply not done. I am sure he is used to sleeping in the open so you should not worry about him." Antonio was incensed by her insulting attitude towards another human being, especially when a large crucifix hung on the wall and a smaller one around her neck. He remembered Sister Maria's comment about some Christians being bad at it. Clearly this was one of them. Instead of arguing, they decided that since they were not allowed to pay for a room for Orovis he would just have to sleep there for free.

After leaving their locker and her bag in their rooms they went in search of transportation to take them to the Vegas. Back in the direction of the docks they had seen several livery stables that were used to deliver merchandise to the various merchants within a reasonable distance of San Juan. Those outside their service areas were forced to drive their wagons to receive their merchandise directly from the ships. The one advantage of not receiving merchandise from the livery stables is that they could save the added charges incurred as a result of the middle man process. Bypassing the middleman meant that no or fewer bribes for the customs agents were required.

After one hour of searching for the best solution to their transportation, they settled on buying a buck board wagon and a horse. Mercedes, who because of her upbringing knew something about horses, selected one about thirteen hands in size. The one she selected had pulled wagons before, which she could tell by the shape of her legs and the length of her stride. She also decided it was best to select a mare because of the opportunity to breed her once they settled where they were going. After paying for the wagon and horse, Antonio went to the bank with Orovis, while Mercedes went shopping. At the Banco Popular they were met with the same discrimination towards Orovis that they had encountered at the guest house. Upon greeting Antonio, the manager insisted that the Taino had to wait outside. This he made clear with a fair amount of disdain. Before Antonio could argue, Orovis said, "I'll wait outside." Antonio presented the bank draft to the manager who received it and looked at Antonio with renewed interest and a changed attitude.

"Mr. Barradaz" he said, "We are pleased to serve as your bank and want you to know that you may count on us to introduce you to the very best people in our city. May I ask, what kind of business are you in?" Ignoring the question, Antonio asked for additional funds and the balance on a new draft note. The manager suggested that he open an account with the bank and that way there would be no risk of his note being lost or stolen. And there was also the matter of earning a small dividend on the deposit. Antonio drew on all of his self control which kept him from telling the man what he could do with his interest. "My funds and my note, the sooner the better" He said The next time they saw Miguel and Mercedes he looked like a husband, loaded down with packages and not enjoying it. Mercedes said that she wanted to change at once into her work clothes so that they could eat in a place where working people ate. Since she had embraced the idea that she was now a working woman, she would start living like one at once. Miguel inquired about the transaction at the bank and shaking his head Antonio replied, "Don't ask. You go back to the Asucena, Orovis and I will return to the livery stable and make arrangements for an early departure tomorrow. Afterwards you can meet meets us at the bar across the street. I am sure that Mercedes will fit right in with the rest of the working people," he said as he turned in the opposite direction laughing.

"Orovis, we need to buy a tent so that we can have shelter tomorrow night wherever we happen to be. What do you think?" He answered by explaining that no tent was needed because he would provide the shelters, one for the couple and another for them. All they would need he suggested, were hammocks, and three Machetes. One for each man. "A machete is not a long knife as you may think. Instead, think of it as the most important tool of the enterprise at this time." After selecting the machetes, Orovis asked the merchant for a burlap sack that he had seen lying in the corner. The merchant gave it to them at no charge, which surprised Antonio. This merchant did not seem to have a reservation about doing business with a Taino. "That is because he is a Jew, and they will do business with anyone, besides he understands rejection better than Christians."

Antonio watched Orovis wrap the handles in the machetes with burlap strips and when finished the burlap appeared to have been weaved into the handle. "You will appreciate the burlap because when your hand is hot and wet it will keep the handle from slipping. No blisters and no accidents. Bad things happen to people whose hands are not firmly secured in their grip of the machete. Some call it accidents, I call it careless. Remember what I tell you; never be careless with your machete or around someone who is holding one near you. When we get to where we are going you will notice many with missing thumbs and other parts. Those are people who were not careful around a machete. Be careful not to draw it in anger because you will be expected to use it, and blood will be spilled. More importantly do not anger anyone holding one because he may use it against you, especially if he has Rum in his eyes."

While sitting at the bar with Miguel and Mercedes who true to her word, looked like a working woman. In fact she more resembled a working man than a woman. Since there were no working clothes to be found for women, she bought what she could find and that was men's clothes. The only problem was that she looked like the only working woman in all of San Juan and if her intention was to fit in, the result was the opposite. Antonio started formulating his plan as a result of the conversation with Orovis. He wanted to buy land that could be deeded and titled. He had read about the consequences of buying land that did not belong to the seller. To ensure the property was completely theirs he would employ a surveyor.

"Two surveyors," added Miguel. It will cost us a little more but it will identify variances between the property lines and plats registered with the magistrate's office, before money is exchanged." Orovis looked at them not understanding a word they were saying. He understood the language alright, it was the meaning that troubled him. He and his people had never owned the land. It belonged to all, it belonged to the gods. In his way of thinking, one owned only that which he could carry with him. In his case he owned his walking stick, his machete and the hammock that Antonio had just given him. It was incomprehensible to him how anyone could claim they owned the land. "They only thought they did. But at the end it owns you," he thought.

As the evening wore on, they never left the bar as they had planned. They soon found out that this was like no other restaurant they had visited. In this one, when they expressed their desired to eat and ask if they had a menu. The owner responded not with a menu but with a tour of his kitchen. There he had various types and size of fish and lobsters, cuts of ham, several kinds of cheese, inland vegetables and several regional fruits. The owner's wife asked them to choose what they would eat and she would cook it. Instead they asked her to do both and returned to the bar to continue their planning and to wait for their dinner. It was past eleven when they returned to the Asucena for the night. This time everything was dark so they simply walked to their rooms and turned in. After some discussion, Antonio won the argument and Orovis slept in the bed while he slept in the hammock. When morning came, they all entered and sat in the small dining room where they helped themselves to hot rolls, cheeses, different cuts of ham, coffee and orange juice. After a while they were noticed by the owner who came to protest Orovis' presence and asked them to leave. "We were leaving anyway because he does not like your establishment, good day," said Mercedes with a grin. Following all of this, Orovis thought that he would like being with these white people.

At the livery stable where they picked up their wagon, they also picked up blankets and comestibles to last them for the next five days. Not knowing what form of commerce existed where they were going, they though it best to carry enough to set up camp and sustain themselves. While they were completing their purchases, Orovis hitched the horse to the wagon and was waiting to help them load when they returned. He arranged the load in a way that was balanced so as to minimize the horse's effort as she pulled.

Mercedes said that they should name the horse before they started so they could address it by name. She suggested they show respect to such an important member of their expedition by selecting a dignified name. The men agreed and asked her to name the horse since it was her idea. "Esperanza," she said, "We will call her Esperanza." Miguel said, "Why call her only hope, why not hope and dreams."

"Because it is too long," she replied.

The front board was plenty comfortable for all three. Mercedes sat in the middle, Antonio held the reigns and Miguel held her hand. Orovis was invited to ride in the back but he refused offering instead to go ahead of them. He simply asked them to keep up with him which they found amusing since he was walking and they were riding. Their amusement turned to marvel when they saw how effortlessly he could walk faster than the horse could follow.

Of course, they thought, Orovis is not pulling three people and a loaded wagon, but still it was remarkable that when they stopped to allow the horse to rest and drink water from a stream, Orovis looked absolutely fresh. When they exclaimed their surprise over his condition, he simply said, "You must remember that I am Taino." The trail had led them to the village of Bayamon which appeared to be a thriving center of commerce. It was the place where farmers would buy their supplies that had been carried there from San Juan. There was a wagon service that was used by all the merchants to ferry materials from San Juan to Bayamon. This wagon was pulled by oxen. They were as slow as they were big but could pull enormous loads. And since volume was more important that speed, the teamsters did not care how long it took them to make the trip. Moreover, since they would only make one run each week, they had all the time in the world to get to the docks, load their materials and merchandise and return to Bayamon.

The village of Bayamon was close to the halfway point between San Juan and their destination. Orovis explained that the place that he was taking them to was named Vega Alta and, was a good day's trek away, and he advised staying the night. Miguel went off to locate rooms for the night while the rest waited. Near them a man was roasting a small pig with a reddish color to its skin and an aroma unfamiliar to them. They approached the man and asked if they could buy some of the meat for their dinner. "In another hour," he replied, indicating that it was not yet done to his satisfaction which turned out to be perfect as they later found out.

Miguel returned to confirm that he had found two rooms for the four of them. Orovis apologized for not having mentioned that he was planning to sleep under the skies. As he explained, given the choice he never understood when there was an opportunity to look at the beautiful night sky, why would anyone chose to sleep in an enclosed room. Antonio agreed with him and said that he too would sleep outside. Miguel was tempted to do the same. But he and Mercedes were still on their honeymoon and required privacy. Something everyone understood without the need for further explanation.

The man roasting the pig had set up a table for them at the side of his small house and there he served them their dinner. He had roasted sweet potatoes and served them along side fried ripe plantains. On separate bowls he had served rice and beans. Finally he produced a pitcher of Mavi. This was a drink extracted from the sugar cane that when allowed to ferment would affect a person before they could realize they were drunk. For this reason, he cautioned them to drink it slowly. Orovis seconded the advice saying that on one or more occasion he had chosen to ignore the admonitions of good judgment and had paid the price for his folly. After dinner the man offered them guayaba paste. This was a regional fruit mixed with sugar and cooked in a rectangular shape. After cooling, it was sliced and served with a very bland cheese. The idea was that the sharp flavor of the guayaba blended with the blandness of the cheese when eaten together offered an extremely interesting taste. This he served with coffee, which they all drank without concern to sleep since their bodies told them that sleep would not be a problem. Orovis slept on the ground while Antonio tied his hammock to two trees near where Orovis laid and thought that he had been right when he asked why would anyone sleep in a room and miss the beauty of the sky. He fell asleep while looking at a shooting star.

Before the sun had set in the eastern sky they were on their way. This time, Antonio decided that he would walk with Orovis just to see if he could keep up. Much to his pleasant surprise, he found out that he could keep up once he got in stride with the guide. His walk was made the easier by a walking stick that had been cut for him by Orovis. The first half of the day seemed that it was all down hill and the balance of the day was all uphill. After they crossed the Rio Plata at a shallow point they began to climb a small and mildly steep mountain that preceded the valley of Toa Baja. The trail confirmed that many wagons crossed over the mountain, often and heavily loaded.

They all climbed off the wagon to lighten the horse's burden, and tied ropes at the front which allowed them to pull along with the horse. Better to pull than to push the wagon because pushing from behind would have put them at risk in the event the horse slipped or the wagon rolled backwards. Orovis once again thought about how he liked these Spanish people. He believed that anyone who was kind to animals would be just as kind to all other living forms. It was important to him because that had been the Taino culture.

They reached the crest of the mountain at around four in the afternoon, and from there saw what they all agreed was the most beautiful valley they had ever seen. They stood for a while appreciating its uncommon beauty.

Birds of all sizes and colors were flying below where they stood as if it were a welcoming ceremony expressly for them. Covered in vibrant greens, yellows and reds the valley was met by two perfectly symmetrical mountains on either side. The mountains appeared as extensions of the valley because at the time the terrain started to climb, the flora was the same as the lower valley and it gave the effect that it was not a mountain but a climbing valley. Looking to the north they could see amazingly beautiful beaches. Similar to the ones in Cuba.

Mercedes was looking at all of the beauty, lost in a world of her own. While the others may have been looking at business opportunities and similar concerns, her mind was focused on this, her new home. This would be the place where she and Miguel would raise their family. God willing they would be blessed with many children. She would raise them to love this land and to fall in love with it the way she was falling in love. She was thanking the stars for her husband who was making all of these dreams possible for her. Some distance away near a cluster of red flamed trees that were more wide than they were tall, and covered in red flowers, she also saw a pond that appeared large from the distance. In her mind she could see their children climbing the trees and swimming in the pond. "Here," she said to no one in particular, "Here is our home, and there, there we will build our house."

Close to the base of the mountain and to the right laid the village of Toa Baja. From their vantage point they recognized the Spanish design for all villages. It had a plaza in the center which led to the entrance of what they thought was an impressive church for such a small town. Looking much farther and due west they saw what Orovis explained was the village of Vega Alta, which from a distance appeared to be bigger than its counterpart; Toa Baja. As they descended it was decided they should stop at the closer town to spend the night and collect as much information as they could about the region. Antonio was pleased when he realized that nobody in Toa Baja, just like in Bayamon did not in any way object to Orovis' presence. It seemed that it was the same way all over the world. He had experienced discrimination in cities that he had not seen in the countryside. He liked the island more and more every minute that he spent on it.

They agreed to meet at the entrance of the church after securing rooms and cleaning up. Mercedes and Miguel left to see about a room while Antonio and Orovis walked to the small stream running alongside the church where they washed. Antonio took the opportunity to shave while at the stream. Three days had passed since he had last shaved and he was beginning to look like someone who did not much care for his appearance, and that was not him. Apparently Miguel had the same concern but for different reasons, he had a wife to think about. He too shaved.

They walked around the plaza for a while exchanging greetings with who they thought were the most welcoming group of people they had ever encountered. Everyone smiled and spoke to them. It seemed that there were no strangers in Toa Baja. This was a dramatic change from the Catalans in Barcelona, where one would be spoken to only after a proper introduction, and then only maybe.

They learned that there was not a bank in the town and that the magistrate's office would be closed until the next morning. The magistrate, who was appointed by the governor, was the official responsible for the collection of all taxes and fees paid to the government as well as the registration of all transactions such as real estate and other forms of properties. The government ensured that their taxes would be collected through the registration system controlled by the magistrate. Moreover, the magistrate was seen as the Queen's representative and as a consequence it would have been safe to presume, easy to dislike.

Towards the early evening they settled on the one an only outdoor café in the plaza. The owners had tried to imitate the Tapas bar atmosphere so commonly found in Spain. Don Pedro José Bermúdez was the owner and by coincidence, a Basque. He had been in Puerto Rico going on ten years having left Spain for as he said, reasons he rathered not discuss. "This place will get to you as it has to me, if you let it. Soon you will stop being Spaniards and will become Puerto Ricans. Boricuas as we like to call ourselves."

He offered a complimentary tray of assorted Tapas and asked if he could sit with them. Much to their surprise, not once did he ask about the old country. Nothing about Spain interested him. Instead he wanted to talk about their plans and to learn about ways in which he could help them. As he explained to them, there was not sufficient commerce to promote economic growth and he saw it as his role to promote it. It was not known if he was an educated man but he certainly spoke like one when he explained his plan to promote commerce between the valley of the Vegas, not through barter but through the use of currency. The challenge was to convince the local farmers to buy and to sell instead of just exchanging goods for services and other forms of barter. Don Pedro José's dream was to start the first bank on their side of the island. He explained his ideas about how capital accumulation would promote the kind of investment that would lead to the economic viability of the region. "Believe it or not, our magistrate is unlike the others. Ours understands that by facilitating commerce, tax receipts will grow. And if he gets to keep a little more for himself the Queen will not mind so long as she gets her's. The magistrate is on our side, I will guarantee that." As they listened to him, Miguel and Antonio could see the wisdom of his vision. The conversation lasted long into the evening. Three hours after Mercedes had gone to bed they decided to call it a night. By then they too had a vision and a plan. They would go to Vega Alta and create the corresponding commerce to Don Pedro José's in Toa Baja. They would contribute to the creation of the commerce on one side that would transact with the other, and through that exchange of goods and services an economy could form and grow.

Once again, Antonio and Orovis slept outdoors, but this time Orovis fell asleep long before Antonio, whose mind was churning ideas about how to form and execute a plan that would have a regional impact. The drawbacks were many. Mainly they did not know anyone and they did not know anything about commerce and even less about banks. Other than that, it could be done and it could be done by them. Of that he was certain. He thought it best to keep their intentions concealed from everyone for the time, until he and Miguel could think it through. All things in due course he thought.

Don Pedro José introduced them to Don Angel Rafael Mendoza, the magistrate of Toa Baja. He was just as he had been described. They were more impressed by what he did not do than by what he did. He did not ask Orovis to leave, instead he invited him to sit along with the others. The magistrate lacked the pomposity of most government functionaries. He was as unassuming a man as they had ever met in or out of a government office. In no way did he resemble Don Mauricio at the Port Authority. "Friends of Pedro José are friends of mine, and so think of me as your servant. Please do not underestimate my ability to help you. Forgive me if I lack in humility when I say that anything in this parts not known by me, it is not worth knowing. Are there any present needs that I may assist you with?"

They explained their intention to continue on to Vega Alta as soon as possible and that once there they would have a more clear definition of a plan. Further, they confirmed their intention to remain in the Vegas and establish themselves in some form of business that could add economic value to the region. At once the magistrate called for his secretary and requested that he prepare a letter of introduction for his counterpart in Vega Alta.

Along the way to Vega Alta, they passed beautiful land due south of the trail as they headed west. There were a few huts with small corrals around them which contained, chickens, pigs, goats and an occasional cow. Each house had a garden, and each garden grew different vegetables. As they looked at them, they understood how the barter system worked. And they also understood how difficult it would be to get the people to change from barter to commerce.

Orovis knew some of the farmers which he had not seen for quite some time. Asking them to stay on the trail and saying that he would catch up with them, he veered of to visit his friends. They could hear shouts of joy as the farmers recognized Orovis, and not wanting to interrupt their celebration the wagon continued on the trail but at a slower pace so as to not get too far from him. As he returned to the wagon, Orovis seemed lost in thought. Apparently, what he had seen during his brief visit had given him cause for concern.

Sensing that something troubled him Mercedes said, "Something is wrong with your friends Orovis, can you tell me what it is. We may be able to help them." Orovis explained that the farmers were suffering hunger because while they grew enough to eat and trade, they were still abjectly poor because they were no better off from one day to the next in their desire to improve their lives. Since they had no currency and the merchants in Vega Alta would not accept payment in tomatoes or corn, they had no way to buy materials for their houses or to add barns, and storage bins, or to buy tools. As they listened to every single word Orovis said, Miguel and Antonio understood that he was confirming Don Pedro José's vision about commerce between villages and a bank.

Upon arriving in Vega Alta, they recognized an identical image of Toa Baja, only bigger in every way. It had a bigger, plaza, a bigger church, many more businesses and more people. They were directed to the Magistrate's office, who received them without delay. The letter of introduction was handed to him by his secretary and soon after, Don Roberto Guardiola Martinez, stepped out to greet them with great warmth and cordiality. He was not surprised at their youth because it was the young who were coming to the region seeking opportunity and fortune. The older people had already made their fortunes in other islands. Puerto Rico represented the last frontier for ambitious Spanish youth trying to find their own way through their own efforts. Don Roberto understood that his role was to act as a resource through which business and commerce could grow. This was also the process through which his and the Queen's coffers would grow, in that order. "My secretary will see to your lodging arrangements and tonight you will all dine at my house. Please, it will be a pleasure to entertain visitors from the old country, so few of our compatriots venture this far inland."

After settling in their rooms, they met in front of the church of the Immaculate Conception at the end of the plaza. They had some time until the Magistrate's carriage would call for them. Orovis had declined the invitation owing to his interest in locating people he had not seen since the last time he had passed through Vega Alta. From his perspective he told Miguel, not much had changed, the rich were still rich and the poor were still poor, but there were more of them. Miguel asked him to try to learn what if anything could be done for these people to the benefit of all. "Just find out what they really need. Not what they want, but what they need."

Innately, Miguel understood the problem. As they had passed the small farms with very small shacks, he knew that people whose main concern is their next meal, had no energy left for planning or thinking about the future. In some yards, he saw more children than chickens. Evidence of the Catholic influence on the population. It is inherent in farmers to have large families since they need the hands to work the farm, assuming they have a farm to work. For the people he saw, the parcels were too small to support a large family. He had been thinking about their circumstances and how to create a business that would optimize the productivity of the farms and improve the lives of the farmers. The first problem would be to create a market to consume the products grown in the farms. Moreover, once a market was created it needed to be sustained at a rate through which demand would slightly outstrip supply. that would ensure that the operation would be profitable. The next problem and one more easily solved would be the creation of a distribution system. He had seen the distribution point at Bayamon and was unimpressed by the absence of urgency in joining the consumer with their goods. Miguel reasoned that accelerating the speed of delivery could accelerate the rate of consumption which would in turn promote the growth of the market. He had much to think about and was regretting having to attend the dinner that evening because he wanted to concentrate in the development of his ideas.

They arrived at the magistrate's house dressed in their suits. Mercedes wore the dress she had worn the morning of her escape from Cuba. Upon entering pass the gates to the house, they were greeted by Mayor of Vega Alta, Don Francisco Vega, and his wife. After the introductions they sat and were served a blend of rum and pineapple juice which they found exceedingly refreshing. The mayor showed great interest in finding out all that he could about these young people. He asked about their origins, how they came to be there, and why. In particular he was curious why they had selected Puerto Rico when there were several bigger islands along the way. With a smile, Antonio explained that he and Miguel had been raised in a convent and when it became evident that they were ill suited for the priesthood, they were sent into the world to do good, and that was their purpose. "Mercedes," he explained, "Is our conscience. She keeps us in the straight and narrow."

"If that is your purpose we celebrate your arrival and let us hope that your stay is a long one. These are uncertain times for all of us. The rumors of war are getting louder each day to the level that we now believe that it is no longer if but when it comes. The Americans are making it clear that they want Spain's possessions and sooner or later will take them. It is what we call Yankee imperialism. We are fortunate that Spain maintains a very small garrison in the island and because of that we do not believe there will be any major battles for or in Puerto Rico. The same is not true of Cuba. There will be serious fighting there and in the end, Spain will lose. It will lose because resupplying an army from three thousand miles is a great deal more difficult than from ninety miles. And so that logistical advantage goes to the Americans. Personally, it is no concern of mine. I am third generation Boricua. My family came here with our founder Don Francisco de los Olivos."

"Dinner is served," said Doña Blanca, the magistrate's wife. As they sat around the table, enjoying a meal of several courses, Mercedes wondered about how long would it be before they could entertain visitors in the same manner. She was more appreciative than envious of her hosts because it was not too long ago that she and her family had hosted similar events in Spain and in Cuba. "Sooner or later," she thought. The evening concluded with an agreement to meet the next morning at the magistrate's office to discuss their plans.

CHAPTER 16

"Mules are the answer." Antonio suggested mules after listening to Miguel's idea about a supply wagon to and from San Juan by way of Bayamon. He thought that mules would be better than oxen for pulling the wagons. Miguel followed with, "What if we could hitch two or more wagons per mule team. That way we could deliver more quantity to and from Vega Alta. Part of the load we could distribute in Bayamon and the rest we could bring all the way here."

"Why don't we try to find a partner in San Juan to open a farmers' market. Through the market we could move a number of products to be grown by the farmers. Initially we could supply them twice a week as crops come in, and as we determine the best rotation between planting and harvesting, we could have something to sell every week." Miguel also thought that instead of buying wagons initially, they could rent them by the day from the livery stable which had several not in use the day they bought their wagon. The mules they would own because that way they would ensure they would be well cared for and fed. They decided to buy two teams of four mules each. This would allow a team to rest and a team to work. Since they remembered the difficulty in pulling their own wagon up the hill before they reached Toa Baja, they would have the fresh team of mules meet the wagons before the climb. That way the fresh mules would do the heavy pulling while the tired mules could rest. This conversation lasted until four in the morning at which time Miguel decided to turn in. Antonio had accepted the room this time because it had been arranged by the magistrate and because he needed a place to wash before changing into his suit. He could not remember the last time he had slept in a bed. Surprisingly, it did not take him long to adjust.

At seven in the morning Mercedes was still asleep but the men were drinking their first cup of coffee at the kitchen of the guest house. Orovis was already waiting for them in the yard next to the wagon where he had slept. He joined them for breakfast and talked about the number of friends that he had been able to find. It seemed that everyone had the same difficulty in breaking the cycle of poverty and hunger. This confirmed Miguel's understanding of a structural problem. Poverty was endemic to the region because of the collective inefficiencies as result of the absence of a system that would promote supply and demand.

They understood that the mountain that separated Vega Alta from the towns to the west and the ports of San Juan represented the same barrier to market that would serve as the catalyst to their business. "If it was easy someone would have done it by now. By the time we have proven the concept we will have gained control of supply, demand and distribution," said Antonio. The first challenge was to control the farmers so that they could control production. To that end they would meet with the magistrate about determining fair market value for the property they wanted. While they had no farming experience, they could tell rich soil when they saw it, and they had seen it between Toa Baja and Vega Alta.

By morning Miguel had completed his list of action items. He had been extremely careful to only include those items that were actionable by them, within their timeframe and their resources. Those that were not yet actionable, such as building a hard surface road or a bridge over the Plata River would have to wait their turn to be placed on the list. First on the list was the need to secure the properties. He thought that by using the current occupants of the farms as their labor force, they would have the best of all worlds. The farmers could have the income they had not been able to realize from their one acre plots that had been allotted to them through the land grant program, and they would have hard working people who would appreciate the opportunity to leave poverty behind while retaining their land. Miguel and Antonio would control the land adjacent to the farmers, who could do as they wished with their acres since they would no longer be needed for their survival. Miguel also thought about the importance of having capital flow through the regional economy. It was essential that people had money to spend, and that would be guaranteed since it was them who would provide the money through wages paid. Moreover, in addition to the decent wages they intended to pay the farmers, they hoped there would be sufficient earnings to pay bonuses either at Christmas or through regular profit sharing disbursements. At a minimum, the farmers could live their lives beyond the constraints that hunger imposes on the poor.

They spent their first Saturday in Vega Alta meeting merchants and people in general, getting the feel of the place, gaining an understanding of how things worked through the flow of commerce. Everywhere they stopped they were well received and made to feel welcome. The word was out through the town that these were young people who had plans for Vega Alta, and since that happened so seldom, their presence was a novelty. Without revealing their intentions, they wanted to learn the things they did not yet know about how commerce was served by transportation and of the merchants' views of the system's shortcomings. As best they could tell, there were exactly twenty farmers who each owned one acre of land and the structure standing on it.

The land had been granted by the governor of Puerto Rico, Sabas Marin Gonzalez, in an effort to attract people to the island in general and to the valley of the Vegas specifically. The same program was put into effect in other regions with the same results. It was clear that someone at one time formed the right vision for how to attract population, but it seemed they had failed in the execution, because once there, the farmers were pretty well abandoned by the authorities. Left to their own devices and owing to their ignorance about managing and growing a farm, they were no better off in Puerto Rico than they had been when they left their original homes. At home, they had been for the most part abandoned by their families who were struggling to feed themselves and simply sent away those who were a burden, to be someone else's concern. And that someone else, mainly the authorities, did not really care.

By this time Mercedes, Miguel and Antonio had earned Orovi's respect and trust. By their kindness towards him and their conduct towards others he had appreciated that these Spanish were not like the ones he had met before. Keeping the discussion short on details they explained their intentions to him in a way that was clear that their plan would benefit his friends. They also made it clear to him that their ultimate intention was to create wealth, but that they would do good for others while they did well for themselves. Orovis, they knew would be important to their plan because of his history with the farmers. He had lived with them, and as them he had known hunger and endless toil for little rewards beyond the day's food supply. With his help they planned to assemble the farmers in small groups or individually to hear their proposal. They could have just offered them jobs, but they wanted them involved and as committed as them. As the day ended they had completed as much as they had hoped to and checked off some of the items from their list.

Sunday, they attended the ten o'clock mass which was the only mass offered at the church of the Immaculate Conception. The church was large by any standards, but was enormous relative to the number of parishioners in it. Apparently, someone must have thought that Vega Alta would one day be a large population center, and built the church based on those expectations. This church was under the direction of the Diocese of San Juan which was controlled by the bishop. Evidenced by the youthful appearance of the priest conducting the mass, serving this church was young man's work.

Either that or this was the place where they sent the priests who had in some way displeased the bishop. He did not look much older than Antonio or much different for that matter. He was a strong looking man whose body indicated that when it came to working hard he was up to any task.

Father Reynaldo Monroig had been sent to Puerto Rico directly from the seminary which he had attended in Santo Domingo. His family had moved to that island from Spain while he was still a young child, and by the time of his fourteenth birthday he started feeling the attraction to the church and hearing the call to the service of God. Starting at the age of ten he had served four years assisting in the masses and at the same time studying the life of a priest. He particularly liked the simplicity that a priest's austere life offered.

He could have been anything he had wanted to be. He had the brains to have chosen any profession and he would have excelled in it. He had the physical strength to have been a soldier and could have been a general. He had the character to have been an outstanding leader in government. He had the charm to have conquered any girl's heart had he set his sights on her. Many were the girls who had dreamt about a future with Reynaldo as his wife, but that was not to be.

Much to the dismay of his mother, everything about the church appealed to him and drew him closer to the priesthood. He was not the only child in his family, but he was the only son. His mother, like all good catholic mothers would have been glad to give a son to the church, but her only son was too much to ask of her. She prayed and pleaded with God to not take her only son, even offered to trade two daughters going into the convent in exchange for her son staying out of the priesthood. All to no avail. Reynaldo finally convinced her that he could not be talked out of it. From that day on she donned a black dress and swore to wear it as long as she lived.

After the mass, the priest approached Antonio, Miguel and Mercedes and invited them to lunch. He asked that they wait until he could see the sexton to ask him to close the church. Since he had been raised on a Caribbean island, whatever trace of a Spaniard's Spanish accent he may have once had, was long replaced by the Quisqueya influence. As he explained to them, just like Boriquen was named Puerto Rico, the real name for the island of Santo Domingo was Quisqueya, its Indian name. Following the introductions he said, "You don't look very much like the brothers that you say you are."

"That's because we are brothers by choice," Antonio explained. "And that is the best kind," replied the priest.

He insisted that they be his guests for lunch but not at his home. Since the church could not afford a parish home, he was forced to live with one of the local families. "I insist that you all be my guest, there is a small place one block north of the church that serves the best food anywhere in the island."

Orovis had left them at the entrance, explaining that he had sworn to never enter another church since he last been in one on the day he whipped the priest. It did not matter that this church was different and so may have been the priest. "Churches are churches to me, and the priests are all the same."

Instead he said he intended to spend the day visiting his friends up and down the valley and planned to discuss their plan with the few who had any influence over the others. "You will not see any of them in this church either. They will not come. For reasons different than mine, but they will not come."

When they sat for lunch, several of the patrons approached to pay their respects and have their children blessed. Father Reynaldo explained that these were all town's people and that it troubled him that the people in the outlying farms never attended. He had been trying for some time to build a chapel near the farmers so that he could minister to them on Sundays and on the other days as needed. Instead of them coming to him, he would go to them. The problem was that the church did not have enough money and the diocese was not contributing anything to the church. On the contrary, he was supposed to send them money and since he hadn't they were unhappy with him. So unhappy were they with him that he had not been able to celebrate the sacrament of confirmation because that required a bishop, and he would not visit Vega Alta until they could make the contribution expected of them.

The owner's wife approached with a plate of thinly sliced fried plantain in the center of the dish. Before placing the plate on the table she asked and received the priest's blessing. Around the outer edge of the plate were slices of blood sausage in a veranda shape. In between the slices of blood sausage the cook had inserted very thinly sliced bananas fried to a crisp. Mercedes, was the first one to reach saying, "Finally, familiar food."

As their lunch progressed they told the story of how they had come to be married, first exchanging vows in the confessionary followed by the wedding at sea on the way to Puerto Rico. "Although it was a sacrilege" the priest said smiling, "I can't keep from laughing. I can just imagine what would have happened if another person had come in and confessed to you, Miguel. How would you have kept yourself from laughing once you heard what comes out of people's mouths? Believe me, you have no idea about the things that people confess to. My oath keeps me from sharing any of it with you, but take my word for it." Further he told them that he would be honored to marry them in the eyes of God whenever they were ready. He also expressed his wish that they would remain in Vega Alta because the town needed young smart people and he could see they were both.

Antonio and Miguel exchanged a look that said they were both in agreement about discussing their plans with the priest. As Miguel explained their ideas, he first focused on what he had perceived to be the needs of the people they had seen, both on the east and west side of the mountains. Next they explained how their business would benefit all, and would make them money. Their main concern was getting people to trust them, and that they knew would not be easy. "Unfortunately, I can not help you there because they do not trust me either. But I can help you by finding you an agronomist. Unless you have farmed for a long time in the tropics, you will need an agronomist. One of the brothers from my order was educated in agronomy before entering the priesthood. He and I are very good friends, and I know he would love being involved in a project such as yours. Next, I can help you with the Mayor and the magistrate. I can promise that you will have their complete cooperation. I know how to approach them. We need to make certain their vanity and greed is satisfied. If they understand that they will make more money with you than without you, they will be happy to help. I just want one thing in exchange for my help. You gentlemen will build me a chapel before the end of two years after we start." The "we" comment caught their attention and before they could reply, the priest called for another carafe of wine saying, "This calls for a celebration and of course the wine is on you."

That evening they met with Orovis after he returned from spending the day with his friends in the farms. It seemed they were all dejected and feeling hopeless about their future. Most felt betrayed by the government that failed to follow through with their promises of support. The loans promised were never made. The seeds for planting were not made available since they did not have the money to pay for them. Not one of the promises made by the governor was kept. Protesting would not only have gained them nothing, but it would have certainly caused them to be evicted from their parcels. "Not one of them looked healthy," reported Orovis. He told them that since there was not enough food in quantity and variety, the children were malnourished and as a result could not contribute much to the farm's demanding work. Difficult though it was for them to admit, the farmers were not unhappy that so many of their children were dying early because there would not have been enough food to feed them all, had more survived. Orovis made the comment, repeating what one of the farmers had said upon looking at a flock of birds, the farmer said, "It seems that only Jacanas grow here," Making reference to the large footed bird that populated the region. "Jacanas and children are the only things that are produced in this land, and we don't have enough to feed either," said another farmer.

Hearing this report, touched Mercedes' heart deeply. Feeling somewhat uncomfortable that the life she was learning about was so remote from what hers had been. How could she had been so blind, she asked of herself. She felt angry that her wealthy country allowed so few to live so well why so many lived in misery. She felt even more anger that these circumstances may have been before her eyes all her life and she like many of her class simply chose to ignore them. The knowledge that she was gaining was adding to her resolve to do well by these people and to support her husband in every way that was needed. Orovis' report further confirmed the viability of their vision, both to build wealth and to help people in a desperate situation to a better life, but not necessarily in that order. The execution of their plan demanded speed and some secrecy, lest their intentions be revealed causing the price of the land to rise. Misdirection, they believed was the best course to follow. Reveal as little as possible to only those who needed to know. The magistrate was intrigued by their interest to purchase the hundreds of acres of unused land between the base of the mountain near Toa Baja and the beginning of the parcels occupied by the tenant farmers. The land belonged to the government and he was more than happy to assist in the transaction. Since he had the power to conduct land sales transactions and because he would act as the agent on behalf of the government and that entitled him to a commission from the sale.

Once they had agreed on the price, the magistrate offered to secure the services of the surveyor who would create the plat to be incorporated with the title to the land. Miguel accepted the offer by the magistrate and suggested that in the interest of accuracy they too would provide a surveyor. As he explained, Miguel would pay for the services of the second surveyor and since the added cost would be of no consequence to the government, the magistrate would have no objections. The official was all the more enthusiastic about the venture when Miguel and Antonio told him they would travel to San Juan the next day and would return the day after with the bank draft to cover the purchase and all related expenses. The next stop was at the church where they asked Father Reynaldo to help them secure three horses for the trip to San Juan, two for them and one for him. Mercedes would be staying behind to visit and meet the farmers with Orovis. "Why do you need me to go with you?," the priest asked. "Do you or do you not want that chapel?," responded Antonio.

On the way to San Juan, as they passed the farms they had first seen as they rode on the wagon to Vega Alta, they had a better appreciation of what they were seeing. Now they understood both the problem and the solution. Antonio had not yet shared his thoughts with Miguel, but he was firmly committed to building a school in their property. He wondered how difficult it would be to convince the parents to allow the children to attend, especially the girls. Hopefully it would be no more difficult than to get the authorities to cooperate maybe even contribute, he hoped. He had not forgotten that little or no effort had been made to teach him to read until he took it upon himself to learn. He thought about how to get the parents to want the children to have a life better than their own. He thought about using Mercedes, Orovis and Father Reynaldo in this effort.

They stopped in Toa Baja where they once again met with Don Pedro José Bermúdez, who himself was a surveyor. He immediately agreed to survey the land they planned to buy, and said that he would begin his survey the next morning. Before another word was spoken, he mentioned the issue of remuneration. He thought that at a minimum he would require a crew of four men, and planned to spend no less than five days on the property. This would not be easy or cheap, not just because of logistics but also because of the cost of labor. He recalled several unfortunate incidents and the fights that had ensued resulting from poor surveying. Miguel listened to it all before telling Don Pedro José that they already had a surveyor in Vega Alta who was also willing to start the next day and he did not require four days or four men. Aware that he had competition, Don Pedro responded by saying that out of consideration of their friendship he would complete the survey in no more than three days and that only two additional men were needed, and that he would cover all costs from his fees. "In that case we can afford to have two surveys. One from Vega Alta heading east and the other from Toa Baja heading west. No doubt that you will meet in the field and can resolve any variances between your maps. That way when we apply for the title we can have one consistent and accurate survey." Miguel went on to express his confidence in Don Pedro José's professionalism, and his certainty that his services would be excellent.

Miguel had not forgotten the value of making people feel more important than they really were. They arrived in San Juan too late to conduct their banking transaction. Instead they went directly to the diocese of San Juan which was housed at the Cathedral of Saint John the Baptist. This was the third cathedral built in the Caribbean Sea region. The first one having been built in Santo Domingo, where Diego, the son of Christopher Columbus was buried. The second one was built in Cuba as the regional economic power was shifting to that Island.

Since Father Reynaldo was persona non gratta at the Bishop's offices, he sent Antonio and Miguel with a note to be delivered to his friend Father Angel, the agronomist. As they entered the gates to the offices of the diocese they came upon a man dressed in working clothes, engaged in masonry work. The man's approach to laying mortar was akin to that of Michelangelo as he sculpted La Pieta. Every motion had a purpose and every stroke equally as important as the previous one. This man obviously saw his work as an art form rather than just manual labor. He had an artist's flare towards his work. He turned, and while standing on the ladder offered to help them. "We are looking for Father Angel, can you please direct us to him?," Miguel asked. The man answered them by saying, "Isn't providence wonderful? You are looking for Father Angel while I have been searching for an excuse to stop working. I am Angel Martinez the Father Angel that you are looking for, at your service," he said as he came down from the ladder and shook their hands after meticulously wiping each finger with a rag. After reading the note from his friend, he asked for a little time to clean up and instructed them to return to La Mallorquina and wait for him there.

Angel Martinez had been born in Puerto Rico and was the son of a very prominent and wealthy family whose origins dated back to the time when Juan Ponce de Leon had been the governor. Their money had been made in shipping and in agriculture. The original Martinez, whose name was Gallardo, had arrived in the Island with Ponce de Leon in the early fifteen hundreds with the rank of captain of artillery. Other than the Taino rebellion of 1511 there had not been much need for artillery. The subjugation and subsequent enslavement of the Taino population had taken very little time and other than the drowning of Diego Salcedo, as ordered by the chief Urayoán, there had been very few casualties suffered by the Spaniards. After the brief conflict, Gallardo Martinéz spent a great deal of time studying and understanding the strategic importance that the island's geography offered to those who were endowed with strategic thinking talents, and he was a strategic thinker. Soon after arriving in Puerto Rico, Ponce De Leon had ordered a topographical survey of the island, focused on recording the flora and the fauna, as well as collecting census information on the native population. This was of particular importance because it was critical to the safety of the invaders to know the numbers of males in the population. In particular, males of fighting age.

It was during the ninety days of the survey of the island that Gallardo Martinez began to think in terms of commerce more so than in terms of martial concerns. Halfway between what was the village of San Juan and what would soon be the village of Ponce, he studied the topography north and south of his location and reasoned that a blind man could see the opportunities. But it would have to be a smart blind man. And while he was not blind, he certainly was smart. Soon after completing his survey, he returned to San Juan and delivered his findings to Ponce De Leon, personally. His report focused exclusively on logistics, defensive positions, fields of fire for artillery positions and the like. Soon after his report had been received, and with great praise, he requested and received his discharge from the army of Spain. His request was granted on the basis that Gallardo was already in his thirties. At that age he was well advanced in years for the work of a captain of artillery and would soon become a liability to the fighting force. By this time, Ponce De Leon had begun to ponder the idea of going after a fountain of youth that he had heard about from the natives of the several islands that he had visited.

Once out of the military's control Gallardo Martinez moved to develop the ports of Ponce and San Juan. Knowing that commerce across the mountains would not be profitable for a long period of time, and for a number of reasons. He built a small fleet of cargo ships that sailed around the island joining north and south and in time east and west as more villages were built around the coast. Because of the favorable trade winds that constantly blew throughout the Caribbean Sea region, he reasoned that once he had the volume, his ships could sail day and night, moving his and other goods throughout the island and the region. Sugar cane is what he had in mind for his main crop and saw that shipping would be the only impediment to commerce. Until he could build his own sugar mill in Ponce, he would ship the cane to Santo Domingo, but the rum he could distill himself. The demand for sugar would be as great as rum, he thought correctly. The English were planning to harvest sugar from their possessions in the American colonies and he knew that Spain would need to compete as England's commercial equal.

Unlike Peru and Colombia, Puerto Rico had been a disappointment to Spain because of the absence of gold, copper and other minerals, but agriculture would prove to be the hidden treasure.

Many generations of Gallardo Martinez's descendants had followed and all had gone into the family business in one form or another. It was preordained that every Martinez male born into the family would enter the business after receiving their education in Spain. This is why Angel Martinez was sent to the University of Zaragoza. This institution, famous for its academic reputation and rigor, was also a Jesuit school. The entire faculty was composed of men committed to learning and promoting knowledge, and all of them were Jesuit priests. Angel was sent to the university to learn agronomy, a field in which he did excel and for which he was naturally gifted, however it was the Jesuit order that reached his heart. He liked the strength of character of its members. They were serious but not humorless. They were austere but not detached, and had a genuine love and affection for all the members of the order. As brothers in the faith they had formed the strongest of bonds. They were very physical men who loved to wrestle and fight with one another as a form of sport.

On several occasions Angel had enjoyed social interaction with females outside of his own family, and while he enjoyed being with them and appreciated their flirtations, the female attraction was not stronger than the call to the priesthood. Finally he wrote to his family that he would be entering the Jesuit seminary after completing his studies. Originally the announcement of his plans caused some consternation because he was the first in their family to enter the priesthood, but after serious consideration the father congratulated his son and offered his support to the future Bishop Martinez or Cardinal Martinez. These dreams of greatness within the catholic hierarchy were not Angel's who just wanted to be a priest.

On their return to meet Father Reynaldo at La Mallorquina, Antonio spotted a book store. At first he was stunned as if he had seen an apparition. Realizing that Antonio was no longer next to him, Miguel stopped to look back at him who was fixed on a store across the way from the cobble stones. Antonio was entering the small store as Miguel caught up to him. They both entered the shop that had few books on display but did have a sign that books could be ordered with a small deposit. Neither one of them found anything they wanted to read. Instead they ordered five books each. Their order could not have been more different in subjects. Miguel's books were all about agriculture, commerce, irrigation and water pumps. He did order two books that he thought Mercedes would enjoy. Teaching was one, and birthing was the other. Antonio's selections were about history, philosophy and a treatise on forms of governments.

As soon as he walked into La Mallorquina the most famous place for sweet rolls anywhere in the Island, if not in the Caribbean, both priests embraced with such fierceness that it was difficult to tell if they were enemies or friends. "You show either great courage or great insanity by showing yourself on this side of the mountain or anywhere near the Bishop. That is why I know this is going to be an interesting and important meeting. As you know things seldom are both. The problem with human beings is that we rarely can tell the difference between the important or the merely interesting. And by the time we can tell the difference it is usually too late to recover the time wasted on the interesting thinking that it was important. But enough of my cynical philosophy, tell me why are you here," said Father Angel.

"I will let them tell you" said Father Reynaldo after updating him on the relationship he was forming with Miguel, Mercedes and Antonio. Over the following hours they discussed their vision and plans for both sides of the mountain, answering many questions from both priests who shared in their vision with greater enthusiasm than their own if such a thing were possible. Father Angel not only liked the plan, but demanded, more than asked to be allowed to be a part of it. His contribution would be to work on the organizing of the farmers' market in the expectation of significantly great volumes of goods and products that would be consumed in the San Juan region, or possibly sold to the ships for their own stores or for export to other islands. After all he came from a family who had started the business in the region, but only servicing the coastal villages, this new plan sought to develop the resources from within the island.

Father Angel believed that competition was the force that propelled markets and economic growth. When he had been sent to the University of Zaragoza to study agronomy, he had also studied economics starting with the Romans in the sixth century. Because of his studies and his own observations he knew that civilization would advance only through commerce, and Christianity would be the beneficiary. "Well fed souls," he said, "are faithful Catholics."

Like Miguel, Father Angel was a firm believer of detailed planning and if such a thing were possible, the Priest was more focused on details than Miguel. Once satisfied that they had discussed all considerations more than once, they agreed to meet at noon after concluding their transaction at the bank. Only then did they realize that the restaurant was closed and that the staff was just waiting for them to leave so they could clean their table and close up. They would have complained, but who would ask two priests to leave their establishment, especially if one of them was Father Angel Martinez. Offering their sincere apologies, they all left La Mallorquina.

Still, the only place where they knew to rent a room was at La Asucena. This was not their preferred choice but it would have to do. Remembering the impression they had made on the owner the first time they had slept there, they thought it would be best for Father Reynaldo to secure the room, while the rest of them remained out of sight. They left their horses at the livery stable where they had originally purchased their horse Esperanza, and the wagon. All three slept in the same room that night. They insisted that the priest should take the bed while they slept on the floor. In the early morning hour all three entered the small dining room, off to the side of the kitchen where they proceeded to slice some of the cheese to eat with their bread and coffee. They hoped that by leaving early they would avoid an encounter with the owner with whom they had the confrontation before, but it was not to be. She approached the table explaining that breakfast was served only to the guests and that they would have to pay for theirs. The priest explained that they had all slept in the one room and were therefore entitled to the breakfast. She protested calling their conduct outrageous and saying they should have been ashamed of themselves. "No madam," said the priest as they stood to leave, "It is you who shame yourself."

"Good morning I am Elias Elizondo, the assistant manager, how may I be of service to you," said the man as he shook hands with all three. In contrast to the first manager that had received them at the Banco Popular on their previous visit, this one had a personality, and seemed to mean it when offering assistance. Antonio presented the bank draft previously issued to them during their visit. Seeing the note, the banker said, "Oh yes, I have heard about you, you were here with the Taino gentleman. Is he not with you? I would have loved to have met him. He is one of a dying breed. I hope that he will be with you the next time you visit us. I have always regretted our conduct towards his people and hope that we can do something for the few that survive."

"How would you like this?," the manager asked. Antonio explained that they wanted a bank draft in an amount sufficient to cover the purchase of their land plus other expenses, and the balance on another draft. Just like the previous visit, the manager recommended they open an account with the bank which was safer and would earn them some interest income while their money was not being used. Unlike the last time, they decided to receive another bank draft for half of their balance, the remaining balance they would use to open the account. They also withdrew additional funds to be used in the purchase of animals, materials and equipment when they returned to Vega Alta.

They later met with Father Angel, at the same bar where they had dined their first evening in Puerto Rico. The priest had invested considerable thought in their plan and had many suggestions about what to grow in their land. He believed that a combination of permanent and rotating crops would provide a rich variety of produce that would allow them to have something to sell all year long. His studies in agronomy had taught him that allowing a portion of their land to go unplanted would sustain the viability of the soil. The land to go unplanted would rotate from one year to the next and that way the soil could have the time to regenerate its nutrients. His plan suggested that coffee and breadfruit trees would be their permanent crops. Pineapples and corn would be the rotating crops. Planting legumes would also help because they gave more nutrients than they consumed. He had a world map that showed that Puerto Rico shared the same latitude as Africa's most fertile region for pineapples. More specifically he believed that the loose soil found in the Vegas regions would be perfect for what they planned to grow. He also knew that the coffee grown in Puerto Rico was acquiring some fame. They were just not producing enough to generate the volume of income to sustain it as an industry.

Lastly he said, "And I am going with you. I will not miss this for all the gold in the world. I am either getting permission because I will convince the Bishop that Father Reynaldo needs help in growing his church or I will anger him to the point that he will exile me to Vega Alta. Either way, I am going with you after I set up the farmers market and the distribution agreements at the docks."

They spent the evening in Bayamon thinking that it would be much too late to do any good in Toa Baja. Their time, they thought, would be better spent in Bayamon talking with merchants and building the relationships they knew were needed as their plans evolved. The merchants' complaints were much the same as the ones they had heard in Vega Alta. There was not much merchandise and what little was there took too long to replenish. Their customers would place their orders and wait from one week to the next to see if their goods had arrived. Since the merchants had no influence over the distribution, they were at the mercy of the inefficiencies inherent in the slow system. All of this served to slow the rate of commerce and to reduce the flow of products and cash turnover between producers, suppliers and consumers. Miguel wondered out loud, why if the need was so obvious to them, why had no one seen and acted on the opportunity. "Someone always has to be first," said the priest.

Instead of stopping in Toa Baja they decided to look for Don Pedro José on the property being surveyed. He was fully engaged in the project. They knew that he knew that he had competition and he was not going to allow the other surveyor to out perform him. Expressing both his surprise and pleasure to see them, he invited them to dismount and share his water. He ordered one of his men to take the horses to the creek for watering. They walked towards a table made out of two boards laid across sawhorses and began to describe his progress and to discuss the attributes that he saw in the land. He explained that the topography was such that flooding would not ever be a concern, because the land sloped slightly upwards and away from the water. The amount of rain required to flood their property would have to be of biblical proportions. As Miguel looked at the map, he began to form the plan for building an irrigation system that would flow anywhere that was needed by the crops. The surveyor went on to explain how the position of the land relative to the mountains would allow them to sustain crops requiring a great deal of sun and those not requiring as much. He showed them how his map traced the movement of the sun at different times of the day. They appreciated the importance of this information and expressed their satisfaction with his work. This surveyor knew his craft.

Don Pedro José's crew had yet to meet with the surveying crew coming from Vega Alta. No doubt they thought, as they had expected, competition promotes excellence and one crew was as diligent as the other. As a result of that diligence they expected the surveys to have marginal variances, if any, and the filing of the deed application to be processed, unimpeded. After all they had the support of the government of both towns and the services of supremely competent surveyors. These were lessons that they would put to good use in their future business developments. Hire the best, pay them a fair wage and allow them to deliver their personal best by among other things not interfering with them or their work.

Mercedes met them in Vega Alta filled with excitement and news about her visit with the farmers. "We need a small dairy," were the first words out of her mouth after kissing her husband and hugging Antonio and the priest. She went on to explain that the milk would help the children with their malnourishment and that the children could help with the milking of the cows. She also talked about how she could organize the women to churn butter and make cheese, all of it to be consumed by the families and the surplus to be sold to the local towns. In addition, there was the value of the amount of fertilizer that the cows would generate. They listened to her ideas more focused on her commitment to her plan than to its merits, because if there was one thing they knew about Mercedes for certain, it was that if she was committed to the idea she would see it through its successful execution. "I'll add it to the list," was all Miguel had to say.

CHAPTER 17

"La Jacana is the name," they told Mercedes as they walked out of the municipal government's office after completing the purchase of their land. Their property extended to six hundred and eighty seven acres. That afternoon they bought three horses and had them stabled with the mayor who thus far had proven himself true to his word and had made certain that all potential problems or errors that could be averted, were. He went so far as to offer to guarantee any loans they needed to propel their business ventures as fast as it could progress. That was a generous offer which they declined, but it gave them the impression that everyone with any influence was committed to improving things in the valley of the Vegas. Maybe they thought it was because they were becoming more Puerto Rican and less Spaniards. And that was the reason why when asked if they wished to name their property, without thought or consultation, Antonio selected the name La Jacana. As he said the name, he looked at Miguel and with a smile on his face, he said, "It sounds Boricua, just like us." Now that they were owners of the land they proceeded with even greater speed in putting other pieces of the plan in place. This included animals, equipment, seeds, feed and people. At this moment they trusted that those things beyond their control were being handled as planned. Large among their concerns was the farmers' market. Without it, the distribution channels for their products would be severely limited. Timing, they knew would be crucial. It would not do to have the market before products were available, or to have products for which there was no market.

As he said he would, in a very short time Father Angel had managed to have the bishop bless his request for reassignment to the church in Vega Alta. In obtaining the bishop's blessing he had appealed to both the good and the bad in the man's nature. He convinced the bishop that with his knowledge and experience in all things agrarian, the Catholic church would accrue some of the credit for helping to grow the economy of the region, and through that process create the source of funds that would land in the church's coffers.

The bishop, on his own, reasoned that the success of Father Angel in the La Jacana project would clearly demonstrate Father Reynaldo's incompetence and thus facilitate his removal. Moreover, it had not escaped the bishop that lending the name of a descendant of Gallardo Martinez to the development of the church in Vega Alta, with all the prestige that came with it would draw him all the closer to that distinguished family. He thought about the importance of having the family's support not only in Puerto Rico, and Santo Domingo but in Spain where the political power of the Catholic church rested, next to Rome. Beyond the certainty of death and taxes, the bishop knew that politics was as real to the church as was the holly trinity. The Father, the Son and the Holy Ghost he knew would be the closer to him, were he to be appointed to the College of Cardinals. He was already dreaming of his red vestments, as he pretended to listen and visualize the picture of greatness being painted before his eyes by Father Angel. The Father could not believe that it would have been possible, but the bishop's sense of urgency about assuming his priestly duties in Vega Alta was greater that his own. "Please be ready to depart within a week, the letter of appointment will be in your hands before you retire this evening. I want to make it clear that Father Reynaldo is to assist you and that you are his superior." It bothered Father Angel that he had acted so deviously to achieve his end but not enough to keep him from smiling after he left the bishop's office.

Father Angel had already lined up the people who would build and manage the farmers' market in San Juan. With his family's connections and influence it had been as easy as he had envisioned. Although he tried not to play on his family's powerful name, he did whenever he thought it was in the service of God. And this was one of those occasions. He first called on his cousin Juan José Martinez with whom he had formed brotherly bonds since childhood. They had grown up together and had remained close through the years. Juan José and Angel Martinez were sent to study at the same university in Spain at the same time. One came back well educated in agronomy the other returned well versed in wine women and song. Much to the family's surprise the roles had been reversed since they had every reason to believe that it would have been Angel who would have given in to a life of license, and not Juan José. It mattered not to the cousins who had done what or failed to meet the family's expectations, their love for one another could not be affected by family or anyone else. One had always been there for the other and nothing would change that.

Juan José was many things but not a dilettante, and he certainly was not lazy. He was the kind of man who would succeed at his task so long as the task agreed with him. The building of the farmers' market was something that took hold of him even before Angel had finished explaining it. His vision had grander scale than the one his cousin was describing. Not forgetting that his family controlled most of the small trade shipping in the region, he began to formulate a plan that when linked to La Jacana's vision would continue to strengthen his family's position in such a way that he hoped would cause them to cease in their never ending efforts to marry him off to someone in whom he had no interest. Lack of interest in women was not the issue, because he had a great deal of interest in a great number of women. It was in the marrying part that his interest lacked enthusiasm. He, more than anyone was surprised that good families were interested in marrying their daughters to someone like him. Unlike most names that circulated through the rumor mill, his misdeeds were seldom overstated. But also unlike most men who enjoyed or suffered from the same reputation he neither confirmed nor denied the rumors which lent an aura of mystery to his persona and made him all the more desirable to the women he met.

Orovis too had been busy, speaking to his friends about these new Spanish people with whom he had been traveling. He believed that all of the farmers would gladly sign up to work at La Jacana. All things considered, there were no better alternatives available to them anywhere. In spite of his assurances that they would all sign on, Antonio and Miguel were determined to sit with every one of them, one by one, and explain their plans and discuss what they could expect from the brothers. By this time, everyone had come to believe that they were brothers in every way. Among others, the principal purpose of the individual meetings was to communicate to the farmers the importance of their contribution to the development of the farm. They remembered that not once in all the years at the docks in Barcelona, not once had anyone in a position of authority had spoken directly to any of the men who worked there. If it had not been for the success achieved by Antonio and Miguel, they too would have been ignored by Don Mauricio and others at the port authority.

The brothers knew that there were a few elements in their venture that they could not control effectively. The weather was beyond their control as was the possibility of war between Spain and the Americans. They believed that no resource would be more important to their venture than the people upon who they relied to work and work hard. Better to invest one's energies on the things that can be if not controlled at least influenced. Further, they knew human nature and believed that these people who for so long had been ignored if not abandoned, would respond to the appeal for their help, especially when they understood how all could profit from their individual and collective labor. Antonio committed to them that they could expect to see him in the fields when they arrived at work and could expect him to be the last to leave the fields at the end of the day. Not because he would be their overseer, but because he needed to learn everything that they could teach him.

He also pledged to them that at La Jacana they could expect a culture of respect for one another, and after having said that, he advised them of what would come to be the first rule ever imposed at La Jacana and that was the rule of no raised voices in anger. He and Miguel had witnessed plenty of yelling and exchanging of insults between men and had seen the results, all of them negative. "You will know that I am angry because I will speak more slowly and more deliberately than usual, and on those occasions when anger gets the best of me, only you and I will know it." After he spoke, Antonio asked them to draw closer and served them all two ounces of rum which they had obtained from Father Reynaldo who did not tell them where he had obtained it. For all they cared, the priest was making his own rum.

Slowly and hesitantly at first, Juan Escobar spoke. His question had to do with the wages they could expect and in what form they would be paid. Since they had arrived in Puerto Rico no money had passed through their hands. That was one of the reasons why their lives could not get better. All they did was to barter with people who were in no better condition and as a consequence, their lives never improved for any of them. Francisco Ferré spoke next and asked about how they would sustain themselves during the time the first crops were planted and the time they were harvested. He was concerned since they would not be working their individual acres there would not be any kind of production, of anything.

Miguel stepped in and explained that everyone would receive a living wage which they could expect would grow as the farm grew. Pineapples and corn would come first because they had the shortest time from planting to market. These crops he explained would sustain them all until the Coffee and Breadfruit trees could produce enough to become self sustaining. In the meantime, they had enough funds to sustain the operation for two years until the farm could generate income. Not that everyone was interested, but he went on to explain the events that were taking place in San Juan as the farmers' market was being formed.

After much discussion about division of labor, they agreed that it would be best to breakdown into small work crews that would work in parallel to the end that no time was lost. They left it up to them to determine who the crew foremen would be. Because they did not know them as well as they eventually would, they themselves would be better at the selection process since they had been in Puerto Rico for a longer period of time. One crew would clear trees, another would clear rocks, another would plow and prepare the soil for planting corn and pineapples, the last crew would dig wells in places where they would eventually be needed. The first of these wells would be dug in a way that every two houses could share in the water. Miguel had been reading about water pumps and knew that if people did not have to walk to the creek to collect water and then walk it all the way back to their homes, the time and energy saved could be put to better use. He had been working on a design for dual distribution pumps. Two pumps connected by one pipe that collected water from the one well shared by two homes would provide a marked improvement on the quality of their lives. Water was life, especially for those who had to toil to collect it.

Guillermo Recondo stood outside waiting for the meeting to end and as Miguel walked out to the yard, Guillermo approached him. After paying his respects, he asked if they could talk for just a few minutes. Miguel asked him to wait by the small garden while he went to get Antonio, so that they could speak together. Guillermo had been one of the first farmers to have received his parcel of land. Both he and Magaly, his wife were in their mid-twenties but looked twice their age. Since arriving they had worked together in raising their farm and their children, failing at both. Their children had all died before reaching the age of three and with them died any hope they may have had for a better life. The bitterness that had set with them was far too strong to overwhelm any opportunity for happiness that may have been presented to them. They were spent in every possible way and while they had not yet left, they had already quit.

He offered to sell his acre and the small house in it for whatever they thought it was worth. Both Miguel and Antonio knew that Guillermo had not lived in his farm the required ten years minimum and as a result the acre was not his to sell. After explaining the conflict to Guillermo who was not aware of the covenant over his property rights, he sunk even lower in his desperation. Since the land was not his to sell, Miguel suggested that instead he should rent it to him. After all he and Mercedes needed a place to live until they could build their house, and riding every day to and from Vega Alta would be both impractical and wasteful. Miguel knew that Mercedes would welcome the opportunity to live with these people whom she had grown to appreciate in the short time she had been amongst them. Guillermo's disposition changed dramatically when Miguel explained that they would rent the place until sufficient time had passed and he could sell the land. At that time, Miguel would buy the acre and the house from Guillermo at the then fair market value. They agreed that by morning, Guillermo would receive the first year's rent and that once settled somewhere, and their address was known to Miguel, the annual rent would be sent to them in the form of a bank draft. "Where do you think you will go after here?," Miguel asked. "We will look for work in San Juan. My wife can work as a maid and I hope to find work in the docks." In the morning of the following day, when they met, in addition to the money promised, he gave Guillermo Father Angel's address and a note to take to him. The following afternoon, Mercedes and Miguel entered their new home. "It may not be much to others, but it is our home to us," said Mercedes.

Their little house was built on stilts and the dimensions were equal on all sides. Since it stood about four feet above the ground, air could flow freely underneath the house, and that helped in keeping the house more comfortable than if it had no clear space. Each wall was thirty feet in length and eight feet in height. The roof was built with boards across the beam which were tarred before laying the thatch over the boards. Every wall had two windows with boards that acted as shutters. These were fixed to the open holes when needed, since there were not window frames. The boards were pressed against the windows which they overlapped, and were secured by sliding four small metal bars into the corresponding holes. These should have been shudders but they would have been too expensive for the previous occupants especially since all they ever did was to trade and that did not generate money. Except for the thatched roof, the whole house was made of wood boards that were joined by tar and nails. The entrance had five wooden steps that rested on top of fairly flat stones which preceded the steps by twelve feet. This distance between the stones and the steps ensured that anyone entering the house could leave most of the dirt outside. This was greatly needed to keep the mud from entering the house. The house itself was spotless, indicating that while the farmers were very poor they were also very clean. Against one wall and in between two windows stood a wood burning stove with one large sheet of metal on top in which the pots were placed. The burning wood sat on top of large stones which served to augment the heat required for cooking. The temperature was controlled in zones by keeping the fire mostly in the center for food being cooked and moving pots to the side to keep it warm. Following the wall towards the entrance of the house was a small bed made out of boards of different shapes and sizes with a down mattress on top. They hung sheets to serve as walls and separate the bedroom from the rest of the house, and from Antonio who would sleep in his hammock which he hung from the rafters at night and removed when he awoke.

As she was wont to do Mercedes took charge immediately and determined that the first thing they needed was a bed, a set of drawers and a heavy curtain to separate the bedroom from the rest of the house. The sanitary facilities would require some work since the shack they used for a latrine looked ready to fall at any time and certainly would not have survived the coming hurricane season of which they had been warned by Orovis. She asked Miguel to have four chairs and a table made. And that would have had to do for the time being. Her next project was grander in scale and in importance. Seeing first hand how the farmers lived, she was bound and determined to do all that she could to help their wives improve their quality of life. Beginning with starting a school during the week that would serve as a chapel on Sundays. She was committed to being the first school teacher at La Jacana and wanted to be the first bride to be married in the chapel.

After supper that evening, she explained all her ideas and plans to her husband and Antonio. Both who knew better than to argue with Mercedes once her mind was set. Besides there was really nothing about her plans that they disagreed with. In fact their vision corresponded to her's, only they wanted faster execution. Miguel expressed his concern that Mercedes was taking on too much too fast. He pointed out that while she was well intentioned about the school she was not a trained teacher. Mercedes' response was to suggest that they would just have to find one. That was when Antonio said, "We do know a teacher, her name is Marisol." The smiles came to all three of their faces at the same time when they realized what a wonderful thing it would be to have Marisol Machado with them. "I will write to the convent tomorrow, and the next time we are in San Juan we will send the letter with a bank draft to cover her expenses." Miguel suggested that the letter should instruct her to respond only if she would not accept the invitation, and to include directions on how to reach Juan José Martinéz in San Juan, who would arrange for her to reach La Jacana.

The following months were a whirlwind of activities all filled with the excitement that a bright future brings to those who not so long before had been without hope. Children became healthier and as a consequence happier. The parents who were no longer overwhelmed with the concerns of survival could now live, for a change. Their energy spoke volumes about their confidence in the owners of La Jacana and although they referred to Miguel and Antonio with the formal "Don," and Mercedes as "Doña," they did so out of respect instead of the fear that authority causes on those who have always been looked down upon. Unlike any other rich people they had ever met, these were different. They had kept every promise made and in every way demonstrated a kind heart and a giving spirit. Upon arriving at a farmer's home, Mercedes, without fail would embrace the women, kiss the children and greet the men. The women after a while became comfortable with the sincerity of her warmth but took longer to get used to seeing her dressed in man's work clothes and boots.

Antonio was the first to work and the last to leave the fields at the end of the day. The flow of work and the sequence of tasks were carefully planned by Miguel, who made a new list each and every day before turning in for the night, ensuring that neither materiel nor efforts were wasted. While men waited for the clearing of the fields to begin plowing, they built stables or cared for the cows, the goats and the pigs that had been added to the farm.

After living at La Jacana for three months they arranged for a celebration with all the families, and invited Father Reynaldo to bless the gathering and to celebrate with them. The Father took the opportunity to baptize all the children who had not been baptized which was all but two of them. During the feast he reminded Miguel that he expected a chapel to be built as promised. "Sooner rather than later," responded Mercedes. Who explained that their plan was to build the school house which would also serve as the Chapel on Sundays. "While you are it, can you build a small room in the back so that we may have a place to sleep on those days that we stay too late or drink too much to return to Vega Alta?" Father Reynaldo asked. "All things in due course," said Miguel.

Antonio arrived at the celebration an hour after it had started. He had been detained removing a stubborn rock that would not yield to the force of two oxen and only gave after the team had been doubled. As he put his horse away, for the first time in his life he heard a form of singing the locals called 'LeLoLai.' There were many opinions as to where this music originated. Some believed that it had gypsy origins; others believed that it had been influenced by the melancholy of the Portuguese Fado blended with African and Caribbean music. Regardless of its origin it came from the heart of the one singing it. The singer was accompanied by a man playing a small guitar that he had made. Shaped exactly as a guitar, the cuatro as it was called, had only four strings instead of the six found in a classic guitar. Her voice was soft and mournful and as she sang about trials and tribulations, disappointments, frustrations, anxieties and broken hearts one would have sworn that it was her life's experiences she was revealing. LeLoLai music is absolutely improvisational and follows no particular rhythm or lyrics. The tempo of the music and the melody comes out of the singer's soul. And in this instance as she sang, Ana Maria Morales' voice cried out with sentiment that brought tears to her and to her audience. She sang as if the songs owned her, and used her as an instrument for the release of pain. The stories she told with her songs were ones that could have been told by anyone at the gathering if they could have sung like her. And since they didn't, they were pleased to hear their sentiments expressed so well, so mournfully. She sang about children lost, about feeling abandoned by God and lives so hopeless that they could not accommodate dreams however small.

Ana Maria continued with her lamentations but the tone turned for the better as she changed to parodies about the mayor, the governor and the queen. Her irreverence towards the authority figures was identical to that of people who had no allegiance to any land other than the one in which they stood. The humor of her songs became contagious as others joined in the improvisation and as it went around the group, one's end marked another one's start.

Antonio looked at Ana Maria trying to divine her origin. She was not a Spaniard, and she was not Taino, and she was not African. She was none of those races and yet she was all of those races. She was Puerto Rican. Her great-grandfather who was a Spaniard from the Canary Islands had married a Taino woman with whom he had fathered seven children. All of them were scattered over the island and throughout the Caribbean region. One of them, a daughter had married an African who had arrived in the island a slave and was eventually granted his freedom. These were Ana Maria's grandmother and grandfather. Her mother had a similar colorful racial mix in her background and as a result when asked about her ancestry she always said "I am pure Puerto Rican and proud of it." Ana Maria had the rich blood that all her ancestors had contributed and it showed in her.

She was the only member of her family who could read. Thanks to the missionaries who had lived in Toa Alta, a nearby village, and to her great determination, she had learned to read. Her father who believed that there was no good reason why a woman needed to learn to read, would punish her for her daring to go against his wishes with additional work. He finally acceded and allowed her to go to school twice a week but only after finishing her chores. Every morning she would rise early and after collecting the eggs from the hen house and milking the two cows her family owned, and the two additional cows her father kept for his brother, she would mount the mule and ride it bareback to the small room that served as the school, chapel and whatever other purpose the community needed. There the priests would feed her and the six boys in her class and teach them to read using the catechism and biblical stories.

Her father was not the only one trying to make it hard on her for wanting to learn to read, her fellow students made it worse. They resented that a girl was trying to be their equal, especially this girl, who was their better. Every day after school as she rode back to continue her work for the day, she would repeat the day's lessons and reading rules, and hoped that the day would come when she could own her own books. Now that she was comfortable reading everything that was given to her, and able to understand what she read, she found the materials the priests covered to be repetitious. From time to time the teachers would slip and make reference to the works of some philosopher or historian, and that would trigger her thirst for more knowledge. One morning she awoke to begin her day's work and prepare to go to school but noticed the mule was not where she always found it. Her Father had been waiting for her after the milking and told her that his brother would be using the mule for plowing during the coming two weeks and that she should give up on the idea of going to school. She said nothing. There was neither disappointment nor hurt, only resolve. For the rest of her time in school she ran to and from Toa Alta and never missed a day or was late. The only thing that changed was that she was hungrier when she arrived. Next her father increased her chores, but not her brothers'. He did this so that she would have less time for school, but she would not be deterred, and she found ways to do more in less time. Finally a truce was called in the contest of wills with her father since the school was closed and the priests moved to Arecibo where they had access to a larger population. The most important lesson she learned was that she was capable. She was capable of anything she set her mind to.

Antonio studied the young woman as the celebration continued. Mercedes took him by the arm and walked him in the singer's direction. Once near her, he noticed her high forehead, a smallish nose, the blackest eyes that had ever looked at him, and the prettiest smile he had ever seen in a woman. She was slightly taller than Mercedes and had large bones. When she looked at him he felt that she was not looking at him, but inside of him. "Anton, please meet Ana Maria Morales, she is from Espinosa near the mountain."

"Don Antonio needs no introduction, Doña Mercedes, I do not believe there is anyone between San Juan and Arecibo who has not heard about the Basque gentleman. I am your servant sir." Antonio knew not what to expect from the girl but enjoyed her spontaneity and candor, and her genuine warmth. Unlike most of the women he had met, this one looked right at him. The strength of her character was revealed to him as if she was on display for him to admire, and he did.

"Don Antonio, I believe that I heard you have books of your own. Is this true?" Antonio first wondered how she could have come by that information and realized that some of the women had helped Mercedes with the cleaning and readying of the house he shared with them. Further, he appreciated that they must have been the topic of conversation in many homes and places. This would not have been the case in Barcelona or Havana or even in San Juan where the population was large and the people's interests were consumed by many more subjects than newcomers. But the same was not true of the valley of the Vegas since the number of people who made their home there was small. The number of people who passed through there was large, but few stayed to call it their home.

"I am pleased that my books are of interest to you and I will be happy to share them with you, but they come with a price," he said with a wide grin, and waited for her reaction. It took a while for her to respond because she felt that she was in a conversation with a man of substance, and she had not met many of those in her eighteen years. After learning to read with the missionaries, she had hungered for knowledge and with her limited time she had tried to engage them in conversation about subjects other than biblical stories. She had read that passage in Luke, in the new testament when Jesus had been asked about taxes and he responded with; "give to Caesar that which is Caesar's and to God that which is God's." After reading that lesson, she asked the priest to speak to her about Caesar. The fact that he said very little increased her curiosity, but there was no way to quench her thirst for knowledge, without books.

"Name your price Don Antonio, but be careful of what you ask for, you may receive it," she said as she looked at him with challenging eyes. He responded by correcting himself and adding that he meant prices instead of price. He said that he expected a good conversation with her after she was through with whatever books, she borrowed. In more ways than one and not yet known to Antonio he was meeting his equal. Her hunger for knowledge was as great if not greater than his. She was driven by the frustration of feeling inept and incapable because of her perceived ignorance. She had been around poor farmers all of her life and had thought about why they never seemed to break the cycle of poverty, to rise above their station to a better life. Ignorance, she reasoned, was the curse that afflicted them all and she was determined to rise above it all through knowledge. "Your condition is acceptable to me. Will you do me the honor of selecting the first book for me."

Seasoned roasted pig was being served on the plates that were brought by the farmers. Since no one had more than the dishes that they used for their daily meals, everyone was expected to bring their own plates and utensils. Sometimes a family would bring only two plates and these would be shared with their children or someone else's. The unspoken rule amongst the men was that women would eat first, and the unspoken rule between all the women was that children were always served first. The pork was served with fried ripe bananas fried in butter and crispy pork rind which was cut from the pig's skin. The ears of the pig were regarded as a delicacy as was the tongue. They were first offered to Mercedes who gracefully declined and passed them to Antonio, who accepted them with grace and joy, and asked Ana Maria to share the honor with him.

As they sat on tree stumps to share their first meal, Antonio expressed his surprise that someone so young could sing so mournfully about life's painful experiences because he could not fathom that they were her own. He had been touched deep in his heart not just by her words but by the sentiment that accompanied her words. He felt that only someone who had endured the pain that she sang about could have shown the emotions demonstrated by her as the words flowed from her lips. "That is because you are still a Spaniard, forgive me, a Basque and as such you do not yet understand the heart and soul of a Puerto Rican. I am Boricua through and trough and everything about me comes from those roots. I believe that some day you will become one of us. From what I heard, Basques are not Spaniards as we know them and so they do not belong in Spain. You went to Barcelona but you are not Catalan and so you did not belong. Now you are here, amongst Puerto Ricans, and here you belong."

When Father Reynaldo joined the festivity his presence seemed to change the mood of irreverence into one more somber. Fully aware of the impact his cassock had on the people there, he removed it and stood before them in a plain white shirt and pants. After changing into his less official appearance he went around to each and every person and after reintroducing himself to them he again blessed all of their children. Next he asked if he could be allowed to contribute a jug of wine that he had carried with him from Vega Alta. As he went around serving all the farmers he apologized that he had to resort to bringing wine in a jug, because as he explained only Jesus was capable of turning water into wine, and that was just once. He also reminded them that Jesus expected them to drink it all, after all he said, "Why do you think they ran out of wine at the wedding in Canaan?," he paused to see if anyone had a guess. "Jesus and the apostles were there." Everyone laughed with an infectious and welcoming laughter. The kind of laughter that said to him that he was welcomed there. Sensing that he had a good opportunity to be accepted by the very same people who had rejected all of his approaches in the past, he relieved the man standing over the pig by handing him his plate and serving him. That act was followed by more gestures of kindness and warmth. He served everyone before he had his first bite and his first drink. Miguel watched the farmers watching the priest and realized that Father Reynaldo knew that he would have to earn the people's trust and that this was an auspicious beginning.

It was well past midnight when the party began to break up with the awkwardness that sets in when everyone knows it is time to turn in but no one wants to be first. Noticing that not all had transportation, Father Reynaldo offered his wagon so no one would have to walk in the darkness as they returned home. For some, it was a short walk but not for all. And for those whose children had fallen asleep, the walk would be hard. "Go on, take my wagon. I will come to look for it tomorrow morning. I only asked that you remove the harness from the horse and let it feed a while. I'll be by in the morning. Go on I too need to sleep." He gave the reins to David Torres, whose wife was holding two of their children, and retrieved his hammock from the wagon. That night he slept with the satisfaction that he had done more good in the last four hours than he had in the previous four years.

As usual, Antonio was in the field before anyone else, except that this time

Father Reynaldo was with him as the men arrived to start the day's work. The priest was dressed the same as he was the night before; boots, pants and a work shirt. The only way anyone may have known that he was a priest was the scapular he wore around his neck. In trying to understand how Antonio and Miguel had come to be so well accepted so quickly, he realized that whatever barriers were there between them and the farmers, they had crossed by reaching out to the farmers as their equals. Reynaldo knew that he had approached them from the implied position of authority represented by the catholic church and the power that it held over people. That had not worked and as a result his church had not grown. He chastised himself for his arrogance and his lack of understanding. In Antonio and Miguel he had seen servile leadership at its best, and the response he had witnessed showed him that not only was it the best way for the shepherd to reach his flock, it was the only way. Removing his shirt he stood bare-chested and worked alongside the farmers for the next two days doing whatever was needed to earn their respect and their trust.

Their baptisms would mean far more to him than any that he had ever performed because these people were baptized because they wanted to not because they had to. For the very first time in his life he felt that he was doing God's work, they way he had wanted him to do it.

Father Angel had arrived that morning since he had spent the night in Vega Alta. Reaching La Jacana at sunrise, he rode his horse first to the dairy. The very first thing he had done upon arriving at the church in Vega Alta was to meet with Father Reynaldo to receive a progress report and to listen to his suggestions about what was needed and in what ways they could help. "Everything and anything was his response." Thirty days had passed since they had met at La Mallorquina. It seemed more like thirty minutes if measured by all that had taken place since that day. But first Reynaldo wanted to know how he had succeeded in getting the Bishop to assign him to Vega Alta. "I promised him that I would horsewhip you each and every day, except for Sundays. I promised him that on Sundays I would whip you twice. Come on let me take you to dinner and celebrate." The next day the priests rode together to La Jacana to begin assessing their needs and to develop a work plan with Miguel. The clearing work was well in process and the earth had been kind in giving up its trees and rocks. For the most part the soil was somewhat lose which boded well for the crops they planned.

In very little time Mercedes had organized the women into a group responsible for the hen house and the dairy. The dairy operation consisted of caring for eight cows and ten goats. This number was surely to change because they had also purchased a bull and two male goats. The women were especially supportive and engaged in the work because through the hen house they could accumulate egg money. This was their private fund to be used for their necessities. For women who have never had anything least of all their own money, egg money was empowering.

Having been around farms all of their lives, the women of La Jacana all knew how to milk cows and goats, and how to gather the eggs. The one thing they needed to learn was how to do it through a production process, one that would optimize all their labor and yield the best results and the greatest personal satisfaction. For women who had lived hopeless lives in which they saw no end to their misery, working for themselves and believing in themselves was a totally new dynamic. All the difference between their hopeless lives and their lives full of hope and great expectations was not because of Jesus, but because of his servant, Father Angel Martinez.

On the first day of his arrival at La Jacana Father Angel asked for a mule. When one was brought to him, he swapped saddles from his horse to the mule, packed two days rations, and headed towards the mountain. Other than the mule, he had Orovis to guide him and to keep him company. Orovis was not yet comfortable around priests, and although Father Angel was not dressed as one, in Orovis' eyes he was and would remain a catholic priest.

No one, not even Orovis knew what the priest was after as he rode towards the base of the mountain. The priest however, did have a plan if not a specific destination. He first rode to the spot where the stream ran nearer to the base of the mountain. After about a one hour ride for him and a walk for Orovis, who would not ride an animal, he finally selected a spot to begin climbing the mountain. He was searching for the spot where a person could climb with ease. He needed a spot where a climbing trail could be carved that would lead to the one spot he really needed. The one he knew Orovis would find for him. As they stopped for lunch, Father Angel drew a map on the ground that covered the dairy farm, the stream and the cave that he was asking Orovis to find. Father Angel explained the entire plan to Orovis, who grew more enthusiastic towards the ideas as he gained a better understanding of the plan. Father Angel's idea was for the dairy to produce butter and cheese and to do that he needed to build a small shack in which the urns would be stored with the cool water flowing around them which would maintain the freshness of the products.

Next he needed a cave in which to store their products as they ripened and matured before being taken to market. Since it would be women who would handle all of the production and storage labor, the cave needed to be close enough to the shack so that the climb with the urns would not place exceeding demands on the women's bodies or their children's. Three hours later, Orovis returned to Father Angel with the location of two caves that he thought would be adequate for his purposes. Upon arriving at the first cave, Father Angel fell on his knees and asked Orovis to join him in thanking the Virgin Mary for their good fortune. "I'll just wait for you to finish," said Orovis.

CHAPTER 18

With the farm starting to yield crops the level of activity was up in every front. The men were happy working in the fields, involved in a number of tasks, one more important than the other. If it was not harvesting the corn and tying it for transport to the farmers' market in San Juan, they were working at crating pineapples for delivery to the market and to the port where Juan José had arranged with the port authority to provision the ships with fresh fruit. Pineapples being a hardy fruit were perfectly suited to be consumed on board ships and to be sold in other islands where the fruit was not available. Their wagon, with which they originally used to deliver goods to and from San Juan, had been so successful that now they had two wagons a day, one going and another one coming. The demand for their transport services had risen as they knew it would because of the need they saw when they arrived in Bayamon for the first time. Just as they thought, increasing the frequency and speed of the wagons would increase the demand for their services, and as a result commercial activity had risen as demand rose to meet capacity. Their aggressive growth coupled with the increased demand for more wagons caused them to add mule teams to the route. These were stabled with farmers who seeing the opportunity built a livery stable to care for the mules that were switched with fresh teams half way to and from San Juan.

The dairy operation had fared at least as well if not better than the farming activities. This created an atmosphere of healthy competition between the men and the women who challenged one another in matching results. Since there was enough milk for all to drink on a daily basis, and the women had money to purchase whatever was not grown in the farm, everyone's health had improved, especially the children's. Not one was lost to hunger or sickness since La Jacana had started operations. Because of improved health, normal pregnancies and healthy deliveries were now the norm instead of the exception.

The women kept all of the funds generated by the sale of eggs and returned the cheese and butter money to the farm. Within two months of starting the dairy farm, they were making sufficient butter and cheese to warrant a wagon to Vega Alta and one to Toa Baja on alternate days. Mercedes had taken it upon herself to invite Ana Maria Morales, the LeLoLai singer, to work with the women for the same pay as the men were receiving. Since Ana Maria could read and write she was responsible for the delivery to locations in Vega Alta and Toa Baja, and points in between, and for keeping accounts. Some of these were customers who paid weekly or monthly for which accounts and records needed to be kept. Little did Mercedes know that Ana Maria was born for commerce. Because of her intelligence, which was evident to most people who met her, very few tried to take advantage of her, and the ones who did found themselves on the losing end of the transaction. The only drawback to the arrangement was that Ana Maria lived with her family in Espinosa. The distance to the farm from her home required her to leave her house long before the sun rose and return long after it set. Further, Mercedes knew that the money being paid to Ana Maria was being taken by her father.

Ana Maria did not complaint, and that is not how Mercedes learned of the situation. She figured it out when shopping together in Vega Alta, Ana Maria's eyes could not hide her attraction to a particular dress she had seen at the seamstress' house, but did not complete the purchase. This was the kind of issue that only a woman would recognize, and so Mercedes offered to lend her the money to buy the dress, but Ana Maria refused and was greatly embarrassed to confess to Mercedes that she could never pay her back because her father took all her money.

That evening during dinner, which was prepared by Angela the daughter of one of the farm hands, that had been hired by Miguel to help Mercedes who spent all of her time managing the business of La Jacana Their decision was unanimous, Ana Maria was to move in with Miguel and Mercedes and sleep in Antonio's hammock. He in turn agreed to move into Orovis' hut where he spent most of his evenings anyway. The next day, when work was done, Mercedes told Ana Maria of their decision. She told her of the plan to bring the wagon near her house in Espinosa and that she was to bring with her as much as she would need to live with Mercedes and Miguel. Ana Maria accepted under the condition that she would do all the cooking for her room and board. They reminded her that she already had Angela and that she needed the income. It would not have been fair to remove Angela just to accommodate Ana Maria. The issue was resolved when Ana Maria suggested that Angela should be paid what she was being paid but that she would only work half days. The later half of the day would be Ana Maria's responsibility who would cook every night for the room and board she was receiving.

The next morning, Mercedes waited for Ana Maria who was not carrying much, but was carrying everything she owned. She did not tell her family because they would have kept her from moving, not because they were afraid of what might have happened to her, but because they were losing the income contributed by their daughter.

Once everyone was settled, they all joined for the first dinner prepared by Ana Maria. She cooked breadfruit, boiled and served covered in olive oil. She also served fried chicken that was reddish in color as if it been covered with saffron. The chicken was surrounded by fried sweet bananas that because of their bright yellow color offered a striking contrast to the color of the fried chicken. Mercedes made a mental note to learn how to prepare the chicken like Ana Maria's. All she had to do was to look at Miguel and Antonio, and look at the plate where the chicken had been served just a few minutes before, to realize that both the chicken recipe and Ana Maria were a success.

The first book that Antonio had loaned to Ana Maria was a history of Charlemagne, that dealt with how his Magna Carta had set civilization on a then unknown course. The concept of rights of an individual, trial by jury, rights to property, rules of evidence and the like were overwhelming to her.

For most people able to read, and most likely in the upper class, reading about the Magna Carta raised the question of why. For Ana Maria the question was, "Of course, why not?" The way that Mercedes had positioned the kerosene lamps around the room, served to offer adequate lighting throughout the house. Ana Maria saw several books on a crate that she guessed belonged to Antonio and asked if she could look at them. "Ana Maria, this is your home. One does not ask when at home," was the answer she received.

"You do not know my home," she replied. Antonio reminded her that he was owed a good conversation about the book she had read before she could read another one. Smiling, as she listened, Ana Maria said, "Since you have asked for it you best be ready because this may take all night." First it had been her singing that impressed him, then it had been her confidence and now it was her challenge that drew him all the more closer to her. If she had any idea of the impact she was having on him she did not reveal it. After all he was white and she was not.

As she had warned, their conversation lasted well into the night, with one question generating more questions rather than answers. There was no contest, and no competition for whose ideas or comments had the greater value or relevance to the subject at hand. Instead they held a conversation among equals. He asked her to please call him Anton, and she replied, "Fine, Don Anton it is." He corrected her and asked that she dropped the Don, and she refused by saying that she saw him as worthy of the Don prefix and could not bring herself to ignore it. He in turn replied by saying that he would then call her Doña Ana Maria because she too merited it. Little did they know that those would be their names for one another for the rest of their lives.

He offered to shake hands as they parted company but she took his hand and pulled herself closer to him and kissed him on the cheek saying, "Thank you for being you and letting me be me." Strangely, he pulled back from her gesture of affection, not brusquely but not without purpose either. They both felt the awkwardness of the moment, she more than him. Naturally she felt the rejection that his body language projected and questioned if she had become more familiar than she should have. She reasoned that she had reacted to the moment and nothing else. And although she felt she had not done anything that was not natural or appropriate to the occasion, she felt rejected. At the moment her lips touched his cheek, he remembered how Dolores had kissed him the same way, the first time, and just as innocently. He still regretted the memory and remembered the pain their affair had visited on him. He also remembered that he had sworn that no woman would ever be made to feel used by him. Still, he felt a strong attraction for the Puerto Rican girl, and knew that there would be more conversations and kisses, but all things in due course.

Sunday morning when Mercedes awoke, she found Miguel sitting at the small table with papers carefully positioned in front of him. When asked what he was working on this time, he answered, "Your house, our new home." He invited her to sit down as he served her hot coffee from the pot he had on top of the stove. The house he was designing showed that he was planning on a large family. It had four bedrooms that filled the entire left side of the house and consumed one third of the total space. All the bedrooms were connected by shared doors, except for their bedroom which was in the corner and had only one door that could be accessed through the living area and not through the adjacent bedroom. Each bedroom also had two windows placed in a way that would facilitate circulation when the entire house was opened. The remaining space was one large open room that ran from the kitchen in the back to the entrance in the front. There was a back door next to where the wood stove would go, the front door and a third door in the middle of the room which would lead to a veranda that wrapped around the entire house. There were two windows in the kitchen. One directly over the stove, and one to its left. The other windows were evenly spaced along the rest of the walls. Miguel had developed a keen appreciation for the Caribbean trade winds and had designed a house that would allow as much breeze as nature could provide.

She asked to see the house he had designed and was struck by the open design and the flow of the kitchen to the open rooms and to the bedrooms, and the veranda that wrapped around the entire house. She remembered that the house in which she had been raised never felt like a home. In retrospect, it never felt like she thought a home should have. Her parents' house had the maid's quarters, the children's rooms, her parents' suite, a large parlor and a separate dining room that was adjacent to the kitchen. Every room seemed isolated from the others as the occupants themselves were isolated.

The house lacked nothing except warmth. She had never felt that a family lived in her parents' house. But she would make sure that her husband and their children would never feel isolated in their own home. Once again Miguel had surprised her with his sense of her needs in everything he thought and in everything he did.

"Where will we build this house," she asked. He asked her if she had a favorite spot in mind. They both knew the answer to the question because they had both looked at the spot where the cluster of red flamed trees stood out on the first day the entered the valley of the Vegas as they crossed from

Bayamon. On that day, at the same time, they both knew where their home would be built. The challenge was in how to build it without cutting down trees or cutting down the smallest number of trees. He understood that there would be some compromises along the way and the trees would be the first one. "And when will we start," she asked, with a certain childlike quality to the question. The way she asked it told him that something was up with her, although he did not know exactly what, he knew she was up to something. The something not yet revealed to him was that she was pregnant. Since he rose and left the house long before she awoke, he had no seen her morning sickness. He answered that he thought they could build it in eight months possibly seven.

The materials would not be a problem since they were readily available in San Juan. Labor would be a concern because most of the men he knew worked at La Jacana. His one additional worry was the fact that he did not know anything about building a house. Drawing up a plan was a far different proposition from actually building one. While he was a supremely confident man, he knew his limitations. They both agreed that it would be best to ride to Toa Baja and speak to Don Pedro José, who would surely help them to find a builder.

As they were dressing for church in Vega Alta, he asked Mercedes to say whatever it was that she was dying to tell him. He knew her better than he knew anyone, including Antonio. He knew her so well that he knew what she was about to say before the words left her lips. He marveled how she could say precisely what he had been thinking only seconds before, and he understood that their connection came from many levels. They were connected in mind, body, spirit and soul. Their closeness was beyond that which love brings. It was an affirmation of all the decisions they had made, all the actions they had taken that brought them to the place where they stood, thinking each other's thoughts. Finally she could hold it no longer and just came out and said it; "I am carrying our first child." His eyes welt with tears the second he heard her say the words. He lifted her from the small stool on which she had been sitting and held her closely against him ever so gently as if wanting to feel her heart beat against his chest and that of the child she was carrying. "Praise God let it be a girl. Let our first child be a girl, so that her mother may be honored by giving birth to her image. So that the child's beauty may reflect your own." Overwhelmed by the expression of his wishes for her, she thought it uniquely Miguel for him to wish for a daughter when all men she had ever known had or would have wished for a son. The feeling of love she had for him at that moment could not be satisfied by the tenderness they were exchanging and they both knew it, as they undressed and began to make love, she said "God will understand why we will be late to church."

When they finally walked out of their little house, both Miguel and Ana Maria were waiting outside sitting on the steps. As they did at the start and the end of every day, they hugged and kissed and wished each other God's blessings. On Sundays the butter and cheese wagon was modified so that the ladies sat on a bench on the rear and the men sat on the front. The ride to the church in Vega Alta usually took no longer than thirty minutes but at the pace the horses were running it would have taken closer to forty five minutes. Mercedes who was feeling in fine form asked that they let the horses run at a faster gallop.

The mass was less than half over when they entered the church, and since they had arrived late they sat towards the rear so as to not draw attention to themselves. Both priests, Fathers Angel and Reynaldo were officiating the mass, and the homily was delivered by Angel. The mass was still sparsely attended since the farmers were not yet coming to church on a regular basis.

Some went on occasion but not regularly. They preferred the open air mass that was held at La Jacana late Sunday afternoons. Father Angel spoke about the impossibility of God. Making the point that the creation of the world and the universe were absolutely impossible except for God whose specialty was the impossible. His central message was that all was possible for those who believed in God and that the rewards that were given to a Christian were commensurate with his faith. When he spoke from the pulpit he always projected complete command of the sermon, never looking at notes and speaking from the heart. Since coming to the church in Vega Alta his presence had been felt by the entire town and Father Reynaldo rejoiced in having him there. At the end of the mass the four decided to remain in town for lunch and to invite the priests. "We hope this does not mean that we are not having mass at La Jacana this afternoon," Father Angel asked. "No, this means that we will hear mass twice and that we wanted to eat lunch in town, which we have not done in a while," responded Antonio. "Besides we are picking up a dress that Ana Maria ordered the last time we were here other than delivering butter," said Mercedes.

"Mercedes, when are you going to tell us," asked Ana Maria. She asked the question after they sat at the small restaurant, in the back of a house at the end of the Plaza, near the church. Mercedes looked as surprised as everyone else at the table and wondered how could Ana Maria know. In the time that Ana Maria had lived with them, she had come to appreciate her as a trusted companion and not as a woman who worked at the farm. She had sensed in Ana Maria wisdom beyond her years and knowledge beyond her education. She appreciated her keen intellect coupled with her kind heart. In Ana Maria she had found a sister. Ana Maria explained that she was a fourth generation midwife and had been delivering babies since her mother trained her at the age of fourteen, and that she could tell a woman's condition sometimes even before the expectant mother knew herself. All the men except Miguel were perplexed by the conversation between the two women, and looked questioningly at Miguel, hoping that he would make sense of it. "Yes, you are right, I am having a child. Miguel wants it to be a girl. And I so hope that I can give him that gift." Antonio was the first to his feet. Lifting Miguel from his chair he meant to say something congratulatory, something appropriate to the occasion, but no words came from his lips, such was his love for them that tears flowed from his eyes as he put Miguel down and reached for Mercedes saying, "I can not believe it. I am going to be an uncle." After everyone had their share of kisses and hugs, Father Angel said a short blessing for the child and the mother, and although he knew it was sudden, he asked them if they had even thought of a name. "If it is a girl her name will be Graciela and if a boy his name will be Miguel Antonio, like his father and his uncle." Early that Sunday evening after mass was said by the Fathers at La Jacana, the celebration started in honor of Mercedes' announcement. That evening the LeLoLai singing was all about joy and great expectations. There were no laments or mournful words coming out of Ana Maria's lips because there were none in her heart. There was no pain to relate and no miseries to share, this was all about the love they all felt for Mercedes and Miguel. This time she sang in a soft voice directing her music to all the women when they had to do with women and likewise to all the men. She named everyone of them in her song before she passed it over to the next singer.

Everyone felt her joy and the honesty of her emotions, and everyone including herself was aware that Antonio had not taken his eyes of her.

At the end of the evening they all retired to rest for the next day's labor, except for Antonio and Ana Maria who sat at the steps of the house. He had asked her to stay as she was walking up the steps. "I have not read the last book that you loaned me so I am not ready to talk about Cicero. But I am willing to listen to you tell me about him." He remained silent taking in her smile while feeling the need to speak and knowing well what he wanted to say, not knowing how to say it.

Antonio was determined to speak to her in a way that would not frighten or offend her to the point that she might withdraw from him. The closeness they had developed since first meeting was moving beyond filial, and he wanted it to progress, to change, but he needed to define what form that change would take. That, he determined would be her decision after hearing his story. Where to begin, how much to tell and how to tell it were as important as what needed to be said.

She sat one step above where he sat, and he began by telling her why he wanted to say the things that he was about to say. He explained that if she could understand who he was and how he came to be that man, she would have an appreciation about his attitudes, his demeanor and his expectations of her and his own. He still lived with the regrets of his affair with Dolores, more so for the disappointment that it had caused Sister Graciela than the pain he may have caused Dolores. First he had to tell Ana Maria not only what Sister Graciela had meant to him and what she had done for him. He began at the beginning explaining how Miguel came to be his brother, and Mercedes his sister in law. He talked about their lives in Spain and how they came to be in Puerto Rico. She looked at him with insightful eyes knowing that asking questions would in no way serve any purpose other than interrupting him. She also knew that by remaining silent he would feel compelled to keep talking until whatever it was that he needed to say, was said. He finally arrived at the Dolores chapter of his life, and with trepidation he began to tell the story of what happened between them, how it happened and why it happened. In a way that seemed to her was harsher than it should have been, he spoke of his regrets not over seducing the girl, but because he had broken his self imposed code of honor. He felt that he had a bond with

Sister Graciela that was founded on the strength of her lessons during his years at the convent, and that the bond had been broken when he laid with Dolores. Although it could be said that he had been vindicated in the eyes of the Sister, evidenced by his inheritance, he still lived with the shame that his conduct had caused him in the eyes of Sister Graciela.

Still, Ana Maria did not speak, nor did she move. She simply waited for him to say more. He did not know what impact if any was his story having on her. The relationship with Dolores as he described it, had escalated with no intention on his part. And although he believed he had done nothing to mislead her in any way, he had not rejected her affections until it was too late for either of them to not follow their natural urges. While Ana Maria was a young woman she was by no means innocent in the ways of the flesh. Although she had no first hand knowledge she had seen plenty through her sisters and brothers and through the women whose children she and her mother had delivered. "I tell you these things because I do not believe that I have ever loved anyone and as a result have no experience about the needs of a woman. More importantly, I do not want any one, especially you to feel used by me in any way. I have very strong feelings for you and hope that you have them for me as well. I just do not ever want you to be made to feel the sadness Dolores felt while being with me." The roosters began to crow, one after the other as the morning's cacophony started. He stood from where he had been sitting for several hours and she did the same, indicating they would retire to whatever little sleep they could get before starting their day. She approached him and holding his face in her hands said, Don Anton, if you want me, I will be your woman. But you must remember, my name is Ana Maria, please remember that." And then she kissed him.

Before anyone else had risen, Antonio and Miguel were hitching the mules to the wagon that had been loaded the night before with the goods and products that were to be delivered to Bayamon and San Juan. On this day, however they were making a stop in Toa Alta to deliver some of their eggs and cheese and to meet with Don Pedro José Bermudez.

"How can you possibly not know that you are before the builder in this region. Let me say that again, I am not a builder, but the builder in this region. Every house that I have built still stands. You have yet to see your first hurricane but when you do, you will appreciate the full meaning of what I have just said to you. Miguel, the house that I will build for you will be a home to you and your children and their children and their children's children." Both Antonio and Miguel knew the man to have been true to his word in everything he had said since they had arrived in the valley of the Vegas. His survey had been as precise as any ever recorded in the region.

"Leave your drawings with me and I will have your plans by the time you return. I know that you must hurry, your wife wants this house before your child is born." Miguel looked at him with curious eyes. "You are probably wondering how I know that your wife is with child, are you not? Well, I just do." It was in the early afternoon when they arrived in Bayamon. As the mules were switched with a fresh team and the wagon was unloaded and reloaded with the deliveries to San Juan they spoke to the locals who only wanted to talk about the coming war. The rumor of war had been spreading all across the Caribbean and the questions were not about the if but the when of the war. Since most of the people were not able to read, the occasional periodicals that found the way to them were of no use. At the end of the day their concerns were no different from anyone else's, mainly they had to do with what it meant to them and their families. They departed Bayamon with the commitment that they would report whatever news they had on their return.

By the time they reached San Juan, the market was closed so they had no choice but to drive their wagon to the livery stable, where they found Juan José. He asked them to look in the direction of the docks. As they looked, the rumor of war turned into a fact before their very eyes. Several frigates were being provisioned with urgency and purpose. Waiting to be provisioned were other frigates just outside the bay. Sailors were loading barrels of gun powder and cannon balls as fast as they were being handed. However, the speed of their actions did not reflect an enthusiasm for their work. Instead, they looked as if they were doing things they would have rather not been doing. They looked defeated. "The only people who profit from wars are merchants. Soldiers never do. The only soldier in the history of my family was Gallardo Martinez and he only profited after he left Ponce De Leon's army. Have no doubt my friends, war is coming, the only question is how will we profit from it." Juan José paused allowing them to absorb his meaning.

They spent the night near the livery stable in a new guest house a block from the bank. Antonio awoke just before sunrise to find Miguel outside the room, sitting in a chair where evidenced by his eyes he had spent all night. He had seen that look on his brother before. It showed that he had been consumed by though. "If whatever you want to say can wait lets have a cup of coffee. Lets go to La Mallorquina."

"Anton, there is going to be a war and Spain is going to lose it. Remember when we sailed into Havana and we saw the fortifications overlooking the bay? And do you remember that we saw the exact same fortifications when we sailed into San Juan and we thought we were back in Cuba? Anton, Spain is not prepared for the kind of war that will be fought. Those fortifications are built to repel an enemy from the sea. But not to fight the kind of war the Americans will fight. You see, the Americans can resupply and support their forces from ninety miles away from Florida to Cuba, while Spain has to cross an ocean of four thousand miles to support its forces. The mayor of Vega Alta is right. Besides, Americans have never stopped fighting wars, Its what they do. Not only will the Americans win, it will be a short war. I have thought about what Juan José said, there is nothing that we can do about this war but profit from it." Once again, and not surprisingly, Miguel showed his strategic thinking talent. He was and always had been a deep thinker. "What do you have in mind?" Antonio asked. Miguel responded by saying that in war there were victors and vanquished, but not only in the field of battle. Spain may be vanquished in battle but we can be victors in commerce. He suggested that they should speculate on the outcome by buying American dollars from the bank while they could.

Since they had to complete their currency transaction at the bank and load and unload at the market before they could leave San Juan, it was late afternoon before they reached Bayamon. When they reached Bayamon, as they had expected their wagon was surrounded by many waiting to hear what they had learned in San Juan. They thought it best to keep their assessment to themselves rather than to frighten people with concerns upon which they could not act.

During the night they could hear the men, mostly young ones, greatly encouraged by the rum they had consumed, carrying on about what they would do to the Yankees if they came. How they would confront them and fight them, and kill them if they had to. This from people who had only seen blood spilled from the hogs and goats they occasionally butchered. Funny, they thought, that it was only the men doing the talking, but not the women. They seemed to know better. Maybe, because they really knew their men, or because throughout history it was the women who were left to bury them.

Much rum had been consumed, and tempers and passions were rising with the talk of war and displays of presumed bravery. One of the women, a young girl not much older than Ana Maria, sat next to Anton and allowed her leg to rub against his. "I do not hear you saying what you will do to the Yankees if they come, why is that?" she asked. He looked at her trying to judge her age, her meaning and her intentions. It was obvious to him that she was Puerto Rican. Her color, size and demeanor reminded him of Ana Maria and because of that he liked her right away. She said, "Look at them, never having heard a shot fired in anger. Or having faced a spear or an arrow, how brave they are. Look at them. They make me laugh. Most of them I know to be cowards. They are only brave when confronting their wives and then only maybe. I think the Yankees are safe in Bayamon." Antonio smiled and looked at her in agreement. At this moment, a boy, not much older than her stepped in front of Antonio and asked why he was speaking with the girl without asking his permission. She stood to speak to the young man but he shoved her aside before she could say a word. Antonio stood up to help her as the young man struck him squarely in the chest with his fist. Antonio barely moved by the blow seemed more amused than hurt. Immediately the noise stopped and the crowd moved towards the conflict in expectation of what would happen next. Out of nowhere the boy brandished a machete and yelled to Antonio to find one and defend himself. Miguel tried to intercede with the young man but he pushed him away as he did the girl.

Antonio looked at Miguel with a look that confirmed he had the situation under control. With every second that passed, the crowd pushed and shoved themselves into position to witness what they believed would be a duel. Sensing he had no options, Anton asked for a machete and one was handed to him. As he turned his back to the young man to reach for the machete he looked at the girl who was now being held by Miguel and gave her a look of confident assurance as well. As soon as he turned to face his opponent, he saw at once the fear in the boy's eyes who understood he had taken it too far but could not retreat.

The boy's chest had deflated and the grip on the machete was not as tight as when he first held it. It seemed that he was more inclined to drop it than to lift it. Antonio did no take his eyes away from the boy and held his blade at his side in a way that offered no indication of his intentions. And waited. Knowing that his opponent was the challenger and it was his move to make, he just waited. The crowd too waited but more in disappointment than in expectation as it became clear that there would be no bloodshed in Bayamon that night. The stalemate continued a few seconds for Antonio and an eternity for the boy.

"Rafael, stop this nonsense right now," a voice shouted. At that moment the boy's mother arrived, slapped him once on the face and twice on the top of his head, took his machete away, hit him on his butt twice with the flat side of the blade, and ordered him home. Turning to Antonio before she walked after her son she said, "Thank you for not hurting my boy, Don Antonio, I am in your debt." No madam," he said, "I am in yours." He walked to Miguel and said, "The girl is right, the Yankees have nothing to fear."

CHAPTER 19

Antonio returned from his birthday celebration all the worst for the wear, and fearing that he may have done some damage to his body, or at least to his brain. In fact there were several instances during that day that he had begged God to put him out of his misery by taking his life. However, he did promise to never again overindulge as he had the night before. A promise that he kept for the rest of his life. The first person he saw was Ana Maria who recognized his symptoms. Although she herself had never been drunk, she had seen the look often in her brothers and father. She had never felt pity towards them, but she did towards Antonio. After all, she may have loved her family, but she was in love with Antonio. "Come with me. I have the remedy for you." And he followed her to his salvation.

War came and went so fast that its effects were not felt at La Jacana or anywhere in the Vegas for that matter. None of the casualties came from the valley, and no one at La Jacana knew anyone who was serving with the Spanish forces. The farm's progress had continued unimpeded and in no way was affected by the war. The commercial activity propelled by La Jacana was having an economic impact throughout the region between San Juan to the east and Arecibo to the west, and started to influence commerce to the south towards Ponce. Unlike when they first arrived and people only passed through the Vegas on the way to somewhere else, the valley was now their destination. The volume of traffic was such that what used to be a trail was now a road. La Jacana was employing many of those who appeared to them ready to work. A bunkhouse had been built for the bachelors, and in expectation of the arrival of new families, Miguel had directed the building of small bungalows that were positioned around the various water wells that had been dug. These clusters of newcomers, along with the original farmers would join and build the new shelters in very little time. All of this growth created the need for a general store, and since Mercedes was reaching the advanced stage of her pregnancy, the store was the perfect place for her. She had never understood the concept of confinement when a woman was pregnant in Spain, and she certainly would not tolerate it in Puerto Rico. Her routine had in no way been altered since she first realized she was pregnant, but it needed to change as she neared her delivery.

The general store went up soon after the school which also doubled as the chapel. They were both positioned near the road, in a way that could be readily accessible to the largest number of residents. Instead of having to wait for goods to be delivered from San Juan or Bayamon, people could now buy them at the store without having to wait any longer than it took to load their wagons, because the store maintained an ever growing number of items in stock. And since the customers were paid in currency, instead of bartering, they had money to spend. Women mostly bought materials with which to sew clothes for their children, their husbands and themselves, in that order. This was a long and painstaking process since it was one hundred percent manual labor. Because Mercedes had made it acceptable, even fashionable, for women to wear work clothes, they could have one good Sunday dress and all other garments were more of the utilitarian variety. Mercedes had ordered and received a sewing machine from a man named Singer in the United States. She had read about his sewing machine through a periodical that had found its way to her. The machine had been delivered through a freight forwarder that serviced and delivered goods from most anywhere in the world. Wars do not always interfere with commerce and such was the case with the sewing machine and the Spanish-American war. The delivery was a fortunate development for everyone and the timing could not have been better. Because Mercedes was now very advanced in her pregnancy and her delivery was imminent, she was not allowed, nor was she able to do much physical work of any kind. It was in her nature to keep busy and idleness rankled her.

The sewing machine filled the void in her days. It came with an instruction manual which included diagrams describing its use, the threading and replacing of needles based on their intended use, and several extra needles. Yet again, Mercedes put her boarding school experience to work, since she could speak, read and write English she became an expert on the workings of the Singer sewing machine. Possibly the first one in Puerto Rico.

It was natural that she would first experiment with making baby clothes. Her enthusiasm for her labor was such that she made enough baby clothes to ensure that if every female in the district had a baby, the child would be well clothed.

"Huracan is coming," Orovis told Antonio and Miguel when he encountered them early in the morning as they approached the pineapple fields. "We must make ready. There is time but not much. Possibly two days, three at the most, but the God of wind is coming. How angry he is I do not know, but we can count on his coming." They dismounted their horses wanting to hear more. If there was one thing of which they could be certain, was Orovis' instincts. While some people claimed a sixth sense, he could claim seven or eight. There had been a few low clouds in the previous day's sky, and the normal breeze that typically flowed through the valley, but on this morning everything was exceptionally still and larger and lower clouds were beginning to form. Other than that, this was a day as normal as any day they had experienced in the valley of the Vegas, but that was about to change.

They heard his horse before they saw Father Angel riding at a pretty fair gallop in their direction. "I am sure that Orovis has already told you that a hurricane is coming. This is not my first one, but I know the same is not true for you, so I suggest that you all listen to me. We must assume the worst and get ready for it. There is nothing that we can do about the crops. Neither the pineapples nor the corn can be picked in time to make any difference. And the coffee and breadfruit trees are strong enough to withstand the pressures of the wind. So let us worry about our people." Antonio and Miguel recognized wisdom when it spoke to them, and their reaction was along the lines of wanting and waiting to be told what to do. Father Angel started by saying that while there was much to do, time was on their side, but it could not be wasted.

The first step was to organize their evacuation plan which consisted of moving everyone into the church in Vega Alta. It was important he said that everyone was accounted for, and that families be transported to the church together because that way they could make certain that every family member was on board the wagons. Secondly, he instructed that they be directed to store all of their belongings in a corner of their small houses. Lastly he ordered that all houses keep two windows opened. This last instruction was readily accepted by the locals, but not really understood by Antonio and Miguel. Never having experienced a hurricane they had no appreciation for the variances between pressures outside and inside the houses. Opening the windows would allow water to enter and wet the house, but it would dry, and the house had a better opportunity to remain intact than if the windows were closed.

Antonio said that he would remain on the farm and seek shelter in the deepest cave where they stored butter and cheese. The caves would be the place to keep the animals, as many as they could. Orovis, who knew why he was really choosing to stay, said that he too would stay in the caves with Antonio and help to move the animals. With Mercedes so near her delivery, there was no way for Miguel to not evacuate with her to the church. Besides, Father Angel advised that his and Mercedes' presence at the church would be a great source of comfort to their people sheltered there. They, along with Ana Maria were the last to leave, but not before she told Antonio, "Don't let anything happen to your books and don't let anything happen to you." By midday of the day before the hurricane struck, everyone was at the church or on the way there. Father Reynaldo, with the help of La Jacana women had set up a kitchen against the wall along the side of the building near the sacristy. Many of the town's people were also sheltered at the church. The impending crisis was serving as a catalyst for the bonding of all the people who up to this point had remained distant. This was the first time that they interacted in any way because town people never went to the farm and farm people seldom visited the town. This isolation was about to change. Thanks to the God of wind, people were congregating in the house of God.

Most of the pews had been converted to beds for the children who worn by the excitement had little trouble falling asleep that evening. The adults, confident that all that could be done had been done, were mostly in a festive spirit, which served to conceal the anxiety they all felt. After all, if not in the house of God, where could they have felt safe? Cauldrons filled with varieties of soups were prepared and kept hot. Since there would not be a formal time in which to eat, families arranged their own schedules and ate when hungry. Fortunately there were two indoor privies in the church, but they would require emptying before the hurricane passed. Other than Ana Maria, Miguel and Mercedes, no one gave any thought to Antonio and Orovis. No one else worried because they knew that Orovis would take care of Antonio. Ana Maria was sitting on a pew when she heard Mercedes say, "Oh my God, my water just broke."

The last two mules were shoved inside the cave, and the barrier to keep them in was raised when the drizzle started. It felt like any other light rain which they had experienced on many occasions. In fact the sun shone brightly as it started to rain. But in the blink of an eye, day turned into night and Huracan arrived. His anger not yet revealed through the strength of the wind, would soon make its presence known. Inside the cave was strangely warm, which was all the more noticeable because of the cold they could feel just one foot outside the cave. The sounds of the wind and the rain as they beat against the mountain, were deafening. Antonio had to place his lips next to Orovis' ear as he said, "This is magnificent. It is everything that I expected." Orovis, who thought he knew why Antonio stayed, now had it confirmed. And felt glad to have shared the moment with him. All through the night Antonio remained mesmerized by the force of the wind and the rain, and if Orovis had not been with him, he would have stepped outside the cave to feel the force of Huracan more directly.

Ana Maria went to work with the motions and actions of one who knew exactly what to expect and what was expected of her. Mercedes, who had been longing anxiously for this moment since the minute she had realized she was going to have a baby, was as ready and as calm as a human being could have been under the circumstances. She spoke clearly, calmly and crisply when she asked Ana Maria to send someone to find Miguel. In the time that he was located and joined his wife, a makeshift bed had been made on a pew, as comfortable as the circumstances could allow. A few standing candles had been placed around her, and sufficient space was allowed for some measure of privacy to be afforded. Soothingly and reassuringly Ana Maria coached her through her breathing and pushing as she felt for the baby's positioning. Her smile told Mercedes that everything was alright and her look to Miguel told him the same. Mercedes at a later time remarked that while she did not know what to expect, she had not expected the birth of her first child to be so easy or under such circumstances.

Miguel experienced the feeling of helplessness that all fathers have always experienced unless they were doctors delivering their own children. All he could do was to hold her hand and pray with his inner voice as loudly as he could, "Please God, Please God, be with us tonight. We are in your house, be a genial host and be with my wife." Over and over a version of the same plea played in his head up until that one second in which he closed his eyes and heard his daughter's cry. Ana Maria lifted her and said, "Mercedes, Miguel, I give you Graciela Mercedes de la Madrid, a child of God born in his house." His dream had come true. The child was a perfect image of her mother. She looked bewildered as she looked at her father with the same round eyes he had noticed when he first saw Mercedes. The baby's hair was lighter than either one of theirs and so was the color of her skin. Miguel, holding back tears of joy, kissed the baby, and after kissing Mercedes gave the baby to her.

Around noon of the next day the Hurricane ended as it had been snuffed in the way one blows a candle. It simply stopped and the sun reappeared. Several of the men ventured outside the church to assess the conditions around them. The wagons had been stationed and tied with heavy ropes against the church's wall and away from the wind. Except for a few loose boards, they were intact. They would later find the horses in great shape as well. Miguel organized an advanced party to ride to La Jacana and assess conditions there. Before leaving he checked on his family and found them surrounded by more women than were needed to attend to a new born baby, but this after all was Graciela Mercedes de la Madrid, and she was special.

The first houses they saw at La Jacana were beaten up but still standing. Not one had collapsed. Owing to Father Angel's instructions to keep windows opened, the houses withstood the pressure of the wind. The corrals which offered less wind resistance were also standing, but the same was not true of the barn which was scattered all over the field. All of the heavy milking cans which had been tied together with rope were still together. Someone had the idea to fill them with rocks to add to their weight and as a result the cans either stood their ground or did not travel far. Miguel asked the men to collect all the debris and separate them in piles based on their possible reuse. Those boards that could not be reused would be burned, when dry, and those that could be salvaged would be used to rebuild. Not one house had collapsed. A saddled horse came out to them from under the nearby trees.

They recognized it to be Jaime's and had no idea how it came to be there since they believed everyone had evacuated to Vega Alta.

Not known to them was the fact that once at the church, Jaime Yasmino had left his family to return to La Jacana for fear of leaving his home unprotected. This foolish decision proved fatal for him. They walked in the direction of the trees from where the horse came and after clearing fallen branches and more debris, they found his body pinned under a large branch. He had a wide crack on his skull where apparently a branch had struck him. They could not tell if the blow caused his death or if he bled to death. The one sad and evident truth is that dead he was. "Move him to his house, and clean him up as best you can, I will go tell Elisa." Miguel thought that it was ironic than on the day a new life had arrived at La Jacana another one ended.

Just before the body was moved, Antonio and Orovis returned with some of the animals and after paying their respects to the deceased asked the men standing over the body to collect the rest of the animals from the caves. The animals needed to be fed and secured in a corral until the barn could be rebuilt. From their elevated vantage point they could see most of the farm, and all things considered, in their judgment, it could have been much worse, the loss of life notwithstanding. "Huracan was not very angry this time," said Orovis, causing Antonio to wonder what real anger would have been like. They had been fortunate because the storm had come from the south and while it dropped a great deal of rain, the wind had been effectively blocked by the mountain. Not yet known to them, San Juan, not having a mountain to protect it, had not fared as well. The damage caused by the hurricane had been far more extensive than in the valley of the Vegas, and since it had many more structures, the property damage was greater.

In San Juan, Juan José Martinez who had lived most of his life in Puerto Rico was well versed in the ways of hurricanes, and although not Taino, he had an understanding and a healthy respect for the forces of nature when unleashed upon a small island. He had taken several precautionary steps. The most important one had been to hire a crew to dismantle the farmers market. So thorough was their work that once finished with the dismantling there was no evidence that a market had once stood on the spot where there was only open space. After organizing the reassembly of the market he rode the horse to assess the situation at La Jacana.

Riding at full gallop, and changing horses in Bayamon, he reached his destination in less than four hours. By the time he arrived, La Jacana was bursting with activity with men and women working side by side, cleaning up and getting things organized. All the children under ten had been left at the church for an extra day, giving adults the opportunity to do their work without distraction. As a result, except for fallen branches here and there most everyone's homes had been restored to their previous condition. Because of the heat, they buried Jaime as quickly as Father Reynaldo had been able to conduct the service and a grave had been dug. His grave was near the chapel, which had also survived the storm. He was the first to be buried in what eventually became the cemetery. By the end of the day following the hurricane everything was as close to normal as it could have been. All that was missing were the children and that was remedied the next day, when Fathers Reynaldo and Angel drove them back from Vega Alta in two wagons that had been left behind.

Juan José drew Antonio and Miguel aside and talked about the opportunities that were now opened as a result of the hurricane. It seemed to him that most of their corn and pineapples, and the individual farmer's plots had survived the wind and rain. He told them that the need for food in San Juan would be great and that if they hurried in picking the corn and harvesting the pineapples, plus whatever else they could gather, they could rush it to market and have it in their stands as soon as the market was raised, which he expected was happening as he spoke. "All of the ships went to sea to ride out the storm, rather than to remain in port and be crushed against the piers or one another." Ship captains knew what to do when facing a storm at sea and knew that little could be done to avert disaster when tied to a dock. Juan José knew the ships would be returning to port and upon recognizing the opportunity they too would try to respond by sailing to other islands and returning to Puerto Rico with whatever goods and foodstuffs they could collect. He suggested sending a rider to Bayamon to buy as much as was available from the farmers there and having that available to load on their wagons when they passed through on the way to San Juan. The same possibilities existed in Toa Baja and so another rider was sent to assess their condition as well. In the event they had vegetables to sell, they too would be sold at their market in San Juan. They also gathered a few pigs and chickens to sell to the restaurants that would need them.

"One last thing," Antonio said, "I do not want anyone to feel we have taken advantage of the situation by charging higher prices than normal. These after all are our people." Like Juan José, Miguel knew that there was an opportunity to double, possibly triple the income from their crops, but knew better than to argue with Antonio about the matter. Miguel knew well why he spoke as he did. He remembered that Sister Graciela had left Antonio the money to do good things with. And at that moment, getting food to people who were going to be hungry was a good thing to do, overcharging them was not.

The rider from Toa Alta returned and said that a wagon should be sent there since there was enough left to warrant the trip. The remaining two wagons were loaded and sent on their way, while another trailed fairly empty to be used for whatever they expected to pick up in Bayamon. The damage to the valley of the Vegas was insignificant to what they saw in San Juan. As they descended from Bayamon they could see a great many number of structures damaged, some with collapsed stilts, others with missing roofs, some with partial roofs and missing walls. Entering the city and heading in the direction of their market, they observed a group of shirtless men, clearing debris and trying to restore some semblance of order in the streets. They were big men, all wearing boots and the same colored pants. These were American soldiers. The first they had seen, since they had not been in San Juan after Spain's surrender. Looking at the men working and appreciating their strength, they could more easily understand why and how Spain came to lose the war.

Off to the side of the men, fully dressed and standing under a tree was a man who by the absence of sweat on his body, and his crisp uniform they deduced must have been the officer in charge of the work detail. He was blond and of fair skin, as tall as Antonio but not as big. Only when he lifted the cap from his head momentarily they recognized the man. They knew that they had seen him before, in Cuba. This was the man who slapped the woman in front of them. The very same man that Antonio had bear hugged to prevent him from hitting the woman again. On that occasion he had been wearing a white dinner jacket and a black tie, instead of the uniform that he now wore. The night of the incident had been a full moon night, and they had then sufficient light to have had a good look at the man and his rage filled eyes as Antonio released him. They turned away from him at the precise moment that he looked in their direction. It was not possible for them to tell if they had been recognized. Although they had done nothing wrong, they preferred to avoid another confrontation with the man. After all he was an officer in the army occupying Puerto Rico.

Soon after unloading at the market, and opening for business, Miguel was approached by Guillermo Recondo, the man from whom he had rented his house. His wife Magaly was standing next to him and looking at her feet. He seemed embarrassed as he approached and soon after he started to speak, Miguel understood why. Things in San Juan had not worked out as they had expected, and as a result he and his wife were living on the streets, sleeping where they could, and eating what they could scavenge. The money they had received for the rent did not last as long as they had hoped and the opportunities for work they thought existed, didn't. Their lives in the valley, which seemed so terrible, were by comparison far better to how they now lived. Even before Guillermo asked, Miguel spoke, sensitive to Guillermo's condition which was causing him to humble himself in front of his wife, saying, "Would you consider helping us at La Jacana we could surely use you and your wife. Mercedes just had a baby, and she will need some help, and the farm will need more hands than we now have. Do you think you could do us a big favor and return with us. Please, I will consider it a personal favor." Guillermo with his manhood restored was only too happy to offer his help. The little that they owned they had with them, so they were ready to return at that moment.

They were out of inventory as soon as they finished unloading. The locals had seen the wagons as they entered San Juan, and spread the word like the wind. The market had been rebuilt and was only waiting for goods to sell and customers and now it had both. As agreed, they sold everything after the hurricane for the same price they had sold it before. Juan José did this against his better commercial judgment, but all the same appreciating the intentions behind the decision to not take advantage of people who had suffered enough Early the next morning, while making preparations to depart for the valley, a blond, tall and lanky man approached Miguel and Antonio as they loaded the last wagon. The man's attempt to speak Spanish which was appreciated by them, was funny nonetheless. They could not tell the origins of his Spanish accent. It certainly was not Caribbean or European for that matter. His Spanish had been learned in the Philippines, taught to him by the women he visited while American ships had been welcomed. His vocabulary was limited mostly to the words used in the transaction between women who sell and men who buy. However, that was enough for him to communicate his interest in speaking to them. And he could understand perfectly. What made his pronunciation all the more funny was the blend of English, Spanish and Tagalog. He said that he had been a sailor in the American navy, whose term of enlistment expired while his ship was docked in Puerto Rico. The navy had suggested that if he wanted to return to his home in the United States, he was required to extend his service. And since he had nothing, and no one waiting for him in Baltimore, and the Caribbean sea region agreed with him, he decided to remain in Puerto Rico.

Before joining the navy he had been a blacksmith and believing he had had his fill of horses biting and mules kicking, he thought he would give the navy a try. It turns out that he disliked the sea a whole lot more than smithing and settled on the idea of picking up his trade and staying a while in the island. "Throw your bag in the wagon and jump in. We can surely use a blacksmith and an American one at that," said Antonio.

CHAPTER 20

While the wagons left ahead of them, Miguel and Antonio waited for the bank to open. It was in the same place, with the same people and even the name, had not changed. They met with the Manager, Elias Elizondo and inquired about their cash position since they had traded for dollars before the war started. The manager looked at his ledger of accounts and told them they had more money than the bank had in its vault. The demand for dollars had been high since the Americans had taken over with anyone holding pesetas requiring to trade them into dollars. Of course the rate of exchange for those late traders was not the same as that of anyone who saw what would happen with the war and acted early. They learned that they had as much money as they did before they bought the farm. "Did I not tell you, did I not tell you, this would happen?" said Miguel. "No," said Antonio, "I only remember you saying this could happen, and besides I do not remember disagreeing with you," he added with a large grin on his face, as he threw his arm around his brother.

"Tell Don Pedro José that we will build two houses. Both of them identical but on different locations. Tell him to double the crews and start right away. I am taking Ana Maria to live in my house." Not surprised by what he had just heard, Miguel asked if Ana Maria would have any say in the decision.

Antonio told him that she already had, it was him who had hesitated, and that he would not hesitate any longer. He had decided to take the Puerto Rican woman for his wife. "I am going to ask her to select the site upon which her house will be built. I will ask her as soon as I see her." They caught up to the wagons in Bayamon, where they had stopped to wait for Antonio and Miguel. And after settling accounts with the people whose goods they had received in consignment, they continued on their way to the Vegas. Antonio caught sight of the boy who had wanted to duel with him, and the girl who had sat next to him. He tipped his hat to both and nodded to the boy's mother who stood to the side of the couple. They only looked at him fleetingly since they were more interested in the gringo sitting on one of the wagons seeming to be taking a nap.

This time, instead of trailing the wagons they galloped ahead and by early afternoon they were at Miguel's house where Mercedes, Ana Maria and Graciela Mercedes sat in the small balcony enjoying the afternoon breeze and breastfeeding the little girl. Miguel and Antonio were impressed by Mercedes' absence of modesty, but nonetheless surprised as she did not move to cover the breast to which the baby was attached. Mercedes responding to their look of surprise said, "This child is Boricua by birth and I am Boricua by choice and this is how Boricuas feed their babies. Why would I do any different?" They both looked at Ana Maria who proudly smiled back at them with a look that said. 'Get used to it.'

There were no idle hands at La Jacana evidenced by the progress made since they had left for San Juan. The dairy was mostly fully restored, not quite, but functional. The same was true of the chicken coop, which was functional enough to start gathering eggs on the next day. The chickens were still recovering from the shock of the storm and delayed laying eggs by the one day. Ana Maria was waiting for the wagons to return from San Juan so that she could get back to her deliveries. Antonio, who was holding Miguel's plans for his house, took her by the hand and asked her to go with him. When they were some distance from the house, they stopped and sat under a red flamed tree which surprisingly had retained most of its branches, at least enough of them to offer shade.

"Take a look at these plans and tell me if you like them." He laid them at her feet and waited for her reaction. She looked at him for a few seconds before looking at the drawings of a house before her. As he asked, she took a good look at the plans and said, "Don Anton, what am I looking at, and why am I looking at it?"

"This, Doña Ana Maria is your house. The one in which we will live, the one in which our children will live, this will be our home." She was not surprised by his words since they were the ones she had hoped to hear. Still she was overwhelmed by the fact that this man who had come from so far, who had done so much in so little time, who could have had any woman he would choose, had chosen her. "Well, since you put it that way, Don Anton. Yes, I will be your woman." They held hands a while, she contemplating what their future would be like, he letting go of his past, letting his great expectations remove his regrets from his memory. Then they kissed. They kissed sweetly, with the confidence and comfort that comes to those lovers who find their mate exactly as they had hoped. They kissed with the expectation of how their lives would be fulfilled by the realization of their marriage. Then they just kissed because their lust overwhelmed them.

Raymond Gossett wasted no time in setting up his blacksmith shop. He first focused on the horses and the mules. Then he went to work on the wagons and the equipment that before his arrival had only been serviced when they broke and failed in some form. His navy training had taught him an important concept. One foreign to La Jacana and possibly to the island. The concept was maintenance, preventive, scheduled and consistent maintenance. He had a disposition that endeared him to all he worked with.

And while his accent still brought smiles to people when they first heard it, his conduct soon earned their respect. Although he did not know it, he was a great teacher. Everyone who stood near him as he worked received a lesson whether one was needed or not. Soon everyone became more conscientious about how they cared for animals or equipment. And just as quickly, the word went out about the American blacksmith at La Jacana. People from Vega Alta and as far as Arecibo brought their equipment and their animals to the American. The growing demand for his services justified his getting apprentices to be trained by him. Those boys not in school, and of age, were sent to him by their families to learn a trade. Everything was as perfect for Raymond Gossett as it could have possibly been, except for his loneliness.

Then he met Elisa Yasmino, and his loneliness ended. It started with her bringing him coffee to the shop in the morning, water in the afternoon and lunch in between. It continued with him showing an interest in her boy by taking him riding with him, every chance he could. Their oblique courtship continued for several months and as they exchanged kindnesses one to the other, they began to want to be with each other more so than with anyone else. Although her husband had not been caring, warm or loving, both Elisa and Fermin, her son, had been left devastated by Jaime's death. The devastation came from the fear that loneliness brings. How to go on? How to raise a child on her own? What would become of her and her boy? It seemed that with the American, the questions had been answered. Raymond who made the formal move by asking Fermin, Elisa's eight year old son if he would approve of his marrying her.

Raymond's mother had never remarried after her husband abandoned her. Instead several men had moved in with her until they too abandoned her. Because of his experience and the pain associated with his childhood memories, Raymond was determined that Elisa's boy would know a better life than he had known. He was determined that the boy would feel loved. Although a child, Fermin had a good understanding of what had happened with his mother from the time his father had been buried to this day. She had stopped smiling then and now smiled and sang all the time. This man who was speaking to him had made him feel loved, as if he belonged. He loved this man more than he had loved his father. With his father he had felt fear, even respect but never love. He said yes. Next Raymond spoke to Antonio and Miguel, requesting permission to marry Elisa. They answered him that it was not up to them to say yes or no, but up to Elisa. Raymond, had always thought that if he ever married he would do things right, and since Elisa had no one but Fermin, they were the next thing closest to parents she had. And so he asked and received their blessing. Next he asked her and she too said yes.

They decided to build their house at a spot near the convenience store. Since Mercedes had less time than before the baby, Ana Maria was managing the store most of the time. She no longer rode the dairy wagon. Instead her brothers were now making the daily deliveries. With the increased volume, they now sent a wagon to Vega Alta and one to Toa Baja every day, except Sundays. At first it was mostly families who bought their products, but as their product improved in quantity and quality, businesses joined in ordering for their stores and restaurants. In particular, a new bakery had opened in Vega Alta and they sold freshly baked bread, lathered in butter and re-baked. People would line up outside the bakery to buy the loaves as soon as they came out of the ovens.

Her brothers came out of nowhere, a week after the hurricane, looking for work at the only place that was hiring; La Jacana. They had not spoken to Ana Maria since she had left them and had no idea she was engaged to one of the owners. Their father had forbidden them to speak to her, but even then they had wished they could have done the same, except that unlike her, they could not read and had nowhere to go. They were the prodigals to the grateful father. Her reception could not have been happier or warmer. When they entered the store to inquire about work, they were stunned to see her. Although she had not changed much since they last saw her, she looked nothing like the girl they use to berate for trying to be better than them. The person before them had the bearing of a woman of distinction. Not presumptuous, but assured and confident of herself. She spoke first and said, "When I got out of bed this morning, I knew this would be a special day. I just did not know just how special." With that she hugged and kissed all three of them, while they held their hats at their front and looked at the ground. They reacted to her as their superior while she spoke to them as their sister. She asked Angela, who was now attending at the store since Magaly, Guillermo's wife was now at the house helping Mercedes take care of Graciela Mercedes, to take over the counter. "Come" she said, "I want you to meet Antonio." They were married at the church of the Immaculate Conception in Vega Alta.

Ana Maria did not care where they were married, but Antonio wanted the wedding at the church for reasons of his own, and she would not disagree with his wish. She wore Mercedes' wedding dress, which required only minor alterations. Antonio wore the same suit he had worn to Mercedes' and Miguel's wedding on board ship. However, he did have to buy new boots for the occasion. When Mercedes heard that he intended to wear the same boots he wore every day to work in the fields, she in no uncertain terms told him just how unacceptable that would be. She finally reached him and he agreed to buy new boots after she reminded him that the wedding was about Ana Maria as well, and that for her sake, he needed to wear new boots. He wore the new boots long enough to be married, because immediately after they returned to La Jacana for the wedding feast, he changed to his old boots.

Their first dance as husband as wife was a Danzón, a combination of Waltz and Mazurka which is an European dance. It had the formality and pomp of a traditional Waltz but the steps were livelier and the dancers stood closer to one another, than European tradition allowed. They did not really dance as much as it was him holding her as she danced, while he stood awkward and helpless. Antonio was quite relieved when her father stepped in to have his turn. Customarily it would have been the father's dance first, but Ana Maria insisted that her first dance would be with her husband. Her father danced no better than Antonio and was just as pained in going through the motions. It did not mattered to her, her main purpose in inviting her father and mother was for them to celebrate her good choice in the husband she had selected. After her brothers had been hired at La Jacana they returned to their home in Espinosa to collect their things and to invite their parents to the wedding. The parents readily accepted once they heard whom their daughter was marrying.

The music was provided by the municipal band, organized by the mayor for ceremonies and special occasions. He had determined that the wedding was a very special occasion and made the music his wedding gift. He also offered, and they accepted the use of his carriage for the ride to the feast. The band was composed of anyone who owned an instrument and could play it. Their music was strongly influenced by the Caribbean region and their repertoire ran from the formal Danzón, to the informal Merengue and the wild Bomba. The Merengue had its origins in the island of Santo Domingo while the Bomba was created by the African slaves who had found their way to the islands of the Caribbean. The Bomba would take possession of those who drank enough Rum to allow themselves to be possessed and driven to frenzy by the beat. Some of the men stayed behind to watch over the several pigs that were being roasted, along with breadfruits, sweet potatoes, and the blood sausages that had been prepared from the pigs' blood.

During the feast, Father Reynaldo, Miguel and Mercedes, holding their daughter in her arms, slipped away to the chapel where lamps had been lit. There, with the music and the celebration in the background, they were married on that day in the eyes of God. There, at that moment the promise was fulfilled and she was the first woman to be married at the chapel in La Jacana. Elisa and Raymond had already been married, and the wedding took place at La Jacana but not in the chapel. Their wedding had been held outdoors.

The feast would continue through the night and was not to end until the roosters crowed and the sun rose over the mountain. Antonio and Ana Maria boarded their carriage and as customary were sent off bombarded by rice thrown at them by the multitude of well wishers. People from Vega Alta, Toa Baja, Bayamon and as far as San Juan had traveled to attend the biggest wedding the region had seen in years, if not ever. When they arrived at their house, Antonio picked Ana Maria in his arms and carried her inside. Once inside the house, he kissed her without putting her down and carried her into the bedroom. The house remained in darkness as they undressed, either out of modesty or because they chose to not bother with lighting a lamp. This was their first time together as husband and wife, but not their first time together as man and woman. That had taken place, soon after their engagement when she invited him to bathe with her in the river. It was as natural an act as could have taken place. And under the circumstances, not making love that night in the river, would have been unnatural. As young people are wont to do, passion overwhelms process, but not kindness or tenderness. That evening it had started with her sitting behind him who was half submerged in the stream. She bathed him with a soft cloth and while reaching to wash his arms from behind, she pressed her body against his and from that moment on, their passion overwhelmed their judgments, and they made love. With the reckless abandon that accompanies youth, that night they made love until they had no more to give and they were spent.

That had been the first and last time they had made love until the night of their wedding. That special night, they committed themselves to kindness and tenderness towards one another.

These were the two conditions prevailing in their bed their first night as husband and wife, and the same ones they would observe every time they made love. Life was good for the two of them in every way. They had lived their lives apart and now would live the rest of their lives as one.

Marisol arrived at the port of San Juan, precisely one week after Ana Maria and Antonio were married. As instructed by the letter she had received, she located Juan José Martinez who had been advised to expect her, but only her. He had been told to expect a school teacher, but the lady in front of him did not match his image of school teachers. This one was lively, self assured, pretty to look at and easy to like. This girl in no way resembled the many girls chosen for him by his family so often in the past. Had they selected the one before him now, he would have been married long ago, he thought. It was hard for him to think of the pretty woman before him in the role of a disciplinarian. He was indeed very glad to meet her and said so. Her ship had arrived on Friday afternoon and immediately after landing she sought out to find him. Because of the late hour, he sent one of his men to collect her luggage which she had left with the chief steward until it could be reclaimed once she knew what was to happen. He then made sleeping arrangements for Marisol and her companion, and scheduled an early departure for La Jacana. Knowing this would be a long ride he selected the best horse to take them to Bayamon where he again selected the best available horse to take them the rest of the distance. Along the way he allowed her to say as much as she wanted to say, and he told her the story of La Jacana since the beginning. It was just past six in the evening on the Saturday following Marisol's and her traveling companion's arrival when they reached Mercedes' and Miguel's house, and there they also found Ana Maria and Antonio who were visiting. Juan José announced their arrival with a loud yell to get their attention.

They had been sitting on the porch and turned to see who was calling. From the distance they could recognize the wagon, and Juan José's shape, but not the other two passengers riding next to him. They could tell one was a female and the other one a small child. They recognized her as the wagon neared but not the young boy. "Marisol, Its Marisol," shouted Mercedes with great excitement as she rushed down the steps. "Our teacher is finally here and it looks as if she brought a student with her." They all stepped down to greet the wagon as it came to a stop, and whatever weariness Marisol may have felt from the day's long ride in a wagon, disappeared as she saw her old friends. They looked wonderful to her, and she wondered how she appeared to them. Antonio was the first to take her in his arms as he helped her down from her seat, and hugged her fiercely after her feet touched the ground. After better than three years since he had last seen her, having her with them was a dream come true. Next, Mercedes and Miguel stepped forward to greet her with at least the same warmth displayed by Antonio. At last he spoke and said, "Marisol allow me the pleasure of introducing you to Doña Ana Maria Morales de Barradaz, my wife, we were married last week." The two women took an imperceptible moment to size each other, before Marisol said, "I am Marisol, please think of me as your sister, Anton has been my brother for many years, but rather than having a sister-in-law, I want to be your sister," then she stepped forward to hug her as sisters do. Marisol reached for the boy who had remained on the wagon next to Juan José, and holding him by the hand she walked the child an stood in front of Antonio. "Antonio Miguel, say hello to your father, Anton Barradaz."

CHAPTER 21

They waited for the boy to fall asleep to ask the many questions on their minds. Who, what, where and how were just the beginning. The how started with the sad and tragic story of Dolores who had died of complications after giving birth to the boy. Her pregnancy had been a welcomed event in her life, but not in her family's. Only because her mother prevailed upon her father she was not thrown out of her house. In her father's eyes she had disgraced the family. Her mother on the other hand understood that her daughter had loved and was in need of love and would not allow her husband to order her daughter out of the house. In no uncertain terms, she made it clear that his order would have caused him the loss of a daughter and a wife. It all seemed normal with her pregnancy and with the birth. At least the midwife thought everything was normal, until she could not stop the bleeding. The midwife, not being a doctor did not have the means or the knowledge to keep her alive. Dolores, bled to death soon after naming the boy, and holding her son against her bosom, she closed her eyes and rested. Her passing had been peaceful, as if she understood what was happening to her, and accepted it.

Dolores's mother would have preferred to raise the boy as her own, but realized it would not be in the boy's best interest for him to remain in her house, since he would have been a constant reminder to his grandfather of the shame and tragedy that his birth had brought to the family. And since the mother knew that she could not protect him all the time from her husband's wrath, she asked Pilar to take the boy to the convent in Barcelona, and there search for the father. Pilar did as instructed, and took the boy to the convent, where upon learning he was Antonio's son the nuns readily received him. Marisol had not been present when the baby was delivered to the convent by Pilar, and had no way of knowing where they child had come from, but she knew the boy was Antonio's son the moment she laid eyes on him, and the baby smiled at her. His head was shaped exactly as his father's and his eyes, black and penetrating seemed to belong more to a Gipsy than to a Basque, "Dolores' eyes," she thought. His hair was as dark an unruly as his father's and it stood in all directions. It had not been practical or possible for the baby to remain at the convent and as a result, arrangements were made for him to be housed at the orphanage of the Little Sisters of Charity, near the church. Out of site was not out of mind when it came to Antonio Miguel Barradaz because Marisol made it her mission to spend every available minute nurturing the child and replacing the mother he had lost.

She had every intention of adopting the boy once she married, but the letter from Puerto Rico had changed all that. She had received it right at the time war was declared on Spain by the United States, and as a consequence, she had not been able to respond to the letter, and not knowing how long the war would last or how it would end she had not given much thought to the idea of what to do with the boy or with herself. And then, all of sudden as quickly as it had started, the war ended.

Since she was a single woman, releasing the child to her was somewhat problematic. On the other hand there was no one at the orphanage or the convent who did not know that Marisol was the only mother the boy knew. Not once, never, did anyone from Dolores' family visited or even inquired about Antonio Miguel in the three years since Pilar had delivered him to the nuns. Either the sight of him was too painful or anguishing to them, but for whatever the reason, he was dead to them. His natural mother's family notwithstanding, the boy lacked for nothing when it came to loving care and attention. Marisol saw to his baptism, and without fail visited him before leaving for work or upon her return. This pattern she followed consistently, except for Sundays, when she would pick him up for the entire day, and return him to the orphanage after he was already asleep in her arms. There was no way that Marisol was going to Puerto Rico without the boy, and so she pleaded with her uncle the Bishop who interceded with the Bishop of Barcelona, who authorized that the baby be given to her. All she had to do was to swear that the baby would be raised Catholic.

Stunned by the story they had just heard, the two men and the two women remained silent, trying to absorb the full impact of Marisol's account, possibly even visualize the entire sequence of events as they understood them. The one thing clear to all of them was Marisol's love for the boy. For that reason Ana Maria needed to tread lightly. Her first impulse was to say that she would assume the mother's role and raise the boy as her own. In a way she felt gratified that something good had come out of her husband's union with the boy's mother. Tragic though her death was, that could not be changed, all she could do, all they could do was to honor her by raising her son to be like his father. And this she would do. Ana Maria insisted that they move into their house. Although still sparsely furnished, and only one bedroom had any furniture in it, she insisted that their bedroom would be Marisol's and the boy's. They would have beds made at once, and they knew the man to make them in Toa Baja. Ignoring Marisol's protest, she insisted that they would sleep in her bed. She and Antonio would sleep in hammocks until the new beds could be delivered. "Marisol, you just met my wife and you have no idea how stubborn she can be, so please honor our home by living with us." Either because of weariness or for gratitude, Marisol simply said, "Let's go to sleep" Antonio was somewhere between bewildered and elated. Who could have told him when he awoke that morning that by the time he went to sleep, he would have a son. Marisol and the boy were fast asleep as Ana Maria and Antonio sat on rocking chairs on their porch. Sensing his mood, and understanding his need to just be with his thoughts she chose not to speak.

Together they sat in silence for the better part of an hour and then he spoke. "What do you think?," he asked. "I was just thinking how fortunate we all are. Antonio Miguel, because he has his father and two mothers. Marisol, because she can rest easy in the knowledge that her boy will be loved by many, for different reasons and in many ways. You, because God has delivered a son to you, and me, because I have never loved a man, and now I love two of them." He simply looked at her and smiled, relishing in the knowledge that he had married well.

With the teacher at La Jacana the school gained form, shape, structure and schedules. All of the underpinnings of a system of education were present in the little building that was a full time school and a part time church. Marisol was in the element of one who was born to teach, and the love she had for her profession was shared by all who benefited by being taught by her. The children of La Jacana were progressing at a pace that astounded their parents. Especially since most of the children, if not all of them could not wait to get to school in the mornings. Books, writing tablets, writing boards, desks and all other items required to outfit a school had been purchased with the dairy fund that had continued to grow at La Jacana. There were many changes taking place at La Jacana but few more noticeable than the increased number of visits by Juan José Martinez.

Soon the school population outgrew the school and a new building was needed. The decision was made to build a bigger structure, with a second classroom and its own water well. The little building would become officially and exclusively, the chapel. Education was not the only thing thriving at La Jacana. Antonio Miguel was growing in every way. Surrounded by people who adored him, and having all the open space a child could need. He was in his element. Some said that although not born in Puerto Rico, he was born to be Puerto Rican. Because of Marisol's commitments at the school, a bungalow had been built for her close to the school but distant from the house where she had been living since arriving. No particular decision had been made, it just happened that the boy remained with his father and his other mother. One second after laying eyes on the boy, Ana Maria's heart was given to him. She loved him as if she had conceived him. She wondered if she would love her own natural children as much as she loved Antonio Miguel. That question would soon be answered since she was in the first trimester of her pregnancy. One day she woke up early, stepped outside of the house, sat on the steps in the back, reached for a bucket, and she knew she was pregnant.

Her husband, like all husbands since there have been husbands was oblivious to her daily rising and throwing up routine. She had thought to wait until he would ask about why she threw up every morning but he never did. With the morning sickness behind her she just told him. "Don Anton, Antonio Miguel needs a brother or a sister and I am going to give it to him."

A smile came to his face and remained there for quite a while. He too had wondered if his love for his children to come would in any way compare to his love for Antonio Miguel. He had hoped so, because he so enjoyed his love for his son, that he wanted more of them. He reached for her hand and pulled her next to him as he laid in bed, and kissed her. He then asked, "Whatever we name the child, the name Miguel must be in it." Ana Maria answered by saying "If a boy, his name is Miguel Antonio, and if a girl, we will name her Ana Graciela, if you approve."

Because of his nature and by choice Orovis kept to himself most of the time. If he was not with Antonio he was alone. He had a curious mind, and for a Taino living in a constantly changing world, his mind was continually reeling. Since first returning to the valley of the Vegas his life had been everything he had wanted it to be. The Spanish people had done everything they said they would do and in ways they had said they would do it. He could look around and see happiness where he had seen desperation. Instead of attending children's funerals he was attending their baptisms and birthdays celebrations. He had not embraced Christianity because his religion had served him just fine. However he did enjoy the fellowship he shared with the priests, and when given the opportunity he participated as long as he was not required to enter a church. The arrival of the young Spanish boy had puzzled him. Although he knew that Antonio had come from Spain he could not fathom how the boy was connected to him. Curious as he was, as was everyone else, he wanted to see the boy. And when he did, he knew what the fuss was about. The child was his father in every way. He walked like him, moved like him and looked at him, the same way Antonio had looked at him the evening they met on board ship. Antonio Miguel had replaced Antonio in Orovis' heart and mind.

It was a fortunate thing for all concerned that the running of La Jacana in all of its forms consumed their time and energy, but not Orovis'. For the first year of Antonio Miguel's arrival at La Jacana and until the time that he came of school age, Orovis would pick him up at the house and teach him about things that could not be learned through school books. Sometimes the best lessons were taught with the help of birds that allowed them to watch as they fed their young ones, other times the lesson was provided by a snake as he ate a rabbit. Other times the lessons were more practical, such as when he would take him to watch Raymond the blacksmith nail shoes on a horse or a mule. Sensing that the boy may have wondered why the horse would stand so still while nails were pounded on his hoofs, Raymond explained that first he needed to gain the animals' trust and then they would let him do as he needed to, just like people. Although only four years old, these lessons would influence Antonio Miguel in his development. Regrettably, depending on whose perspective, the boy reached school age and the time for their activities was curtailed. Still Orovis would meet the boy every day after school, holding a pineapple, a papaya or a mango for them to share.

Miguel Antonio was big for his age and as a result played with boys the same size but older in age. It was then as it has always been the nature of boys for the big to pick on the small or the older ones to pick on the younger ones. And so it was that this dynamic was in play on an afternoon, when leaving school and walking towards Orovis, Antonio Miguel was shoved from behind by a boy for no evident reason. He did not fall as much as he rolled on his shoulder and used the momentum from the fall to charge at the boy, who surprised and off balance went down with his intended victim on top of him. That was the last time that anyone misjudged Antonio Miguel Barradaz. In fact, when arriving home from school his mother would ask him." Son, how was your day today," to which he would respond by saying, "I had a good day mother, no one hurt me and I did not have to hurt anyone."

As victors go, the Americans were benevolent ones. Instead of dictating and forcing their ways upon the Puerto Ricans, they allowed the local authorities to remain in place and conduct their business as usual, with minor, if any interference by the occupiers. As vanquished go, Puerto Ricans offered little resistance and seemed to not have cared that their dominion had passed from Spain to the United States. Long ago, Spain had stopped caring about the island and its residents, who reciprocated in kind, and in due course lost all identity with their European origins, and were more Puerto Ricans than Spaniards. As a result there was no resistance on the part of the general population to the American's occupation. What little resistance was offered by the small garrison of Spanish soldiers was eliminated in a few days. The presence of the Americans was not felt in the way that a conquering army reminds the vanquished what losing a war meant. The American presence was felt at La Jacana only through the patrols that occasionally passed through the valley on horseback. Occasionally they bivouacked on La Jacana property. On the occasion, when they helped themselves to a goat, a pig, or some ears of corn, they would always make an effort to pay for what ever they consumed. In San Juan, at the farmers market, the Americans had become the best customers. So great was the need that the market could barely keep up with the demands of the quartermaster who was responsible for the feeding of the troops garrisoned in Puerto Rico.

"We need to face reality," Marisol spoke to Mercedes. "The Americans are here to stay, and we need to prepare our children for the new world that is coming. Americans are here and English is their language. I do not speak it but you do." In a million years, Mercedes would have never guessed that her years in the English boarding school would have prepared her for the present circumstance. Marisol and Ana Maria were having lunch, Miguel, Antonio, Orovis and Antonio Miguel had gone to help Raymond to brand the new cattle in their growing herd. They originally had enough cows to support the dairy, now the American army needed beef and La Jacana was pleased to supply it. Whenever Ana Maria was asked about her expected delivery date she would answer, "Any day now," but now, when asked, she would say, "Any minute now."

"Marisol is right," she said. Ana Maria's hunger for knowledge and books had in no way decreased since marrying Antonio. On the contrary, the books that they had accumulated had caused them to think that they may have needed to add a library wing to their house. She had read about America and the Americans in various books, and was amazed to learn that they had defeated what had been the greatest army in the world to gain their independence. Since then, gradually and almost stealthily they had continued their expansion. One president, Monroe was his name, had established a doctrine essentially designed to preclude all other countries from interfering with American interests.

Mercedes listened to all comments but did not need them to appreciate how important the English language would be to all Puerto Ricans. Ignoring it would in no way change the reality that they were occupied by people who spoke English. She felt as if she was in limbo. She was born in Spain but was no longer a Spaniard, she was living in Puerto Rico but there was no Puerto Rican country as such, and for all she knew she would probably end up an American. "You are right. We owe it to our children to prepare them to live in this new world. We must teach them English." Right there and then it was decided that she would meet with the governor general and ask for his help to obtain books to be used to teach Puerto Ricans English. Marisol insisted in traveling to San Juan with her. She expressed her concern over Mercedes' pregnancy. Not knowing that pregnancies to Mercedes were like long walks to most people. Ana Maria smiled and asked Marisol if seeing Juan José Martinez had anything to do with her desire to travel to San Juan.

In the carriage borrowed from the mayor of Vega Alta, the very same that had been used by Antonio and Ana Maria on their wedding day, Marisol and Mercedes set out to meet the military governor, in San Juan. Two riders were sent to escort them on the long ride. One of them, Raymond Gossett, had tied a cage with pigeons to the back of the carriage. He had come upon the idea of using carrier pigeons to send and receive messages between La Jacana and the market. He had been sending the same pigeons with the wagons for the better part of a month. This was the process required for them to learn the route. This trip to San Juan was to be the last one before they were put to work carrying messages.

In San Juan they were met by Juan José, whose pleasure in seeing Marisol could not be concealed even if he had wanted to. His familiarity with Mercedes was such that it made a hug and a kiss on both cheeks appropriate, so he decided to test if the same was true with Marisol, and it was. It was no accident that their lips glanced as they switched cheeks. He escorted their carriage to his family's house where there were to dine and stay the night. The escort riders then took the carriage and the horses to be cared for and made ready for the next day's return trip. Claiming exhaustion because of her pregnancy, Mercedes excused herself immediately after dinner and retired. Her real motive was to give Juan José and Marisol time alone. The same kindness was not extended by Juan José's mother who either intending to protect her son from Marisol, or her from him, sat with them until they all retired.

They stood before the desk of an aide de camp to General Guy Vernor Henry, Military Governor of the island of Puerto Rico. Struck by the elegance of both ladies, who were exquisitely well dressed, he rose to greet them and even saluted them. Their business they informed him was to request an audience with the governor general, and to discuss the need for support for their school. Not having and appointment, nor a recommendation from one of the local functionaries, their presence was most irregular. The meeting would have been difficult to arrange, had it not been that the general himself strode into the office, at the very same moment the aide was going to send them away. Mercedes had never met a general officer from any army but reasoned that it must have been him, since everyone stood at attention as he entered. "General Henry, I am Doña Mercedes De la Madrid, and this is Señorita Marisol Machado, we come from La Jacana in the valley of the Vegas, it is our farm that has been feeding your troops since soon after you arrived in Puerto Rico. May we please have a brief audience with you, sir?" To say that the general was impressed by the lovely and elegant ladies standing before him would have been a serious understatement. He felt as if he should have worn his dress uniform instead of what he was wearing. Moreover, general officers anywhere, from any army are not accustomed to being spoken to by civilians who do not follow protocol and the chain of command. These women were different. He had never spoken to Spanish women in English, and certainly never with one who spoke English with a British accent. These were obviously well bred ladies, and pretty at that. He spoke to them while looking at the captain standing next to him, and said, "Captain Caldwell will see you to my office, where I will join you in a minute." While they walked into his office, the general stepped near the window to have a second look at the carriage tied to the hitching post outside his command headquarters, and the two men standing next to it. While trying to assess the situation, he was surprised that one of the men was evidently not Puerto Rican, and not a Spaniard, he definitely looked American, and yet he was speaking in Spanish to the other man. Not having any answers to the questions in his mind, he figured he might as well ask the women what their visit was about.

Since arriving in Puerto Rico on December 1898, he had done very little other than to wait for orders from the war department. The battles that he had envisioned they would fight never materialized and the people whom he had expected to be hostile to Americans, weren't. Under the circumstances there was little need for an infantry general, and even less for a governor. It seemed that the island had managed to function very well without any authorities. All things considered, this was about as interesting an event as he had encountered since assuming his post.

"Ladies, I apologize for keeping you waiting, I hope that my aide has made you feel comfortable. Please tell me again who you are. I already know your names, but I am more interested in knowing who you are." Not a word of this made any sense to Marisol. She simply kept her hands folded on her lap and smiled at Mercedes, which gave the general the impression that the English speaking woman was the spokesperson for the quiet one. From the start of the meeting, to the end, General Henry had no idea that Marisol had no clue what was being said. Her occasional smiles and nods gave the impression that she was following the conversation.

Getting straight to the point, Mercedes stated her request for assistance with her project to teach English to Puerto Rican children. She made the case that if the United States was there to stay, it would serve everyone's best interest if English could be taught in the schools. She underscored the fact that other than the schools supported by the Catholic Church, there was not much of a formal educational system in Puerto Rico. Her specific requests were for books, educational material and anything he felt would serve their common purpose. Nothing could have been further from the general's mind when he had turned in the night before or when he awoke that morning, than the building of an English based education program for Puerto Rican children.

While they had encountered minimal resistance since occupying the island, no one was holding parades welcoming the American army either. For that reason, the request he was now considering was as surprising as it was welcomed. A feather in his cap for certain, he thought. Moving forward with the Americanization of the population through the teaching of English, and to have that be a local initiative, would surely be well received by the department of war, which had not quite decided what to do with the Island of Puerto Rico. While the Philippines had been strategic because of its position in the Pacific Ocean and Cuba because of its proximity to the United States mainland, Puerto Rico's value was yet to be determined.

Mercedes continued by asking for fifty books appropriate for the teaching of English to ages five to twelve. Further she asked the General for teaching guides that could be used by her in developing lesson plans. Sensing the General's enthusiasm for what he was hearing, she sealed the agreement by saying, "And of course, this being the first school to teach English in the Island, I insist that it should be named after you." Her understanding of human nature had never failed her and it certainly served her well on this occasion. The General responded to her request by calling for his aide and the clerk and ordering books and materials. Following those orders, he directed Captain Cawdell to assume responsibility for the delivery of the materials ordered to

La Jacana. Since the captain had learned Spanish before being posted as the General's aide, he would be the liaison between the General and the school. You should have all that you need in no longer than two months." Mercedes did not have a great deal of experience in commerce, but knew that once she had what she came for, it was best to leave. And so they did, after allowing the General to kiss both their hands.

Captain Mathew Cawdell did not embrace the General's orders with the same enthusiasm with which they were given. The truth of the matter was that he had always resented being the General's aide, as much as the general resented having a West Point reject on his staff. The captain had been forced upon him because of his family's connections in Washington; otherwise the General would not have allowed the captain in his ranks, under any circumstance. Captain Cawdell had originally been assigned to the quarter master corps. In the army, an officer was assigned to the quarter master corps either because he was exceedingly good at logistics or exceedingly bad at fighting. The captain was not good in the former and terrible at the latter. His expulsion from West Point was the culmination of many transgressions which he had committed all of his life. That time, his family could not protect him. The charge had been assault and battery and attempted rape of a female visitor to the academy. And although it had been too dark for the girl to identify her attacker, in the process of covering his tracks, he had lied about his whereabouts on the night the assault was committed and was expelled on an honor code violation for lying. His bitterness had followed him along with his reputation and now he was stuck in a little island far away from where decisions of great consequence were being made, and as he believed, through no fault of his own, he was being excluded. The first time he visited a Caribbean island was when he went to Cuba on his honeymoon, but that too had been an unpleasant experience because his wife filed for divorce on the day they had returned to the United States. Just another unfortunate event in a long list of similar misunderstandings.

CHAPTER 22

Marisol was finishing her lessons when Father Reynaldo arrived at the school, and asked if he could have a word with her. Since her arrival at La Jacana, they had been introduced but had not spent much time together in any setting, neither at church nor at the farm. She asked him to wait until she had assigned the next day's lessons and dismissed the children. As it was her custom, every school day started with a prayer by one of the children and concluded with a prayer by her. Her closing prayer always recognized by name the students whose performance merited the recognition and by anecdote those who needed to be recognized for different reasons. Father Reynaldo was greatly impressed by the children's response to her. It seemed to him that all eyes were on her and all ears listening to her every word. "Wish that I had that magic," he thought. "May I walk you to your house, Señorita Machado," he asked as she walked out of her school. There was never any effort to lock any doors because it was inconceivable that anyone would have dared take anything from the school. Instead, she just closed the doors. "Yes you may Father, but my name is Marisol, and since you are good enough to escort me, will you not join me for a glass of lemonade? Assuming the answer is yes, please stop at the well and draw a bucket of cool water, I'll go squeeze the lemons and then we can sit down." As if ordered by a superior he followed her instructions and brought her the fresh water as requested.

After mixing the lemon juice with the water and sugar, they sat on the steps of her house and remained silent for a time. Not long enough to be uncomfortable but long enough to border on awkward. Almost as if taking the measure of one to the other, they seemed uncomfortable with one another. The kind of response expected between two people who at that moment realize who they were and the impact one was having upon the other. Instead of one speaking and another listening, they both spoke at the same time. Finally she pointed to him, with a signal that indicated the floor was his.

The reason for his visit had been to try to solicit her support for his own purposes. His pastoral duties, he felt had been neglected as they concerned the children. Mainly because he had been having so much fun being part of La Jacana that when there, with the farm hands, he had to remind himself that he was not one of them, he was their priest. His problem was that he drew greater satisfaction from being with them as their equal than he did from hearing confessions and serving communion. These very personal thoughts were not shared with Marisol, instead he said, "This concerns the children." Specifically he wanted to introduce religious education to the children in a way that was reflective of the whole educational experience. He wanted to create a curriculum that would be compatible with the secular materials used by Marisol. He sought to make his lessons seamless, to the end that to the children it would be not necessarily religious education, but education. Marisol remembered how it had been for her to sit through catechism classes and how she could not have been less engaged. For her the experience was more endured than enjoyed, and it was not until she came under the influence of the sisters in Barcelona that she got religion, as it were.

The priest mainly wanted her support by allowing him access to the children who were already assembling in her school every day. He wanted an hour on Friday afternoons. Fridays worked best for him because he could remain at La Jacana for pastoral visits after work. He proposed to align her lesson plans with relevant Christian teachings so that the children could receive the lessons in a way that promoted a positive disposition towards their religion. He told her that long ago he realized that teaching the fear of God when it came to children, was not as effective as teaching the glory of God. "Let them learn the fear of God on their own when they are older. Let us make their childhood all the more joyful by promoting the love of God in them." She looked at him with a measure of surprise. The very fact that he was articulating his thoughts in the way he did, would have been heresy back in Spain, but this was Puerto Rico, and a new world required a new approach to teaching. Finally he said, "You and I are joined by our love of God and our love for these children. Together, we can do great things for him and them." He could not have been more right in more ways than he had yet to know.

The books arrived as promised by the General and were delivered crated, on board a wagon escorted by the Captain and two soldiers. Also as promised, the General had sent writing tablets and all sorts of additional materials of a greater variety and volume than requested or expected. Since he spoke Spanish, Captain Cawdell was able to find the school house by asking directions. There he found Marisol and the children outside, enjoying their recess. He was especially pleased to have met her, since he had found her alluringly attractive when he first saw her in San Juan. His arrival was met with great excitement and one of the boys was sent to find Mercedes and bring her to the school house so that she could personally thank the captain. While the books were unloaded, uncrated, and taken into the school house, he attempted to engage Marisol in conversation of an insinuating nature. The kind that made her feel great discomfort. The captain sensing her rejection to his advances made up his mind that this one too needed to be taught a lesson and he would do the teaching.

Miguel drove the wagon to the school house with Mercedes at his side. He recognized the officer at once, but the captain did not seem to recognize him. On the evening of their intervention with the captain in Cuba, Miguel's back had been mostly turned towards him, and his face could not be seen. Mercedes stretched out her hand to greet the captain while thanking him at the same time. The very next thing she did was to ask him to report to the General that he had seen the sign with his name on it, nailed to the wall of the school house. After that, she invited the men and his soldiers to stay for lunch before returning to San Juan. The captain declined, saying that they planned to make Bayamon before nightfall and continue to San Juan the next day. Having said that, they departed, but not before he gave Marisol one good last look.

Sensing a different than normal disposition on the part of her husband, Mercedes asked Miguel why he had remained in the background during the Soldiers' short visit. Asking for Marisol to join them in the conversation, he told them that he knew the officer and how he had come to know him. Mercedes knew the story of the encounter in Cuba because she had heard it on board the ship as they traveled to Puerto Rico, but not Marisol, and so he retold it. Marisol was shocked by what she heard from Miguel and felt the need to wash her hands after having touched the captain's. Hopefully, they said there would be no need to see him again. But they were wrong.

Mercedes was now teaching English two days a week using the materials provided by the Americans. The children at first responded with giddy laughter when asked to repeat the alphabet, over and over again, followed by counting to ten, over and over again, followed by singing short songs, over and over again. Soon they were exchanging greetings in English and using short sentences when asking for things. Mercedes who was a stickler for discipline would not respond unless the children spoke to her in English. They always had a good laugh when the same rule was applied to Marisol since she was also trying to learn English and was required to follow the rules of the class as did all the students.

She was seeing more of Father Reynaldo because he either had lunch with her or would stop at her house during his pastoral visits. Her house was always the last stop of his rounds, so that he had more time to visit with her than he did his other parishioners. As time evolved their friendship grew stronger and their conversations gravitated more towards their personal stories, dreams and aspirations. With no sense of shame, as if she was describing someone else's life, she related her life's story to him, and he reciprocated in kind, including the doubts he was having about his priestly calling.

Juan José's visits to La Jacana were always justified by some pressing matter that merited Antonio's and Miguel's attention, or by whatever excuse he could conjure so that he could visit Marisol. The fact that the carrier pigeon system created by Raymond the blacksmith was fully operational, eliminated the need for most direct conversations. The birds flew every morning and every afternoon as regular as the sun. Because the pigeons facilitated communications concerning orders or requests for goods and produce, these were ready upon the wagons' arrivals. The quick turn around lead to increased volume of business at a faster rate. La Jacana was a fully functional business operation with every one of its elements performing at peak levels. The general store was being attended to by Mercedes with Angela's help. Ana Maria, who was now past her delivery date, stayed at her house waiting for the big event.

Antonio had a feeling that they had not seen the last of the American captain. He suggested to Marisol not to be alone with him if he ever showed up at the farm again. Antonio just had a bad feeling about the man. He shared his thoughts with Ana Maria and with her mother who had moved into their house in expectation of Ana Maria's delivery which had been imminent for a week. The precise date of birth for a child had been as unpredictable an event as any in humanity. At best it was a close enough kind of proposition, and Ana Maria had been close enough beyond the expected date. Her mother suggested inducing the birth with a mixture of herbs and roots, but Ana Maria remembered seeing the effect the mixture had had on other women and refused. Her pains started just after midnight, shortly after her mother had left to attend to someone else's delivery. Being the only midwife between Arecibo and Bayamon, her services were in great demand. There had been times when she had delivered two babies on the same day, and sometimes more.

Antonio's first response to his predicament was in the form of anger towards the midwife, mother-in-law or not, until Ana Maria assured him that she could talk him through the procedure and besides, his anger in no way would alter their situation. Except for Antonio Miguel, who was asleep in their room, they were alone and that was their reality. Or so they thought until they saw Orovis at the entrance of the house. He had seen the wagon leave with Ana Maria's mother and decided to be near the house just in case he was needed. His sixth and seventh senses active as usual, placed him at the right time where he was most needed, and he was needed now. Glad to see him, Ana Maria directed him to pump water into two buckets, and then asked him and Antonio to wash their hands. "Don Anton," she said, "Look at me and do exactly as I tell you, Orovis you come to the side in case we need you." As calmly as if she were exchanging recipes for rice and beans, she talked them through the birth of their first born. This boy was in every way Puerto Rican. It seemed that every single form of ancestry in his blood was there for all to see. He looked exactly like the two of them. He had his mother's curly black hair and his father's Basque nose. His skin was dark complected but his eyes were of a clear blue color. He was all of those things, but most of all he was all theirs. After he completed the unpleseantries that immediately follow the birthing of a child, he once again washed his hands and reached to take the boy from her. "Would you like to name our son, Don Anton?," asked Ana Maria. Antonio had been cleaning the boy, after cutting the umbilical cord, he lifted him as if it were some form of ceremony. Mainly he just wanted a good look at him, so he lifted him up to the light and said, "Miguel Antonio Barradaz Morales, welcome to the world and to our lives." Their oldest son who had slept through the birth of his brother, walked into the room. His mother said, "Antonio Miguel, come and meet your brother Miguel Antonio." The older boy tentatively approached the new born who was about to receive his first feeding, placed his hand on his brother's head and smiled from ear to ear. No sooner were they all asleep when Ana Maria's mother returned and asked, "Did anything happen while I was gone?"

The new born was three weeks old by the time of his baptism and already had a reputation. According to who spoke, he had the longest fingers, or the strongest grip, or the greatest smile, the list of his qualities was long and special. Antonio was relishing in all of the attention because of his very private oath that his children would never, not for a moment feel abandoned and unloved as he and Xavier had felt. He remembered as an adult the pain he felt as a child not by his mother's absence but by the absence of her love and attention. It had hurt when they were sent away by their father without any regard about how they might have felt about leaving. He thought about his brother Xavier, and wondered if he had a family by now and if he felt the same way as he did about Ana Maria and his children. He quietly restated his oath to give his children a life better than the one given to him. Xavier he thought, "If he could see me now."

Orovis watched him as he entered La Jacana and followed him to Marisol's house where he saw the captain tie his horse out of the way, so that it could not be seen from the front of the house. He then saw the captain walk to her house but not before looking around to make certain that he had not been seen. Orovis walked away from his vantage point quietly and with great care. Once cleared, he retreated away from the house and turned to run in the direction of where he had last seen Antonio, who had been with a work crew, trimming bushes, machete in hand. Upon hearing Orovis' report, Antonio slid the machete in the scabbard attached to the saddle, and mounted his horse. Orovis did not have to describe the man he had seen entering Marisol's house. Antonio already knew who it was, and why he was there. He had known since he saw the officer in San Juan that he would see him again. By the time he arrived at her house, he could hear Marisol shouting, "Get out of here." Antonio ran into the house, just as Orovis who ran alongside his horse, caught up with him. What he saw, was the captain leaning over Marisol, who was pressed against her small table, as the man was attempting to tear off her blouse. Blocked by the man's body, she did not see Antonio until he stepped closer, stood behind the American, and grabbing him by his hair pulled him away as he struck him on his kidney. The force and the placing of the blow, caused the man to release her and drop to one knee, as air exited his lungs. From the kneeling position the man turned to look at his assailant and his face registered shock and surprise when he recognized the man who had grabbed him from behind in Cuba. He started to speak, but before a word came out of his mouth, Antonio struck with a downward blow that caught him squarely on the right temple. The blow made a cracking sound indicating that bone was being broken. The captain's cheek bone swelled in the blink of an eye. So large was the swelling that it caused the man's right eye to close almost shut. Antonio's rage was now beyond control as he raised his boot to stomp on the man's head, Marisol shoved him away saying, "Anton don't kill him, he is not worth it. Please think of your children, stop this now, I beg you in the name of Sister Graciela." Her face flushed and covered with tears, pleaded with him to listen to her.

Collecting himself and now fully under control and as calm as he had been before Orovis had come to find him, he asked Orovis to hitch a wagon and to take Marisol to his house. They picked up the semiconscious captain, placed him on his horse, slapped it, and sent him on his way. What to do next was on his mind. Whether to report the officer to his commander or to the local magistrate raised jurisdictional issues that he did not understand. Ignoring that the incident had taken place was not an acceptable option because it would further embolden the man to try it again. Along with his horse, he walked in the direction of where he had last seen Miguel, whose counsel he now needed.

Antonio had walked for a half hour and was now on the trail in the middle of thick trees when he saw the soldier, sword in hand, waiting for him. "Twice you have attacked me from behind like the coward that you are, but this time you will meet me face to face. Twice you have intervened between me and women who were none of your concern. Twice you have humiliated me, but never again. I am going to cut you to pieces, and send your head to your girlfriend." Although he spoke Spanish, this time the man was speaking to

Antonio in English. No interpretation was required for Antonio to understand everything that was being said to him. The captain's face was swollen almost beyond recognition, but not to the point that his intentions were not made clear. He intended to kill Antonio.

Antonio reached for his machete, which had been sharpened to a fine edge, and while it was no match for a soldiers' sword, in this instance agility would prevail over ability. Clearly the soldier had the advantage of training and experience but what he lacked was the cold blood that coursed through Antonio's veins. He examined himself as he looked at the soldier who was now walking towards him and would soon strike. He was surprised by how controlled he felt, his blood was not rushing and his heart felt as if it had slowed below its normal pulse. Antonio was ready for battle. The captain soon learned that in hand to hand combat rage is your worst enemy and anger is not your friend. Calm behavior was required and that all fell to Antonio. Captain Cawdell raised his sword straight up and charged at Antonio, with the intention to slice in whatever direction Antonio moved, but Antonio did not move. This caused the captain to hesitate as Antonio made his body smaller by crouching. The captain cut downward with his blade and forced out of balance by his own momentum, overran Antonio who from the crouched position, sliced backward and cut the captain's tendons at his right ankle. The captain screamed from rage more than pain as he fell to one knee. Antonio was now standing behind the man, as he attempted to stand. His ankle could not sustain him but still he attempted to charge at Antonio with the same result, only this time his left tendons were cut by a slice of the machete to his lower leg. The captain now on both knees attempted to stand using the sword as a cane, but his legs did not respond.

Now defeated and understanding what was about to happen to him, he stared at Antonio, but this time with a smile. He laid his sword to his side, placed both hands on the ground as if attempting to rise, but instead with a surprisingly quick motion, he reached for his holster and removed his army issued Colt revolver. Antonio remained where he stood and made no attempt to run towards the captain or away from him. He was just not afraid of death or its method. The captain still smirking raised the weapon extremely slowly wanting to extend the pleasure he was deriving from the moment. Angered and disappointed that his target showed no fear nor begged for mercy as he had expected, he waited a few more seconds to squeeze the trigger. In the next instant he was staring at his weapon that was lying on the ground, with his hand attached to it. He saw an Indian standing next to him holding the machete that had killed him. The Indian seemed impervious to what he had done. He showed no anger and no concern as he was watching him die. His cut had been so clean that the machete in his hand had no blood on it. The speed with which he struck the wrist was so swift that the hand was already on the ground before captain Cawdell realized he had lost it. He remained stupefied and incredulous of his circumstance until the very last drop of blood left his body, and he dropped dead. Not a word was spoken between Orovis and Antonio about this event ever, other than when he told Antonio to leave everything to him because he would ensure that neither the horse nor the rider would ever be found. And they never were.

CHAPTER 23

Juan José traveled from San Juan because he had the need to confer with Antonio and Miguel about the need for a second market to be built towards Puerta De Tierra, a village a short distance east of San Juan where general stores similar to theirs had been opened. In the exact same manner in which their commerce had led to the opening of the general store in the valley of the Vegas, the one in Puerta De Tierra had been formed. Juan José wanted to extend his supply runs from La Jacana all the way to where his new customers were. More and more customers were clamoring for more products as the population was expanding beyond San Juan. Unlike the Spaniards who taxed everybody for everything, the Americans did not tax anybody for anything. They believed that if people were allowed, they would find their own way to sustain their economy. After completing his business transaction he headed in the direction of Marisol's house where he wanted to fulfill the real purpose of his trip, to propose marriage to her.

He found her in the company of Father Reynaldo, engaged in lively conversation and enjoying herself with the priest in a way she never did with him. A twinge of jealousy touched him, as he saw her so happy with another man, albeit a priest. They did not notice his arrival until he was upon them. They were sitting on a small bench which had been built alongside an avocado tree near the door to her house. He actually had to speak for them to be aware of his presence. "Juan José, what a wonderful surprise to see you. You have no idea how great it is for me to have you here because now I can have dinner with my two favorite men." She rose to hug him, but this time her greeting was more fraternal than romantic. He sensed that something had changed and that the progress he thought that he had been making was now stalled. He did not think of Father Reynaldo as competition, after all he was a priest. Still he felt uncomfortable and his disposition showed it when he declined the invitation with the excuse that he needed to go on to Vega Alta to see his cousin, the other priest.

After Juan José had disappeared from sight, Father Reynaldo said, "Too bad he could not stay because I am cooking for us tonight. He is going to miss the best Chicken Fricassee served in these parts." She protested with a measure of faked anger, but also somewhat appreciating the fact that a man was offering to cook for her. Even if the man was a priest. This had never happened before, and not knowing if it would happen again, she accepted with delight. Although he insisted that she wait outside while he cooked, she refused because as she said, she was not about to miss seeing a man cooking. While she had lived at the convent, all the meals for the priests were prepared by the nuns. This she believed was an extension of the role of the female, even if it was a convent that made this event all the more remarkable. She appreciated how comfortable he was around her small kitchen. Not once did he ask where to find anything he needed. He simply looked until he found what he wanted. Of course, it made sense to her, he and Father Angel lived alone in the back of the church, and they had no caretaker, and so out of necessity they must have cooked for themselves.

"You may step outside so that I may officially call you for dinner. Please step outside." She did as he asked her, and with great pomp he said it, "Dinner is served." In the ten minutes that he made her wait outside, Father Reynaldo had set a lovely table, one so charming that she thought only a woman could set, or a sensitive man. The dinner was as succulent as he had promised, and she so much enjoyed it that she felt moved to offer a toast. As she spoke she transitioned from having dinner with a priest to having dinner with a man. After her very kind remarks concerning the quality of the meal and of the man who had prepared it, she closed by raising her glass saying, "To what ifs." He asked what she meant by that remark and she spoke of the irony that only two men had really impressed her in her life, and neither was available. He knew of whom she spoke in both instances and held his silence.

Drawing up on his courage and fully aware of the blasphemy he was about to commit, he declared his love for her. By telling her that being a priest had not made him the lesser man, and that while he had struggled with his vows he had also struggled with his love for her, and she had prevailed. He had confessed his dilemma to Father Angel, with whom he had spoken at length following his confession. Father Angel admitted to Reynaldo that while he had loved women, he had never been in love with one. And as result he could add nothing but to counsel Reynaldo to follow his heart as well as his conscience. And that was exactly what he was doing as he asked her to marry him. He added, "Please do not be concerned about me leaving the priesthood for you, I am leaving it for me." She had dealt with the guilt and anxiety that her what if thinking had brought to her. The what if became the what now. After a few minutes of silence her dilemma was solved, she held his hands in hers, kissed his lips and softly whispered, "Yes."

Reynaldo and Marisol were surprised by the absence of their surprise when they sat across from Ana Maria, Antonio, Mercedes and Miguel and disclosed their plans to marry. According to them, the love between Marisol and Reynaldo had been a secret only to the two of them, because everyone else at La Jacana spoke in terms of when they got married, not if they got married. Mercedes said, "You were silly to think we had not noticed how you beamed when he came to the school and how he puffed out his chest every time he saw you. In fact, we were calling Reynaldo the rooster."

The night was still young, but Reynaldo did not want to delay the conversation he needed to have with Father Angel. His best friend, the very same one with whom he would lose all contact after his excommunication was ordered by the Bishop. By morning he was back to La Jacana and dropped his belongings in Marisol's house. Since it was an impromptu event, and Mercedes' pregnancy restricted her travels, and Miguel was staying close to her, they stopped to collect Ana Maria and Antonio as their witnesses. By half past one in the afternoon, they were standing before the magistrate, who although he thought it was most irregular that the groom was the priest, married them anyway. At precisely three in the afternoon they entered their house as man and wife, and started their honeymoon. That evening they were assaulted by fifty well wishers. Assaults were a Christmas tradition through which unsuspecting couples would be visited by a large number of people that they were required to receive and feed and provide drink for. This assault was different in that the visitors brought everything that was needed for the celebration. As the bride and groom walked outside to greet the well wishers they remarked that it wasn't even Christmas, to which Elisa Gossett responded, "It is to us." The next day Reynaldo posted a letter to his mother with the big announcement, asking her to join them in Puerto Rico. Tears of joy ran down his mother's cheeks when she read the news of her son coming back to her life, after so many years. Her only thought was concerning Marisol, and it was; "I hope that she is pregnant." Her celebratory disposition had in no way changed when she arrived at La Jacana and met her daughter in law. The first thing she said as she hugged Marisol was, "Thank you for returning my son to me." His mother had stopped wearing black.

Reynaldo's letter of resignation was delivered to the bishop by Father Angel and it was not well received by the Bishop, neither was the news of Marisol's marriage when he informed Juan José, who received them calmly and with resignation. "I waited too long," he said. And he had. He believed that he had lost the only woman he could have married, and he did. For the rest of his life, he remained a bachelor, much to the consternation of his family and the families of those girls who they envisioned would have been perfect in the role of Juan José Martinez's wife.

Antonio found it curious that the army had not come to look for the Captain. Surely in the four weeks since their fight, they would have missed him. Their failure to search for him west of San Juan was because the Captain had signed off on leave and registered his destination east of San Juan. Since he knew what he was planning to do, he must have thought it best to conceal his real destination. As a result all the search efforts focused in the swamps in the region of Fajardo and Luquillo. Both densely covered by vegetation and made inhospitable by the number of swamps that existed between the river and the sea. Finally, giving up on their search east, they decided to search in points west, hoping that someone had seen the man. Much to the detriment of their search efforts, Captain Cawdell had done an excellent job in keeping from main trails or any locations where people gathered, so no one had seen him. The soldiers conducting their search were severely limited because of the language barrier and the overall uninterested disposition on the part of the people.

Finally, their search lead them to La Jacana where they knew English was being taught and where they hoped to get information. Upon arriving at the farm, the first people with whom they came in contact were Raymond Gossett and Antonio, who were fixing a wagon wheel in the blacksmith's shop. The soldiers dismounted and walked in the direction of the shop. As they neared, Raymond shouted to them to tie their horses near the water trough and to let them drink. They looked twice at Raymond because from where they stood they could not tell that he was an American like them. He wore a wide straw hat and his skin was as dark as that of the natives and his face was covered in soot. It was only after he dragged a rag across his face that they could see his features and realized he was one of them.

Antonio did not have to understand the conversation to know the reason for the soldiers stopping at La Jacana. Pretending to be impervious to their visit, he continued with his work. While he could not understand what was being said, he guessed it when he saw Raymond walking the soldiers towards the main road leading towards Vega Alta and points west, and heard the name Arecibo. Raymond was telling them that he though he had seen the man a few weeks ago, passing through on the way to Arecibo. The man he said wore captain's bars and seemed to be in a hurry. "No sir, I never saw him return, not through here. But that does not mean that he could not have taken the costal trail that follows along Cerro Gordo and Dorado. That sure is a lot of terrain to cover for a small patrol." Because the information was coming from a fellow American, the sergeant was favorably disposed to agreeing with Raymond's assessment. He thanked him, ordered his men to mount their horses, and departed in the direction of Bayamon, effectively giving up on the search. Raymond returned to his shop where Antonio raised his head and saw the American wink and nod to him as he too returned to work. The General ultimately listed Captain Matthew Cawdell as missing, possible desertion.

The years that followed were a whirlwind of progress and growth in every front. Ana Maria and her mother were kept busy by the number of births not only at La Jacana but all along the valley of the Vegas. Three of those were Marisol's and Reynaldo's children. Four of those were children born to Ana Maria and Antonio, and three more were born to Mercedes and Miguel. As envisioned by Miguel, their enterprise would generate enough commerce to promote economic growth on a regional scale. Consequently, people of all trades and skills had moved to the valley. Guillermo Recondo and his wife Magaly had gone back to occupying the house they had rented to Mercedes and Miguel. And seeing the traffic building along the road to Vega Alta, opened the first restaurant outside of the surrounding towns. It started with one pig per weekend which was roasted on the open fire, and served with boiled breadfruit, sweet potatoes, and oven fresh bread made by Magaly at their house. Soon, what started out as four sheets of zinc, overlapping and nailed to four posts, became the place to stop and eat on Saturdays.

Underneath the roof they had two long tables and corresponding benches, all made by them with the help of their neighbors. Not long after opening they began to run out of food long before closing time. Recognizing a business opportunity when he saw one, Miguel loaned them the money to expand the restaurant with actual walls, doors and windows and more long tables with benches and a makeshift bar. Their menu did not change, only the number of people they served. Not only did it become a favorite place for the locals in which to eat, it also became a favorite place for American soldiers and civilian engineers who while working on the road had their first taste of the food and kept returning for more.

The Americans had undertaken the building of roads. One of them was between San Juan and Arecibo, which saw the dynamiting of the mountain that had stood between Vega Alta and Bayamon. The mountain was now a gentle hill, in between two very large walls. In 1917 the United States congress granted American citizenship to the residents of Puerto Rico.

For most Puerto Ricans that was a non-event. The people who had sought it were those whose strategic visions served their political designs and they were the only ones who celebrated. The newspaper, El Territorio the weekly publication printed in San Juan could now be distributed through out the island. Communications in many forms were introduced to the island and along with it, politics. The telegraph had been installed but was not yet widely used by the general population. Instead, it was mostly used for communications by the authorities, both civilian and military.

Political parties were formed, each with an agenda to influence American policy towards its territory. Some preferred a closer alliance through annexation and ultimately statehood, others wanted independence. Regardless of what each faction wanted, at the end of the day the United States would do what it deemed to be in their best interest.

At La Jacana none of those changes were of any consequence to their lives. They were a country unto themselves. Their little chapel had to be expanded because it was bursting at the seams. Since Reynaldo's separation from the Catholic Church and the subsequent decree of excommunication, the Catholic Church had ceased to provide a priest to minister to the residents of La Jacana. Their intention was to force the residents to attend mass in Vega Alta. Instead, a Pentecostal minister turned up, and the residents believing the word of God was the word of God, regardless out of whose mouth it came, enthusiastically welcomed their new minister and their new faith.

The school that had been started by Mercedes, and grown by Marisol and Reynaldo were now schools. There were three of them and whereas before education stopped at the age of twelve, now it went all the way to sixteen. Moreover, whereas before only English was taught in English, some history and some arithmetic was taught in English as well. The idea being that the practical application of the use of the language outside the framework of a language class would promote fluency in its use. At first, Reynaldo joined with Marisol in teaching, but as the number of students and schools expanded, the need for an educational system was manifested, and he became the first principal of the La Jacana school system. What gave even a greater source of pride to the residents was the fact that it was self funded.

The money earned through their collective efforts sufficed to provide them a good standard of living and a good education for all the children. Not going to school at La Jacana was not an option for children of school age. A system of rural schools had been ordered by the Spanish government before ceding Puerto Rico to the Americans, who continue to promote its development throughout the island. Since education was not compulsory and the schools were located mostly in towns with large populations, the school system at La Jacana continued to function excluded from the government's influence, by choice.

The Americans were particularly partial to them because they were producing bi-lingual students at a rate much faster than the other schools, and with greater proficiency. This became readily evident, when the first University in Puerto Rico, originally named the College Of Agriculture and Mechanical Arts in the town of Mayaguez, was opened in 1911 and started welcoming La Jacana students. So well recognized were the schools at La Jacana that when Governor Beeckham Winthrop learned about it, he made it a point to meet the Principal and the Head Mistress early in his administration, while touring the Island.

Along with progress came roads followed by automobiles and other forms of motorized vehicles. The first one in the region went to La Jacana and was purchased by Raymond Gossett whose inquisitive mechanical mind just had to have one. Not because he needed one, but because he needed to know how they worked. Always the clear thinker, he saw the automobile and knew he was seeing the future. The very first mechanical shop in the region was his. It was located next to his blacksmith's shop where his apprentices continued to service horses and wagons, while Raymond made himself an expert on the new method of transportation.

The train service which had been initiated by the Spaniards a few years before losing the war to the Americans, was extended to service most of the island, and its availability created new and greater market opportunities for La Jacana causing Miguel and Mercedes to feel nostalgic for the good old days when they used to have time to enjoy their lives, their families and each other's company. Miguel now had accountants who worked for him.

Antonio had foremen who reported to him, and as a result he spent more of his time telling than doing, delegating more than executing, and enjoying his life less than he used to.

Never intending it, Ana Maria's kitchen became the community dining room. Thanks to Antonio's habit of greeting people with the same question; "Have you eaten today?" It never mattered who it was, or if they were locals or visitors. Every one was asked the same question. Upon receiving a negative reply to the question, he would simply send the person, man, woman or child to the house by simply saying, "Go up to the house and ask Doña Ana Maria to feed you." Antonio and Miguel continued as the beacons that attracted people to the region. Their reputations for fairness and kindness were legendary and through word of mouth their stature grew. While Miguel gravitated to the management of the business, Antonio focused on the people's issues and concerns. None more important than the development of his own children.

He made sure, that his boys, Antonio Miguel, Miguel Antonio and Miguel Angel spent a good amount of time under Orovis' tutelage. And when not with the Taino, then with Raymond whose influence was just as important to character building in different ways. Orovis' teachings were about nature and inner strength. Raymond's were about work ethic, doing things right and keeping one's word. Together, and along with Antonio they prepared the boys for life. The raising of his two girls, he had left to Ana Maria who had made certain of their development for a love of learning in all of them. They did build a wing in their house to hold their library, and required all of their children to spend an hour after dinner reading with them. It did not matter what they read, so long as they read. Reading had been a hunger in both parents' early lives and that was one hunger they made sure their children shared.

CHAPTER 24

His resentment of the Americans had been building since killing the captain, and continued to grow as more intrusive orders were issued by the American Government. One of these was the adoption of English as the official language of Puerto Rico. The other was the order for compulsory military service issued by President Woodrow Wilson. The taking of 20,000 Puerto Rican boys to fight the American war in Europe was deeply felt in the Island and regretted at La Jacana because some of their boys who went to serve in the Great War, as it was called, never returned.

In part, and in silence Antonio blamed the draft on the teaching of English to Puerto Rican boys. The way he figured it, if the boys had not spoken the English language the Americans would not have taken them. The end of that war confirmed to the whole world, what they already knew in Puerto Rico. The United States was the new world power, replacing Great Britain, France, Germany and Spain.

These thoughts were on his mind on a Sunday afternoon as he was enjoying a glass of brandy and a cigar, while reading his Sunday copy of the El Mundo the most recent newspaper printed in the island. Sitting on his rocking chair next to a hammock, in which Ana Maria slept, he looked at her as he often did when she was unaware and relished the company of such a splendid woman. She was and continued to be the love of his life. There had never been a moment in the twenty two years since they married in which he had not felt honored that she was his wife, and in which he did not refer to her as Doña Ana Maria. Not once had he spoken to her without the title. When their private tradition started on the day they met, it was just courtesy, now it was to honor her. Next to Sister Graciela, she had been the driving force in his life, his rudder and his compass, she was his guiding light. Many had been the nights when heavy rains fell and without discussion they would walk outside and bathe naked in the rain. They did not need to be quiet since the sound of the rain falling on the roof blocked all the noise they made. Many had also been the nights when they walked to the river to bathe after their children had fallen asleep. Their bathing in the river was almost a commemoration of the first time they had known one another. On that night more than joining their bodies they bonded their souls. He recognized that he had married a woman of great style and substance. One whose principles never wavered. He admired his wife because of her great nobility. Her's came not from royalty or lineage, she was a gift from God, for him through her.

Although having had several opportunities, as women made it known that they were available to him, not once had he ever thought about betraying her or their love. Their marriage vows meant more to him with the passing years than they did on the day they repeated them to one another.

There was an article in the newspaper which captured his attention. Up to now he had not had any interest in the local or national politics or in anything that had to do with government. He believed that all politicians placed their personal interest first and last, and any words to the contrary were just words. Moreover, he could not and would not trust any of them. The jockeying for position and political gain since the Americans had been allowing bits and pieces of autonomy, was now at an almost frenzy level. The worst thing was that political parties were now printing their own newspapers as the way to advance their propaganda, making everything he read suspect.

On this Sunday, in particular he was drawn to an article written by a man named Manuel Calero Gallardo, who seemed to have no bias towards one view or the other. The article dealt with the announcement of the formation of the Puerto Rican Nationalist Party. The founder, according to the article was a man named Pedro Albizu Campos, whose sole objective was total independence. Unlike all the other parties that harangued the population with various forms of platforms promising some variation of continued connection to the Americans, the Nationalist party wanted no less than absolute independence from the United States, and they wanted it now.

A man that looked to be in his mid twenties, but no older than twenty seven, approached his house driving a carriage pulled by a beautiful stallion. He wore a white linen suit, a white shirt and a black tie. At his side, on the seat was a straw hat with a wide brim and a black band around it. It was clear to anyone who knew him that the man consistently gave a great deal of thought to his appearance, or if not, this then was a special occasion. The man stopped and tied his horse to a low hanging branch from a Mango tree. One the many surrounding their house. He walked up the steps as Antonio stood to greet him, newspaper in hand. "Don Antonio," the man said, "My name is Manuel Calero Gallardo and I have come to ask for your permission to court your daughter Lola." Actually, her name was Ana Graciela, Lola was her nickname. She acquired it when as a little girl she had wanted to be a Lelolai singer, like her mother, but instead of Lelolai she said Lolalai, and the name Lola stuck.

Antonio looked at the article he had been reading, and realized that before him stood the writer. Upon hearing her daughter's name mentioned by their visitor, Ana Maria stood, pushed the hammock away, attempted to brush the wrinkles our of her skirt, tried to conceal her bare feet and invited the man to come up to their porch and sit down. She offered him some lemonade, but he declined, and asked if he could have a brandy instead, like the one Antonio was drinking. He extended his hand to her first and then to Antonio who received it still not over the surprise caused by the young man's presence. It was not often that a man visited Antonio Barradaz for the purpose of asking permission to court his daughter. In fact it had never happened. His surprise was all the greater when he understood that the man had not actually met his daughter. "I believe her name is Lola," the man said causing Ana Maria and Antonio to realize that he did not know her. As he explained to them, he had seen her the week before at the feast of the patron saint in Vega Alta, while she was walking around the plaza with her girlfriends, made inquiries about her and here he was. Ana Maria had to struggle to contain her laughter as she watched Antonio dealing with what was happening, and not knowing how to react. Instead she responded for the two of them, and invited him to sit down. "Is she home?" he asked. "If not, I do not wish to interrupt your Sunday rest." Lola was not home, but was expected for dinner to which he was invited.

Since he was not dressed as a farmer, she surmised he was not one, so Ana Maria asked what it was that he did when he was not calling on girls for the purpose of courting them. Antonio knew from the moment he had seen

271

him that he was a Spaniard, more than likely from Madrid, was his guess. "I studied law at the Inter American University here in Puerto Rico. It is a Presbyterian school." Ana Maria looked at her husband and said, "Well Don Anton it seems that we will be dining with a lawyer this evening. "A journalist," he corrected her. "I studied law, but do not practice it, I write for El Mundo, mostly I write about politics." They both knew that this was a most unusual man. They both also decided that they liked him. He seemed mature beyond his age, which they did not yet know for certain. Ana Maria thought that it did not matter how they felt, it only mattered how Lola felt, and they were about to find out as she approached walking alongside her horse. At first Lola thought her parents had company, but was surprised when she did not recognize the man speaking with her father, because she thought that she knew all of her parents' friends. She walked the horse to the stable, removed the saddle from the horse, threw some feed in the stall, brushed her dress and her hair, and walked to meet her future husband.

"Don Manuel, may I introduce our daughter Lola," said Ana Maria. Lola offered her hand as she spoke of her pleasure in meeting him. While that was a commonly used phrase when meeting a gentleman, in this instance Lola meant every word of it. He responded by expressing the same, and meaning it just as much. And then said, "I have come expressly for the purpose of meeting you." She was struck by the gravity in his voice, and the precision with which he spoke. This was a well bred and educated man, she thought. She was also struck by how tall he was. Manuel was as tall as her father, but more slender in build. His hands were the hands of a man that did not do manual labor. He was an impressive man, and she was impressed by him. "You said that you came for the expressed purpose of meeting me, why is that, may I ask?" He told her that he had been sitting on his family's house balcony in Vega Alta, the previous Saturday, and had seen her walk by with two other ladies, and that right there and then, he made the decision to find her and meet her. "Don Manuel, I am still curious, what is the reason why you wanted to find me?"

They were still standing as they exchanged remarks, with her parents looking on as spectators in a play. He had not yet released her hand when he said, "So that I can become your husband and you can become my wife." Neither him nor her moved to release their hands. She could have said yes at that moment but decided to wait. He felt that he knew the answer without asking the question. To him being a Spaniard, it mattered not that she was Puerto Rican. The same was not true of his parents.

Manuel's father, Don Franco Calero was an engineer who directed the operation of the local sugar mill just west of Vega Alta. They had moved to Puerto Rico after a few years working in Venezuela. He and his wife Maura, were both born and raised in Madrid, where they had been raised alongside each other since their parents had been best of friends. Although they did not come from royalty, they thought themselves to be aristocrats nonetheless.

Both having been educated in the best schools in their native country, and raised with all the comforts that their families' wealth provided them. Short of having titles, they saw themselves as better than most. Especially Maura, who had deeply resented the freeing of slaves. Some of them, who had been owned by her when they were slaves, were now employed by her, and while she did have to pay them she treated them no better than she had when they had been slaves in her house. She was a proud and strong willed woman who believed that nothing or no one was good enough for her children, and she certainly did not agree that Ana Graciela Barradaz Morales was good enough for her son. She was not even white, she protested when Manuel announced his intention to marry the Puerto Rican girl. "I refuse to have half breeds for grandchildren. I simply will not accept them," she protested.

"Don't worry Mother," said Manuel. "Maybe they will not want you for a grandmother." Neither of his parents, or relatives close or distant, attended his wedding to Lola Barradaz.

The last thing that Antonio Barradaz ever thought was that the day would come on which he would give his first born daughter in marriage to a Spaniard. But then again he himself was a Spaniard who had married a Puerto Rican girl. History, he believed, does repeat itself. In deference to the bride, the wedding had been held at the church of the Immaculate Conception in Vega Alta, the same one in which he and Ana Maria had been married. The celebration took place at the bride's parent's house. It started at eight in the evening and lasted until eight the next morning. During the celebration Antonio asked his new son in law to join him for a brandy and a short conversation. Once they were seated he went right to the point. He started by telling Manuel some of his family's history beginning at their arrival in Puerto Rico to the present. Making certain that his son in law could appreciate what his family meant to him. He added, "In all of these years since I have been a father, I have never laid hands on a child, male or female. Never wanted to, never needed to and never did. And I certainly would resent it if anyone were to lay hands on any of them, especially one of my daughters.

The reason I tell you this is because I have known anger and I have known rage and when caused by my wife, I simply walked away until I could find the kindest way through which I could communicate my most negative thoughts. I will thank you to bear this in mind and to do the same when angry with Lola." Manuel appreciated Antonio's quality for plain speech. There had never been a time when they had spoken on any subject that he had not understood what had been said to him. And this was one of those times.

When they first married, Manuel and Lola lived at La Jacana in a small bungalow where two of their four children were born. The other two were born in the town of Dorado, where they had moved to when Manuel accepted the position of district superintendent of schools. He did it not for the money, or the prestige the position afforded him. He did it because the job needed to be done. Three of the four children had been delivered by Ana Maria. The second child, a boy, born at La Jacana was named Manuel Antonio, and was delivered by Antonio because Ana Maria was away delivering another child when her grandson was born and Manuel was away at work. Antonio performed as well as he had the time he delivered his first born son with Ana Maria. All that would have been needed for history to be repeated was for Orovis to have been there.

The next one of Antonio's and Ana Maria's child to marry was their younger daughter Gloria. She married Andres Guardiola, a man who while working on the road to Arecibo spotted her clearing her mother's garden. He was seventeen, exceedingly tall, had short curly hair, enormous hands and was illiterate. His family's circumstance had demanded that he and his siblings work to sustain the family and as a consequence he had been doing some form of physical labor since the age of seven. He was almost run over by a bulldozer when he stopped to stare at the pretty girl picking tomatoes, about two hundred yards from where he stood. Water was the excuse he used to get to meet her. He walked to where she was, and asked if she minded if he drew some water from their well. Not only did she not mind, she went into the house and brought him a glass of lemonade. He sipped on the glass of lemonade instead of drinking it so that he could prolong his stay and her company. "You might as well sit down and rest, if you have the time." As much as by her beauty he was impressed by her kindness. He knew that she was one of the Barradaz daughters, and knew of her father, although he had never met him, he knew his standing in the valley of the Vegas. The following Sunday, he found himself sitting behind her at the ten o'clock service in the chapel. After several weeks of small talk, his intentions were known to everyone who witnessed his oblique approach to courtship. It was not until he turned eighteen and she turned seventeen that he approached her parents about courting Gloria, and when he did, he brought his own parents with him for support.

What Andres lacked in education, he made up in common sense and intelligence. He had been endowed with both in volumes. Some said he was a born engineer. There was no construction challenge that could overwhelm him. Pretty soon after joining up with the construction crew he was directing work crews with men twice his age. Whatever resentment they may have harbored by being ordered by a boy, was kept in check, by his size. Andres Guardiola was one large man. People looked up to him because of his size first and then his stature. He was big by both measures. When he finally asked for her hand in marriage, her parents set one condition. He needed to learn to read and write before they married. Under Marisol's tutelage, Andres learned to read and write at a rate faster than most. Not only did he learn to read, he learned to love it. In fact it became a sore point with Gloria, when Andres came to visit and spent more time with her father in the library than with her.

Their children came in rapid succession, but they were prepared for a large family, since Andres had built their house in his spare time on a plot of land given to them by Miguel and Mercedes as their wedding gift. His friends, which included Gloria's brothers, would join him after work and on weekends to help him build his house. Gloria and her mother would make certain that a pot of rice and a pot of beans were always at the ready so the men could eat before or after work. Rural electrification had reached the valley of the Vegas and an ice making machine had been installed at the general store. In addition to making blocks of ice, the machine kept beer cold. The 'La India' brewery had been opened just a few months before and beer had reached La Jacana. Until then they had never felt the need for ice, but beer changed all of that.

The two sons, Antonio Miguel and Miguel Antonio had grown as closed as two brothers or half brothers could have been. Orovis had a great deal to do with their upbringing and he always imparted the importance of taking care of one's family above all else. Other than the four and a half years that separated them, they were identical in every way. They both had their father's build and his curious mind as well. The word "why" was the most commonly used in their vocabularies. This pleased Orovis and Antonio almost as much as seeing the boy's disposition towards others. Although everyone knew they were Barradaz boys, and would act with deference towards them, the boys would quickly convince them of their equality. Their father had drilled the concept of servile leadership on them since an early age, and they had learned it well. On one occasion, when Antonio Miguel was twenty two and Miguel Antonio was eighteen years old, two American soldiers made the mistake of insulting one of the waitresses, at Guillermo's and Magaly's restaurant. The girl was Raymond's and Elisa's daughter, and had been raised with the boys and gone through school together.

The soldiers made the wrong assumption that they could not be understood as they heaped insults and lewd remarks upon the girl whose English was sufficient to cause her to burst into tears from the embarrassment. All through the episode, Antonio and Miguel's anger and rage had been building, but remembering the lessons from Orovis and their father, they waited until they had absolute control of themselves. And the time came. They approached, Belen, the waitress who was in tears. Took her by her hands, one to each side, and walked towards the soldier's table. The soldiers, oblivious to what was about to happen to them became even more insolent. Antonio and Miguel were intending to ask for an apology before making them regret their behavior. Instead they decided to ask for the apology afterwards. As usual, alcohol gives an added measure of courage to fools, and these soldiers were foolish not to recognize what they were facing. Before the first one spoke, Antonio Miguel landed a punch across his windpipe. The second soldier made the mistake of taking his eyes off Miguel Antonio, because when he turned to look at his friend, Miguel drove his face down on the hardwood table. Four or five of his teeth cracked and flew out of his mouth. The few remaining teeth bit his tongue. He did not even have time to realize his tongue was bitten and bleeding when Miguel landed the second blow to the man's nose, breaking it in two places.

Finally it was over, from the first blow to the last, the fight lasted less than one minute. So efficient had they been about their violence, that no perceptible damage to property was caused. Next they loaded both soldiers on a wagon, tied their own horses in the back and drove them to their garrison. There they met the sergeant of the guard who after looking at the soldiers' shape asked how many were in the fight. "Just us," answered Antonio. They expressed their regrets over the incident, but added that it could not have been avoided since they did not think the soldiers would have apologized. Still incredulous that these two boys had done what they did to his two men, he thanked them for bringing them back.

Signs of the depression that afflicted the United States began to appear in Puerto Rico. Unemployment climbed at an alarming rate and almost over night the island of Puerto Rico was immersed in poverty and desperation such as it had not experienced in a long time. Everywhere, people were living not day to day but hour to hour. Everywhere the people's main concern as they awoke to start their days had to do with finding food. Everywhere, but at La Jacana. Their stores were fully stocked and thanks to great land and animal management, the hunger that afflicted the island did not affect them. Their policy of self sufficiency was paying off, and while their commerce had dropped off considerably, because of their abundance, the people at La Jacana lacked nothing.

"We can not just sit here and pretend that we do not have a duty to help the many who are in need. We can not allow them and their children to go hungry when we are so well fed." These words were spoken by Ana Maria at a gathering at the chapel following the Sunday morning service. Many thought that they needed to worry about themselves, but no one argued against the idea of helping those who so badly needed their help. The discussion was about how to manage the distribution of food and other goods in a way that would not promote consumption beyond their ability to replenish their stocks. For starters, breakfast would be served to all children at the chapel six days a week. Sunday's it would be served to the whole family when they came for the service. Next, they created a program of work for food, for those who wanted to work at La Jacana.

Instead of money they would receive more food than they could eat so that they could trade what they did not consume for things they needed. This added labor which would serve to grow more varied fruits and vegetables solved the problem of demand outstripping supply. It would have been useless to try to sell the surplus food since other than the United States army nobody had any money with which to buy. Another idea that they put in place, was to sell on credit. People could purchase the essential items they needed but could not be grown, and a ledger would be kept. The idea was that eventually when things improved the debt would be settled. To no one's surprise when the economy finally improved, most debts were paid. At the end of the day the self regenerative economic engine at La Jacana saved a good number of people. Sister Graciela's wishes were once again honored.

For Manuel's family the recession had been extremely hard. Gone were the servants, gone were the status symbols that wealthy people so often take for granted, gone was the income from the sugar mill and lastly, gone was the food. They were starving. When Ana Maria learned of their situation, she waited to speak to Manuel during the family's Sunday dinner. Their tradition was for the whole family to gather from the early afternoon to the early evening at the Barradaz home where not a moment of quiet was experienced nor wanted by Antonio and Ana Maria. They sat at the end of their porch after dinner, Manuel, Lola, Antonio and Ana Maria, who spoke first. "Manuel we know that your parents are in a terrible condition, and while they may think that they are not part of our family, we know better. And we must help them, tell us how." These words coming from the woman his parents had so often rejected and insulted with their slights. They did not even come to his wedding, they had never received his wife in their home, never laid eyes on his children and now that they were in need of help, it was not coming from their relatives or their wealthy Spanish friends; it was coming from Puerto Ricans. Never had he felt so ashamed by his natural family or so proud of the family into which he married. The only solution for his family was to close their house in town and move to La Jacana. That was the only logical solution. How to achieve it was an entirely different matter because the move would confirm what everyone already knew; they were poor.

He drove to his parents house in Vega Alta the next day and walked up to their door with a basket filled with fruits, breads, cheeses, eggs and a bottle of Brandy. The brandy had been Antonio's idea. When Maura his mother, who had neither spoken to nor seen him in the five years, since he married the half-breed as she called Lola, saw him walking towards their door, she rose and retired to her bedroom. Don Franco, genuinely glad to see his son, opened the door. Manuel set the basket down and kissed his father. He spent no time talking about his family since he knew it would only open a wound that should best remain closed. Instead he spoke to his father as one speaks to an engineer which his father was, straight and to the point. He told his father that he knew their situation was desperate and he could not permit himself to continue to ignore it. His father knew of the abundance of La Jacana and had it not been for Maura's false pride he would have made attempts to contact his son before now. "We have a small house for you at La Jacana you and mother will lack nothing. In fact the house is far away from the main house so that mother need not see her benefactors." The arrangement he proposed was for them to pay rent when the economy improved, if they wished, otherwise it was not required. "After all, we are family," he said with a smile.

They lived at La Jacana for one year until the sugar mill reopened and Don Franco could return to work. During that time, Ana Maria never once set foot in their little house, instead she would send a roast or a cake, or a pot of soup or a hen. Every day, milk, cheese or butter was delivered to them. To Maura Calero this was the ultimate insult, accepting charity from a half breed. Don Franco, on the other hand would stop in to visit Antonio, and partake of his cigars and Brandy. Both were men of knowledge, formal and informal, and enjoyed lively discussions. In time, Don Franco changed his views to the point that his Spanish origin meant absolutely nothing to him. He actually liked and embraced the Puerto Rican culture to which he had been so blind. The same was not true of his wife, whose bitterness had increased. She had learned that Don Franco was keeping company with a woman at La Jacana. A woman who had been abandoned by her husband and whose house Don Franco would frequent in the afternoons, Diega was her name.

She could have forgiven the transgression, after all he was a man, and to seek comfort was in man's nature, but with a Puerto Rican woman, that she could not forgive. She grew increasingly bitter and the more kindness she experienced from others the more bitter she grew. When they ultimately returned to their house in Vega Alta, Don Franco's disposition towards those he had believed to be the lesser people changed dramatically. Now he saw them as just people. He would on occasion, after dinner walk to the place where the locals gathered in the plaza and join them in a drink and conversation or a game of dominoes. Doña Maura's resentments continued to grow. Now in addition to hating everyone who was not a Spaniard, she also hated her husband.

CHAPTER 25

The role of District Superintendent of Education had taken increased importance among the population of the Dorado district, and as a result Manuel found himself spending a great deal of time listening to people's concerns and problems and helping them as best he could. He had developed a strong and very real affinity for the Puerto Rican people, more so, since marrying Lola. In fact he loved them. The marriage had brought him in full contact with people who while they had always been around him, he had never seen. Although he was effective in the eyes of the people he served and tried to help, Manuel felt inept and unequal to the task. His hopes and aspirations for them were far greater than his or their resources could support. The one thing he knew was that equality would only be reached through education. The reason people remained poor, he believed was not for lack of desire, or lack of effort, their greatest impediment to a better life was ignorance. And only education would overcome that. He also believed that people were the island's greatest resource. It was not the climate, or the soil or the topography, none of those factors added together amounted to as much as people did. The challenge was in how to raise the people to the level that their collective contribution would make a difference on the future of the Island. These words he spoke during a speech he offered at the opening of a new elementary school in the town of Dorado. His summation explained his view that the Americans, purposely or inadvertently had provided the opportunity for unparalleled growth for Puerto Rico, but only if the educational standard could be elevated.

The Americans had expanded the use of the telegraph, created a telephone system and brought large scale and widely distributed electricity to the island. These were great technological advances that could be leveraged to the benefit of the people but only if they could be educated.

Compared to other islands in the region, Puerto Rico was no different. He reaffirmed that the only competitive advantage the island enjoyed came from its people, but only if the people could give their best value to the country by getting an education and through that process elevate the standard of living. He sensed that there was a great strategic opportunity for the island to leverage the American's ambivalence. It was his very private view that the United States did not know what to do with or about Puerto Rico. The 1917 Foraker act that gave American citizenship to Puerto Ricans was at the whim of their congress and not under the protection of the constitution of the United States. This he thought sent a clear signal that for all political intents and purposes, Puerto Rico was in limbo. His impassionate plea for the community to join him in the fulfillment of their potential by making an all out effort to promote education by giving it the priority it deserved was heard with great interest by all who were there, but none more intently than Luis Muñoz Marin.

Luis Muños Marin's father, Luis Muños Rivera was the founder of the El Territorio and La Democracia newspapers and also the founder of the Unionist Party of Puerto Rico. He had been one of the most prominent politicians and had never hesitated in his efforts to gain power in any way that he could. The son, who was a great strategic thinker in his own right, had begun to assemble the framework of what would become the most dominant political party in the island for decades to come. The basis of his framework was to create a form of government that would allow the semiautonomous status for Puerto Rico, which while enjoying the benefits of American protection and capital investment, would allow Puerto Ricans to be Puerto Ricans. Luis, the son, heard Manuel speak and knew that he wanted him in his soon to be formed government. He sensed in Manuel the oratory gifts that would attract intelligent and educated people but also appeal to the population in general. His balanced approach to political reform offered hope to many who would listen. And many were listening. Luis had to have Manuel on his side, in his party, but had to proceed with caution. In the discharge of his responsibilities as Superintendent of schools, Manuel had not revealed his political preference or biases if he had any, nor had he engaged in any conduct that could have even hinted of a conflict of interest.

One thing was clear; Manuel Calero Gallardo was a force to be reckoned with and a bigot. He was a bigot against malice and waste, and was absolutely incorruptible. Luis knew that the only way to attract Manuel to his side was to offer him the power that would allow him to do the best for the people, not just power for power's sake. He would offer him a seat in the senate.

As events were unfolding throughout the island, La Jacana did all it could to remain unaffected by it all. When the Americans decreed that municipalities were required to fund a public school system, the schools at La Jacana decreed themselves private school status. And since their curriculum and their results were far better than that of the public schools, the government had no basis for complaints. Besides, La Jacana schools had long ago ceased to ask for help from any source. They were buying their own books and materials, and on more than one occasion had loaned those to the public schools. When President Theodore Roosevelt decreed that Puerto Rico was free to trade with other countries, La Jacana had already been engaged in trade selling its coffee to European countries. It was a known fact Edward VII, the King of England and his consorts enjoyed a cup of La Jacana coffee every morning.

Many visitors from different political affiliations and persuasions and with many and varied agendas had come around trying to enlist Antonio and Miguel to one side or the other. On several occasions they had tried to appeal or convince Miguel or Antonio separately, but to no avail. Their desire for independence was deeply rooted in experience. They remembered the times in Spain when every time the government sought to help the people, the opposite resulted. Antonio had never wanted any part of any political activity and had made it known to all who offered or promised him great power and influence in the soon to be formed governments based on which party was to prevail in the upcoming elections. He was even offered a seat in the senate that was being created when the Americans allowed Puerto Rico to form its own bicameral legislature.

Deep down he felt absolutely Puerto Rican and his love for his country was unmatched. His love of the land, and its people and the love for his wife were so deeply rooted that nothing less than absolute independence appealed to him. And the only man promoting that platform was Pedro Albizu Campos, the founder of the Nationalist Party. He once heard him speak at a rally at the plaza in Vega Alta and was impressed by the man's impassionate plea for a Puerto Rican nation and identity. Being Americans he believed would have only made Puerto Ricans second class citizens of a first class country. In his speech, Pedro Albizu passionately and clearly spoke of the sacrifices required for Puerto Ricans to be free. At the end of that speech Antonio approached the nationalist, offered his hand and his services.

The following Sunday after dropping Lola and two of their children at his in laws house, Manuel drove with the older two to visit his parents in Vega Alta. His father had met his grandchildren on several occasions when he had visited Diega, his mistress at La Jacana. He continued to visit her more for the quality of her company than for his physical comfort. Contrasted to his wife, from whom he had grown increasingly distant, Diega gave him everything Maura was unable to give, warmth, love, and respect for others.

The first time he saw his grandchildren was when on the way back to Vega Alta, and he had stopped at the house to visit Antonio and Ana Maria. Antonio and Franco both had a love for dominoes and it did not take much to get a game started. Upon seeing him on that Saturday afternoon, Antonio sent for Raymond and one other hand to join them for a game. About an hour into the game he saw Orovis, the Taino Indian walking with four children alongside him. So soiled were they that it was anybody's guess what the color of their skin might have been. All four ran to Antonio's arms laughing and all talking at the same time, and all at the same time saying "Bless me Papá, bless me." Franco stared at the children not knowing whose they were. Antonio asked Orovis to take them all to the pump by the well and wash them, half dressed as they were, and continued with their game of Dominoes. Still Franco did not know who they were, and was curious. It was not until they had washed and returned that he saw his own son in the boy. The girls looked like their mother but the boy was an identical replica of his father at the same age. "Franco," Antonio said, "Is it not high time that you bless your grandchildren? Children, come meet your other Papá." Manuel approached his parents' house holding each child by the hand, as they climbed the steps towards the door. The idea for the ice breaking visit was Lola's who had met Manuel's father during his visits to La Jacana.

Lola knew well that Diega was not the only reason why Don Franco frequented the farm, he had allowed himself to fall in love with his grandchildren. She suggested to her husband that he test the water with two of the children instead of all four, lest Maura be overwhelmed.

When the maid opened the door, the children, first Mercedes older than Manuel Antonio by one year exclaimed "Papá, Papá," and ran to him followed by her brother both asking for his blessing, which he readily and profusely gave, saying, "May God bless you my children." Maura stood at the door of the kitchen watching the scene between her husband and their grandchildren. She stared at the girl whose fair skin and light brown hair was markedly different from the boy who was dark skinned and had black curly hair. She walked straight to the girl hugged and blessed her, and completely ignored the boy. After all, she only had affection for white children. Recognizing what was happening Franco picked up the boy and hugged him while telling him how pleased he was to see him. There were more visits to follow and eventually by the whole family, but Maura's behavior did not change. She never looked at Lola when she spoke to her and only had affection for her white grandchildren. One afternoon after the customary Sunday short visit to his parent's house, and while driving to La Jacana where their children could have fun, Manuel spoke of his frustration with his mother's behavior. Lola, with her arm placed her arm around his shoulders, which was her custom when she was in the car with him, said, "It is not your fault that your mother hasn't a drop of the milk of human kindness in her, it is a good thing that you have so much of it." He recognized that she had spoken the truth, but more importantly he was impacted by the realization that he had just heard his wife's harshest expression about anyone and made him appreciate her all the more.

After the late afternoon dinner, the children returned to their play with Gloria's and Andres's children, their cousins. The women, as it was their custom lingered at the table before starting to clean dishes and putting them away. Antonio Miguel and his younger brother excused themselves claiming they had business to attend to in town. No doubt their business wore dresses, of that their father was certain. Andres departed because he needed to drive to the El Yunque Federal Reserve where he was building a road. Only Manuel was left and he followed Antonio to the rocking chairs for their customary cigar and Brandy. "How strange," Manuel thought that this man from such a different background had come to replace his father in his heart.

It was to Antonio that he turned for consultation, not because he did not love his father but because he loved and respected Antonio. "Don Antonio," Manuel spoke as he lit his father-in-law's cigar and then his own, "I need to consult with you on some matters of great concerns, but before I do so I need to establish some ground rules. First, that if I do not follow your advice you will not think that I do not trust your judgment; only that I may trust mine more. Second, that we can disagree without being disagreeable." This second rule brought a smile to Antonio's face, "Third, I ask that our conversation be confidential. Strictly between us two."

"You have my word," said Antonio. He said that he too had rules and mainly they had to do with needing a commitment to absolute honesty in their discussion. Antonio had spent a great deal of time reading about Socrates, Plato, Julius Caesar and Machiavelli. These readings had caused him to require intellectual honesty and to give it as well. He had learned about the consequences of deceit.

Manuel discussed his plan to leave his post as superintendent of schools because he believed that he had built an organization filled with people who were genuinely committed to educating the children. He followed that disclosure with his plan to return to Journalism, this time as the editor of El Mundo the fastest growing and best newspaper in the island. Lastly he reached the subject that he had wanted to discuss all along; his political future. He disclosed his conversations with Luis Muñoz Marin as they concerned his senate seat opportunity. It seemed inevitable that the Popular Party of Puerto Rico would win the election and that would have assured Manuel's senate seat. His problem was that he did not want it. He had spent a great deal of time considering the issue of Puerto Rico's relationship with the United States and determined that the best course of action was to petition the United States congress to grant statehood. The main barrier, he believed, was the fact that the American civil war was still an open wound in the heart of southern legislators, and because of that he was going to propose a series of measured steps to move them towards statehood. "Move who," asked Antonio. "The people. Through the political party that I intend to form, The Puerto Rican Pro-Statehood Party." Antonio remained silent for what seemed a long time, and before speaking, asked Gloria if she would serve them a second glass of Brandy. He reminded Antonio of all of his posturing in his speeches about the issue of Puerto Rican identity. What happened to that he wanted to know. He also wanted to ask why Manuel believed that Americans would be any better masters than Spain had been. More importantly, Antonio spoke of his vision for the United States and it was not a promising future. "Manuel, I have read the treaty of Versailles, the one written after Germany's surrender, and my view is that as a result of that agreement, the world will soon be involved in another world war. I remember also reading that the one that just ended was the war to end all wars. Well, the Americans, the English and the French have made sure that a bigger war will come. Because of that, I believe that it is in our best interest to separate from the United States as a sovereign and independent country, and go our separate way." Manuel sat in absolute silence absorbing everything he had just heard. He was contemplating the tactical and strategic considerations, which were many. But mostly he had just realized how far apart he and his father-in-law were with the question of Puerto Rico's future. Manuel replied explaining the things that he had heard and read were happening in Cuba since they were declared independent. "Cuba is not Puerto Rico," said Antonio as he stood signaling the end of the conversation. That night, Antonio tossed in bed for a long time. So troubled was he by the talk with Manuel that he even declined Ana Maria's invitation to bathe in the river.

As projected, Luis Muñoz Marin's party did win the election and surprisingly, the Pro-Statehood party founded by Manuel and his friend Miguel Angel Garcia Mendez showed very good results and they both made it to the senate. The conversation that Manuel had with his friend Luis to end their political affiliation had been controversial but not confrontational. Their mutual respect for each other's views and their love of country were bonds too strong to be dissolved by political disagreement. The whole political campaigning process had been a surprise to Manuel and an even greater surprise to Lola. Her renown as the daughter of the midwife that had delivered hundreds of children and her own as a Lelolai singer had attracted many to their rallies and to their party. People for the most part did not really understand the issues but the fact that Doña Ana Maria Barradaz's daughter was supporting the statehood party was good enough for them.

Manuel had returned to journalism and was now the editor of the El Mundo newspaper which was published in San Juan. The newspaper had achieved wide distribution through the use of public cars. These were vehicles whose drivers followed a route and picked up people willing to pay five cents and take them to any point along their route. Manuel had gotten the idea by reading about the American Pony Express, and reasoned that if it worked for horses carrying mail, it could work for cars delivering papers.

The year was 1948 and Lola and Manuel were still living in the town of Dorado and had four children ages eight, seven, five and two. Little did he know when he kissed them goodbye that morning, that the events that would unfold would have serious consequences for him and his family for years to come. It started with his morning coffee accompanied by the powder sugar roll for which La Mallorquina had become famous. As he was leaving the restaurant, he was greeted by two men whom he had met at a meeting with Luis Muñoz Marin, the now Governor. These men were aware that Manuel and the governor had experienced a major political falling out and as result they surmised that they were mortal enemies. What Manuel heard from the two men left him absolutely cold. From their lips and in a very secretive way he had just learned that his good friend the Governor, was to be assassinated that morning. The assassination was funded by the nationalist party who sought to overthrow the government by means of violence. As the men told it, there were men in paramilitary units waiting to hear the confirmation of the governor's death to move to occupy strategic objectives. Radio stations, newspapers, police stations were to be occupied upon receiving the signal. Their objective was to convince the Americans that Puerto Rico was not worth their troubles and that they were better off without it.

It would not have been unusual for Manuel to carry his Cobra Colt 38 snubbed nose revolver. He had bought it after an incident in which his family was threatened, and while he was a man of peace, he was no coward and would not tolerate the threats to his family. On this day, he wished he had it with him, but it was in his office. The time that it would have taken him to reach his office to collect his weapon was time he did not have. As soon as he finished the conversation he ran in the direction of La Fortaleza, the governor's residence and executive mansion where the executive power of government resided. Although he drank often and heavily, and smoked a considerable number of cigarettes in a day, the strength he needed was there for him on that morning. Because he was a well known senator and newspaper man, he reached the commander of the governor's security detail with great ease. Incredulous though he was, the man needed to consider the source of the information that he was hearing. The man still did not move as fast as he should have or needed to, so Manuel told him in very measured words, "Escort me to the Governor's office. Should I be wrong you can charge me with whatever violation you can think that I have committed, and I will be embarrassed by it. On the other hand should my fears be confirmed you will be the hero who saved the Governor's life. Take me to his office and decide what is it going to be as we walk." The two men who were seated across from the Governor's secretary were well dressed and had the look of bureaucrats waiting to meet their boss. They seemed as normal as any two men could be, except for the bulge showing from one of their suits pockets. Bypassing the men at an unhurried pace, Manuel and the officer walked into the Governor's office, without an announcement by the secretary. Before the governor had time to raise his head, Manuel was standing before him. After explaining why he was there he got the Governor to order his security officer to ask two more officers to come to the office and to enter from the Governor's private entrance, that would keep the men in the lobby waiting to see him from being alarmed. With the additional security in place and standing behind massive curtains in the office, the secretary asked the men in the lobby to enter the governor's office.

The taller of the two men, walked hurriedly towards the desk where the governor was standing, and with a slow and deliberate motion, reached for his gun. The security guard nearest the assailant moved and placed the barrel of his pistol on the back of the man's head. The second man reflectively raised his hands in an act of surrender, Collazo and Torregrosa, the two would be assassins were taken away.

"Manuel, how can I repay you," the Governor said. "Name it and it is yours. I owe you my life." Luis Muñoz said these words as he turned and embraced him as they had done hundreds of times. Except that this time it had to do with life or death. "Luis, by now I should hope that you know me well enough to know that I could not allow a murder to take place, if I could stop it. Yours or any one else's. No Luis, nothing is owed to me. What you need to think about is how this attempt will reflect upon your newly formed government and how the Americans will respond."

CHAPTER 26

Mercedes had heard about some of the political animosities developing through out the island. As a result of greatly improved communications in Puerto Rico, news were traveling at increased speed, especially if they were bad, Through their general store they were able to hear every rumor about anything on any subject, confirmed or not. She could hear about concerns in Bayamon and political affairs in San Juan. She heard it everywhere all the time. If not through the rumor mill, then she would hear it on the radio. While she understood that radio had taken the form of an entertainment medium and as such it lacked in credibility, nonetheless it was influencing the people that it was entertaining. The cacophony of politics was overwhelming all other forms of public discourse. Even the Catholic churches were engaged in the most intrusive political speeches disguised as homilies. What disconcerted her most was that nowhere was the voice of reason being spoken or heard. It was all about feelings and emotions and those topics removed all possibility for facts, figures and common sense to be heard. "The country that we have helped to build may be collapsing before our very eyes," she told Miguel. He had heard similar sentiments and concerns but from different sources. He had noticed a change in Antonio. Gone were the isolationist practices that they had both believed in and promoted. While Miguel had been the commercial brain behind the success of La Jacana Antonio had been and was the heart and soul not just of the enterprise, but of the community. In particular he had noticed that Antonio's detached attitude towards political developments had changed. Whereas before Antonio had been agnostic to all forms of government initiatives so long as they did not affect La Jacana now he seemed to have a bias towards all things anti-American. It mattered not to him, if it benefited people or not. If it was an American initiative, he would reject it regardless of its potential merits. On the other hand, Miguel had noticed Antonio's positive disposition towards any idea, program or policy that was anti-American. At the end of their conversation both Miguel and Mercedes agreed that a talk with Antonio was in order.

Automobiles were now the most common form of transportation in Puerto Rico. It seemed that everyone had a car or knew someone who did. Cars were seen everywhere in the island. They were seen in use for public, commercial and private transportation or for emergency vehicles. They were used in many forms by many people, but not by Orovis and seldom by Antonio. When Miguel found them, they were returning from the coffee fields, both walking. Antonio holding the horse's reigns and Orovis following alongside. It seemed to Miguel that only he and Antonio had aged because Orovis looked no different than he did on the day he had led them to the valley of the Vegas, so many years ago. He reached them as they were approaching the stables and drove his car next to them. Antonio knew Miguel so well that even before he spoke, he asked Orovis to stable his and Miguel's horse. He turned to Miguel and asked if they were about to have a one or two Brandy conversation. "Two, to start," Miguel said Sitting on Antonio's rocking chairs where most decisions of any consequence had been made in the last thirty years, Miguel spoke first. Throughout the years, ever since that evening at the port of Barcelona, the bonds that they had developed had been made all the stronger by their natural ability to think each other's thoughts, this conversation was no different. The fact that Miguel had been troubled by the political events in Puerto Rico made them all the more important to Antonio. "Tell me, what is on your mind?" Antonio asked.

After the incident at the governor's office with Collazo and Torregrosa, a great deal of effort had been invested in keeping the attempted assassination a secret. The assassins had been held in solitary confinement and while a forceful effort was made to learn who else had been behind the conspiracy, they revealed nothing. The men who had been waiting for the signal to attack never received it and no uprising developed. At the end of the day it was decided that the best option considering all political implications was to deport the assassins to New York and to never allow them to return to Puerto Rico. Absolute secrecy was of course impossible to maintain.

The facts were known to the governor and his security staff, and to Manuel as well. Most damaging was the fact that the events were also known to the conspirators. The newly formed government, with only two months in office, lacked the security and intelligence resources to launch a complete investigation. Besides, a large scale investigation would have given greater exposure to the secret they needed to maintain. Instead the government engaged in a program of discreet surveillance. Through the use of paid informants they kept secret vigilance on those they considered suspects. Namely, Pedro Albizu Campos, Lolita Lebron and Antonio Barradaz.

It had taken Antonio's personal intervention to keep his daughter Lola from becoming a young widow. When the conspirators learned about Manuel's interference which caused their entire plan for insurrection to collapse, their first reaction was to order his murder. Antonio himself was suspect for the failure until it was learned how it was that Manuel had come by the information of the assassination plan, that morning outside La Mallorquina restaurant. Antonio personally appealed to Luis Albizu Campos for the life of his son in law. He made a compelling case based on how much he had contributed to the nationalist cause and how much more he intended to contribute. He also convinced Albizu that his real problem now was restoring morale to his comrades, since it had fallen so low after the failure that many had withdrawn from the movement. He further argued that the killing of Manuel Calero would only serve to attract more unwanted attention and possible persecution of members of the party. He further argued that as the leader of the nationalist movement his energies needed to be better spent in reorganizing the forces and in improving their keeping of secrets until the next attempt.

In listening to Antonio's arguments, the party leader understood that this was not about one thing being the truth while another was not. Everything Antonio said was true. Albizu personally issued the order retracting Manuel's death sentence. He did this but not before admonishing Antonio to make certain that Manuel Calero would never interfere with the nationalists again.

This experience signaled to Antonio the need to isolate his loved ones from his political activities. He had no intention of withdrawing from the nationalist responsibilities and duties, but needed absolute secrecy. While supporting the party, he needed to be less visible in his actions. It was essential that no one in his family knew about his activities. The problem with subterfuge was that it required deceit. He needed to deceive Ana Maria. He had never lied to her about anything and how to do so now was a matter of great concern to him. It was also troubling to him that while he was not yet the target of an overt investigation, he had to recognize the real possibility that he was targeted by a covert investigation. For that reason he had to change from the open and accessible man he had been, into one who could trust no one, for safety and security reasons. His and his families.

The conversation he was now having with his brother Miguel de la Madrid brought to the forefront those very issues he wished had remained in the background. He had no certain knowledge of how Miguel had learned about the incident at La Fortaleza, but there was no doubt that he knew as much as anyone who had been there on that morning. Antonio could not ignore that some of the La Jacana boys were police officers and national guardsmen and undoubtedly some of them may have been on duty while the attempt on the governor's life was thwarted.

"What is on my mind, is what is always on my mind. Our families, our businesses and our future. But today all of those concerns I have set aside. Today it is you that is on my mind." He told Antonio in the least confrontational way what he thought about his involvement with the nationalist party, because of their platform of independence through any means, non violent or violent. He pointed out by name that most if not all of the leaders in the party had little or nothing to lose, and as result they could afford to be reckless or careless. Neither one of these luxuries were afforded to Antonio. He then struck deep into Antonio's conscience when he reminded him of Sister Graciela's wishes. Antonio continued to listen in silence as Miguel closed with; "There is nothing that you could do that will cast me or Mercedes away from you and from Ana Maria. Regardless of the consequences, I will remain your brother. We will stand by you against all who threaten you, whether justified or not, I only ask that you trust me enough to let me help you by keeping you from making possibly grave mistakes. Please do not shut us out, we are your family." A deafening silence rolled in like a thick fog that represented a wall that obscured one from the other's view.

Antonio remained silent and Miguel did the same. For Antonio the moment for subterfuge, deceit and lies came sooner than he expected and he was not quite prepared to lie to his brother. Inevitable though he knew it was, he nevertheless hated himself for what he was about to do. "Miguel," he said, "Please be assured that I had nothing to do with the attempt on the governor's life. Yes, I sympathize with the nationalist ideas, but also realize that overthrowing a government supported by the strongest power in the world would be an exercise in lunacy at best and pure suicide at worse. Let us have another Brandy so that we may speak of more pleasant subjects. Has Mercedes heard from her family?" Miguel, saddened by the notion that Antonio had lied to him, declined, finished his Brandy and returned home.

Mercedes had learned through correspondence with the convent in Barcelona that her family had fallen on hard times and that their economic situation was a disaster. While her family had given up on her the same was not true on her part. She was troubled that she lived in great comfort while her family might have been living in depravation and possible destitution. She longed to reunite with her family because it was the element needed to complete her happiness. Through the years she had remained close to the convent by way of contributions and communications. Using the sisters at the convent as brokers in the reconciliation she asked them to approach her parents about the possibility of a conciliatory dialogue. Their response had been a heartwarming, most assuredly yes. The latest development was that she was expecting her parents to visit for a long visit and possibly a permanent stay in Puerto Rico. Her brother was not part of the plan because he had disappeared some years back. Driven out of Barcelona by his enormous gambling debts he simply chose to disappear leaving the father to honor his son's debts and in the process experience personal bankruptcy. Mercedes and Miguel had arranged a comfortable house near theirs. Built with all the comforts they could surely afford and share with her family, the very same ones who had sworn their daughter was dead.

The arrival of Don Genaro and Doña Carmen Gabriel to Puerto Rico was met by a delegation of dignitaries from Vega Alta and San Juan. When they boarded the Packard automobile for the ride to the welcoming reception at La Jacana they were impressed by the luxury of the car. They were even more impressed by the love and affection they received from all the Puerto Ricans they met. Mercedes' mother had not stopped crying since she saw Mercedes and it only got worse when she met her grandchildren and their children. She finally stopped crying when Miguel spoke to her thanking her for making their lives complete. Here, before her, stood the man she had hated so intensely, giving her life back to her. At that moment she parted with all her regrets and decided to dedicate her life to make amends. It was also at that moment that they decided to never return to Spain.

Manuel was surprised, almost shocked when his secretary entered his office to announce that his father-in-law was outside wanting to see him. He was all the more surprised by how Antonio looked. He wore a dark blue suit with a freshly starched shirt and a red patterned tie. His boots were highly polished, as was his custom. He had never felt the need to purchase shoes when he was a poor boy in Barcelona, and his current economic condition in no way changed that. Although probably not on purpose, Antonio was wearing the colors of the Puerto Rican and American flags. As it was their custom, both men shook hands and embraced. Only this time the intensity in their exchange of affection was stronger than ever. They had never disappointed each other in any way. Manuel had been everything that Antonio could have wished for in a son-in-law, and to Manuel, Antonio was far more than a father-in-law. He was, next to Lola, his best friend. He was his father by choice. As they separated and sat across from one another, all of their affection, all of their history together was about to end. It saddened them both.

"May I offer you a whiskey Don Anton? While I am not certain what is the purpose of this visit, I do know that it is worthy of celebration, the very fact that this is the first time you have visited me at work does merit a drink." Antonio smiled and asked for a Brandy instead. As Miguel turned to the cabinet to reach for the glasses and the two bottles, Antonio's smile left his face and sadness replaced it. What he was about to do, he needed to do for his love of country, but how unfair he thought, that his love of family was threatened by the love for his country. The man that now served him his brandy had been everything he had expected him to be since the day he arrived at his house seeking permission to court his daughter. He remembered at the end of that evening as he and Ana Maria retired how pleased they were by the quality of the man who was attracted to their daughter. Rectitude was an appropriate word to describe his son-in-law. His honorable conduct and his willingness to help all those that he could brought him closer to Antonio's conduct as well. Why, he wondered, was the coming rift necessary.

There was no need to inquire about family or children since only the day before they had spent the afternoon together as they gathered for their Sunday dinner at La Jacana. Antonio spoke first, saying, "It is pointless for us to pretend that we do not know about the events at La Fortaleza last month. Destiny has dealt me a bad card, a serious blow, but those are necessary as we men make decisions of consequence. It was destiny that placed you outside the restaurant at the same time that two fools could not keep a secret. They were foolish in that they did not know you well enough to believe that you would have acted as you did. Your actions have placed you in great danger. Possibly your family as well. It is for that reason that I come to ask that now that you know the intentions of the nationalist party that you refrain from interfering in the future. Manuel, there are forces in motion that can not be stopped. We will have our independence and this will be a sovereign nation. That is the inevitable truth."

"I had wondered when we would get around to having this conversation."

Manuel served himself another glass of Whiskey and poured more Brandy in Antonio's glass. "With respect Don Anton, it is your actions that have placed my family in danger. But that which is done can not be undone, so let us deal with our circumstances. I had hoped that while we have become political enemies, we could remain a family. However, we have to recognize that the course of action that you will follow will not allow for that to happen. I believe that as political leaders we have the duty to persuade those who oppose us, to our point of view. Your party chooses not to do that. Instead of following the process of discourse and changes through the legislative process, you will pursue the process of instant gratification. You believe that change can only come through violence and the fear that it engenders. You believe that in this instance, violence is a virtue, but it is a vice, I tell you. You ask me to be a silent observer, to sit backstage and take no role in the tragedy that is unfolding before our very eyes. That I can not do, because my love of country is as great as yours and so is my love for my family." Manuel finished speaking and Antonio realized that he had his answer. He stood to leave and exchange their customary embrace, only this time they both had tears in their eyes.

CHAPTER 27

When Ana Maria opened the door in response to the knock, she was surprised to find Raymond Gossett standing in front of her. He declined the invitation to enter and sit, but asked for Antonio. "Don Anton is out at the dairy this morning, you can find him there, I am sure." Raymond thanked her and left to find Antonio. Ana Maria who was an excellent judge of people and of their character sensed that her visitor's countenance that morning was out of character with that of the Raymond Gossett who always had a smile on his face, even when not intending to. He had been a Godsend to the farm and to Elisa. God knows what would have happened to that girl and her boy if this good man had not married her. His behavior since arriving at La Jacana was totally inconsistent with that of the wild sailor he had been prior to arriving in Puerto Rico. What had made the change so striking was that he had become more Puerto Rican than American, and while he still spoke Spanish with an accent, it became less noticeable in time. Elisa, his wife, had grounded him in ways that a woman knows to do when she sees a better man inside the person than his external demeanor denotes. She had seen right through Raymond Gossett the very first time she saw him around her son, and knew she was seeing a good man. She had had a good life with him. The three children they had together had been great blessings. They had even visited his family in Baltimore and had been well and warmly received. She could not have imagined a better life than they had experienced at La Jacana, but now they were leaving.

Antonio heard Raymond's reasons why they were leaving La Jacana and moving to Rio Piedras, which had become the largest population center next to San Juan, and where he planned to open a gasoline service station and auto repair shop. As he explained, he and his sons would run the business together and capitalize on the great demand that existed for his services. The many cars that had been purchased in Puerto Rico did not have the corresponding number of mechanics required to maintain or fix them. Antonio did not have to be told the real reason why they were leaving. Raymond had eyes and ears and as an American had felt sentiments in the valley that made him feel unwelcome, not because of his conduct but of what he represented. He envisioned the ensuing conflict between forces that would surely come, and instead of putting himself or his family in an at risk situation he thought it best to leave. He had shared his thoughts and feelings with Elisa, who shared them with Ana Maria and Mercedes during an afternoon of coffee and conversation before leaving La Jacana.

Ana Maria hoped and prayed that a confrontation with Antonio could somehow be avoided. But it was not meant to be. It was she who broached the subject when she said, "Don Anton, in all the years that I have been your wife there has never been a time in which I regretted my decision to take you for my husband. You have honored me greatly by giving me your name and for fathering our four children. There has never been a day that I have not thanked God for all his blessings and the joys that our family brings to us. The reason that I say these things to you now is because this is the only time that I have felt insecure for our lives and our future. The recent events give me cause for great tremor and fear. When I think of the course that you may be setting for us, I fear for our children and their future. Not for me, but for them it is that I beg you to rethink what you are doing. Did you think that I would not notice that only Lola and her children come to visit, but not Manuel. I know of your involvement with the nationalists and of your conversation with Manuel at his office and I reproach you for both." First she wiped her eyes, next she sipped on her glass of Rum, and looked at him with pleading eyes.

"Doña Ana Maria," he said, "Since coming to this island, everything that I have done and said has been honorable in every way. Since meeting you, nothing has been more important to me than your love and respect. And my conduct has been guided by them to the end that our honor and our good name could never been challenged or derided by anyone. The births of our children and their upbringing have filled me with greater pride than I could possibly describe. And all of the credit for who they are and what they are, I give to you. It is I who feels honored to be Doña Ana Maria Morales' husband. I could not imagine my life in any way other than as your husband.

I tell you these things so that you understand that my decisions and corresponding actions are not taken lightly. I am not a child, in fact, I was not a child even when I was supposed to be one. I know first hand what it is like to feel abandoned and unloved. It is my life's experiences that caused me to want to give my family a life far better than the one I had as a child. And it is precisely that which causes me to participate in the movement to liberate Puerto Rico, at all costs. This land, this island, this country deserves no less." Ana Maria saw intensity in his eyes only rarely seen in all their years together. One thing that she knew about Anton Barradaz was that he was a serious man, and the subject at hand was as serious as it could get. They had read many of the same books with different perspectives. In the history books found in their library there were many accounts about political and military events in the development of the world's governments. And while Antonio focused on the strategies, objectives and results of the protagonists in the world scene, Ana Maria focused on the consequence of the events in the eyes and hearts of mothers and wives. They had both read about Napoleon and the Duke of Wellington at Waterloo and while Antonio spoke of the strategic errors that caused Napoleon's defeat, she could only see the fields of battle with the thousands of bodies strewn about, most of them in pieces, and the few wounded survivors begging for a merciful death. She had wondered if the women who had given birth to those dead or dying in the battlefields would have given birth to sons had they known their lives would have ended as they did. Knowing that there was nothing that she could do to alter her husband's course, she raised her concerns about the lives that would be lost in pursuit of independence. Antonio replied that men had and would always stand ready to give their lives for the good of the country. "Not my sons. I will not allow it. It is too high a price to pay," was her reply.

A similar conversation but of a different tone was taking place between Miguel and Mercedes. Knowing that what was to happen was inevitable their conversation centered on how to best protect their family, theirs and the Barradaz family from the consequences of Antonio's actions which were certain to end in disaster. Miguel, as always the strategic thinker, and as always produced a list of concerns. This time his first item of concern was the safety of both families, followed by how to protect their assets from the retributions that were sure to follow. His concern was about how to protect the La Jacana people from involvement in things they did not really understand but would do out of loyalty to Antonio. His plan was to keep the men of fighting age busy with irregular schedules so that they could not be relied on for the Para-military training which would surely be required of them. Mercedes had been consulting with Ana Maria whose main concern was to keep her children safe, and suggested that she send them to a university in Florida to study and through that process keep them out of the island. Next, Mercedes told her family, every one of them, that they would be going on a long cruise around the world. Weapons had been purchased and buried in a section of La Jacana known only to Orovis and a few others, who did not have any affiliation to political dogma, only to Antonio. Orovis knew the caves in which to conceal the weapons, and in the interest of secrecy few others shared in the information. The nationalist, funded by Antonio and other supporters, had raised a small but ineffective military unit. War making in all forms is a combination of art and science, requiring great discipline, desire and training. The units had been assigned specific tasks and trained accordingly for the execution of their missions. The first order of business was to recruit a number of men and to provide the weapons with which to fight. Ideally for the attackers, in combat situations there are a number of advantages. The number of men, the number and quality of weapons and the element of surprise. None of these would be to the advantage of the nationalist on the day the attack was launched. The training of the few men they had recruited had been conducted in an isolated field and without the benefit of live ammunition or even blanks for that matter. For fear of attracting the wrong kind of attention, noise was restricted to the shouting of commands and orders.

The importance of realism in training can not be sufficiently stressed because it breeds familiarity and comfort in the combatants. In this instance and for this engagement the concept of asymmetrical warfare was to be the determining factor. One side was decidedly more powerful than the other. Enthusiasm for battle does not overwhelm competence, training and ordnance. And in the attempt to take over the government of Puerto Rico all of those favored the authorities. Training nevertheless continued although no date for the attack had been set.

Regrettably for Ana Maria, the attack would take place before she had the time to send her sons out of the country. Antonio understood why she was sending his sons to Florida, and offered no argument opposing it. As they neared the date of the attack, Pedro Albizu and Antonio visited the training camp, and much to his surprise Antonio saw both his sons at the gathering. He understood that the leadership was testing him by seeing if he was willing to sacrifice his sons in the way he was asking others to sacrifice theirs. His first thought was with his wife whom he knew would never forgive him for allowing her sons to participate in the battle that was coming. No words were exchanged between father and sons, only their look of support and his of resignation, accepting circumstances that he could not change.

Griselio Torregrosa and Oscar Collazo had been deported and kept from ever returning to Puerto Rico, but that did not keep them from participating in the conspiracy. Their role was to assassinate President Harry Truman on November the 1st, 1950. The men failed in the attempt and Torregrosa was killed. The objective behind the president's assassination was to create such disruption in the United States so as to prevent them from responding to the events taking place in Puerto Rico, on October the 30th. On that day there were a number of poorly coordinated attacks by poorly trained rebel forces with predictable results. The main attack started in the town of Jayuya where only the rebels believed that their secret had been kept, because it certainly was no secret to the government forces who readily responded with air bombardments and troops with heavy weapons. The rebel's main weapon was the Springfield 1903 single shot rifle. Certainly no match against automatic weapons of which the army and the police had plenty. The rebels had succeeded in keeping the date of the attack secret but not the targets. In battle the advantage falls to the one who knows what is about to happen and prepares for it, far better than it does to the one who has to initiate the attack, pretending they have the element of surprise. The government had already distributed the operational orders, and the focus of their preparation was in boxing the rebels in the town which was fairly isolated and inaccessible and a poor location from which to launch an attack.

The attack in Dorado had fared no better. Surprise attacks are best launched as shifts change so that confusion has a good opportunity to prevail or in the early morning hours when troops are less alert. This one started at mid-morning when the opposing force was well prepared to repel an attack.

The rebels intended to attack the police headquarters and the National Guard armory simultaneously. The evidence that no strategic planning had been considered was overwhelming. When conducting that type of attack a diversionary tactic is used and usually results in the isolation of the targets, thus preventing one from supporting the other. In the town of Dorado, both objectives were across the street from one another. Also lacking in the planning for the attack were alternative plans for actions in regrouping in the event the initial attack did not succeed. So confident were they of the element of surprise that they had made no preparation for the repulsion of their initial attack. Within two minutes of the attack ten of the twenty rebels were killed or wounded. The defenders having been prepared for the attack had assigned fields of fire to their snipers and as a result just as soon as the attackers exposed themselves they were cut down. Five took off in a wild foot race against bullets, which they lost. The remaining rebels took refuge in the balcony of a house at a corner between the police and the National Guard armory. There they collected to wait for the end because no one on the other side was asking them to surrender. There were no plans for taking prisoners on that day.

Things were no better at La Fortaleza where Antonio was leading the assault. Reflective of their poor training the two hand grenades they threw to signal the start of the attack, were thrown with their pins still in place. In the absence of the detonating signals Antonio had no choice but to initiate the attack without the intended shock that should have been created by exploding grenades. Theirs too was the expectation of surprise but like in all other fronts on that day, surprise was nowhere to be found except on the side of the rebels. Antonio instructed six of his men to provide covering fire while he and Orovis tried to reach the main guardhouse. Thinking that control of the guardhouse would allow them the opportunity to gain control of the main gate. That would allow the rest of the force of fifty men to advance and penetrate the executive mansion. For God knows what reason they expected that there would be some sympathizers in the government forces who would join their side. If such was the case they must have taken the day off because instead of sympathy they encountered withering fire from well placed automatic weapons being used by well trained men. Unlike a single shot rifle where there is a need to select and aim at a specific target, an automatic weapon aims to a sector and kills everything in its field of fire. The men in Antonio's unit never having experienced the devastation that an automatic weapon causes were petrified by the thought of what was about to happen to them. At that point recognizing that his unit was disintegrating, Antonio needed to take the initiative to rally his men. In one instant he had ordered Orovis to follow him. In the next he was holding Orovis' lifeless body in his Arms, shot through the head. At that moment he came to grips with the full impact of his actions. "Oh my God what have I done," he said before the stock of a rifle hit him square on the back of the head.

As soon as Lola heard the gun fire across the street from her house, her instincts reacted to protect her children. They were having their late morning snack of a bowl of coffee and crackers lathered with fresh creamy butter. Her state of shock caused by the explosions froze her for only one second before she flew into action. She ran to the bedrooms and dragged the mattresses from all the beds into the kitchen. That being the room farthest from the action. No sooner she had placed all her children underneath the mattresses that bullets began to fly through the front of her house. The children looked to their mother for indications of what was happening and how to behave.

The oldest was eight and the youngest, Rosa was her name, who was only A baby. Too ignorant to be terrified by the danger but not by the noises which they had never heard, the children remained silent. Lola did not know that they would have to remain in their kitchen under fire for almost four hours, but her concerns at that time were not about the length of time that they would be threatened, it was all about her family under the mattresses and her husband, who had no way to know what was happening at his home.

The rebels who had taken cover in Lola Calero's house were being decimated, by the government's forces superior fire power, and the outcome was already known to those still alive. Antonio Miguel called to Miguel Antonio for the condition of his weapon and ammunition. Other than two smoke grenades, they both had rifles and side arms and very few bullets left in each. They also knew that any attempt to surrender would result in their immediate death. Miguel Antonio, the younger of the two, asked Antonio Miguel for his thoughts on their predicament. The older brother said that he believed that the soldiers would wait them out rather than to risk a charge.

The outcome was not in question. Only the hour in which the fight would end. To their advantage, the soldiers did not know how many rebels they were facing. They did not know how many had taken cover in the balcony, or that only two were still alive.

During the lull in the fighting, Lola recognized her brothers' voices as they were discussing their situation and options. Leaving her children where they were, she crawled towards the living room and pressed herself against the door at its lowest point. She called out to them, who in the excitement had failed to recognize that they were in her sister's balcony. Not surprisingly, since they had only visited her twice before and both times at night, they actually did not know where they were, although it would have made little difference since they were seeking cover from the murderous fire that would have surely killed them had they and their comrades not jumped over the concrete veranda.

Upon recognizing their sister's voice they asked if she was alright, and she responded with the same inquiry. "You need to get in here," she whispered behind the heavy wooden door. They declined for fear of putting her at risk, "You have already put me at risk, get in here now," she replied. Antonio Miguel expressed his fear that if they saw them opening the door, the soldiers and the policeman would commence firing. At that moment they had a slight advantage because the soldiers did not know for sure how many were there or how many were still alive. It was Miguel Antonio who came up with the idea of using both smoke grenades to conceal their movements and give them the time to enter the house. The idea worked because in the space of time between the deploying of the smoke from the grenades and the soldier's response they were able to enter the house undetected.

The town of Dorado was placed under martial law until the authorities could give the all clear. That did not keep Senator Manuel Calero from being driven to his house in an army jeep. Believing that it would not have been safe for a civilian vehicle to drive through the combat zone, his car was left at the entrance of the town. He arrived at the same time that three bodies were being taken away from his house. The officer in charge of the clean up detail recognized him at once and offered his assurances that they had done all they could have to minimize the danger to his family and the damage to his property. He also explained that out of concern for his family they had kept from launching an all out attack on the house or from using grenades.

Manuel heard only half of what the officer said to him and listened to none of it. He entered his house and called for Lola who slid out from under the mattresses and quietly slipped into his arms, which made her feel safer than she ever had in her entire life. Only after she was certain they were really safe did she ask their children to come out and kiss their father.

Manuel stepped outside to confer with the officer with whom he had spoken before, and to the one who had escorted him to his house. He asked for an estimate of the length of time before an all clear could be expected. Not knowing if the hostilities were over, he asked if an armed guard could be stationed at his house at least for the next twenty four hours. He thanked the officers for their courtesy and walked back into his house and hugged Lola once more. "My brothers are in our bedroom," she informed him.

At approximately one in the morning Lola's sister Gloria, was driven to Manuel's house also by a National Guard jeep. She entered the house soaking wet from the storm that had started just after midnight and promised to last for at least a day. The reason for her being there so late was that she needed help with the weapons. "What weapons?" Manuel asked. Gloria did not know where the rest of the weapons were hidden, but knew that they were there, on their property. Some had been hidden in caves and some were buried. These were the weapons the rebels planned to use to arm the men whom they believed would join the rebellion once they had taken over the government. At once, Manuel understood the implications. Were the weapons to be found at La Jacana the entire property would have been confiscated by the government. Andres, Gloria's husband could not help because he was stuck in the El Yunque project and probably unable to travel because of martial law restrictions. Manuel was the only one who could help.

Once again playing on his prominence and on the fact that he was the founder of the pro-American statehood party, Manuel approached the officer in charge about borrowing an army vehicle for an emergency having to do with rescuing animals. As he explained to the officer his own vehicle would have been stopped every fifty yards and that is why he needed the army's help. After conferring with his superior officer and the chief of police, both, Antonio's personal friends, the officer called for a half ton truck and had it delivered to the house. After the soldiers and the police had left, only the guard was left behind. Antonio drove the truck to the back of the house, while

Lola stepped out onto the balcony to offer hot coffee and a ham sandwich to the guard, who gratefully received it and sat down on a rocking chair to eat. This distraction was necessary in order for Antonio Miguel and Miguel Antonio to hide in the covered truck under a tarp that had been folded in the back.

Exiting the town of Dorado had been as simple as Manuel thought that it was going to be. Not once were they stopped by anyone as they crossed the various check points and barricades that the government had set up. "You are taking us to the weapons after we drop Gloria at her house." Gloria protested and the brothers agreed to help. Antonio knew better than to argue with her sister-in-law because he knew there was no way she would relent. Gloria was too much like his wife. Instead of taking Gloria home, they drove to one of the tool sheds positioned throughout La Jacana where they collected shovels and picks. Although the ground had been softened by the rain, they carried the picks just in case. All four arrived at the first cave, located at a small elevation, and covered with branches to conceal the entrance. There they found thirty rifles still in a crate, and carried them down to the truck. Two more stops were made where an even larger number of weapons were found and loaded them on the truck. By this time it was past four thirty in the morning and little time was left before the sun rose and their cover of darkness was lost. Assured by the brothers that no more weapons were left on the property, they drove along the river until they could be certain they were outside the boundaries of La Jacana. Driving in the dark in sometimes blinding rain made their progress dangerous and slow. Finally, they reached the river where the weapons were dumped and they watched the crates floating away from them, in the direction of the sea.

What to do with the brothers was his next concern. Manuel drove them to hide in the one place he knew they would never be found. He stopped the truck at the alley next to his father's house. He knew that he was taking a great risk because of his mother's antipathy towards the Barradaz family. But he had faith that given the circumstances, his father would do the right thing. "Maura, Sit down and shut up, and do not speak another word." Manuel's mother was shocked and outraged by the intrusion and what she felt was the invasion of her home. "Maura, we are going to help these boys and you will be quiet about it." The way that Franco Calero spoke those words had an accompanying chill about them, and it had their desired effect because his wife sat down and remained quiet.

Next Manuel drove Gloria to her house, hugging her as they parted. He had always liked and loved his sister in law, now he had the deepest respect and admiration for her courage and character. Next, he returned the truck to the chief of police, thanking him and adding that he would never forget the favor. Thinking that the man would be curious about the use of the truck, Manuel added that all the animals had been rescued, thanks to his help.

CHAPTER 28

For the next two days, the authorities concentrated on arresting all potential suspects. Under martial law, the need for habeas corpus was suspended as well as any rules of probable cause or evidence. The involved and the uninvolved were rounded up and thrown in jail pending investigation. Among those was Miguel de la Madrid, who had waited too long to leave on their planned cruise. He along with many others was taken to La Princesa prison where they were interrogated many times by different officials who would then compare notes trying to find inconsistencies in their answers. Fortunately, none were found in Miguel's and he was released after one week in custody. While in prison he had not been able to see his family, nor could he see Antonio who along with the other leaders of the rebellion were being held at El Morro, the fort from which the Spaniards used to hang pirates. The very same one that had so impressed them as they entered the bay of San Juan when they first arrived in Puerto Rico.

Marisol approached Juan José Martinez for help with an escape plan. The two brothers had remained in hiding at the Calero home in Vega Alta. The government had left no stone unturned and re-turned for the sons of one of the rebellion's leaders. They retraced all of their steps since the attack in Dorado. First believing that they had been killed, but not finding the bodies, the police changed their status from killed in action to fugitives. She appealed to Juan José was for his help in taking them to Santo Domingo where Reynaldo's family would hide them. They had not seen one another since she had married the priest, and while wounded by her decision, Juan José had conceded that Marisol had married a good man. That knowledge in no way assuaged his love for her, and as she now asked what she was asking; to put his life at risk for the sons of Antonio and Ana Maria Barradaz, he could do no less.

At two in the morning on the tenth of December, 1950, Reynaldo delivered the fugitives to the pier in the coastal village of Fajardo. The men knew they were leaving the island but not to where, how or by whom were they being helped. They left the Calero's house in the same way they had entered, and that was without Maura Calero's blessings.

The secrecy had been imposed by Reynaldo because in the event they were captured the least known the least could be confessed. Since he and Marisol were well known school teachers who had never engaged in any sort of political activity, they were not under suspicion, and as a result could move with some freedom. Reynaldo's idea was to isolate as many people from the escape plan as possible. In fact while Marisol knew the destination she knew nothing else. Even Ana Maria had not been given any information for fear that she would attempt to see her sons, which would have been a fatal mistake, since she was been kept under close and continuous surveillance. She was only told by Marisol that her sons were uninjured and leaving the country. Further, she told her that she would have to wait a while longer to learn where they had gone. This was necessary, she explained to Ana Maria, for the benefit of all concerned, her's included. For Ana Maria, that was enough.

By four in the morning, the truck loaded with vegetables arrived in Fajardo. The choice of the vegetable truck helped in the deception because it left La Jacana very early in the morning every other day to replenish the farmers' market in San Juan. For that reason, neither the police nor the soldiers would have thought it unusual for the truck to be on the road at that hour. Once beyond Bayamon, Reynaldo turned north towards the coastal road and headed east. The plan was that in the event they were stopped, he could explain that they were picking up fresh fish to deliver to San Juan, as well. All the while, the boys laid underneath a tarp that had been covered with produce. Juan José and another man met them at the pier and escorted them to the boat. He had readied a sail boat with a small outboard motor, which would be used to troll out of the bay unnoticed. The usual heavy traffic in the bay of Fajardo would serve to their advantage. His first heading was in the direction of Culebra Island, steering away from Viequez Island which was occupied by the American navy and marines. Half way to the island of St. Thomas and under full sail the boat changed its heading, but this time in a north, north west heading which took them away from San Juan and out into the Atlantic Ocean.

Sail boats in that region were a common site during the fall and winter seasons because many wealthy Americans living in the north of the country, and Canadians, sailed those waters when it was too cold in their countries.

Three days later they reached Puerto Plata in the Island of Santo Domingo, where they were met by Reynaldo's brother, who took him to his house on the outskirts of Ciudad Trujillo and gave them their new identities.

Frustrated and anxious for information, not rumors, but real information, Antonio paced his cell at El Morro fort. He knew for certain that the effort to assassinate the American president had failed and so had their efforts to create a crisis in Washington. He also knew that every attack carried out in Puerto Rico had failed and that many from his side had been killed, and only a few of the soldiers and police had been killed or injured. The one thing he did not know was the status of his two sons. At El Morro, as it had been the case in all prisons since there have been prisons, there was an active information network. However, in this case the flow of information between outside and inside the walls was marginal at best. Antonio only wanted to know about his sons. They had been attached to the unit attacking in Dorado, and to the best of his knowledge there had been no survivors in that battle. Owing to that piece of information, he had to assume they were dead. His next concern was for his wife. He had not spoken to her in six weeks and wondered if he would see her at his arraignment, or if anyone but the accused and the accusers would be in the courtroom.

She was there looking at him, and sitting with their daughters as he walked into the courtroom. There were more security guards in the courtroom than anyone in the island had ever seen, in one room. All who entered had been searched and no bags or packages were allowed in. Pedro Albizu Campos was the first one brought in, followed by Antonio and two other leaders.

An attorney recommended by Manuel and hired by Ana Maria, sat a table where he was joined by Antonio. There was a common sensation felt in the courtroom, and it was sadness. This was a sad occasion for the defendants and the accusers. The prosecutors as well as the judge were all Puerto Ricans and the sadness felt by all indicated that if they could all have turned back the clock to October the 29th, knowing what they now knew, the events causing the trial would have never taken place. Puerto Ricans killing Puerto Ricans had been a terrible experience for the island and now the experience would be extended by the judicial process which was about to begin. Modesto

Pantana, Antonio's attorney made a plea with the court and requested that his client be released from solitary confinement. This the judge denied because after the hearing the accused were to be transferred to La Princesa prison and there the potential risk that Antonio could run among the general prison population needed to be considered. Next, the lawyer asked for the judge to grant visitation by his immediate family. The judge agreed to consider the motions and to rule at the end of the hearing.

All through the discourse between prosecutors and defense attorneys, Antonio held his eyes on his hands which were placed on the table. While he had been issued a clean uniform, and was made to shave in preparation for his court appearance. He had aged a hundred years in the passed six weeks and looked and felt defeated. His thoughts were not about him, but about his sons and Ana Maria, because he feared and dreaded the next encounter with her. Finally all preliminary motions were heard and it was time for the reading of the charges. One by one the defendants were made to stand and hear the same charges read to them individually, followed by a request for a plea of guilty or not guilty. Not guilty, they all plead.

The request for visitations was granted and Ana Maria traveled to La Princesa for the first visit with her husband since the events that caused his incarceration. Concerned by the context and substance of their first meeting, and wanting to spare her daughters a potentially unpleasant circumstance, she went by herself. She was driven by Miguel, who understood her desire to speak to her husband alone. The meeting took place in the prison court yard, and while they could speak openly, they were not allowed to touch or the visit would end. The sadness that was so pervasive in the courtroom during the arraignment was even stronger between them in the courtyard. The meeting made all the more difficult by the no contact rule, became increasingly intense. She wanted to cry, but tears would not have been helpful, strength is what was most needed in that courtyard. The first words out of her lips were, "Our sons are safe. I do not know where they are. They are out of the island. They were not hurt during the battle. Manuel and Lola rescued them." The tears that he had contained in himself burst out of his eyes uncontrollably. He sobbed as she had never seen him sob. She looked at the guard who had been assigned to watch them. He read her eyes and looked away so that Ana Maria could hold her husband. In that moment and through that embrace everything that needed to be said between them was said. They broke their embrace, and she continued with the account of how the weapons had been removed from La Jacana followed by an account of Miguel's actions to protect their business interests and their land. Finally they came to the inevitable subject; their future. He asked her to recognize that if he was not executed he would be in prison for the rest of his life, and suggested that she think about a divorce. "In addition to all the stress that you have put me under you now choose to insult me. If you know anything about me, is that I never quit on anything especially my husband." When the hour ended they parted company better than when they first saw each other that afternoon.

The deal offered by the prosecutor as related by Modesto Pantana, his attorney, was for Antonio to plead guilty and be spared the death sentence. Instead, the court would impose a life sentence without parole if he answered all their questions truthfully. Antonio agreed to the rules for the plea but on the condition that he would only answer those questions that related to his personal actions and interactions with the other leaders. He refused to answer questions concerning anyone not already charged with the assaults and conspiracies. Moreover, he would only confirm what they already knew, but would not implicate anyone not already in custody or charged. Further, he demanded that none of his family members would be persecuted in any way.

More than anything, the court and the United States government wanted to put the entire matter behind them. And they wanted the whole mess handled by the local authorities so as to eliminate any semblance of colonialism in their dealings with Puerto Rico. There had even been talk in the United States congress of revoking the United States citizenship from Puerto Ricans. These and other reasons propelled the government to accelerate the prosecution of the case and to accept Antonio's terms, including his final one; to serve his life sentence in the island.

Prison life imposes a form of routine upon all concerned, the jailed and the jailers. The prisoners' loved ones just have to adjust. As such, the Barradaz family had settled into the routine of visiting Antonio in jail every Saturday.

This was the day of visitation for all prisoners, and while it was restricted to two visitors inside the walls, the visits took place in the open courtyard, so that those not allowed inside could see and be seen. During her visits Ana Maria always remarked about his loss of weight and his lack of enthusiasm for matters in general. In effect, he had given up and they both knew it.

No one could have been more surprised than Ana Maria when Manuel arrived at her house on a Friday morning. After Antonio's incarceration, Manuel had returned to the Sunday visits ritual at La Jacana. Since the events in Dorado, Lola had delivered another baby, a girl. The first one in the family born in a hospital. The birth of the new child had brought a sense of renewal to the whole family, signaling that hope is eternal. She asked him if everything was alright and why was he there, the day not being a Sunday. "Doña Ana Maria," Manuel said, "Let's go and get your husband." Stunned by what she just heard, she placed her hands on a chair to support herself. He did not say lets go and claim your husband's body, and he did not say, let's go visit your husband, let's go get your husband is what she had heard.

On the way to the prison to collect Antonio, Manuel related his visit to the Governor, one month before. Precisely eleven months after Antonio started to serve his life sentence. Manuel had visited the Governor in his private residence and along with him, recalled the day when he had saved the governor's life. Manuel reminded Luis of his very own words on that day, after Luis Muñoz Marin realized how close he had come to being assassinated. His words had been to the effect that Manuel could name his price and the governor would grant it. Now Manuel spoke saying, "I want you to commute Antonio Barradaz's sentence at the end of December that would be the end of his first year in prison." The governor looked at his glass full of Chivas Regal whiskey, his and Manuel's favorite brand, and held his silence. In his mind the question was not if to grant the request, but how to grant it. Since the federal government had left the matter under Puerto Rican jurisdiction, there would be no interference from the United States government. His other concern was about how the pardon would be seen by the island's population who had been fractured since the rebellious attempt. By the end of the bottle and of the night, the Governor decided to commute the sentence because of Antonio's 'grave' medical condition. The posturing of the decision based on the medical condition of the prisoner would appeal to the heart of the population who was prone to kindness towards the elderly. Manuel's second request was equally as controversial. This one had to do with the dismissal of charges against the Barradaz brothers on the basis of insufficient evidence. This request merited the opening of the second bottle.

"Your sons have been hiding in Santo Domingo with Reynaldo's family. They will be here this afternoon. Miguel and Lola will meet them at the airport and bring them to you." It had been a struggle to get Antonio's signature on the release agreement which called upon him to never be involved in any form of political activity, ever, including voting. His refusal to the request ended when he learned that his sons could come home as part of the deal.

What Ana Maria was hearing was beyond answered prayers. This was in the realm of lives restored. Escorted by Modesto Pantana, his attorney, and holding a small box with books and the rest of his belongings, Antonio walked ever so slowly into Ana Maria's arms. The notion that he could ever be free again had never entered his mind, and for that reason he felt and acted like he was in a dream. He pressed her arms, kissed her and held her against him as if trying to make sure that he was not dreaming.

One hour later they were sitting in their porch watching the celebration that Lola had organized once it was confirmed that her father was coming home. The better part of the afternoon and evening was spent getting reacquainted with all his family and friends. Franco Calero had traveled with Miguel and Lola to meet Antonio Miguel and Miguel Antonio, and now they were driving on the road to meet their father. Since their failure in Dorado, they had lived with the shame that they had let their father down, and it weighed heavy in their hearts as they climbed the steps of the house into Antonio's arms. No words were said, only feelings exchanged. His, that his sons were alive. Theirs, that they were finally home. "Franco," Antonio said, "I have learned of what you have done for my sons. There is no way that I can repay you for your friendship and loyalty to my family."

"You already have," said Franco. "You produced the woman who has given me my grandchildren." Then they embraced, as Manuel stood at their side enjoying the site of his two fathers embracing as brothers.

Upon arriving at La Jacana and before joining the celebration, they had stepped out of the car, allowing Ana Maria to proceed ahead of them. As it is often the case between honorable men, gestures are far more important than words. Antonio nodded to Manuel and he did likewise to Antonio and never was there a word said about their past.

It was inevitable that the most prominent Lelolai singer in the region would be asked to sing. Out came the cuatros, a space was cleared for her to stand, and silence was observed. She began by singing about crisis and struggles, she continued by singing about the human spirit that can rise beyond anyone's expectations and she sang about the power of love, and the power of God's redemption. Lastly she sang about resurrections, Jesus' and her family's. Next, Lola joined in and sang about the hope that children represent, and she sang about the joys of loving and being loved. The celebration went on past three in the morning, when finally everyone retired. That night it rained.

CHAPTER 29

After a year in jail, Antonio had no difficulty adjusting to a new routine. Jail had taken a great deal of his energy and of his health. While he did gain some of his weight back, his strength and agility were not the same. He dedicated himself solely to running the general store. Many more stores had opened in the region, and much larger than his. The concept of the old general stores had been overwhelmed by larger ones such as Gonzalez Padin and Sears & Roebuck, which was now in Puerto Rico. Twice a year Sears would publish their catalogue which was printed in English. Twice a year Antonio would collect the catalogue, drill a hole through it and with a wire hang it in the out house. It gave him some pleasure to use sanitary paper with English written on it. He might have violated his commitment to stay away from politics, but this was his very private protest.

Running the general store was more about passing time and staying in touch with people, than about making money. Many were the women who would stop in to buy ten cents worth of rice and five cents worth of beans. As usual, everyone who stopped at the store would be asked if they had eaten. And if they answered no, he would say, "Go to the house and tell Doña Ana Maria to give you breakfast or lunch, or whatever the meal was according to the time of day. And as usual, Ana Maria kept a pot of rice and a pot of beans, along with fried pork chops or fried chicken ready to be served to whomever entered her kitchen. Many parents would send their children to the store in the morning not because they could not feed them, but because they knew how much Antonio and Ana Maria enjoyed receiving them.

On Saturday mornings, Antonio enjoyed a walk on La Jacana for the purpose of counting cows as Ana Maria used to call his outings. He always carried a rope, a walking stick and a thermos full of coffee. This was his walk into the past. He knew every inch of that land and remembered every change since he, Mercedes, Miguel and Orovis had arrived at the valley of the Vegas. Orovis was never too far from his mind, and he had deeper regrets for his death at La Fortaleza than he did about the failed attempt to overthrow the government.

To his way of thinking, every one on the farm was his family. He knew everyone and their children by name. For many he had stood as their baptismal godfather. In the Puerto Rican tradition when one was a godfather, you became a co-father. The title was compadre. Because of the honorific title, many people called him compadre Anton instead of Don Anton.

He never really counted cows as Ana Maria liked to tease him, but he did feel protective of everything and everyone at La Jacana. It had been that way when they formed it and it was still that way now. He first heard, and then saw a cow that was standing next to a thick briar patch. As he walked closer to the cow he saw what the problem was. A calf about two months old was stuck in the briars and could not get out. Antonio hit the cow on her side with his stick, to get her out of the way so that he could reach her calf. A machete was what he needed, but he had not handled one in a long time. He pushed through the briars with his walking stick and reached the calf which had a bewildered look in her eyes, consistent with the condition in animals which causes them to panic over things they do not understand. Antonio tied the rope around the animal's neck and attempted to pull her out into the clear. The calf was stronger than him, and he could not get it to budge.

Finally, he came upon the idea of using the cow to pull the calf, so he tied his end of the rope around the cows neck, gave her a few blows with the stick and the force of the cow pulled out the calf. Feeling pleased with himself, he walked to the cow first and released her from the rope. He then looped the rope around his hand several times. He intended to guide the calf back to the herd but before he could turn it in the right direction, the calf spooked, probably by a snake, took off in the opposite direction, dragging Antonio on his back. He was attempting to rotate so that he could be pulled forward rather than backwards. Forward he could rise and stop the cow, backwards he was being dragged uncontrollably. Realizing that his attempt at a change of direction was not going to work, he started to loosen the rope from his hand, and wait for the animal to tire out. Just as he was about to let go of the rope, the animal dragged him across a large stone which struck his head killing him instantly.

His vigil was held at their house with hundreds of people dressed in the uniform of the nationalist party; long sleeved black shirts and black pants. His body too was dressed in that way. During his eulogy Miguel spoke and said that mourning is for those whose life was not worthy of celebration. Such was not the case in the life of Antonio Barradaz. He spoke of his brother as they met in Barcelona, their adventures at the docks, their joining with Mercedes and lastly their arriving in Puerto Rico. He expressed his deep regrets to those people who had not had the honor and pleasure of having met Antonio Barradaz because if they had, they would have known true love and true friendship. "Antonio lived his life in a way that would allow us not to mourn him, but to celebrate him, let us go forward and live our lives in a way that will allow the same to be said of us, when we too pass." Antonio Barradaz is buried at La Jacana, in Espinosa, Puerto Rico.

The End